Praise for

THE BAD MOTHER'S HANDBOOK

"*The Bad Mother's Handbook* reminds us that there is neither the perfect time nor the perfect way to be a mother, and that life, in fact, is what happens when you're busy making other plans. For the sheer laughter and love and crankiness of the entire parenting endeavor, spend some time with the three generations of Cooper women. This is a book for anyone who's ever been part of a family (and you know who you are)."
—WHITNEY OTTO, author of *How to Make an American Quilt* and *A Collection of Beauties at the Height of Their Popularity*

"Charming, funny . . . [with] saucy humor and resourceful characters." —*Booklist*

"*The Bad Mother's Handbook* is a bittersweet comedy, a glimpse into the lives of three generations of women that gives the reader a poignant reminder of the highs, the lows, and the sheer bewilderment we all experience in love, life, and growing up. A must-read for mothers and daughters everywhere."
—GEMMA TOWNLEY, author of *When in Rome . . .*

"This is a book to press tearfully on all your friends saying how much it will make them laugh. Kudos to Kate Long!"
—SARAH SALWAY, author of *The ABCs of Love*

"A book about mother-daughter relationships and the raw emotions that they can unleash . . . [Long] mixes heartbreak and hilarity with a finesse that will have readers cringing and laughing simultaneously." —*Library Journal*

the
BAD MOTHER'S
HANDBOOK

a novel

Kate Long

Ballantine Books   New York

2006 Ballantine Books Trade Paperback Edition

Copyright © 2004 by Kate Long
Reading group guide copyright © 2006 by Random House, Inc.
Excerpt from *Sky Messages* copyright © 2006 by Kate Long

Published in the United States by Ballantine Books, an imprint of The Random House Publishing Group, a division of Random House, Inc., New York.

BALLANTINE and colophon are registered trademarks of Random House, Inc.
READER'S CIRCLE and colophon are trademarks of Random House, Inc.

This book contains an excerpt from the forthcoming hardcover edition of *Sky Messages* by Kate Long. This excerpt has been set for this edition only and may not reflect the final content of the forthcoming edition.

Originally published in slightly different form in Great Britain by Picador, an imprint of Pan Macmillan Ltd: London in 2004

ISBN 0-345-47966-1

Printed in the United States of America

www.thereaderscircle.com

2 4 6 8 9 7 5 3 1

Text design by Laurie Jewell

For Lily

In the battle between handbag strap and
door handle, far better to ruin your handbag
than let the door handle feel it's won.

the

BAD MOTHER'S
HANDBOOK

chapter 1

NAN DREAMS

When I was twelve I fell and broke my elbow. It was election day 1929, and we were mucking about on top of the wall by the polling place. It was about six feet up and you were all right as long as you sat astride the top, only I'd turned sidesaddle in order to spot the people who'd voted Conservative; my dad said you could see it in their faces. Jimmy nudged me and we started singing:

> "Vote! Vote! Vote for Alec Sharrock,
>   He is sure to win the day.
>   And we'll get a salmon tin
>   And we'll put the Tory in
>   And he'll never see his mother anymore."

I swung my legs to make the words come out better, and the next thing I knew I was sprawled on the ground with my arm underneath me. Jimmy tried to make a sling out of the yellow muslin banners we'd been waving, but I screamed and he started to cry in panic. It hurt so much I was afraid to get up in case I left my arm on the floor.

The following day, when we heard the Labor Party'd got in, Dad got so drunk he couldn't open the back gate.

"I'll go and let him in," Jimmy volunteered.

"You'll not!" said Mother. "Leave him where he is."

So I lay on the sofa with my arm all strapped up and watched him struggle. Finally he fell over and my mother drew the curtains on him.

It was funny, we'd never known him to touch a drop before. His vices lay in other directions.

1997

The day after it happened, everything seemed normal. Even from behind my bedroom door, I could hear Mum going on at Nan. She tries not to get cross, but it's the only emotion my mother does these days.

"Come on, Nan, it's time for your bath."

"I can't. My arm hurts."

"No, it doesn't. You've been dreaming again. Come *on*."

Ours is a house of lost things; keys, hearing aids, identities. There was an argument about sausages this morning. My mum had cooked two sausages for Nan's dinner and left them on a plate to cool. Then the window cleaner came to the door, and when she got back they'd gone.

"What have you done with them?" she asked her mother (patient voice).

"I han't touched 'em."

"Yes, you have, you must have."

"It were t' dog."

"We haven't got a dog, Nan. Where are they? I just want to know, you're not in trouble. Have you eaten them?"

"Aye, I might have done. Yesterday. I had 'em for my tea."

"How can you have had them yesterday when I've only just cooked them? God almighty, it's every little thing." My mother ran her hand wearily over her face and sighed. It's something she does a lot.

"By the Christ! There's no need to shout. You're a cranky woman. You're bad-tempered like my daughter, Karen. She blows her top over nothing."

"I *am* your daughter Karen," Mum said.

"Hmph."

It was me who found the sausages next day, wrapped in two plastic bags inside the bread bin.

Not that Nan has the monopoly on confusion.

I know my name is Charlotte and that I'm seventeen, but on a bad day that's as far as it goes. "Be yourself," people—older people—are always telling me: yeah, right. That's *so* easy. Sometimes I do those quizzes in *Most!* and *Scene Nineteen*. Are you a Cool Cat or a Desperate Dog and what's your seduction style; how to tell your personality type by your favorite color, your favorite doodle, the hour of your birth. Do I (a) Believe this crap? (b) Treat it with the contempt it deserves? Depends on my mood, really.

Sometimes Nan thinks I am her own childhood reincarnated. "Bless her," she says, rooting for a mint, "her father beat her till she were sick on t' floor and then he beat her again. He ran off and her mother had to tek in washin'. Poor lamb. Have a toffee."

This drives my mum up the wall, round the bend, and back again. She doesn't like to see good sympathy going to waste, particularly in my direction, because she thinks I live the Life of Riley.

"You have chances I never had," she tells me. "Education's everything. How much homework have you got tonight?" She bought me a personal organizer for Christmas but I lost it—I haven't had the nerve to tell her yet. "You must make something of your life. Don't make the mistake I made."

Since I am part of her Mistake ("I was a mother by the age of sixteen, divorced at twenty-one"), this leaves me in an unusual position: I am also her redeemer, the reassurance that her life has not in fact been wasted. My future successes will be hers, and people will say to me, "Your mother was a clever woman. She gave up a lot for you." Or so she hopes.

Actually, I'm in a bit of a mess.

When Nan walked in on me and Paul Bentham having sex yesterday afternoon she didn't say a word. She's surprisingly mobile, despite the bag. The colostomy was done dog's years ago, pre-me, to get rid of galloping cancer.

"The Queen Mother has one, you know!" the consultant had shouted.

"Ooh. Swanky," replied Nan, impressed. "Well, Ivy Seddon reckons Cliff Richard has one, an' he dances about all over."

I thought she might let it slip that evening while we were watching *Coronation Street*. Suddenly she said, "She were too young, she didn't know what she were doing. I towd her, Musn't fret, I'll tek care of it." My mum, coming in with a cup of tea for her, banged the saucer down so that the tea spilled on the cloth, and gave me a look.

Christ, Nan, please don't say anything or I'm done for. (*A thirty-three-year-old woman was today formally accused of bludgeoning to death her teenage daughter with what police believe may have been a personal organizer. Neighbors reported hearing raised voices late into the night.*)

It still hurts a bit. I didn't know it would hurt like that. I knew there'd be blood because I read somewhere about them hanging the bedsheets out of the window in olden days so that all and sundry could see the bride had been *virgo intacta*. I used an old T-shirt and rinsed it out afterward; if she asks, I'll tell my mother it was a nosebleed.

I'm not a slut. It's just that there's not a lot to do around here. You can walk through Bank Top in fifteen minutes, a small dull village hunching along the ridge of a hill and sprawling down the sides in two big estates. From the highest point it affords panoramic views of industrial Lancashire: factories, warehouses, rows and rows of redbrick terraces and, on the horizon, the faint gray-green line of millstone-grit moorland. To the south there's the television mast where a German plane is supposed to have come down fifty years ago; to the north there's Blackpool Tower, just visible on the skyline. I used to spend hours squinting to see the illuminations, but they're too far away.

There are three types of housing in Bank Top. Small Victorian houses, two rooms upstairs and two rooms downstairs, line the main street, while on the fringes of the village it's all modern boxes with garages and uniform front lawns. None of the people in these prestige developments talk to one another, but you can hear everything your neighbor's doing through the cardboard walls, apparently. Beneath these shiny new houses the foundations shift and grumble over defunct mine shafts—the last pit closed forty years ago—making Bank Top a sink village in every sense.

Then there are the semi-detached duplexes built in the thirties as public housing, where dogs roam free and shit on the pavement with impunity. This is where we live. We bought our house in the boom of '84 (also Divorce Year), and my mother celebrated by having a Georgian front door fitted and mock leaded lights on the windows. The front storage room, upstairs which is my bedroom and minute, looks out over the Working Men's pub parking lot; some odd things go on *there* on a Saturday night, I can tell you.

In the center of the village is the church and the community center and a rubbish row of shops, a newsstand, a launderette, a grocery store. Two pubs, more or less opposite each other, battle it out, but one is for old people and families from the new neighborhoods with quiz nights and chicken tikka pizza, and the other's rough as rats. I don't go in either. For kicks, I get the bus to Wigan from a bus shelter smelling of pee. Fuck off, it says over the lintel, so I generally do.

I don't belong in this village at all. Actually, I don't know where I do belong. Another planet, maybe.

So there I was, on my back, entirely naked and rigid as a corpse, when Nan totters into my bedroom and says to Paul, "A horse has just gone past the landing window."

"Which way did it go?" asks Paul.

"*Which way did it go?*" I said later. "What are you, mad too?"

"I was only trying to make conversation." He shrugged his bony shoulders under the sheets. "What's up with her? Is she mental, like?"

"No more than a lot of people," I said, a bit sharply. I get defensive about her, even though she is a nuisance. "Some days she's more with it than *me*. She's just old. You might be like that when you're old."

"I'd shoot myself first."

"No, you wouldn't. That's what everyone says, but they wouldn't."

Part of the problem in this house is hormones. There are too many undiluted women for one small ex-council house. Huge clouds of supercharged estrogen drift about and react, sending showers of sparks into the atmosphere; the air prickles with it. Nan hasn't got any left, of course, although she hung on to hers longer than most (had my mum at forty-six! Didn't realize people even had sex at that age), but I've got more than I know what to do with. Certainly more than my mother knows what to do with. She suspects I have tart DNA (passed on from her, presumably). If she finds out I've been having sex she will kill me. Really. This would be my worst nightmare: Mum, finding out:

Bloody bloody bloody hell. *Bloody Nan for making a mess on the bed. Again. Not her fault but I* don't care, *nobody cares about me. Come off, you bloody fitted sheet, bastard son of a sheet*—hell. *Trailing this armload off to the washing basket and*—hell, *I've dropped a pair of tights*—hell, *I've dropped a pair of underwear trying to pick up the tights, whole bloody lot's gone now, all over the floor. Navy sock in with the whites, that was a close shave. Charlotte* will not *put her dirty clothes in the right baskets; what kind of a slut have I produced? You'd think she'd have more consideration. Dying for a cup of tea, cotton with prewash, heavily soiled, everything's heavily soiled in this house. Not Nan's fault, that bloody tape doesn't stick to her skin if she gets Nivea under it. What's this, what's this? What's just fallen out of the dirty pillowcase onto the floor?*

Oh, Jesus, it's a condom. Charlotte's been having sex.

I've known Paul Bentham since primary school. Funny to think of all the small events that lead up to a big one. Once, when I was about ten, we girls were down watching the boys play soccer. Paul went for an extra big kick, got it wrong, and smacked me really hard in the face with the ball. The girls all marched off to tell on him, and he thought he was in big trouble. Even his ears went red. But I didn't cry, even though I thought my nose had changed shape. I think he appreciated that.

Then there was the Valentine's Day before we changed schools. I knew he'd made a card for me—his friends had all been teasing me about it—and I waited: morning recess, lunch, afternoon recess. It wasn't till four o'clock he thrust it into my hand, and even then he'd changed the words on it:

Roses are red	*Vilots are blue*
Vilots are blue	*Roses are red*
If you go with me	*If I went with you*
I'll go with you.	*I'd be off my head.*

I wasn't that annoyed, though. I knew it was Martin Hedges who'd made him do it.

I was more upset when he didn't dance with me at the graduation disco. We knew we were off to different secondary schools, him to the comprehensive and me to the grammar, so I thought he might be up for a kiss, but he never came near me, just raced around hitting his friends with balloons and stuffing streamers down their backs. I told my mum about it afterward (we got along in those days). She said, "Well, what can you expect? He's a little boy." It made me wonder when he'd be grown up.

Luckily, it's impossible to avoid anyone in a place as small as Bank Top. We'd meet at the bus stop, blank each other out, and sit as far apart as possible on the red leatherette seats, so I knew there was a chance he was interested. When he was with his friends he'd spread himself out over the back of the 214 to Wigan and talk loudly and swear a lot, writing on the windows and converting the sign EMERGENCY EXIT to VIRGIN EXIT by scratching off bits of the lettering. Then the boys would say to one another, "That's *your* door, that is. That's the door *you* should use." Such a stigma.

Now neither of us could use it.

I thought it would make me feel different, not being a virgin, but mainly it's made me feel scared.

"Have you done this before?" he asked, as he unzipped his jeans.

We knew what was going to happen. It was my New Year's resolution and I'd told him. I don't think he could believe his luck.

"No. Have you?"

"Does it matter?"

I didn't trust myself to answer, so I took my skirt off. Like we were changing for PE; hand your valuables over. I was sure we should be undressing each other, or at least kissing, but that seemed too intimate. I started to shiver with nerves and the cold. "Can you stick the heater on? You're nearest."

Click went the thermostat, and we got into bed.

Then time seemed to hang for a moment and I was back at last August's carnival, sitting on our front wall watching the streamered floats go past and waving at toddlers dressed as bees, when he came sauntering over with his bucket of coins. He was wearing a pirate costume and he'd drawn a black curly mustache over his soft top lip, but the skin only looked more smooth and bright, almost girlish. "It hurts, this eyepatch," he said, peeling it off and rubbing at the red mark on his cheek. "I'm sure I'm doing myself damage. And these boots are killing me, an' all."

So he sat down and we chatted shyly; then we walked to the field together to hear the judging and watch the endless teams of high-stepping knee-socked majorettes waving giant pom-poms about. The megaphone squawked the names of princesses and queens. "Why is there always a fat one in every troupe?" he'd said, and the brass band played "Oh, When the Saints" while the air glittered around us. Little children ran about screaming; teenage girls lay on the grass and exposed their midriffs to the sun. Before he went home he said, "You'll have to come over sometime and we'll listen to some CDs or something." The sun flashed on his dagger. "Yeah," I said. "All right."

Click.

He was fumbling between my legs and pushing a finger inside me—then, Christ, two—stabbing and rotating clumsily. (Wasn't that what the boys boasted about, the girls at school said, how many *fingers* they'd managed?) No. I'd changed my mind. This was a bad idea. Stop. I looked for his gaze to tell him to slow down, to abandon the whole thing and go downstairs and watch *The Simpsons.* But the fierce desire in his eyes paralyzed me. I'd heard of people's eyes burning, but I'd never seen it in real life. It was like all his maleness concentrated there, shocking.

Suddenly he paused and half turned away. My heart lurched; then I realized he was rolling on a condom. His vertebrae were clear through his skin, and I followed their curve down to the shadow at the base of his spine. Were all men so angular?

Click.

Then he turned back to me, grasped his cock like he meant business, and forced his way in. Ow, *ow, ow!* It stung so much it was all I could do not to cry out. A soccer ball in the face was nothing compared to this. I held myself rigid and clung to his back, wondering why something so universally billed as brilliant could be so awful. Why didn't they warn us at school? I'm sure if some teacher had said, "Oh and by the way, it feels like someone sandpapering your cervix," they needn't have bothered with all the AIDS warnings and morality stuff. I'd certainly have thought twice. He came quickly with a series of great shudders and then collapsed onto me, hiding his face against my neck.

It was at this point that Nan walked in, so all credit to him really that he managed anything coherent at all.

Afterward it was embarrassing. Even though I ran over and locked the door, I still felt the horror of Nan's blank stare and half smile. Neither of us knew what to say, and there was blood and we were still naked. Down the landing we could hear Nan singing:

> *"You know last night, well, you know the night before,*
> *Three little tomcats come knockin' at the door.*
> *One had a fiddle, another had a drum,*
> *And the third had a pancake stuck to its bum."*

"Don't put that in the trash bin!" I shouted, as he scooped up the condom and neatly tied a knot in it. "Hell's bells, if my mother finds that in with the tissues . . ."

"So what am I supposed to do with it? Do you not want to keep it forever?"

He dangled it from his finger, then made as if to throw it at me. I screamed and flinched. He lunged and we rolled about on the bed, then somehow it became a pillow fight. I bet that never happens in my mother's romance novels. His ribs moved under his pale skin and his blue eyes shone, and I thought, He's still just a boy, really. He was panting and smiling, and I knew then I'd done the right thing.

At last we rolled into the headboard. He banged his chin and I knocked a picture off the wall that fell down the back.

"Aw, shit, sorry. I'll get it."

He dived under the bed, all sharp shoulder bone, and brought out the photograph: two hand-tinted ginger kittens in a basket above the legend HAPPY HOURS!

Hoping always for a meeting
With a friend I love so true,
Dear, I send this simple greeting:
May the world deal well with you.

"The frame's a bit jiggered." He handed it over. The thin black wood was split at the corner and the glass was cracked.

"I can get a new one. Best not let my mother see, though." I opened the bedside cupboard and slid the picture in under some magazines. "I know it's tacky, but it's got sentimental value. It's one of Nan's birthday cards from when she was little; she used to have it in her room and I always wanted it. I nabbed it when her mind began to go. Sort of a way of preserving a piece of my childhood, do you know what I mean? Against all the change. . . . She's never noticed."

"Very nice. Do you want to come over on Saturday? Everyone'll be out so, only I've got to get back to let Darren in now. Sooner he gets his own key the better."

He was pulling on his sweater as he spoke.

"Can you not stay just a bit longer?"

"Sorry. Little brothers and all that. Have you seen my sock?"

I scrambled to put something on, we found the sock, and then he went home. I lay on the bed wishing he'd kissed me good-bye instead of ruffling my hair. Should've asked. Or maybe that's not cool. What are the rules, anyway? Perhaps some men just aren't all that demonstrative; it doesn't necessarily mean anything, it's the way they are.

So there it is, the great seduction. I suppose I've made the whole thing sound pretty gross. Some of it was. But the point is, the point is I'm a woman now, an adult. Perhaps people will be able to tell just by looking at me (God, I hope not! The girls at school used to say you walked funny afterward). But the point is I have a life that is not my mother's, and it is the beginning of some big changes around here.

I know things are going to be different from now on.

I'd met Billy when he ran across the street to help me carry a basket of washing. It was blowing about, a great white sheet on the top, and I knew if it hit the ground and got dirty my mother would scold me. It happened once before when I was little and Jimmy had hold of one handle and I had the other. We were staggering down the street to Dr. Liptrot's with his week's wash when a big gust of wind took two or three shirts right off and they fell in t' road. We were doubled over laughing as we picked 'em up, but when we got home and showed my mother she laid her head on the table and wept.

Billy had been courting a girl he'd met in the TB sanatorium, a bonny woman, but it made no difference. We had ten for the wedding tea, then caught the train to Blackpool. At Chorley some lads got in and saw all the confetti in my hair so they started singing, "We have been married today, We are on our honeymoon all the way." When we got to the bed-and-breakfast I gave a fish to the landlady so she could cook it for our supper. The next evening she said, "Mrs. Hesketh, are you ready for your fish now?" And I never took her on because I wasn't used to the name.

When I got back to the mill I had such a color all the girls said I must be pregnant.

Where's Charlotte? Gone to Wigan for the afternoon, no doubt to spend money she hasn't got on crap she doesn't need. Nan? Asleep in the chair, legs apart, mouth slightly open. God, if I ever get like that. And why are there never any pens in this house? You put them down and they walk. Useful Drawer; what a flamin' mess. I don't know why we keep half this rubbish. Sandpaper, candles, napkin rings—like we're ever going to use *those*—Stain Devil's leaked all over the clothes brush now. Had a big row with the vacuum cleaner and a table leg today; broke one of the attachments, so that'll be something else to sort out. Bingo! Black ballpoint, bit fluffy round the nib; still, be all right. Here goes nothing.

Love 'n' Stuff

Finding You a Partner for Life's Adventure

Outline Questionnaire

Please try to answer as honestly as possible

Name: Karen Cooper

Status: Divorced. *Very low, actually.*

Address: 21, Brown Moss Road, Bank Top, Nr. Wigan, Lancs WI24 5LS. *Moving in with my mother was supposed to be a fresh start.*

Age: 33. *Feel about 60 sometimes.*

Children: One. *17-year-old madam.*

Occupation: ~~Teacher.~~ Part-time classroom assistant. *At my old primary school! My life's just gone around in a big loop.*

Educational Qualifications: 10 O levels. *Yes, 10. I could have had a degree if I'd wanted. What the hell does it matter anyway? I've been to the University of Life (though I had originally set my sights on Leeds).*

Salary (approx.): Crap. *Funded this caper out of Nan's present (I just withdraw it from her savings account, Merry Xmas, Happy Birthday, etc., even buy my own damn card).*

Do you consider yourself to be:

▢ working class   **X** middle class
▢ upper class   ▢ not sure

Political Persuasion: *If push came to shove I suppose I'd say Conservative. I mean, they're going to be in forever, aren't they? Anyway, if it wasn't for Maggie Thatcher we couldn't have bought this house (although I can't say I rate John Major much). Truth is, nothing ever changes for people like us, no matter who's running about in Number 10.*

Religion: None. *Mum'll put in a good word for us all when she gets to heaven.*

Physical Appearance

Height: 5'9". *That's going to put a lot of men off for a start.*

Weight/dress size: 12/14. *Depends on how difficult Nan's being. Some days I can eat a whole packet of cookies at one sitting.*

Hair color: Brown. *Currently. I'm always looking for the perfect hairstyle, the one that'll solve my life for me. Growing out a perm in the meantime.*

Eyes: Sort of gray. *Charlotte's got her dad's blue eyes. Nan's are brown. None of us bloody match in this house.*

Special Interests: Reading, drinking, watching TV. *Doesn't sound too clever, does it? But believe me, when the alternatives are changing your mother's colostomy bag or arguing with your daughter, there's no contest. Always*

meant to take up something worthy, but there you go.
Actually I do read quite a lot: Joanna Trollope, Rosamunde
Pilcher, that kind of thing. It helps.

Personality

Do you consider yourself to be any of the following?
(It may be useful to ask a friend or relative.) *You*
must be kidding. Charlotte would wet herself laughing if
she saw this.

- extrovert
- shy
- optimistic
- loyal
- generous
- patient

- thoughtful
- down-to-earth
- organized
- creative
- spontaneous
- understanding

To be honest, none of these seems quite right.

Please feel free to add your own ideas below:
Exhausted, bitter, unfulfilled, self-sabotaging. Hence this
questionnaire.

What kind of relationship are you hoping might
develop out of our introductions?
Christ. Just forget it.

My last date was a classic. We'd met at the Working Men's pub.
It's a bit common, but I go there occasionally because it's cheap
and local, and if Nan gets up to anything really crazy, Charlotte
can nip across the road and let me know. Sometimes I need to
get out of the house in a hurry.

Anyway I was sitting at the bar cradling a Bacardi Breezer and feeling bleak when he came over. Grayish—well, gray—but not balding, normal shape, about my height. He was wearing a checkered shirt, with the sleeves rolled up, and jeans, which gave no clues. I clocked hairy forearms, no wedding ring, clean fingernails as he proffered his money to the bartender.

"Can I get you a drink while I'm here?"

That gave me license to have a better look at his face. He just seemed ordinary, pleasant, not weird or anything.

"Thanks. I haven't seen you in here." It was true; it's always the same faces at the Working Men's.

"No. I used to live up Bolton way; I'm revisiting old haunts. What about you? Is this your regular?"

"Not really." God, what a thought. "I just drop in from time to time. When it all gets too much." I laughed loudly, but really I felt like banging my forehead against the bar. Stupid thing to say.

He only smiled, which made his face crinkle up. I wondered how old he was, not that it mattered. I get like that sometimes: desperate.

See, I know you shouldn't look for a man to solve your life for you, but it's easier said than done when you're out in the throng on your own. Sometimes it would be so nice for somebody else to take the flak for once, never mind have some decent sex. A hundred million sex acts a day worldwide, there are supposed to be; you'd think one of them might waft its way over in my direction. Nobody in our house understands that I have Needs as well; it's like Montel Williams says. He was on Channel 4 yesterday afternoon, a show called "I Hate My Mom's New Boyfriend." "Doesn't Mom have a right to some happiness too?" he kept asking these sulky teenagers. The audience was all clapping. I nearly called Charlotte down but she was studying for her midterms.

Six Breezers later, and for all his gray hair I was out in the parking lot kissing him long and full, putting off the moment when I had to go home and change Nan and face Charlotte's scowls. Even light rain and sweeping headlights weren't putting me off my stroke. It was so nice to be held, even for a few minutes. Then a car nearly reversed into us, which broke the mood slightly. I disentangled.

"I'd invite you back but my daughter's around. . . . It's a bit difficult."

"Can I see you again?"

Jackpot.

He fished in his back pocket and gave me his card, very slick, and said there was no pressure but to give him a call "soon." I liked that, it seemed gentlemanly; also it meant I didn't have to sit around waiting for him to ring me. I should have known it was all looking too good.

The next day at school I was telling Sylv, the secretary.

"He wasn't sex on a stick, but he was all right. I'd see him again."

"*What* was his name?" she asked, with a funny look on her face.

I gave her the card.

She studied it and pursed her lips. "You do know this is Vicky's ex, don't you?" She handed it back smugly. I don't like Sylv anymore. I never really liked her. She draws her eyebrows on and wears skirts that are too tight.

"Vicky? Deputy Head Vicky? Vicky Roberts?"

"Yep."

"The one she divorced just before I started here?"

"The one who couldn't *get it up* unless he wore *special rubber underpants.*" Sylv dropped her voice and mouthed exaggeratedly.

"Jesus."

"Wanted her to wear some kind of *mask,* too. That's when she asked him to leave."

Sylv smacked her lips with satisfaction. She'd be dining out on this for months, I could tell. I am never going to tell her anything personal again.

I wanted to sink to my knees and beg her not to pass it on, but I knew it would be a waste of time; Rubber Man would be all around the staff room by lunchtime. For once I was glad I was on playground duty. So instead I said, "Well, he was too old anyway."

"So you won't be seeing him again, then?" she called after me as I swept out of the office.

It's just as well Sylv didn't catch me photocopying my practice run at Love 'n' Stuff in school. I guess perhaps I'm ready to do the questionnaire properly now.

Never let it be said that when things are looking their grimmest, they can't get worse.

I was sound asleep when I heard the crash. I struggled with the bedsheets, tangled from some overheated dream, threw on a bathrobe in case it was an intruder, although I knew it wasn't, and hurried downstairs.

It was completely dark in the living room, but there were

muffled sounds coming from the kitchen. I opened the door and blinked in the light.

"What are you doing, Nan?"

Actually, I could see what she was doing. She was pulling out drawers and emptying Tupperware boxes onto the floor. Six tins of salmon were stacked at her feet.

"Are you looking for something to eat?"

"I've lost my key."

"Which key?"

"To the back door. Bloody hellfire." She wrestled with a plastic lid and flung it across the tiles. Then she sat down wearily.

"You don't need a back-door key. What would you want to go outside for? It's the middle of the night. And it's freezing."

"I need to check the trash bins."

"No, no, you don't. You did them this morning. Don't you remember? Charlotte helped you."

What it is, she worries if we put envelopes with our name and address into the trash bin, in case someone roots through and takes them. "Then what, Nan? What would they do with the envelopes?" "Ooh, all sorts," says Nan mysteriously. "There's some wicked people about." It clearly worries her, so we let her rip them up into tiny pieces. It's one of our routines that has become normal. This nocturnal activity was something new, though.

"Come on, Nan, come to bed, you'll catch your death. I'll clean up in the morning."

"The bins!"

"We did them. Tiny pieces. And the garbage men come tomorrow." And I'm bloody cold and Christ it's twenty past *three* in the morning and I've got to go to work in five hours and no-body cares that my life is a complete fuckup.

"I'll just put this salmon back."

"*Leave it!* Just *come* to *bed* and *leave* this mess. Please." I used to cry before the divorce, but I don't seem able to anymore. I get angry instead. She didn't move, so I lunged over and pulled her up roughly. She's small and pretty light. We staggered together, and I fell into the edge of the counter and banged my arm.

"Hell."

Nan looked up with watery eyes. "You'll want some comfrey for that."

"Shut up." I was trying not to swear at her.

"Or Dr. Cassell's Miracle Cure-All Tablets. They cured Uncle Jack, and he had malaria. Caught it in Mesopotamia during the Great War. He always had to have the doors shut and a big fire. When he emigrated he sent us a lamb. My mother took it to the butchers to be jointed up, but she never got back what she should have done."

"Will you come to bed!"

She turned and stared at me, trying to focus. Then she put her face close to mine.

"I don't have to do what you tell me," she said quietly. "You're not my daughter. Your mother was called Jessie. Didn't you know? You're not mine."

D id you have an orgasm? I want to give you an orgasm, Charlotte." Behind him, David Beckham grinned confidently; no sexual hang-ups for him. We were lying under a Manchester United duvet and it was four weeks since we'd first done it. Outside, children were screaming and an Alsatian barked from behind the chain-link fence in next door's yard. His house is no quieter than ours. I glanced up at the window (Man U curtains).

"Is it snowing yet? It's cold enough. Snow's about the only thing that makes our neighborhood look any better."

"Did you hear what I said?"

"Sorry. Yeah. Well, no. It doesn't matter. It was nice."

"Nice? Is that it?" Paul rolled away onto his back and gazed at the ceiling, hands behind his head. He had little tufts of hair under his arms that I loved to stroke. "I want it to be fantastic for you, fireworks going off, that kind of stuff. I don't feel you're always . . ."

"What?" I leaned on an elbow and watched his face struggle.

"Sort of—I dunno, *with* me. Oh, I can't explain. It's not like it is in the movies, is it?"

"Nothing is. This is Life." I lay back down and put my face close to his. "It's loads better than it was, though." This was true. It wasn't painful anymore, for a start, especially now that I'd sorted out the cystitis. And when we did it at his house it felt more relaxed; no leaping up and legging it afterward, no fear of interruptions. Paul's mum left two years ago, and his dad was so laid-back about his son's sex life I got the impression we could be going at it on the living-room carpet and he'd only complain if we got in the way of the TV screen.

"Yeah, well. Practice makes perfect, eh?" He reached over and ran his hand over my breasts. "These are great." He circled a nipple with his finger and watched it firm to a peak. "Brilliant." Then he moved sideways and put both palms flat over my chest. He sighed happily. "You'll get me goin' again."

It was thrilling, this power I never knew I had. I pushed the duvet back and watched his cock grow and twitch against his pale thigh; it wasn't scary anymore. I felt like the goddess of sex. I wriggled against him and he groaned.

"Touch it."

I still didn't know the proper technique but it didn't seem to matter. Whatever I did he rolled his eyes back, as if he was having a fit, and panted. There was all this loose skin below the tight, shiny stalk. I fiddled experimentally, and he began to swear quietly.

"Like that, yeah. Fuck. Fucking hell."

When my hair fell forward and brushed his stomach, he drew his breath in sharply.

"Wait a minute."

He groped around on the bedside table and snatched up a condom, which he dropped with shock when I dipped my head and kissed his navel.

"I'll get it." I leaned over and retrieved the little foil packet from off the floor.

"Put it on for me. Go on. It'd be so sexy."

I must have looked doubtful.

"I'll show you how."

I thought, You have to learn these things if you're a woman; it'll be another string to my bow.

He tore off the packet end and squeezed out the slimy ring. I watched closely, the way I used to in science lessons when Bunsen burners were being demonstrated. Then he handed it to me. I tried not to flinch.

"Keep it this way up. Pull that pointy thing in the middle, just a bit, gently. Gently! It's my last one. Now, put it on the top like this"—he guided my hands to his groin—"and, that's it, roll it down—Jesus—"

And then he was on me, in me again, jerking his hips and burying his face against my shoulder.

"I'm going to make you come," he whispered savagely. It sounded like a threat.

I moved my hips under his and he slowed his pace, adding a sort of grind to the thrust.

"What does that feel like?"

"Ni—fantastic," I breathed. But I was panicking. I didn't know how to rise to the occasion. Perhaps I had come and didn't realize it. No, because the girls at school said you definitely knew when you'd had an orgasm. It was like a sneeze, Julia had said. A *sneeze*?

Meanwhile, Paul ground on. "Ooh, that's so good."

"Mmm."

Should I fake it? I tried panting heavily and moaning a bit, but I didn't have the confidence to pull it off. He would guess, and then it would be awful. But what to say?

He humped away and I stroked his back absently, gazing around the room at his collection of soccer programs pinned to the walls, his red and white scarf draped over the lintel, the rosette stuck to his computer. The rhythm of his pelvis became a playground skipping song: *Keep* the kettle *boil*ing, *keep* the kettle *boil*ing—

Suddenly he stopped. "Have you come yet?"

There was a brief pause; then I smiled dazzlingly.

"No, but it was great. Have you?"

He looked hurt. "Yeah. Ages ago. At the beginning. I was only keeping going for you. Do you think you might be close?"

"I don't know," I said truthfully.

"Do you want to try a bit longer?"

I shook my head and tried not to shudder.

"Look, Paul, it really doesn't matter. It'll—it'll sort itself out. I probably just need to relax more. Don't worry about it. I'm not." I smiled again, reassuring. "It's great. You're great."

"Okay, then." He grinned. "God, I'm exhausted." He pulled away; then, "Shit."

"What's the matter?" He was looking down in a horrified sort of way. "Have you hurt yourself? Have *I* hurt you?"

"The condom. It's"—he gestured at his limp and naked cock—"it's still . . . can you . . . ? Look, I think it's still inside you. Bloody hell. Do you want to—er, have a feel?"

I was seeing stars of panic but I did what he said. I lay flat on the bed, drew my knees up, and put my fingers gingerly inside myself. "Don't watch!" It felt raw and strange in there. I kept trying to take deep breaths and not clench up. "I can't. . . . Oh, God! Paul!"

"Let me have a try. I'm at a better angle." He giggled nervously.

As he turned back to me I closed my eyes. It was like being at the doctor's. Once there'd been a girl at school, in the first year, who'd got a tampon stuck up her and a teacher had had to fish it out; I remember the horror of simply being told. I wanted, now, at this very moment, to die with fear and shame. I opened my eyes a fraction, as he probed and concentrated, and saw his tongue poking out slightly between his lips.

"Got it!" He pulled out the slimy thing and held it up for inspection. Then he nodded. "Phew! We're okay, it's not busted or anything. I'll stick it in the bin." He threw it across the room.

I hoped he wouldn't shout *Goal!* like he normally did, but he didn't. He just said, "Christ, I can do without that!"

You can, I thought, rolling miserably up in the duvet. That was, would be, without a doubt, the worst moment of my entire adult life.

"Cheer up. It weren't nothin'." He ruffled my hair. "I'll go and get us some cookies in a minute. I'll stick the kettle on too. Do you want to play Tomb Raider when you've got dressed? I nicked it off Darren this morning."

He was throwing on clothes as he spoke. So it must be all right, then. But why don't they tell you sex can be so bloody *embarrassing*? I have to admit, it isn't like I thought it would be. Perhaps I don't love Paul enough, or perhaps it's me. Either way, I need some answers, and I think I know where to get them.

The question is, is Nan telling the truth? And if she is, what then? I have to, *have to*, find out.

chapter 2

$\mathcal{B}$y God, Bill was a clever man. I don't know what he saw in me. Sometimes, when he was a lad, they sent him home early from school because he'd done all his work. Teacher used to say, "Bill Hesketh! Come out with your sums, an' if they're not finished, you're in trouble." An' he'd go up front and it'd all be done, all correct, and he'd be sent home at half-past three instead of four. He should have stayed on, he had a head for learning, but he had to leave at thirteen for the wage, same as me.

So he went down the mines, like his father had, and hated it. He never got any proper rest. In the evenings he used to go to Bob Moss's grocer's shop and pack orders, then take 'em around in a wheelbarrow. Then he started with TB and that was it, off to the Co-Op Convalescent Home at Blackpool, where he met his fiancée. Her name was Alice Fitton, she lived up Chorley way, and she was a good woman. She was brokenhearted when he finished with her to start courting me. I should have felt sorry but I didn't. I had what I wanted. I'd seen the way my mother suffered and I knew the value of a good man.

After we married he got a job at Cook's paper mill and took up with Bank Top Brass Band, playing tenor horn. He used to say they were one of the finest second-class amateur bands in the league. They practiced every other day in a barn over the smithy and paid a penny a week into funds. Once they played at the Winter Gardens at Southport, in front of an audience of four thousand, and won a cup; it was the first time ever. The conductor, Mr. Platt, was overwhelmed. By the time they got back home it was past midnight, but he insisted they play Sousa's "Semper Fidelis" as they walked through the main street. "I don't think as we'd better. We'll wake everyone up," Bill had said. "Well, then," Mr. Platt told him, "we'll take our shoes and socks off."

His chest stopped him playing in the finish; there was the TB, and he'd been smoking since he was thirteen. It kept him out o' the war too, more or less; he stayed at home and was an ambulanceman for th' Home Guard. We were never short of crepe bandage in this house. But it was his lungs that killed him in th' end. He was only sixty-three. We'd been married forty-two years. And it was a happy marriage, oh, it was. Except for the one thing.

Where do you go to get the answers when you're seventeen? Well, you start by pushing your way through the Enchanted Forest of people around you who *think* they know the answers: parents, teachers, solve-your-life-in-twenty-minutes magazine-article writers. Mum thinks screwing up her own life makes her an expert on mine (now where's the logic in *that*?), but what she fails to see is that I am about as much like her as she is like Nan, which is, not at all. To look at us both you'd think I'd been found under a hedge. Bit of a relief if I had been, in some ways. It would certainly explain a lot.

Dad, of course, is conspicuous by his absence. Oh, I *know* where he lives, and it's not far away, but if I turned up on the doorstep and started asking for advice about my personal life, he'd have kittens. It's not his field. Anyway, I think I scare him.

Teachers, they mean well, most of them, but they just see everything in terms of exam results, as if your A-level grade printout will have magically at the bottom a projected résumé to tell you exactly where you're going next: A A B B: Accountancy at Bristol, followed by a meteoric career with Touche Ross, marriage at twenty-six, a nice house in Surrey, and two healthy children by the time you're thirty (suggested names Annabel and Max).

I suppose a normal girl would ask her friends, but I only have acquaintances, people I hang around with but never *talk* to. Is it geography or psychology? John Donne wrote, "No man is an island," but he didn't live in Bank Top. Lucky bastard.

Part of the problem is that the village is at the back of beyond and no one else from my grade lives there. All the other kids from my class at primary school swarmed off to the comprehensive school, sneering over their shoulders at me as they went; I see them around but they don't want anything much to do with me now I'm officially a snob. Most of the people who go to the grammar school live on the other side of Bolton (in, it's got to be said, much bigger houses). I can't drive—no money for lessons and, though Dad's promised faithfully to teach me, I know this will *never* happen—and the buses stop running at 10:30 P.M. Mum can't be ferrying me about because she doesn't like to leave Nan unattended for fear of mad accidents. So here I am. It's never worried me till now.

Don't get me wrong, I'm not Billy No-friends, I know where to sit in the school lounge, I go out (and return early). I just don't seem to have that need for intimacy that some girls do. Strolling around the field at lunchtime, sharing confidences? Not my thing. But maybe I'd be like that wherever I lived. I was always on the outside at St. Mary's, the one helping Mrs. Ainscough in the library at lunch break rather than playing Nick and Jessica by the trash bins. "You spend too much time in your own head," my mother once told me during a blazing row over nothing at all, and I hate to say it but I think she was right.

So where was I going? Here, to this ordinary-looking modern duplex on the outskirts of Bolton, a mere bus ride away from our house. Behind this front door with its glass panels of tulips, a figure moved.

"Hang on a sec. I'm trying not to let the cat out." The door opened a fraction, and a woman's plump face appeared, squashed against the crack. "Can you—oh, damn!" A gray shape squeezed past our feet in an oily movement and was gone. "Never mind. Come in."

I stepped into a white hallway full of swathed muslin and stippled walls, church candles and statuettes, *Trading Spaces* gone mad.

"Hiya, I'm Jackie. Is it Charlotte? Great. Come through. Watch the crystals."

I dodged the swinging mobiles as she led me along to a room at the back. This was all black and red and stank of patchouli. On the walls were pictures of Jackie when she had been younger (and slimmer), together with framed testimonials and a poster of a unicorn rearing up under a rainbow. The table was covered with a scarlet chenille cloth. Jackie lit an incense burner in the corner.

"Now. Take a seat, and we'll start with a palm reading."

We sat with the corner of the dining table between us, and she took my hand. The contact made me shiver and it was all I could do not to pull away.

"Relax," she murmured, touching the soft pads of skin carefully. It felt really freaky. What the hell am I doing here? I thought. Jackie's blond head was bent and I could see her dark roots. Her nails were immaculately manicured and her fat fingers full of rings.

"I bet you're wondering what you're doing here," she said, without looking up.

Shit, shit, shit. "No, not at all." I could feel myself blushing. "You were recommended. A girl at school, you told her not to panic when suitcases appeared in the hall, and then her dad left home but he came back two weeks later. She was really impressed. She's been telling everyone."

"Right." She shifted her bottom on the chair and leaned back, scrutinizing my face. "Only a lot of people feel self-conscious consulting a psychic."

"Yeah, well, I'll be honest . . . I don't know what to think.

Does it matter? Am I going to interfere with the vibrations if I don't—er, completely believe?"

"No." Very assured. "What is it you want to know, Charlotte?"

"I—um, oh, God, now you're asking. I think I need to know what to do with my life. I want somebody to tell me how to get out of Bank Top, 'cause it's a dump, and where I'd be happy. Is there, like, somewhere I should be headed? Point me in the right direction. Show me how to change things." She was really listening, which unnerved me, I wasn't used to it. "Because I thought I had, but everything's just the same. . . . Does any of this make sense?"

Her lids and lashes were heavy with makeup as she frowned, leaned forward again, and studied my hand. Then she began to talk quickly and confidently, her gaze still fixed on my palm.

"You're an independent person. You are surrounded by conflict. You have moments of confusion, and at times you feel nobody understands you."

Welcome to the world of the average teenager, I thought.

"There are a lot of choices coming up for you. You don't know which path to take. Difficult times are ahead, but things will resolve themselves by the end of the year."

Presumably I'd have sorted out my university application by then.

"You need to take particular care of your health over the next twelve months."

"My mother's always on at me to eat fruit," I joked. No reaction.

"Your love life will be complicated. Basically you have too

soft a heart, but you try to hide it. You will find true love in the end, though."

Yeah, well, I wouldn't have expected to hear anything else. She wasn't going to say, "You'll shack up with a one-legged dwarf from Addington and he'll beat you nightly."

My lips were forming a cynical smile when she pulled in her breath and whispered, "There's somebody from the Other Side looking after you. He's here now."

A faint sad cry, like a child, made me freeze.

"Oh, God." I half turned round, appalled. "A dead person?" But there was only my reflection in the patio doors and the gray cat mewing to be let in.

"A little boy."

She waited for my response. I shrugged.

"About eight or nine, I'd say, dressed in old-fashioned clothes: a cloth cap and short trousers. Big thick boots, like clogs. He won't tell me his name, he's too shy. But he's holding out forget-me-nots to you." Jackie's face had gone blank-looking and she was focusing on a spot by my shoulder. It was beginning to spook me.

"I don't know any dead children. God, this is so weird."

"He's cold, very cold. He says you're lucky, you're a lucky person. He says you should make the most of your opportunities in life."

The tension made me laugh. "He's been talking to my mum. It's a conspiracy."

Jackie glared at me and let go of my hand. "He's gone now." She made it sound as if it was my fault.

"Good."

"But he's never far away."

"Christ, don't say things like that, I'll never sleep at night."

"He's a friend."

"Right."

She got up and pulled the curtains across roughly. I could tell she was annoyed with me, and I smirked nervously in the gloom. Then she lit candles and brought over a tarot pack.

"Do you want me to carry on with this?" She had a penetrating stare; I felt like I was back in the first year at school.

"Yeah, absolutely. Sorry." Might as well get my money's worth.

"Pick a card, then," she said.

"Dirty little bugger," said Paul, when I told him. "Here, this'll shift him." He aimed a sneaker at the empty space by the end of my bed. "Shoo. Go spy on someone else, kinky devil. Go back to your cloud and play with your harp or your pitchfork or whatever."

"Do you think there could be anything in it?" I was sitting up with the duvet wrapped around me. I hadn't felt properly warm since I'd come home. *Well, it's the middle of bloody winter, in't it?* had been Paul's response when I told him.

"Ghosts in cloth caps? Sounds like one of the Tetley Tea folk. Get a grip, Charlie."

I giggled in spite of myself. "I didn't believe her up till then. But she went sort of creepy after that. You'd have been rattled. You *would*. Stop laughing."

"And how much did you pay this old hag?"

"Shut up. I only told you because I thought you'd be interested."

"I am. Take off your bra."

I unhooked resignedly. "I know it was all just a load of rubbish. . . ."

"So stop worrying." He was kissing my neck and shoulders, and his body heat was wonderful.

"Anyway, you're in the clear."

"Mmm?"

"She told me a dark-haired boy would hurt me 'more than I'd ever been hurt before.' It was in the cards. So you're all right."

"How do you mean? Because I'm blond?" He took his mouth away from my skin reluctantly.

"Yeah."

"Smashing. Do you want to stop talking now?" he said.

There wasn't the usual mad scramble afterward because Mum had taken Nan for a hospital appointment and the Metro had died so they'd gone by bus. The journey to hell and back, I'd have thought.

"Did you get that picture fixed?" Paul asked, his eyes roving round the room. We were getting better at the postcoital business. "The one you broke that time."

"The one *you* broke, you mean? While we were scaling the heights of passion? No. Although I did get as far as buying a new frame. I couldn't get the old one off so I gave up."

"Bloody feeble girly. Do you want me to have a go? Give it here."

I fished about in the bedside cabinet under the magazines and brought it out.

"Couldn't get it off? What is it, Superglued or something?"

"Just you have a look."

He turned the frame over in his hands and examined the back. "Jesus. I see what you mean."

Wires crisscrossed the thick cardboard; they had been stapled to the frame at irregular intervals. Blobs of ancient brown glue bulged from the corners. "I took off another layer of card and clear tape to get to that. I thought I'd damage the picture if I went any farther. Does it need a screwdriver or something to lever the staples out? We have got one but I don't know where."

"Nah, a penknife should do it. Pass me my jeans."

He set to work, absorbed. I watched him and thought about my little ghost.

Finally the sections eased apart. "There you go. Just needed the masculine touch." I took the pieces in my hands and laid them on the covers. "If you toss us the new frame, I'll put it on for you."

"Hang on a minute." I was taking off the layers of cardboard. "There's something in here. My God, look at that, it's a letter." I unfolded two sheets of thin yellowing paper. "It looks like . . . shit, listen to this." And I started to read:

Dear Miss Robinson,

Re: Sharon Pilkington

Thank you for your letter informing me that the Adoption Committee has accepted this little girl for a

direct placing adoption. I am as certain as it is possible to
be in these cases that the mother is quite definite about
the adoption. She will not change her mind.

Yours sincerely,
P. Davis

"Sharon Pilkington? Who are these people? Somebody's cut
the top off so you can't see the address or date." I turned the
paper over but it was blank. "Let's have a look-see at the other
one."

Notes for the Information of the Case Committee

Name of child: Sharon Anne Pilkington
Weight at birth: 7 lbs. 2 oz.
Date of birth: 13 March 1963
Present weight: 9 lbs. (at 3 weeks)
Child of: Miss Jessie Pilkington
Occupation of mother: millworker Aged: 16 years
Natural father: Aged:
Whose occupation is:
Recommended by: Mrs. P. Davis
Child is at present: With mother at Mother and Baby
Home, Hope Lodge, 46 Walls Road, London N4

General Remarks

Jessie Pilkington is unable to keep and support her baby.
She is only 16 and has several young sisters and brothers at
home. She feels it would be unfair to her parents and

particularly her mother to bring up another young child. She is unwilling, or unable, to supply the identity of the father, so there is no possibility of support from that quarter. Therefore Jessie feels it is in the child's best interests to be adopted and have the chance of being brought up in a happy family atmosphere.

She has asked that the baby be placed with an acquaintance of hers, a Mrs. Nancy Hesketh, who is unable to have children of her own. Jessie feels sure that she has made the right decision to give her baby up and will not go back on it.

Particulars of Mother

Character: good character and reputation
Appearance: good complexion, 5 ft. 7 in., gray eyes
Health: a strong and healthy family

Particulars of Baby

Mrs. Davis has seen this child and says she is a nice little baby with light brown hair and gray eyes. Her skin is slightly dry in parts. She has a tendency to colic but a lovely smile.

Additional Notes

No history of mental illness, nervousness, alcoholism, bad temper, brutality, delinquency, or crime in the mother's family.

"So what do you reckon to all that, then?" Paul was busy fanning out all the blades on his penknife and admiring them. "Charlie? Y' all right?"

I didn't know what to say for a minute so I read the pages again. "Oh, Paul . . . I don't believe this . . ." I went back up to the date of birth at the top and my throat went tight. "Paul, stop a minute. I think this is my mum."

"Who?"

"This Sharon Pilkington. Because—because Nancy Hesketh is Nan, and it's the right birthday, let me just count on . . . 63, 73, 83, 93, 97, yeah. And, oh, God, it all makes sense. Nan was really old when she supposedly had my mum, and everyone said it was a miracle because she'd tried for years. That's the word Nan used to use herself, *miracle*." I'd put the letter down on the bed and was holding my head between my hands. "I can't take it in. She doesn't know, surely? My mum, I mean. Oh, Jesus, Paul, this is just amazing. It means Nan's not my grandmother. It's this Jessie woman. Whoever she is. Wherever she is."

Paul shrugged. "Well," he said closing up his penknife with a click. "There's something your psychic didn't mention."

here's blood in your shoe." I spotted the smear on Nan's tights as she knelt to pick up half a cookie she'd spotted under the table. Her joints really are amazing for her age; the doctor at the hospital couldn't believe it. Wouldn't believe me either when I told him how demented she gets, because, Murphy's law, she was on top form and completely coherent, chatting away as if she'd known him all her life. Even flirted with him. "I feel champion today. Are you courtin'?" she asked him. "You're a good lad. Have you a car?" He thought it was sweet; I thought it was monstrous. I wanted to hit her over the head with a bedpan, only that would probably have got me admitted instead. Maybe that wouldn't have been such a bad idea.

I spotted the blood in the morning as I was opening the mail. Sylv thought—I know I said I'd never tell her anything again but she's got this *way*—Sylv thought I could just write off for a copy of my birth certificate, and that would tell me who my mother was. So I'd been running to pick up the letters from off the mat ever since.

"Have you hurt yourself?"

"No. Where?" She turned her head this way and that, trying to see down her own body.

"Your leg, your ankle. Sit down a minute. Leave the cookie. Sit, Mother."

She sank down and pulled at her tights. "Where? I can't see owt."

Then I saw her heel was filled with blood.

"Oh, God, lift your foot up." I squatted down and gently eased off the shoe.

"That's not my blood," she said immediately.

"Well, who the hell's is it?" I didn't mean to shout so loudly.

"Eeh, you're cranky. I know what's up with you. What you want is another baby."

"Jesus, Mum, you are so wrong. What would I want with a baby when I've got you, eh?"

In the end it was only a scab she'd knocked on her ankle and nothing as bad as it first looked. But pulling her shoe on again, I thought, Why am I doing this for you? Who are you, anyway? And when I went back to the mail, there it was: my birth certificate. And she was right. I'm not her daughter. I'm Sharon Anne Pilkington from London, from limbo.

1. When and where born
Thirteenth March 1963, Hope Lodge Mother and Baby Home,
46 Walls Road, East Finchley

2. Name, if any
Sharon Anne

3. Sex
Girl

4. Name and surname of father
_____

5. Name, surname and maiden surname of mother
Jessie Pilkington, 56 Prentis Road, Wigan

So my mother—real mother, birth mother, whatever you call it—is from around here. What I was doing popping out in London, God only knows. She must have run away. I can understand that. Only it's funny I ended up back in the north. Perhaps it was policy then. Maybe they thought babies with northern genes needed weaning on calf's-foot jelly and gingerbread. Or maybe they didn't want me polluting southern stock.

I'd like to say I still can't believe it, except that's not true. It kind of confirms a feeling I've always had: that I never fit in. When I was little and Dad was still alive, on winter evenings we used to draw the curtains and all sit around watching rubbish: *Wheeltappers and Shunters* or *Bullseye* (super-smashing-great!). Mum's favorite was *The Golden Shot*. I'd have a bottle of pop and a big bag of toffees to pass around, and there'd be this crackly telephone voice droning on: *left, left, stop, right a bit, down, stop, up a bit, up a bit, fire!* Silence, groans, or the rattle of coins and cheers. Once Dad dropped his coconut mushrooms in the excitement, and there were white flakes in the rug for weeks.

Happy times, sort of, but even then I used to feel I didn't really belong. Somewhere out there was a Beatrix Potter sort of a childhood that wasn't like mine, dandelion and burdock and Bob Barken. I can remember thinking, Is this all there is? So perhaps I should have stayed in London. With my *mother.*

I imagine her looking like Julie Christie, swinging her bag and wearing a short belted raincoat and black eyeliner. I bet she sat in cafés and looked soulful when she was pregnant, with the rain lashing down outside and people hurrying past. Everyone's always in a hurry in London. Or maybe that's just an image from some film I've seen. It seems like a real memory, now I know the truth. Can you do that, tune into other people's memories?

The next step, apparently, is to contact the Adoption Register. It's a list of people who want to trace each other, so if Jessie Pilkington wants to find me, she can.

I'm sure she'll want to. I can hardly wait.

People were moving as if they were underwater, ponderously. The air was thick and warm; you could tell it had just been in someone else's lungs. The beat of the music pummeled your chest, and then the strobe started up, making everything look jerkily surreal. I closed my eyes, but the light cut straight through the lids.

Fifty-five minutes to go till closing.

I was in Krystal's Nite Club in Wigan, and it was one of those times where you think, I should have stayed at home.

Gilly Banks's birthday, and at least half my classmates were there, maybe all of us; I hadn't exchanged two words with her since the beginning of term and *I'd* got an invite, so she wasn't being particularly discriminating with her guest list; "+friend" it had said on the gold-colored card, but I was on my own because I'd had a row with mine.

"Do you think we ought to try something different?" Paul had said, after the last session. When his hair's all ruffled from sex he looks almost too pretty, like something out of a boy band. That day, though, it was irritating, not cute.

"What, you mean like actually going out somewhere? Or talking to each other? That would be a novelty." I'd been in a bad mood all week, what with the burden of the Nan revelation and the next History course coming up, and feeling sort of generally not myself. He'd also managed to locate the only Valentine card in the universe that didn't have the word *love* on it.

"All right, there's no need to take my head off. We'll go to the movies if you're that bothered, bloody hell. I just meant we could try some new positions. I've been reading up on it." He pulled out a magazine from under his bed and began to flick through. "There's this one where you get on top but face my feet."

"Sounds charming, what a view."

"No, come on, don't be like that. It's supposed to mean you can—er, control your own pleasure. Or something. I can't remember exactly. Oh, forget it." He flung the magazine across the room and began feigning interest in a ragged fingernail. "I just thought . . ."

"What?"

"Nothing."

"It's this orgasm thing again, isn't it?" I reached for my underwear so I could argue with more dignity. "Why do you keep going on about it? What's the big deal? It's not an issue. But I'm beginning to feel like there's something wrong with me."

He opened his mouth and the words dropped out. "Well, you could nip down the doctor's and get yourself checked over. Check there's nothing . . . amiss."

"You okay?" shouted Gilly over the racket. *"Having a good time?"* She was breezing past on her way to the bar, birthday girl, in combats and a little vest, bra strap showing. She's one of those people who doesn't give a toss. I bet she has loads of orgasms.

"Oh, yes. Excellent. Nice one." I raised my glass through the smoke and smiled at her, and Paul's voice said again in my ear, *Get yourself checked over.* Bastard!

.   .   .

"Bastard!" I'd shouted at him, before pulling on the rest of my clothes in a frenzy. "I can't believe what you just said! What the hell are you suggesting? That I'm *abnormal*?"

He lay there chewing his nail and watched me struggle with my trousers. I'd got my toe caught in the hem and was pushing at the stitching, making it rip, wanting it to rip.

"You want to watch it, you'll tear 'em."

"Jesus!" Some threads gave and my foot shot out. I staggered against the bed end.

"All I meant was, it's not been—oh, you know. Like you hear it's going to be." He looked embarrassed but resolute; he was going to say his piece whatever. He held out his hand to me in a gesture that might have been meant to reassure. "Do you not think the same, though, really?"

"And could it not be"—I put my burning face close to his—"could it not perhaps be that it's *you* who's getting it wrong? That it's *your* amazing technique that's failing to deliver?" I nodded at his flaccid cock, which lay across his thigh innocently. "That your mighty equipment is not quite *up to the job*?"

He pulled the sheet across himself and flushed.

"No," he snapped. "It isn't, actually."

"Really?"

"No. And I'll tell you why."

"Go on." I sensed what was coming.

"Because. Because Jeanette Piper never had any trouble, that's why."

So I finished dressing and let myself out. Past next door's sad

Alsatian, past the bench with no slats left and the tire-marked roadsides, past the shattered bus shelter, and home to my room, where I cried for half an hour.

It's true, he never actually said he was a virgin. But then again, he didn't say he wasn't. I should've kept asking, only what do you do if you don't hear the answer you want? "Stop, it's all off, put your underpants back on; I only sleep with the undefiled!" I don't think so. And it's not something he could have done anything about; you can't rewind time. Once it's gone, it's gone. I should bloody know.

No, it wasn't the fact that he was one step ahead, though to be honest it's not nice knowing he's dipped his wick elsewhere. (Thank God I don't even know this Jeanette Piper; I think she lives in Standish. He did say she was a bit of a dog before I slammed out, but that was probably only to make me feel better.) No, it's what he said before. About me. My defective body. What if it turned out to be true?

"Over there, by the bar. I think you've got an admirer!" Gilly twinkled as she squeezed past, a pint glass in each hand.

I squinted across the room, but it was all heads and bodies and there was a great fat man in front of me. I stepped backward into a bit of a gap and immediately stepped on someone's toe.

"Sorry. *Sorry.*"

It was Daniel Gale, recently arrived in our class from somewhere down south and already dismissed as a boring nerd. He swept a hand through his wild hair and grinned weirdly. What was someone like him doing here, for God's sake? He should have been at home chasing Internet porn.

"Actually"—he leaned closer—"it's a prosthetic."

"A *what*?" I was still trying to see over to the bar.

"Galvanized steel and platinum bonded. Bionic. I had it fitted after a terrible freak accident. You could drop a Mini Cooper on here, and I wouldn't feel a thing. It's fully magnetized too. If you dropped me in the sea, my toes would point north."

"You *what*?"

His shirt lit up dramatically as the ultraviolet came on; it made his head look disembodied and wobbly. I don't know what my face was doing, but I don't think it was registering anything very positive. His glasses flashed reproachfully at me and he opened his mouth, then shut it again. *"Joke,"* he finished sadly, and drifted away, shoulders hunched.

It was then I spotted him: a tall guy leaning against a pillar, watching me. Black jacket slung over his shoulder like a catalog model, dark curly hair, thin nose, might have been all right but it was difficult to tell from a distance. He waved. I looked away. I looked back. He started to come over, smiling. Shit, I thought. Then, Well, why the hell not? Teach that bastard Paul, wouldn't it?

It wasn't till he got really close that I could see the leather pants.

Now, the only thing I know about leather pants, not owning a pair myself, is what I heard some stand-up comedian say once: that they turned your privates into a fiery furnace. As he got closer I could see he was quite nice-looking, but the thought of the turkey-neck testicle skin and the accordion-wrinkled penis cooking gently in there persisted, and my brow furrowed.

"Penny for them," he said, as he reached me.

I could hardly say I was thinking about his genitals.

"You look like you're in another world, you do. With your big eyes. Like you're waiting to be rescued. Like a princess." He put his hand on my arm. I didn't move. "So where *do* you come from?"

I couldn't think of an appropriate reply to this—there was no way I was going to utter the words "Bank Top"—so I reached up and glued my lips to his. Out of the corner of my eye I could see Daniel Gale watching us, so I shifted around and put my back to him.

This guy knew how to kiss, that was for sure. No bits of escaping spit, no feats of ridiculous jaw-stretching or clashing front teeth, just a nice lazy action. I let myself go with it, and after a while we found ourselves a corner and settled in for what was left of the night. The leather pants felt odd under my hands but also safe, in a reinforced sort of way. You couldn't feel anything *personal* through them, just the lumps and bumps of folds where they creased. We had the last dance together—well, we stood on the dance floor and necked while slowly pivoting— then the lights came on and we were suddenly blinking at each other and looking sheepish. It was then I realized how much older he was.

Outside, in the quiet cold air, his pants squeaked.

"Can I see you again?" he murmured over the creaking. My ears were still ringing slightly, and it took a moment to register what he'd said.

"How old are you?" I found myself asking. Around us crowds

of people moved into knots and couples, shouting or embracing, slapping passing cars on the roof. Someone was throwing up in a shop doorway amid cheers.

He held up his palms to me, head on one side. I was sure I could see crow's feet in the lamplight. "Hey. What's up? Does it matter?"

Does it matter? That's what Paul said when I asked him if he'd done it before. And yeah, it bloody well did, as it turned out. So not a great question, Rawhide.

"I'll take *your* number. I'll give *you* a call."

He shrugged. Then, with difficulty, he extracted a pen from his back pocket and wrote it on my hand, held on to my fingers afterward. He was staring into my eyes.

"I'm twenty-eight, if you must know. God." He shook his head. "Still don't see what the deal is. Why, how old are you?"

"Like I said, I'll give you a call." I loosened my hand from his grip. "See you." And I joined Julia and Gilly at the taxi line, feeling as if, somehow, I'd got one back. On somebody.

See the doctor? Not bloody likely!

It was only a dance at the Mechanics', but I got in a row over it. It was a regular thing when I was about sixteen. I'd throw my lace-up shoes and best frock out of the window, then tell my mother I was off to Maggie Fairclough's. Her mother used go out drinkin' and we could do as we liked. So then we'd walk it into Harrop and go dancin'. The last time, though, it was the Carnival Dance, and when I got back home I had confetti all in my hair and cuffs. I kept brushin' it out but it clung. My mother spotted some of it on the floor, and I got a good hiding and sent to bed. She was always angry and tired to death, bent over her washtub or her scrubbing board or her wringer. And shamed. You see, she could never hold a man, never had a home of her own. I think she were terrified I might end up the same.

I made a trip into Wigan to find out what I already knew.

There was a time—late sixties, I suppose—when approaching the town was like driving through a war zone. Nan and I would get in the bus, and I'd stare out the windows at rows and rows of shattered houses, brick shells, piles of rubble. Sometimes there'd be a square of waste ground with just a line of doorsteps along the edge of the pavement, or ragged garden flowers sprouting through the masonry, or a tiny patch of floor tiling in the mud. On the horizon there would always be those huge swinging metal balls on cranes. It made me shudder to think what they could do. That was the progressive period, when they were busy putting people into high-rises (I don't know what they called the period when they moved everybody back out again).

The journey through all those ruins always unsettled me. We'd have reached the Market Hall by the time I felt right again. Nan would visit each stand, chatting and joking with the stallholder over every purchase, and I'd turn on my heel and gaze upward at the steel rafters, where pigeons fluttered and escaped balloons dawdled tantalizingly. You could smell the sarsaparilla from the health-food booth, and ginger, and herbal tea. If I was good, I had a hair ribbon off the trimmings stall, and I got to choose the color.

So now I drove through the outskirts of a reinvented Wigan with grassed-over areas and new prestige neighborhoods with names like SWANSMEDE and PHEASANT RISE. Imaginative chaps, these developers. I got through Scholes and onto the one-way road, over the River Douglas, past the Rugby League ground, under Chapel Lane railway bridge. Huge billboards promised faithfully to change my life if I bought a new car, cereal, shampoo: if only. Then I was out the other side, glancing over at the A–Z map spread out on the passenger seat. Finally I was turning into Prentis Road.

Streets like this used to be cobbled, but the government paved them years ago. At the beginning of the road, two short blocks of row houses nudged the pavement. I know these back-to-back houses; there's enough of them in Bank Top. The flat red fronts, the white doorsteps that nudge the pavement, and, at the back of each house, a flagged yard walled round six feet high and a door opening onto a cinder track. The original outside privies would all have been demolished in the sixties, and little narrow kitchens built on to free up what had been the parlor. Then in the seventies everyone had to go smokeless, so the coal sheds went. While they were at it, most people had the two downstairs rooms knocked through and folding screens put in (so much more versatile!). Anything so long as it didn't look Victorian. (You want to get them picture rails taken off and all.)

This was where my real mother grew up.

I parked the car and walked slowly along the pavement.

I started counting door numbers, although I could see, ages before I got to the end, that I was going to run out. Number 28 was the last in the row; then there was a grassy space with a sign saying HOLLINS INDUSTRIAL PARK. Past this was the first building, a sort of hangar, Naylor's Body Work Repairs. A row of courtesy cars was parked outside, and one of those revolving signs turned sluggishly: OPEN/SUNDAYS. A young lad in overalls came out, saw me staring, and shouted over.

"Y' lookin' for something? Boss is out the back."

"It's okay," I called.

He shrugged, climbed into one of the cars, and started revving the engine with the door open. I walked a bit farther, to where I thought number 56 would have been, and silently blessed my mother. I knew she wouldn't be here. I'd known it all along. She was in London, with a *life*.

Speaking of which: I'm supposed to be holding out for Mr. Right, but what do you do in the meantime? I was prepared to settle for Mr. He'll Do For Now while I was waiting. Love 'n' Stuff had sent me Davy, looked a bit like that actor who played Jesus of Nazareth in the seventies, only not so holy. Same age as me but a completely different attitude to life. Dressed young, smoked hand-rolled cigarettes. Tall and lean. I'd seen him twice, once for a quick drink at the Wagon and Horses (he had an appointment with somebody), and once for an Italian meal in Bolton (we went dutch, but that was okay; it *is* the nineties). Right from the word go, he let it be known that he had a full and active social diary. Well, I thought, I bet you don't have a mother with a high-maintenance colostomy and a daughter ready to hurtle off the rails at any moment. I just smiled and said, "Good for you. Hope you can fit me in somewhere," which sounded tacky and desperate (again).

At Luciano's he told me he was divorced—which I think even now was probably the truth—and that he'd been in a few different dating agencies, but Love 'n' Stuff was the best so far (he gave me a little wink when he said this line). Then he did some tricks with a breadstick which I thought were screamingly funny, although in retrospect I'd had quite a lot to drink by then. He also said he was a sales rep, so the only way he could be contacted with any regularity was through his cell phone. Yeah, well, I know it's the oldest trick in the book, but when you want to believe someone, you do.

I wouldn't have brought him back to the house but he claimed to be Mr. I-Might-Fix-Your-Metro too. Also, it was Saturday afternoon, Nan's nap time, and I knew Charlotte had gone into town as usual, so the coast should have been clear. Hah. When is my coast ever bloody clear?

He'd not been under the car two minutes when Nan appeared at the front door. I motioned her to go back inside but she only waved back, put her hand to the jamb, and lowered herself down the step. Then she waddled down the path holding some bit of paper aloft.

"I've won a Range Rover," she said, pushing a letter in my face. "Charlotte can have it, she can have it for school."

I thought there hadn't been any mail that morning, but Nan had been up before me.

"Let's have a look." I whipped it off her and scanned the contents. "Load of rubbish. No, you haven't, Mum. It's junk mail. And it's for me anyway."

"It never is." Nan looked cross.

"Look, what does that say?" I pointed at the address window. "See?"

She peered forward and huffed at me. Then she spotted Davy, who had wriggled himself back out from under the chassis while we'd been talking. "Who's this?"

"Davy, Mum."

"Jamie? Eeh, you favor a German." She reached down and touched his leg. "Is he foreign?"

"No. Come on back inside and I'll make you some tea."

She gave him a glazed smile before retreating. "You want to watch them swanky pants," was her parting shot. "Don't get muck on 'em."

We went back up the path, me holding her elbow to stop her escaping, and I got her ensconced in her chair and put the TV on. *Love Boat,* ideal. Then I came out again.

The Ribble bus went past and stopped at the corner. Charlotte got off, face like thunder.

When she got close enough, she held up a shopping bag and snapped, "They wouldn't take it back! Can you believe it? Just because I'd washed it! I tell you what, I'm never shopping there again, bunch of rip-off merchants."

She stepped angrily over Davy's legs, then paused as she realized they were coming out from under my car.

"Bloody hell," she said, staring down. "Mum? Mum, who is this?"

"It's Davy. A—er, friend of mine."

She shot me a withering look.

Davy shuffled out, grin at the ready, wiping his hands on the oily rag. Then his face fell. There was a pause.

"Jesus, Mum, we've met, actually," said Charlotte, in icy tones. "Last week, at Krystal's. I'm sure you remember, all those *teenage girls*. God, how disgusting. Twenty-eight, my ass! You're really wrinkly in the daylight, Mr. Leather Pants. Don't you ever wear anything else? They must be beginning to *stink* by now."

The penny was beginning to drop.

"You old, sick bastard," she said, and turned on her heel. I gaped after her. *Charlotte?*

"Small world," said Davy.

"I'll give you small world," I snarled. My leg twitched with the effort of not kicking him. "You should be reported. Get your hands off my car and leave my daughter alone, or I might do something vicious with that tool set."

"You'll laugh about this one day," I heard him saying as I walked away.

When I got inside, Charlotte had stalked upstairs but Nan was still watching *Love Boat*. A soft-focused couple was embracing to a backdrop of blue sea, and from the bridge a little boy was watching them, a big smile on his face. The captain put his hand on the boy's shoulder, and a tear twinkled in his eye. "I guess your mom's found what she was looking for, Freddie," he said, as the music swelled and the credits rolled.

"I forgot to tell you, I've won a Range Rover," said Nan, pulling out an envelope from under the cushion.

"Jesus Christ," I said, snatching it off her. But this time it wasn't junk mail. It was from the Social Services Adoption Department.

chapter 3

I didn't know what to do.

If I contacted Paul first, would that make me look like a total Sad Act? Would it be reported to his friends that I was turning into some mad stalker, unable to accept the bleeding obvious, that her boyfriend had dumped her? Because he had, hadn't he? Or was it me who gave *him* the boot? Or was it neither?

Or what if I'd got it all wrong and he was sitting alone in his room, brokenhearted, too dispirited to pick up the phone? After the initial fog of anger had cleared, I'd got to thinking we'd make up, maybe sulk for a few days but then fall into each other's arms, and out of the ether he'd pull some magic words that would wipe my head clean forever of Jeanette Piper and her writhing limbs and panting cries.

But that had been two weeks ago. Oh, *why* hadn't he been in touch? Even to finish it. You know, if you've shared bodily fluids with someone they ought at least to tell you where you stand. Surely it's manners. It wasn't just my pride, there was my hymen too. Or perhaps best to forget about that.

Bloody Paul bloody Bentham, bloody men.

In the end I went around to his house.

I practiced all the stuff I was going to say before I went, and on the way as well, trying to get the inflections exactly right, the face, the body language. *I just want to get things cleared up,* I told my bedroom mirror, folding and unfolding my arms to assess the different effects.

Clothes had been a problem too. I didn't want to wear anything that implied I'd made an effort, only for him to break up with me; that would make me look really pathetic. On the other hand, I didn't want to look like something the cat dragged in, in case he had wanted to get back together but changed his mind when he saw the state I was in. God knows, I didn't want him to think I'd been *pining* for him. In the end I'd settled for washing my hair and worn my second-best jeans.

I think it's best for both of us, I told my friend the Alsatian, and it wagged its tail slowly and grinned. Then I marched up and rang Paul's doorbell, shaking. *Paul Bentham is no good, chop him up for firewood,* my head kept chanting, which wasn't exactly helpful. There was a funny metallic taste in my mouth.

Chimes echoed in the distance, but no one stirred. I waited a long time, then turned to go, half relieved, only to hear the door open behind me.

"Sorry, love, I was on the toilet." Mr. Bentham, naked to the waist, barefooted, embarrassed and embarrassing. I tried not to look at his pink rubbery nipples, and the line of wiry hair that came up from inside his trousers and touched his paunch. His face was shiny and he had too much forehead. You could tell he'd been pretty once, like Paul, but everything had begun to blur and slide. It made me think of my dad, about the same age, mid-thirties, but sharp-featured, built like a whippet, all his own hair—extra, actually, if you count the recent mustache. I hate it when old people let themselves go.

Mr. Bentham stared at me for a moment. "He's not in. Went off to Bolton, I think. He'll be back about dinner time. Shall I tell him you called?"

"Yeah." My heart sank. I was going to have to go through all this palaver again. "No. Actually, can I just scribble him a note? I won't be a minute." I smiled nicely.

"Aye, all right, love. Come in." I followed him down the hall to the back kitchen. "Want a cup of tea? There's one brewed."

I glanced around the mess and took in the dish of gritty butter; the weeping brown sauce bottle, top askew; the open bag of sliced bread stuck on the table. I knew without looking what state the sink would be in. Even if it was clear of dirty pots, there'd be Christ knows what clogging and breeding in the drain. My mum has her faults, God, but at least our house is fairly clean. Three men living on their own: possibly even worse than three women.

"No, thank you, I'm all right."

Mr. Bentham followed my gaze. "I work shifts," he said simply. "Oh, you'll need some paper."

We doubled back and stopped at the telephone table, which stood under a rectangle of lighter-colored wallpaper, a little hook still protruding at the top. "Used to be their wedding photo," Paul had pointed out on my very first visit. "You'd have thought he'd have stuck something over it," I'd said to Paul, who'd shrugged.

"Anyway, give me a shout when you've done. Like I said, he's gone off to the shops. After some video or something, I don't know." He shook his head. "He doesn't talk to me, you know; I don't have a clue what he's up to from one day to the next. But that's boys for you." He scratched his neck and dropped his gaze to the floor.

"Thanks." I brandished the pen and pad. "I won't be long."

Mr. Bentham wandered off into the lounge and *Grandstand* came on.

Dear Paul,

I ~~came~~ popped around to say can I have my CDs back sometime? If you want we could ~~get together~~ meet up for a drink and a ~~talk~~ chat (but only if you've got time). I've got loads going on at the minute and I bet you have too!! Give me a ring.

Love ~~Charlie~~ Charlotte

This masterpiece of literature took me nearly ten minutes to draft; I kept thinking, At any point Mr. Bentham's going to re-emerge to check I'm not up to anything dodgy, like rifling through his wallet. And what if Paul came back early and caught me off guard? A Royal National Institute for the Blind envelope came though the letter box, and I jumped about a mile. "Get a grip," I remembered Paul saying, which irritated me so much I lost my train of thought even more. But finally it was finished.

"Shall I leave it in the hall?" I shouted toward the lounge.

Mr. Bentham ambled out. "No, give it here, we put them on a board in the kitchen. See?"

"Oh, yeah. Right."

I thought that was a bit civilized, but then I registered the gingham frame around the cork and realized it was just another bit of Mrs. B she'd left behind. He impaled the note with a map pin, underneath a takeout menu and next to, oh, God, next to a note for Paul, written in childish handwriting, must be Darren's, saying, *Phone Chrissy about Sat eve!*

Of course, Chrissy could be a bloke. Or a friend. No need to panic.

I wanted to get back so I could read the letter from the adoption agency again, just in case I'd missed something, because I still hadn't decided what to do. But shopping with Nan takes forever because we have to stop and chat to all and sundry. Forty-five minutes it took us to walk back up from the butcher's—we could have done it in ten—blood seeping all the while out of the cold chops and pooling in the corner of the plastic bag. Little Jim by the post office, with his flat cap and muffler, wanted to know how Reenie Mather's operation had gone ("She were the color of this envelope when th' ambulance men carried her out; she was, honest"). Then he detailed his own ailments for us. (Why should he think I want to know about his prostate? Nan was all ears, though.)

Next it was Skippy, our local tramp, so-called because he spends a lot of time ferreting about on the municipal garbage dump. He was turning on his heel outside the library, begging for change and spitting on the pavement.

"All right?" Nan asks, cheerful as anything. I can never tell what Skippy says, so I left them to it and went in to see if the new Mary Wesley novel was in (it wasn't). When I came out, Skippy was on his hands and knees making a sort of yipping noise and Nan was doubled over; Christ knows what was going on there. I didn't stop to ask, just dragged Nan away. "Eeh, he's an odd one," she said, wiping her eyes with a hanky. "Filthy old deviant, more like," I muttered, but she was blowing her nose and didn't hear.

Then, when we were on the home stretch, up pops Mr. Rowland, the newish vicar. Don't know what it is about vicars, they always make me feel guilty, then annoyed with myself for feeling guilty. I mean, I know I don't go to church, but on the other hand I'm not especially sinful either. Not on the world scale of evil, anyway.

"Lovely to see you," he calls across the road, like he means it. Nan beams, and he bounds over and starts to describe at length how the vicarage is shaping up and how Mrs. Rowland's knee has been poorly because she fell off a stepladder trying to get to a cobweb and it's started an old hockey injury off again. Nan tuts and shakes her head sympathetically while I lean on the wall and look over his shoulder. Hanging baskets are going up in the High Street; they'll last all of two minutes.

He finally remembers some appointment and dashes off (where does he get his energy from? God, presumably). Nan watches him go fondly. "Now, *he's* a good man. Not like old

Mr. Speakman, or the one who came next, playing guitars and tambourines, what have you. I'm not surprised *he* didn't last long. Clapping in church! He went off somewhere foreign in the end, didn't he?"

"Surrey, Mum. The old vicar went to form a charismatic group in Farnham. You told *me* that."

"Nay, I never did. Are you sure? Well, who was it went to Japan?"

"I've no idea." I bundled her up the step and shut the door. I felt like I'd run the London Marathon. "I'll get the kettle on. Give me your coat."

I pulled the letter out of the table drawer and took it into the kitchen to scan it again while the water boiled.

In the past it was thought best for all concerned that an adopted child's break with his birth family should be total. Parents who placed a child for adoption were generally told that a child would not have access to the birth record. The current legislation reflects increased understanding of the wishes and needs of adopted people. It recognizes that although adoption makes a child a full member of a new family, information about his or her origins may still be important to an adopted person.

People adopted before November 12, 1975 are required to see a counselor before they can be given access to their records because, in the years before 1975, some parents and adopters may have been led to believe that the children being adopted would never be able to find out their original names or the names of their parents. These arrangements were made in good faith, and it is important that adopted people who want to find out more about their origins should understand what it may mean for them and others.

This means that *if you were adopted before November 12, 1975,* you will have to see an experienced social worker called a counselor before you can obtain further information from your original birth record.

There was something in the phrasing that had made me pause. *What* might it mean for me? And who else was it going to affect if I began my search properly? The Adoption Contact Register had drawn a blank. All they'd said was that "my details had been entered in Section 1," so that must mean there was nothing in Section 2 that matched up. But Jessie Pilkington probably didn't know the Register existed. Why should she? She'd been told nobody could trace anybody when she handed me over, and that was that. However you looked at it, I was going to be a bolt from the blue. Best not to overanalyze the situation, really. I mean, if you went through life examining the minute consequences of everything you were about to do, you'd end up so bloody paranoid you'd do nothing. We might as well all live under the table.

I shut the letter inside a cookbook and shoved it to the back of the cupboard.

"Phyllis Heaton's had a hysterectomy, did I tell you?" Nan was playing with a piece of toast left over from breakfast; God knows where she'd stowed it.

"No, Mum. No, she hasn't. She's gone *ex-directory.* You misheard." I was going to be explaining Phyllis Heaton's unlisted phone number for the next six months.

"And she can't accept it." Nan carried on as if I hadn't spoken. "If you ask her, she denies it. Eeh, it's a shame for some folk. We don't know as what we'll come to, any of us." She gnawed at the toast like a terrier.

It was then I noticed the amaryllis.

"God, Mum, what's happened to my flower?"

Instead of two brilliant red trumpets, a naked green spike rose two feet into the air and stopped. The pot had been pushed back to the left of the windowsill, behind the curtain, so I knew who'd done it. I leaned across the table and slid it back out.

"Mum? Mum, look at me. Mum, what happened to the flowers on the end? Where have they gone?"

Nan laughed uncomfortably. "I was closing the curtains and I must have caught it. It came away in my hand. It'll be all right."

"How can it be all right when you've knocked its head off? Honestly! I can't keep anything nice in this house. If it's not you it's Charlotte, with her magazines and clothes all over the floor. I ask her and ask her to tidy them up, but she takes no notice; neither of you do. What's the point of me reading *Homes and* bloody *Gardens* when you're busy mutilating my plants and hiding bits of food around the place?"

Nan glanced guiltily at the sofa.

"Oh, hell, you've not got butter on the cushions, have you?" I flipped them up angrily, one after the other. But it wasn't toast, it was the amaryllis, tattered and flaccid like a burst balloon and sporting a little tape collar round the base. I held it up, speechless.

"It'll be all right," said Nan. "We'll just stick it back on. It'll be all right." But she didn't sound convinced.

"No, Mum. It won't be all right." The flower heads came apart and I squashed them hard in my palms, feeling the cool petals bruise and smear. When I opened my hands it was like the stigmata. Nan stared. I looked over to where the letter was hidden, waiting. "There are some things you can't mend."

There is *no privacy* in this house. My mum, probably just to spite me, has the phone wall-mounted in the hall, which is just about big enough for two medium-sized people to stand chest to chest. Since there is no room even for a chair, let alone those swanky telephone seats she drools over in the catalogs, I have to sit on the stairs to have a conversation. It's bloody freezing, too. I don't know why we bother having a fridge, we could just keep the milk on the doormat. The letter box doesn't fit properly and she's never got around to fixing it (waiting for a man to sort it for her; dream on, Ma), so it blows open at the slightest breeze. You can, of course, hear everything that's going on in the next room and vice versa. So all in all, it's pretty crappy. I'm *definitely* getting a cell phone for my birthday.

I could have sneaked out to the public phone booth, but knowing my luck my money would jam or run out, or there'd be some pervo outside listening in. I needed this call to go well; I had to be on top of it. I didn't want to lay my heart on the line in a stinky glass box.

As I dialed the number, I could hear Mum picking on Nan again, something to do with some stupid flower. Like it matters. I pulled Nan's scarf down from the hook above and wound it round my neck. It smelled of Coty L'Aimant.

Ringing. Ringing. Click.

Paul: Hello?

Me: Hello.

Paul: Hello?

Me: It's me, Charlotte. I was—

Paul: Oh, yeah, right, Charlotte.

Me: Yeah . . .

Paul: I was going to give you a ring.

Me: Did you get what you were after?

Paul: You what?

Me: Your video. Your dad said you'd gone into Bolton.

Paul: Oh, yeah. Oh, I see what you mean. Yeah, *England's Pride,* top twenty goals of the decade. Narrated by David Beckham. I've not watched it yet.

Me: Sounds fantastic. Look, when you do, can I be the first to borrow it?

Paul: Ha bloody ha. It's better than a video on, I dunno, makeup or something, girly stuff.

Me: Fuck off. Look, did you want to meet up for a drink sometime? Only . . .

Paul: Oh, yeah, right, that would be great. Um, yeah. I'll give you a ring . . . we'll get something sorted. Maybe next week. If it's not too busy. All right?

Me: Yeah. All right. Well . . .

Paul: I'll call you.

Me: Paul?

Paul: What?

Me: Who's Chrissy?

Pause, click, dial tone.

The door to the living room opened and Nan wandered out. There were crumbs all down her front.

"Phyllis Heaton's had a hysterectomy," she said sadly, and sat down on the step next to me.

I unwound the scarf and draped it round us both. I wanted to cry.

"There's some things as can't be mended," she whispered.

Well, you wouldn't catch me even thinking about it," said Sylv, swinging her knees to and fro on her swivel chair like she does; one of these days she'll unswivel herself completely. I was sitting in the office to cut out my thirty daffodil shapes, because Year 6 was watching a science program on TV and the classroom was too dark to see what I was doing, not that it was exactly taxing stuff. Sylv, however, had been delighted to see me. "I *mean,* what if they want your bone marrow?"

"They what?"

Sylv looked at me as if I was stupid. "Don't you watch the news? When these long-lost relatives meet up, there's always someone wanting your bone marrow or your kidneys or what have you, and then if you don't give it to them *you're* the villain. I was reading about a case in *Woman's Own* last week. This woman didn't even know she had a twin brother until he turned up on the doorstep wanting her organs. It's a hell of a risk, Karen. I wouldn't touch it in your shoes."

Thanks, Sylv, I thought, these heart-to-hearts we have are invaluable. You've helped me make up my mind. I'm going to find my birth mother if it kills me.

Just then the Headmaster came into the office with a letter for typing. Sylv quivered like a pointer.

"What do you think, Mr. Fairbrother?" She ignored my desperate expression and plunged on. "Do you think Karen should try to find her natural parents?"

Give him his due, Mr. F didn't bat an eyelid. I suppose he's used to it; he sees Sylv all the time, whereas the rest of us only consort with her at break times.

"I really couldn't give an opinion," he said, and put the letter down on the desk. "Can you get this out to Gavin Crossley's parents by the end of the day? We'll have to have them in; it's no good. Daryl Makinson's had to have stitches." Then he turned to me. "A difficult decision for you. Not one I should like to be faced with." He gave me a nice smile and left us to it.

"Such a shame," said Sylv, as soon as the door was shut. She means because he's past forty, possibly fifty, and still single, and used to live with his parents till they both died, and now he lives on his own in that big house up Castleton Road and must rattle around in it—why he doesn't buy a little bungalow?—maybe he's homosexual but doesn't realize it, not that it matters in this day and age. And he's losing his hair, poor chap. I've heard Sylv's musings on the subject more times than I can count. But he's actually a pleasant man and really quite okay as a boss, especially when you think the staff are all women: you'd think we'd drive him mad. He's great when I need to take time off for Nan, and he buys us all Christmas presents, just bits and pieces, but it's the thought. This year it was cacti. Sylv got a squat, spiky number. Mine was tall and sort of hairy, as if a gang of spiders had run amok over it. I don't like them as plants, I tend to think they're a bit common. You never see cacti on *Inspector Morse.* So I put Mr. F's effort on the back kitchen windowsill, behind the terra-cotta garlic jar, but I didn't throw it out; that would have been ungrateful.

The bell was about to ring for break so Sylv tottered off to the Ladies' to redo her lipstick and rearrange her underskirt, and I gathered up my daffodils and set off for the classroom. As I got to the corner, some of them began to escape and flutter to the floor. Any minute now and they'd be stampeded by a bunch of ten-year-olds, so I put the rest of the pile on the nature table, got down on my hands and knees, and began swishing up the little paper shapes with my hands.

"Let me help." Mr. F, with his clipboard and stock-cupboard invoices under one arm, was stooping to pick at a lone petal that had welded itself to the gray vinyl floor tiles. "Tricky customers, aren't they? Look, I'm sorry about earlier."

I must have looked blank.

"In the office. Sylv." He lowered his voice. "Sometimes her enthusiasm to—um, *help* gets the better of her."

"It's not your fault; you've nothing to apologize for."

"Well. Rest assured, it won't go any further." He handed me my daffodil. "And if you'd like someone to talk it through with sometime, someone objective . . . I can see it must be a difficult situation, with your mother being as she is. . . . Anyway, I'm usually in the Feathers of a Sunday lunchtime; the Fourgates Ramblers meet there. It's quite a nice atmosphere; I don't know if you've ever been in. No jukebox, which is a rarity these days."

Before I had time to do anything other than smile vaguely,

we heard the click of heels behind us. Sylv's face, newly drawn on, was eager with news. "You might like to know we're running short of paper towels in the Ladies'," she said, as she drew level. Mr. F gave a small salute and walked off toward his room. "He's very much on the short side for a headmaster, isn't he?"

My dad always says, "As one door shuts, another one slams in your face." Mind you, he's not nearly as bitter as my mum, because according to her he didn't have anything like as much to lose. He was an apprentice with British Aerospace when she got caught, and he just carried on, finished his training, and got a full-time job there. He's still on the machines, despite waves of layoffs and his appallingly casual attitude. "He thinks it's beneath him," my mum often says, and we know who to blame for that idea. A blue-collar worker? Nah. She wanted to land a professional, a doctor or a lawyer, that sort of league.

Anyway, he's wrong. About the doors. I was asked out by someone else the very next week.

I was in the senior library; I often am. I love it in there. It smells of furniture polish, and the wicker-bottom chairs creak under you as you lean back against the radiator to chew your pen and think. On sunny days the light makes beams of sparkly dust that drifts like random thoughts. The calm is intoxicating. It's about as unlike our house as you can get.

The one thing my mum can't get at me for is, I *do* work. I'm after four As, mainly to get me away from her. Don't know if I'll get the grades, but it won't be for lack of trying. There was another midterm coming up and an essay to get out of the way (what I want to know is, why can't teachers communicate with one another so you don't get about twenty deadlines at once?).

So I had my Keats out and my Brodie's *Notes* and my Oxford pad, and I was just getting into my web diagram when someone put an illegal cup of hot chocolate down on the desk next to me.

"Absolutely *no* food and drink to be consumed in the library," said Daniel Gale brightly. "It's okay, the librarian's outside arguing with Mr. Stevens over the budget. She'll be there for the duration. Cheers." He produced a Kit Kat and snapped it in half. "There you go. Eat up."

Out of the corner of my eye I saw two Year 11 girls half turn to gawk.

"What's that for?"

He ran his hand through his wiry hair like he does and pushed his glasses against the bridge of his nose. "You looked in need."

"Of what, exactly?"

"Chocolate."

"I think you ought to know I never accept sweets from strangers." I bit into the Kit Kat and felt better. "Thanks."

"My big sister always swore by chocolate. Contains iron and antioxidants, boosts your immune system, and relaxes your arterial walls, making strokes less likely. Really. It ought to live in the medicine cabinet. And, most importantly, it lifts your mood through the mystic power of everyone's favorite chemical neurotransmitter—*ta-da!*—serotonin."

The Year 11s were hunching their shoulders suspiciously and nudging one another. Girls that age are *so* immature.

"Right. Do I look like a miserable bugger, then?"

He had the grace to look uncomfortable. "I overheard Julia telling Anya that you'd split with your boyfriend. Although, and I know I'm almost certainly going to regret saying this, he was somewhat lacking in sartorial discretion." Daniel sat down opposite me and leaned forward across the desk. "He dressed like an idiot."

I was genuinely confused. He didn't even know Paul.

"Spooky leather trousers. Give you crotch rot. Apparently. Not that I've ever worn them."

"Oh, I get you. He—it wasn't—" I stopped. If I started to explain, he'd think I was a right tart. Bloody hell. Why did I attract these weirdos? What bloody business was it of his anyway? "It's not really your place to comment," I snapped, and stuffed the rest of the Kit Kat into my mouth.

For a moment he seemed crushed. "No, fair enough. Scrub that bit. Foot in bloody mouth again. The Aztecs used cocoa beans as a simple form of currency, you know." He snatched up the hot chocolate and took a deep swig. Then he put the plastic cup back down on my web diagram and grinned hopefully. I scowled back. He took the scrap of silver foil and scrunched it deftly into a four-pointed star shape, which he stuck on the end of his finger and waved around. The star dropped off and skittered away, leaving a red dent in his skin. Finally he picked up my retractable ballpoint and began clicking it on and off rapidly.

"Right. Well, having fucked up big-time I might as well go the whole hog." He fixed his gaze on me. "Would you—*go out with me*?"

It seemed to me he shouted those words and they went

echoing round the ceiling, because the hum of chat suddenly dropped, like it always does exactly when you don't want it to.

I was completely amazed. It wasn't only that he looked a bit odd and talked pure nonsense, it had been popularly assumed since he arrived at school that he wasn't interested in girls. Electrical gadgets, maybe; human relationships, no. He'd been here a term and a half and never asked anyone out, never made out with anyone at a party, never even seemed to notice the opposite sex in any way. Julia had reckoned he might be one of these Jesus freaks. There was an intensity about him that made you feel fidgety. He certainly wasn't like anyone else.

"Shit, shit, shit. I've done it wrong, haven't I? I ought to have said, 'I've got two tickets for a gig,' or 'Do you fancy coming for a drink sometime?' " He threw down the pen and crumpled up the Kit Kat paper in anguish. "And then you'd say, 'No, sorry, I'm bathing the dog that night,' and I'd crawl off and die quietly in a corner somewhere. Much as I'm going to do now." He flushed and rose to his feet, scraping the chair loudly on the parquet so that the Year 11s put their pens down and turned right around to watch the show. "Don't know what I was thinking of. Sorry. Catch you later," he muttered. Then he slunk off, banging the double swing doors behind him.

I slumped forward and bowed my head till my brow touched the wooden desk. Absolutely fucking marvelous. Just what I needed at the moment, to be responsible for someone else's misery.

That lunchtime I watched him in the lounge. He was sitting, as usual, with the Two Nerds (subjects: Math, Further Math, Math with Knobs On, Complete Bastard Math). One's tall, the other's short, but they both have bad haircuts and crap clothes and look about forty. Daniel looked almost elegant beside them, with his good suit and expensive shoes (I don't think they're short of money in his house).

The nerds were playing chess and Daniel was making a show of reading an Asterix book. There was this *aura* of unhappiness around him. I edged my chair closer to Julia and laughed loudly at something Anya said. The realization made the hairs on my neck prickle: he reminded me of myself.

I didn't mind school, on the whole. Now our Jimmy hated it. As soon as it was time to go, he'd want the toilet. He'd stay in, and when the factory whistle went at nine he'd come out. Of course it was no good then, 'cause you got the stick across your hand if you were five minutes late. He was the worst on Monday mornings when his class had to go through the books of the Old Testament. *Gen*esis, *Ex*odus, Le*vit*icus, *Num*bers. He had a block, he said; he could do them at home. *First* and Second *Sam*uel, *First* and Second *Kings*. You could hear him chanting it through the toilet wall. But the minute he got his bum on t' long wooden form with th' others, it went straight out of his head. So he'd get t' stick again.

One day there was a bit of excitement. The big lads in the top class—some of them were fourteen, and tall—turned on the headmaster, Mr. Avis. He was a vicious man; he had it coming. He used to cane pupils for nothing, humiliate them just to show who was boss. Nobody ever learned anything in his class, you were too frightened. Six of 'em carried him to the window, opened it up, pushed him out, and held him over the sill by his ankles. It was his good luck that there were some workmen in the hall below who heard his shouts and came running. The pupils pulled him back in sharpish and sat down meek as you like at their desks, so by the time the workmen arrived, the only evidence that something had been going on was Mr. Avis's red face and his broken suspender. He was far too embarrassed to admit the truth in front of them, it would have finished him in the village, and we weren't going t' say anything, so he picked up his cane, laid it across his desk, and said he was going home because he felt unwell. He resigned the same day. I think he went to teach at Lytham in the finish.

Startin' work wasn't much of an improvement. You still got the stick—well, you did at our place, and across your legs too. At thirteen I started in the cotton mill. It was that or the bleach-works or pickin' coal at Pit Brow; you hadn't a lot of choice in the matter. I had to clean under four looms before they started up, and you got sixpence extra for that, what they called your "spender." But it meant gettin' there early, and you had to walk it in all weathers. You got put with a woman who'd teach you you how to piece ends, that was called tentin', but if you were slow she'd rap your legs. They got paid by how much cloth they wove, you see, and they didn't want to waste time on sortin' out people like me. And every mornin' the boss'd be waitin' outside, ready to knock money off if you were late, which was worse than any stick.

They say the Good Old Days, but they weren't nice times, not really.

I think worries are like Russian dolls: Almost anything can be eclipsed by something worse. You think a terrible emergency is, say, a monster pimple or a bad grade, but that would be nothing if your house burned down, which would still not be as bad as if you found out you had incurable cancer. (I suppose the only calamity that could top that would be full-on nuclear war.) So it's a matter of scale.

I wondered, as I searched desperately for my completed Keats essay that Thursday night, why on earth I'd ever been concerned about a loon like Daniel Gale. I'd left the essay home on my desk, in a blue folder, ready to hand in next day, which would leave the weekend free to do some last-minute studying for the exam. But it had vanished. I looked in all the pockets of my schoolbag, my course books, my Oxford pad; I got down on my hands and knees and peered under the bed, moved magazines, shoes, clothes; schoolbag, course books, Oxford pad, and under the bed again; then downstairs: house magazines, table drawer, letter rack, under the sofa, under the chairs, in the sideboard, kitchen counters, kitchen cupboards, bread crock, trash bin inside, bin outside (quickly, because it was dark and smelly), laundry basket, bathroom cabinet, top of the toilet tank. There aren't that many places in a house the size of ours. Then I really started to panic.

"Mum. Mum! *Mum!*" I bounded back up the stairs and burst into her bedroom.

"God, Charlotte. Is there no privacy in this house?" she snapped, shutting the wardrobe mirror quickly. I vaguely took in the fact that she was wearing a black miniskirt and a shiny white blouse, like a waitress, and she'd been blow-drying her hair in a sad attempt at a Rachel. "Do you think you might knock before you come barging into my room?" Angrily, she pulled on her old gray sweater over the blouse; it was nearly as long as the skirt. She saw me staring. "I'm only thirty-three. Look at Madonna."

"Thirty-four tomorrow. What's Madonna got to do with it? Look, Mum, I'm desperate. Have you moved a blue folder from off my desk?"

She noticed the state I was in. "Give me a minute," she said, reaching for her leggings.

We both knew it was Nan. "Let me talk to her, you're too hyper." She went into Nan's room, and I heard low voices. Please, God, let her remember where she's put it, I prayed, as I hung outside the door biting my thumbnail. But Mum's face was glum as she came out.

"Oh, God, Mum! I spent *hours* on that essay! I haven't even got my notes anymore! Can't you have another go at her?"

We could hear Nan singing, so I knew it was hopeless.

> "Oh, the moon shines bright on Charlie Chaplin:
> His boots are crackin'
> For want of blackin'
> And his owd fustian coat is wantin' mendin'
> Before they send 'im
> To the Dardanelles."

"I know where we'll find it." Mum's expression was suddenly bright, and I noticed then she had lip gloss on.

"Go on."

"The Tin."

She slipped back into Nan's room and I heard the wardrobe door open, a scuffle as Mum shifted footwear aside, then the lid of the large cookie tin Nan keeps full of Spam and canned baked beans in case of war. I twisted impatiently and peeped around the jamb. Nan was flat out on the bed, staring at the ceiling.

At last Mum stood up. "Sorry, nothing. We'll try downstairs again."

"Jesus! Why do I have to live in this bloody hole?" I exploded at her. "You can't put *anything* down without someone interfering with it. I'm completely *sick* of this house! When I get my A levels, which I probably won't do at this rate, I'm moving out so fast it'll make your head spin. God almighty! What am I going to tell them at school? My nan ate my homework?" I was close to tears. "I *can't* do all that work again. I'm *so* tired. And what about my reviewing? I haven't *time* to do both, I'm just going to fail. I don't know why I *bother*."

"You're hyperventilating. Calm down. We'll have another look, and I'll write you a note." She squeezed past me and began to go downstairs.

"A *note*?" I shouted over the banisters at the top of her head. "Do you know how old I am? It's not like I need to be excused from games! A *note* won't do any good."

She turned her face up to me. "Do you want me to help you or not?"

"Christ!" I turned on my heel and threw myself into my bedroom, slamming the door. Papers fluttered off the desk, but not the right ones. I sank onto the bed in a jumble of self-pity. No one else had to put up with this continual family sabotage. Why hadn't I been born into a different life?

Except, I nearly was, wasn't I?

I'd been trying not to think about it, because the implications were too big and too scary. Only you can't *not* think of something, it's impossible. By making a conscious effort to block it out, you give it life. Try *not* thinking of a blue elephant. See?

Later on, it must have been about 2 A.M., I crept in to see Nan. She looked awful without her teeth, her head lolling, little snores coming from the back of her throat. Close up, you could see the pink scalp through her thin hair. One day she'll be dead, I thought, she'll be lying like this but there'll be no breathing and her skin will be cold. I took her small hand, loving and hating her at the same time. I'm here, in this house, in this life, because of you, I told her. She didn't stir.

Just before I went to sleep I remembered Mum's birthday present. *The Stately Duplex: How to Achieve the Neo-Classical Look in the Suburban Home.* She's forever decorating, trying to paint over the public housing, rag-roll away her roots. I supposed I ought to wrap it, so I tiptoed downstairs for some tape and there, as I clicked on the light, sitting on the table were some narrow-ruled sheets covered with my handwriting. My heart leaped. It wasn't the essay, it was only my notes. There was orange spaghetti-bolognese sauce on the top page, which my mum had tried to wipe off. She must have trawled through the trash bin after I'd gone to bed. I wrapped the present quickly and left it for the morning.

What is it about kids? I'd lie down in front of a train for Charlotte without a second thought, but most of the time I want to beat her about the head with a blunt instrument. Do all mothers feel this way?

*W*hen they laid her in my arms I thought I was going to die with happiness. I used to wheel her up the street in that big pram, and old Mrs. Moss would be leaning on her gate, and she'd say every time, "Whose babby's that? Wheer's tha getten it?" And I'd say, "She's mine." Mrs. Moss would suck her teeth. "She's not." I'd look down at the little fingers poking out over the top of the crocheted blanket. "Oh, yes, she is. She's mine. She's mine."

*N*ot enough sex. That's what causes aggression in middle age." Daniel Gale was twittering at me as I blew my nose into his enormous handkerchief. "It's true. Those ones who write in to *Points of View* to complain about the pronunciation of *controversy* or constantly moan on to the neighborhood council about their neighbor's hedges, those maniacs shouting their mouths off in restaurants and reducing the waitresses to tears, those are the types you know just don't get laid enough. You've got to feel sorry for them, really. I mean, Mrs. Stokes must weigh over two hundred pounds, and she's got that mustache. We know there's a Mr. Stokes, but I don't suppose he's panting to exercise his conjugal rights of an evening. That's why she was such an A-One bitch. Nothing to do with you at all." He hovered at my chair, not touching it, not sitting down. We were in the library; he'd followed after seeing me storm out of cow-bag Stokesy's office.

"But I've never been late with a piece of work for her, *ever*." I was still crying with temper. "She said, 'Oh, I'm sorry, Charlotte, you're the fifth person today with an excuse. I can't make an exception for you. Monday, nine A.M.' So *I* get penalized because of someone else's laziness." I put my head down on my arms. "And I'm *so* tired. I want to sleep all the time." I'd been too angry to be embarrassed with him at first so he got it all, blow by blow, from Nan downward. Now I'd finished, though, I wanted him to go away. "Here." I lifted my head up and gave him back his handkerchief. I knew my mascara must have run, so it was imperative I get to a mirror as soon as possible.

"You can keep it, if you like."

"No, really."

"You've got a bit of . . ." He gestured to his own cheek. "Do you want me to . . . ?" He was wrapping the hanky round his finger, the way mums do with messy toddlers.

"No! Sorry, no, it's okay. I need to wash my face anyway."

"Right."

"I'm fine now. Nothing a hat pin and a voodoo doll won't cure." I smiled feebly.

"Right." He hesitated. "See you."

"Yeah. And thanks," I called after him faintly. He didn't acknowledge me.

·   ·   ·

But on Monday, after I'd handed in my essay and before the exam started, he found me again.

"You been here all weekend? Sorry, stupid joke. I won't hold you up." He nodded at my open textbook. "I just wondered if this was any use." He plunked a plastic bag down on the table. I peered in and nearly swallowed my ballpoint in shock.

"My God, Daniel, it's a laptop! You can't give me this!"

His hands went fluttery, and he swept his hair back several times. "No, no, it's simply a glorified typewriter. We've had it for ages. My dad was literally throwing it out—well, he was going to put it in the loft anyway. He doesn't bother with it now he's got the PC. It's yours to borrow—indefinitely—if you think it'll help."

"How do you mean?"

"You can save your essays on disk as you type them. That way it wouldn't matter if you lost a copy; you'd always have a backup. It's an absolute breeze to use. The instruction booklet's in there, and I've formatted a couple of disks for you so it's all ready to go. Just be careful not to pull the cord out while you're in the middle of something; that deletes it all. Best to save your text as you go along." He was babbling now. "Oh, there's this as well." He fished out a small cardboard box and flashed it at me before dropping it back into the bag. "Iron tablets. You're probably a bit anemic, that's why you're so tired. My sister used to take them, before she ran off to join the circus—well, study medicine at Birmingham. Not these actual tablets, obviously. I'm not trying to palm drugs off on you that are past their sell-by date." He gave a high-pitched laugh. "Anyway, give them a try—or not—as you like."

He let go of the back of the chair he'd been gripping and stalked off toward the doors.

Well, I'll be damned, I thought. You've got to give the guy credit for trying.

I picked up the bag and ran after him, *squeak squeak* across the parquet. Everyone looked.

I caught up with him outside and held up the typewriter.

"I understand. You can't accept it. Say no more." He sighed and made to take the handles of the bag.

"No, no, it's fab. I'm really grateful. Tell your dad thanks. And—if you want, if you're not doing anything on Saturday afternoon, I usually go to Tiggy's for a coffee about three. Do you know where I mean? So—"

"I'll see you there." He grinned manically and all but ran off down the corridor.

Right away I wished I hadn't done it. He was bound to get the wrong idea.

In the event, it didn't matter. Not at all. That Saturday, at about three, Daniel, the essay, the exam were a million years ago. I was in my bedroom, among the posters and the pictures of impossibly beautiful women, staring at my naked body in the full-length mirror. Downstairs, Mum was lecturing Nan at top volume, and through the chink of curtain I could see the light of a keen bright spring afternoon.

I was trying to see if my breasts had gotten any bigger. I had to contort a bit because of the old Take That stickers, which refused to peel off the glass properly. Robbie Williams leered at me unhelpfully but Gary Barlow looked sympathetic, even though the top of his head was missing. I turned sideways to check out my stomach. I grabbed some flesh and pinched. Impossible to tell. Then I let out my breath. That did look pregnant. I sucked in my muscles again quickly.

I heard Mum pounding up the stairs; thank God I'd locked the door. She was shouting down to Nan to stay where she was or she'd get it all over her clothes. There was the sound of drawers slamming, then footsteps on the stairs again. I blanked it out and continued gazing.

I wasn't sure where the idea had come from. I hadn't felt sick in the mornings, but my bra had definitely got tighter. If only I had X-ray vision. What would I see? A little fishy tadpole thing, wriggling its limbs and nodding its outsize head? Probably the length of a baked bean, if I was right about the dates. Oh, please let me not be right. Would it have *implanted* itself in me yet? Burrowed in? God.

It was paranoia. I looked exactly the same. There was no baby. I started to put my clothes back on and checked my underwear once more for blood. Virgin white, alas. Still, I'd been late before; that meant nothing. My jeans still fit, so it was probably all right.

Suddenly there was a clattering noise from the hall. I pulled my sweatshirt on, unlocked the door, and ran across the landing to see. Mum was bending down to pick up the pile of CDs that had been posted hastily through the letter box. I saw her open the front door in puzzlement and, beyond her, Paul's retreating figure hurrying across the road.

Without a second thought I dashed down the stairs, whipped a pistol out the pocket of Nan's Welsh wool coat, which was hanging in the hall, and fired. In the distance Paul crumpled into a denim heap.

"Nice shot," said Mum admiringly.

No, not really. What actually happened was that together we craned to watch him disappear around the corner. Then I turned and ran back into my room, slamming the door shut.

chapter 4

I stayed put in my room for two hours and would ideally have spent the rest of my life there, only the need to pee drove me downstairs.

The table was set and tea was in progress, the TV blaring. Next to the pepper mill sat a neat tower of CDs.

"They catch seagulls off the garbage dump and pass them off as chicken," Nan was saying.

"Charles Darwin!" shouted my mother, oblivious to everything except *University Challenge*. "*The Magic Flute!*"

I hurried through and reached the bathroom. Nan had taken all the guest soaps out of their little pot and lined them up along the top of the toilet tank, as she always does. Usually I put them back, it avoids another row, but this time the lavender perfume pushed right up my nostrils and made me feel queasy. I leaned forward and laid my forehead on the rim of the cold sink. There was still no blood.

At last I got myself together and went to face the inquisition.

"You tell me." Nan was poking a drumstick around her plate and shivering theatrically. "You tell me what chicken has four legs. It's never right, that: four legs."

"They came out of a bag of chicken pieces off the market." Mum was busy eyeing up the TV host, Jeremy Paxman. "There were three wings as well."

"Good God."

"Yours is in the fridge, Charlotte, under some plastic wrap." Mum tore herself away from the screen. "Oh! What's happened to your head?"

In the mirror over the fire I could see the red furrow left by the edge of the sink. Christ.

"Nothing!" I said venomously and plunked myself down in the armchair.

And waited.

Bleak House. A. A. Milne. The Dissolution of the Monasteries.

"Was that the boy you were seeing before Christmas?" she hazarded finally.

Hah, Mother! You know *nothing*! You have no idea how long it's been going on! You miss what's *right under your nose*. You'd have a *blue fit* if you even knew the half of it. I *never* tell you anything because you'd always construct the worst (and OK, in this case you'd be right, but that's *not the point*). It's none of your business. I'm an adult. Get yourself a life; then you can stop interfering with mine!

I said, "Yeah."

"I take it . . . it's finished?"

I wanted to wrestle her to the ground and bang her skull repeatedly on her precious white marble hearth.

"What do *you* think?" I hunched my knees up under my sweatshirt and pulled in my arms so that the sleeves hung empty. I waited for her to say *Take your feet off the chair,* but she didn't. I hated her so much I could hardly breathe.

"They eat frogs' legs in France," said Nan, jabbing a fork in the direction of the TV. "The dirty buggers."

"He's not French, Nan, I've told you before. He does *Newsnight.*"

"Of course he is. Look at his nose."

How long would I have to live in this madhouse, I wondered, before my head caved in?

I was in the bedroom trying on clothes again when the telephone rang.

I'd just been thinking, Maybe I don't look so bad for my age; actually, you see a lot worse on reality TV. I haven't got those road-map veins you see some women with, and my teeth are all my own. You've got to be realistic. Anyway, I guess we could all look like Jennifer Aniston if we had a few million in the bank and a personal trainer. I wasn't fat, not *fat* fat. Size 12 isn't fat. I pulled my stomach in and turned sideways to the mirror. That didn't look bad at all. If I could stand in this pose for the rest of my life, people might think I was quite slim. I did a movie-star smile at myself and arched my eyebrows. Then I tilted my head and tried a wistful gaze: nice. If I ever released an album, this would be the cover shot.

I fluffed my hair up—currently mid-length, lightened, Brauned to within an inch of its life—and slicked some shimmery lipstick on my pout. You see, I told myself, if you had the *time* you could look half decent. But it's so hard with Charlotte and Mum. Sometimes it's like a conspiracy. I only have to get the can of shaving cream out of the cupboard and there's some domestic crisis, so back it goes on the shelf, and I get hairier. Thank God for opaque tights.

Charlotte would have had a fit if she knew how much I'd just spent on the catalogs; thank God you get to pay by installment. So What If I'll Never See Thirty Again, I've Got Legs, favorite outfit of the new batch, lay on the bed slinkily; I'd have to get the razor on my shins for that. You should have seen Charlotte's face when she saw me in it. Bit of a shock for her, seeing her mother look like a proper woman for a change. Serves her right for barging in.

She's a sly devil, though! Some daughters talk to their mothers, I've seen it on *Trisha,* but Charlotte's like a clam. I never know what's going on in her mind. Then again, if I'm being absolutely honest, I don't want to. It's not worth the row to ask, anyway. She'll snap your head off if you ask her what she wants on her toast, never mind how her love life's going.

You walk on eggshells in this house.

And this boy, nice-looking but cocky; I can't say I particularly liked him. I think his name was Paul. She used to go to St. Mary's with him, years ago. I'd only met him twice and even then she whisked him away before I could say much to him.

What would you say, though? *Paws off my daughter till she's finished her education?* She wouldn't thank me for that.

I wish I could have told her *It doesn't matter, you're better off without him,* but that would have sounded pretty hollow coming from me. We might be about to enter a third millennium, but a woman's still a nonperson without a man in tow. At least that's been my experience.

Anyway, the phone rang while I was still wearing *Semi-Casual Sunday Luncheon in a Pub with Mr. Fairbrother.* No chance of Charlotte stirring her stumps at the moment, she's far too traumatized, and Nan can't hear through the receiver properly so she won't touch it: probably just as well. The ringing continued as I wrestled with the top button. "Buggeration!" I yelled at my reflection. Album-cover girl had vanished. My face was hard and cross and my hair had gone all staticky.

"Telephone!" Nan shrieked up the stairs.

I gave in, shoved my slippers on, and nipped down to the hall. It was a woman from Bolton Social Services.

"We just need you to give us a couple more details. I think you missed a page on the form. Have you got your National Insurance number?"

I dug it out of the Useful Drawer in front of Nan's glassy stare and returned to the phone.

"I thought you were ringing to tell me you'd found my birth mother," I said, knowing it was stupid. They'd only had the forms a week.

The woman gave a short laugh. "We have to process the information first. Then you get assigned a social worker and have an interview. It's the procedure."

"Will it take long?"

"You should hear back from us in two to three months' time. Give us a call if you haven't heard anything by then."

"Two to three *months?*"

"It's the procedure."

"No sooner?"

"We're very overstretched at the moment."

Aren't we all, love? I felt like saying.

Nan opened the door as I was hanging up. She was focusing again and gave me the once-over. "Ooh, swanky. Turn around. You're a bonny woman when you want to be. I never see you in a dress." She stroked the sleeve thoughtfully. "You want a nice pair of pumps with that. Did you know you've a button loose?"

"You're one to talk," I said. "If anyone's got a button loose, it's you. Now, look, I'm going upstairs to reinvent myself. Stick the TV on and *don't* touch the kettle till I come down again."

A miracle! A bloody miracle! Well, two actually, although one's quite small-scale. And Fate can go stuff itself. Start the clocks again, open the champagne, exhale.

We were in the hall for the last assembly of the semester. We'd had the sermon, some nonsense about how all the people in Hell have to eat with six-foot-long chopsticks—where do they get this crap from? Then it was the hockey and soccer re-sults, then some Year 7 kids got a road safety award, and finally it was the dismissal prayer. The Headmaster put his fingertips together in that way that always makes me want to give him a good kicking, bowed his oily head, and began.

"Lord, thou knowest how busy I must be this day. . . ."

I prayed: *O God, please make me not be pregnant, please please; I'll make such an effort with Mum and Nan and I'll study really hard and never have sex again until I'm at least twenty-five, and then only with the pill, a condom, and a cap as well; please, God. Amen.*

Someone was digging me in the ribs.

"Get a move on, deaf ears," Julia hissed, and I looked up and saw the line of upper sixth nearly out the door and a big gap where I should have been following. I lurched forward and scuttled after them, aware that all the Year 11s behind were watching and snickering. "What's up?" asked Julia, when we got outside.

"Nothing. Just . . . I've got to go somewhere."

"Not coming into town with Anya and the twins?"

"Gotta go straight home, sorry. Thanks."

I knew the bus was waiting, but first I had to go check the state of my underwear.

The stall was narrow and the lock put up a fight. I closed my eyes, pushed my underwear down quickly, and stared. Blood. *Blood.* Thank Christ. My knees buckled and I sat down on the toilet rim, still staring. Not much blood, but that didn't matter. It was okay, everything was going to be okay. Outside, girls came and went, tanks flushed; then it all went quiet. I'd missed the bus but I didn't care. Catch another one. I could fly home, if it came to that.

Oh, the other little miracle, hardly worth mentioning really but one less thing to worry about. I'd been dreading seeing Daniel Gale and having to invent some lie about why I stood him up. Then, when he wasn't in on Monday, I began to wonder if he'd chucked himself off a highway bridge or something;

that'd be just my luck. Any minute now, I thought, the head of sixth is going to walk into the classroom with a stony face and ask us if we knew of any reason why he might have been feeling depressed. Then he was in registration on Tuesday, a tad paler than usual, perhaps, but definitely not dead. He kept trying to catch my eye, and I kept staring at the floor. I tried for a quick getaway out of the common room but he beat me to the door and put his hand on my shoulder, all breathless and earnest. Here we go, I thought, clenching my teeth.

"I am *so* sorry," he began, making my mouth drop open.

"What?"

"About Saturday. God! I hope you didn't wait for long. I know you must be really angry with me, I mean it's the most awful manners, you must think I'm unbelievably rude—"

"No! No, not at all—"

We were hustled through the door in the general throng. Someone pushed between us with a large art folder; then the bell went off above our heads. We grimaced at each other until the din stopped.

"Look, I'll be quick." He pushed his hair out of his eyes and blinked. "I did try to contact you. I went through the directory, but there were loads of Coopers and my mum was on the phone most of the night anyway. The thing is, we heard on Friday night that my grandfather in Guildford had died. Mum wanted to go down straightaway but Dad persuaded her to wait till Saturday morning—"

"Oh, God, I'm really sorry."

"Yeah, well. Thanks. These things happen. He was a nice guy but pretty old. Mum's a mess, though, and so is my grandmother, so you can imagine, it was all a bit hectic over the weekend, traveling down there and back. But I really am sorry about leaving you in the lurch like that."

I tried not to seem joyful. "Forget it. Honestly. It must have been awful for you." I laid a hand on his arm and he looked down at it in surprise. I took it off again hastily.

"The thing is, I was really looking forward to it."

"No bother. Some other time."

"We're down there again this weekend. The funeral's on Friday."

"We'll catch up at some point. I'm in town most Saturdays." The corridor had gone worryingly quiet.

"So, what, the Saturday after?"

"Whatever, yeah. Look, we'd better get a move on, it's nearly twenty-five past. Last day or not, Stokesy's a complete bitch if you're late for any of her classes; she keeps records, you know, and then makes sarcastic comments on your report."

"And I should be in physics, which is right over the other side, which means it'll be half-past by the time I make an entrance. Hardly worth going, in fact." He furrowed his brow. "Do you fancy ditching, just for this class?"

"*What?*" Daniel was even more law-abiding than me.

"I don't mean leave the building or anything rash like that. We could just go back to the lounge and have a coffee. Quite a minor crime. *I'll* be okay, I can say I was overcome with sudden grief, and I'll put on an innocent expression and swear to Mrs. Stokes that I compelled you to stay and counsel me. You'd get away with it because you're normally so good. And they think I'm so weird they wouldn't pursue it for fear of sending me into a mad fit."

I began a laugh, then looked away in embarrassment.

"Sorry. I shouldn't be so flippant about my grandfather. I'm not, honestly. He was a great guy, and I'll miss him. Only it's so bloody serious at home—awful, actually. Scary seeing your parents show their feelings."

I thought of our house, where feelings flowed like hot and icy water, constantly. I realized my mouth was open again and shut it.

"So, what do you say?" He cocked his head and looked at me over his glasses.

"You're full of surprises, aren't you?"

"I like to think so." He turned to go back through the door. "Coming?"

"Nope. You might be a genius, but I have to work my tail off to get a half-decent grade. She's going over past papers today and I need to be there. That's the trouble with me; I'm just so bloody conscientious." I smiled and he smiled back. "Enjoy the coffee, though. And I will use you as an alibi, if that's still okay."

"I'll be ready to prostrate myself with misery at break time."

And he did. And then I bled. Happy Easter.

I t didn't get off to a particularly auspicious start, that Sunday. I'd downed a couple of gins for luck and put the new dress on. Then I stood in front of the wardrobe mirror, trying to decide on earrings: studs or danglies. Downstairs Nan was belting out "Tell Me the Old, Old Story"; presumably they'd had it at church that morning. From behind her bedroom door, Charlotte was moaning like a cat in pain, which meant she must have her headphones on. And me? *Well, tonight, Matthew, I'm going to be*—I breathed on the glass and waited till the mist cleared—*Celine Dion!* (Sounds of cheering, clapping, murmurs of amazement, et cetera.) Pouting at my reflection, I took a deep breath. I had to admit the new highlights did look good.

"Baby, think twice, for the sake—"

The smoke alarm began to go off in the kitchen.

"Fucking hell," I said to Celine in the mirror, and dashed down the stairs. Nan met me at the bottom.

"Karen! The toaster's set afire. What do I do?"

I shouldered her aside and barged into the kitchen. Black smoke was rolling from the toaster slot. Nan appeared at my shoulder, wringing her hands.

"I was just mekkin' a bit o' dinner—"

"I was *going* to do it, if you'd just waited for two minutes!" I yelled, and she shrank back into the living room.

I wrenched the plug out of its socket and flung a dishcloth over the toaster. The smoke stopped. I opened the back door, put on oven mitts, and carried the thing to the step, then stood looking at it. Thirty seconds later Charlotte came in, sniffing.

"What's that awful smell?" she said. Then she spotted the trail of crumbs across the tiled floor, the dishcloth bundle. "Oh, right. I bet Nan's been putting the cheese spread on again before the bread goes in. I caught her trying that one last week. She scrapes it on about an inch thick, and it welds itself to the element." She put on a sorrowful face. "Poor old Nan. She doesn't understand; it's not her fault. Do you know she's crying on the sofa?"

I ignored her; it was that or stab her to death with a fork. I didn't know why she was being so bloody reasonable all of a sudden, but I could do without it. The doorbell rang.

"That'll be Ivy. I'll go. By the way, you've got odd earrings in, Mum."

"And Ivy is?" Mr. Fairbrother, my boss, took a sip of his pint. He'd moved his chair a little off from the rest of the Fourgates Ramblers, and we were sitting at the end of a long table in the lounge bar of the Feathers. Thank God he'd seemed pleased to see me. Thank God he'd been there at all.

"One of Nan's friends from her Mothers' Union days. Ivy Seddon and Maud Eckersley take her up to church every Sunday, then Ivy comes and sits with her in the afternoon. They take her to the Over Seventies' Club on a Wednesday across at the Working Men's, and Maud visits on a Tuesday morning and stays for her dinner. And if one's ill, the other comes; they never let me down. Then I have a woman from Crossroads Carers on a Monday and a cleaner for three hours on Thursday, which I pay for out of the allowance. I mean, I could leave her with Charlotte, and I do sometimes, but I try not to. Anyway, Charlotte's at school most of the time, so I couldn't even do part-time work without some help. It's funny how these things creep up on you. Ten years ago, even five, Nan was fine, just a bit forgetful, then . . ."

Mr. F looked sympathetic. "Your mother's lucky to have a support network. That's the marvelous thing, though, about community. Our parents grew up in a time when everybody knew everybody else in this village. Times may have been hard, but they all helped one another out. There's too much isolation these days."

I nodded, thinking of myself. Where was *my* little network

of support, my social life? At age fifteen there was a big group of us, out every weekend. More energy than we knew what to do with, on the phone all hours. It used to drive Nan mad. We all had plans; we were going to set the world on fire. Then Dee, my best friend, moved to Cheltenham, and I got pregnant, and there was just this *gulf* between me and the other girls, even though they tried to be nice about it.

Some of it was not understanding. They got fed up with me moaning about always being tired, and they didn't see why I couldn't leave the baby and just go off places at the drop of a hat. And I couldn't confide about the horror of veins all over my boobs, peeing when I sneezed, the big jagged purple lines on my tummy.

Some of it was, too, they were scared it might happen to them, that they might "catch" my pregnancy. I always remember one of them, Donna Marsden, coming to see me in the hospital. She'd gotten a little rabbit suit for Charlotte and she'd come all prepared to coo. But she barely looked at the baby. What she couldn't keep her eyes off the whole visit was my saggy stomach, bursting out from under one of Nan's old nightgowns. She was clearly appalled. Finally she slinked off down the ward in her size 6 jeans and I sat in the metal-framed bed and cried my eyes out.

The bottom line was, I was going to be married with a baby while they were all running off to college to screw around and do things with their lives. And by the time some of them came back to Bank Top to settle down and do the family stuff, I was divorced and they didn't much understand that either.

Mr. F was still speaking, fortunately, and didn't notice the tears of self-pity pricking my eyes.

"Sorry?"

"And, of course, your mother's lucky to have you. Too many people walk away from their responsibilities these days." He smiled at me approvingly, and I thought his face looked nice, fatherly. He was wearing an Aran sweater, canvas trousers, and hiking boots. It was odd to see him out of a suit. "By the way, I take it you've had lunch?"

I glanced down the long table and took in the dirty plates and screwed up paper napkins. Bloody hell, him and his rambling mates had already eaten.

"Oh, yes. I had something before I came out," I lied, praying my stomach wouldn't rumble.

"Then I'll get you another—what was it, vodka and orange?"

"Lovely." I'd have to scarf some peanuts in the Ladies' room soon, or I'd be drunk as a lord. Pace yourself, I thought. On the other hand, the quicker I drank this round, the sooner I'd get something to eat.

"So how long's your mum been a widow?" Mr. F's brow furrowed as he handed me my glass and sat down again.

"God, let me . . . nearly twenty years it'll be. January 1978, my dad died."

"I'm sorry."

"Yeah, it was pretty grim in the end. Lung cancer. It seemed to go on forever, him being ill, but then I didn't really know all the details. I was only fourteen, and Nan kept a lot of it to herself."

"She sounds like a strong woman."

"Oh, she is. They built them tough in those days. Once, when she was a little girl, she broke her elbow and she never cried. Her brother, though, went into hysterics, apparently, and they all thought it was him that was hurt because he was in such a state he couldn't get the words out to explain."

Mr. F smiled. "But you're strong in your own way."

"Not really." If only he knew the truth. But it was flattering all the same. *This* date I wasn't going to spend the whole time dissecting my own inadequacies, I'd done enough of that in the past. His niceness, and seeing him in these unfamiliar surroundings looking like a real person rather than a boss, made me ridiculously nervous. I swigged at the vodka like it was going out of fashion and grinned inanely.

"Yet to cope with losing your father at that age. It must have been traumatic."

The grin fell off my face. "Yeah. It was, actually. We were really, really close; he'd have done anything for me. . . . At least he didn't live to see. . . . But then he'd have loved Charlotte, he really would. I think it's what pulled Nan through in the end, having my baby around. She was, I have to admit it, brilliant with Charlotte. I used to walk out of those screaming rows with Steve, go around to Nan's, and dump the baby in her arms. I don't know how I'd have coped otherwise."

"And yet you still want to look for your biological mother?"

I paused, and Mr. F looked concerned.

"I'm sorry, do tell me if I'm stepping out of line—"

"No, not at all. It's nice to have the chance to talk it over with someone. I was just thinking. . . ." I drained my vodka and stood up. "Um, while I'm up, shall I get some more drinks?" I glanced at his pint. Mr. F had drunk about two inches. He tried not to look surprised.

"No, not for me, thanks."

"Well, I'll just—"

I got two packets of dry roasted and headed off to the Ladies'. Actually, peanuts take longer to eat than you think. I leaned against the sink and munched like a demented hamster; then a door opened and I nipped into a stall. Several years later I finished the first packet, tore open the second, and poured them into my mouth. Next door the other person pulled the chain, and the shock sent a peanut nib down the wrong way. I started a choking fit, scattering bits of mashed-up nut and spit everywhere. Finally I got my breath back, but by then I'd totally gone off the whole peanut thing. I threw the plastic packets in the loo and flushed. They floated back up. I waited till the tank filled, the theme tune to *Countdown* running through my head, and flushed again. When the bubbles cleared, the packets had vanished but two stubborn peanuts still lurked in the bottom of the pan. Screw it, that'd have to do.

I opened the door cautiously and saw my reflection in the mirror. My cheeks were bright red and my eyeliner had run. I moved over to the sink and started to repair the damage, trying not to catch the eye of the other woman, who was making a big production of washing her hands. Sod off, I told her silently. But she went on standing there and, I thought, taking sneaky glances at me every so often. Then, just as I thought she was finished, she sidled over and murmured, "You can get out of it, you know."

"What?" I hadn't a clue what she was on about.

"I used to be like you." Since she was about ten years younger and a heck of a sight more glamorous, I wondered what she meant. She lowered her voice to a whisper. "I used to have an eating disorder." She laid a comforting hand on my shoulder. "You can break out of it, with help."

Light dawned. She thinks I've been making myself sick.

"It's nothing to be ashamed of. Princess Diana—"

"Thanks, but you've got me wrong."

She smiled and began rooting in her handbag. "I always carry these. When you're ready, just give them a ring. Admitting you've got a problem is the first step." She squeezed my elbow and placed a little card in my hand, then went out. THE BULIMIA HELPLINE, I read. TOGETHER WE CAN CHANGE TOMORROW.

What about changing yesterday? Now that really would be worth calling about.

I got myself a spritzer and rejoined Mr. F. Across the room the lady from the toilets gave me the thumbs-up.

"You were saying?"

"About my mum? Yeah, well. . . . It's difficult to explain, you probably won't have the foggiest what I'm babbling on about."

He looked worried again. "No, please."

"Well, it's like—no, you'll think I'm crazy."

"Go on."

"Well . . . do you ever think you might be living the *wrong life?*"

He leaned forward, as if getting his forehead closer to mine might help him understand.

"I mean, who we are, where we live, the jobs we do—

everything, really—it's all just down to chance, isn't it? The lottery of where we were born and who to. It's like the same person could be born into two completely different homes—well, not *really,* but imagine it." I started shuffling the coasters purposefully around the table. "In one home you might get loads of encouragement, go to a posh school, end up all confident and successful in some top job, while in another you might have scummy parents who don't care about you, you might get in with a bad crowd and go to a rotten school and end up in prison or something. . . . Am I making sense?"

"The Prince and the Pauper?"

"Yeah, that's it, sort of." I leaned a pair of coasters into a wigwam. "I don't mean I've been living like a pauper, God knows Nan did her best, but I've always felt like I belonged elsewhere. I mean, I'm nothing like her. She's never been that interested in my education, for one thing. As long as I behaved myself at school, that was enough for her. The comprehensive school was okay, and I'd probably have done really well if, if—"

I had a sudden flash of memory, Steve in school uniform leaning against the iron gates, arms folded: that was the afternoon before the First Time. I shook my head and the image cleared.

"But she'd never have even thought of sending me to the grammar school, and I didn't because of my friends. . . . And she's got—it's not her fault, it's the way she was brought up—oh, God, I sound like such a snob but she's got terrible taste. In everything. Calendars with kittens in baskets, plastic flowers in miniature wheelbarrows. I knew what kitsch was before I ever realized there was a word for it. I try and keep the house nice, you know—improve it—but no one else cares. I've got this vision of my real mother in a lovely drawing room somewhere, fresh flowers, long white curtains. Like the cover of a Mary Wesley novel. Because I think she'll be like me, she'll understand me. And then, then—"

The wigwam slid apart and collapsed.

"What?"

"Then I can go on looking after Nan without hating her."

I heard myself say it, and I couldn't believe it.

"Oh, God, I didn't mean that. I did not mean it, just pretend I never said it—"

But Mr. F was putting his hand over mine.

"It's all right," he said gently. "You forget, I've been a caregiver too. I know what it's like. It's perfectly natural to feel as if you're at the end of your rope sometimes. When you love someone, that's when the other emotions are at their strongest. It's the most difficult job in the world. I know. But you're marvelous, keeping that house running, and your clever daughter—"

I started to fill up. His kindness was too much. "I must run to the bathroom again," I said huskily, and went off to splash cold water on my face.

When I got back there was another vodka on the table for me.

"I got us some peanuts too," said Mr. F. "Dry roasted all right?"

"Mmm. . . . Then again"—I plunked myself down and carried straight on, unstoppable—"it might be a real can of worms. I mean, she might hate me—my real mother, I mean. Or Nan. Nan might hate me for finding this other woman. Not to mention Charlotte. She's unstable enough at the moment. But who do you live your life for, in the end? You've got to take some risks, or you might as well be dead. Don't I owe it to myself? Don't I owe it to my birth mother? What if she cries herself to sleep on my birthdays, or kisses my picture every bedtime? There's more than one sort of duty."

By now I was talking quite fast. I made a conscious effort to stop, took a deep breath, and asked, "So, was it very hard, caring for both your parents?"

Mr. F began to talk in a low, sad voice and I let my eyes unfocus. I felt very tired and slightly sick. After a while I realized he'd stopped speaking.

"Sorry?"

"Are you all right?"

My eyes smarted from the effort to keep them open. "Mm, yeah. Fine. Look, it's been nice, it really has, to talk, but I'll probably have to make a move soon." The idea of getting up and walking anywhere seemed impossible. I could have put my head down on the table and gone straight to sleep. I let out an enormous yawn. "Sorry."

"Do you want me to walk you home? If you're not—if you're a bit tired."

"I'll be fine, really." I reached around the back of my chair, then remembered I'd left my jacket at home; it had been a perfect spring day when I set out.

"Haven't you got a coat?"

"No. Well, it's gotten so mild. You'd never think it was only March."

The pub door swung open and a middle-aged couple came in, shaking snow out of their hair.

"Don't worry. I always carry extra rain gear." Mr. F rummaged in his backpack, drew out a little package of bright blue material, and began to unfold it. "You'll need the hood up by the looks of things."

I struggled into the shiny sleeves and he zipped me up. The other Ramblers looked across and nodded at us.

"Do you think it's possible to love somebody and hate them at the same time?" I asked, as he pulled the toggles tight.

"Oh, yes. Very much so. Now, out into the frozen wastes." He squeezed my hand briefly, then steered me to the exit.

"This is getting serious," sang Celine, quite out of the blue. Mr. F looked puzzled but politely held the swing door ajar and ushered me through.

"I have to say—" I began, but then with the icy air a wave of nausea swept over me and I had to stop and press my hand against the wall.

"Do you feel faint? Best to put your head—"

I didn't hear the end of the sentence because I found I was throwing up peanutty vodka against a half barrel of pansies. Mr. F's arms were around me as I bent and heaved, and when I stood up he offered me a hanky and turned away while I sorted myself out. "It must be something I've eaten," I mumbled.

He took my arm and we walked home mutely through the blizzard, my small circle of exposed face getting redder and redder and my wet bangs sticking to my forehead. My feet, in their unsuitable pumps, were agony. At my gate he said briskly, "So, I'll see you tomorrow," and I thought, Not if I go upstairs now and slash my wrists, except I'm too bloody cold to hold the knife steady and my veins have all shrunk to nothing anyway. I just smiled weakly. He gave his half salute and strode off into the swirling white like Captain Oates at the South Pole.

Ivy Seddon opened the front door as I trudged up the path. "They're smashing, them folding raincoats, aren't they?" she shouted. "We saw you coming. Be quick and get by t' fire. And can you check her bag? I think it's come away again. I'll mek a brew."

Jessie'd only been at the mill two weeks, but I'd had her down as a hard-faced madam, sixteen or not. Then that Monday morning she went off for a break and didn't come back, and I found her crying out by the bins, nearly hysterical.

"T 'int fair!" she sobbed. "He only has to hang his trousers ovver th' end o' t' bed and I catch on. Me mum'll kill him. She'd no idea it was still goin' on. An' she'll want me t' see that foreign doctor in Salford again. I can't go through wi' it. I thought I were goin' t' die last time. They pull all your insides out; you're bleedin' for weeks and weeks after. I'll run away first. No one's layin' a finger on me, not this time!"

And I put my arm around her. "You'll be all right. Me an' Bill'll look after you," I said.

Mum had said to take the washing in if it started to rain and I wouldn't normally have bothered, but my best jeans were out on the line. So when Ivy shouted up that it was snowing I crawled out from under the duvet and thumped downstairs. I'd forgotten about the toaster on the doorstep and, in my haste to get at the jeans, accidentally kicked it, sending it skidding across the stone path. Crumbs and what looked like bits of singed paper sprayed out of the slot. I ran across the lawn, tugged at the clothes in turn till they pinged off the washing line—pegs left swinging on the blue nylon rope or catapulted onto the lawn, I didn't care—then laid the bundle over my arm and scooted back to the house. It was bitterly cold. On the way I scooped up the toaster, American-football style, and carried it under the other arm. I slammed the back door behind me and dumped everything in a heap on the floor.

"Nan says you're getting a Range Rover," Ivy called from the living room.

"Yeah, right," I shouted back. Total bloody nuthouse. I started to examine the toaster.

Dear Mrs. *charred bit*

Imagine what you could do with a loan for £10,000! A new *charred bit* perhaps, *charred bit charred bit* or maybe the holiday you've been promising yourself.

I extracted the rest of the letter and flipped open the trash bin where it could go with all the other loan offers we'd had that week. Even Nan gets them. God knows what she'd spend £10,000 on. Pontefract cakes, maybe, except she's not allowed them because licorice plays havoc with what's left of her bowels. Then I turned the toaster upside down and gave it a good shake. More flakes came out, devil's confetti, but there was something still wedged inside. I took it over to the window and picked a table knife up off the draining board. I could definitely see folded paper when I tilted the slot toward the light. I fished around, got the blade underneath, and eased the thing out.

"What's so funny?" asked Ivy, from the doorway. She moved over to the pile of clothes and automatically began to pick them up one by one, smooth them out, and stack them neatly on top of the fridge. "Something's tickled you."

"It'd take too long to explain," I said, unfolding the ruined Keats essay and watching as it disintegrated in my hands. My shoulders shook uncontrollably, and tears of laughter started to run down my face.

"Eeh, I like to hear her laugh," called Nan. "She has a bonny laugh, but we never hear it these days."

"Well, she's certainly laughing now," commented Ivy, as I lay down on the tiles, helpless, and put the essay over my face.

Jessie went down to London first—the story was she were going to try for an actress—and I handed my notice in two weeks later. We'd found her a place at a Mother and Baby Home run by a charity, though they wouldn't tek her till she were six months. So we stayed down t' road with Bill's sister Annie in Finchley; she'd been widowed two years before, and she was glad to have the company. She had a funny daughter, Theresa, with a face like a line of wet washin'; she must have been about sixteen too but very backward, and she kept asking why Jessie was so fat. I heard Annie telling her afterward it was because Jessie had been a bad girl, and to watch herself or she'd end up the same way. Except I don't think any man ever went near her, she was so sour.

Hope Lodge, they called the home. I'd heard about it through the Mothers' Union: never dreamed I'd ever have anything to do with it. It wasn't a nice place, though. Big Victorian brick house, slippery floors, long dark corridors. I can smell the disinfectant now. They had their own rooms, the girls, but that made it worse; you could hear 'em cryin' at night, Jessie said, behind the doors. She'd not been there two weeks when she said, "I'm not stayin' here, Nance. Let me come back to Annie's wi' you. It's awful. We're not allowed to use t' front door, did you know? And they make you go to church on Sundays but you have to stand at t' back so none of the congregation can see you." I talked her around. I said, "You have to stay where there's nurses and doctors. They have to keep a special eye on you, with you bein' so young. You'll get t' best care here, love. I'll come every day, look after you." I were terrified she'd change her mind. Or disappear, or do herself a mischief. I knew she hadn't thought it through.

When she went into labor, five weeks early, it was at night and I didn't know. It was quick, too, just over four hours. The nurses said she was really sharp-tongued. "I've never known such a foul-mouthed creature," one of them told me, "and we hear some things within these four walls, I can tell you." Jessie said they were cruel, wouldn't give her anything for the pain. "It was unbelievable. I'm *never* goin' through that again, I'll tell you that much. An' the doctor, he came in near th' end and never spoke a word, not one word. I hope he rots in hell, I hope they all do."

I couldn't think of anything except that baby. "Do you still want me to tek her?" I asked. My heart was in my mouth. "Oh, yes," she says straightaway, "you can have her. I don't want her." And I went hot and cold all over.

Bill came down to bring me home, stayed a week, and when I got back everyone was agog. He'd told everyone I'd been nursing a sick relative. So then I said that was a white lie because, though I was thrilled to be expecting finally, I was worried it might go wrong, what wi' my age. I don't know if they believed me or not. It didn't matter. No one ever really asked, whatever they thought in private. A nine-day wonder, that's all it was. And that first Sunday when they said prayers at church for me and t' little one, I didn't feel a bit guilty. "It's our secret," I told the Lord. "I won't say anything if you don't."

We have no radiators in our house, of course, nothing so useful, so I had my snow-covered jeans laid out on the bed with a hair-dryer nozzle up one leg. Downstairs the front door banged and I heard Ivy's voice, then Mum's (sounding strangely muffled). I transferred the nozzle to the other leg and thought about meeting up with Daniel, that it wasn't going to be the ordeal I'd first thought: I could almost say I liked him. Not *that* way, of course, he was too fucking weird. Funny, though. He seemed to understand me more than anyone else at school. Maybe *I* was the weirdo.

I switched off the hair dryer, and in the sudden silence heard Mum's bedroom door click shut. Ivy shouted up, "I'll bring you some milk of magnesia in a sec, love, you put your head down for half an hour. I'll just hang your raincoat up to dry." Another crisis, then.

When I felt the ankle cuffs, the denim was more or less dry, so I pulled down my tracksuit bottoms, eased the elastic over my feet, and stepped into my jeans.

I stopped. Looked at myself in the full-length mirror. Something wasn't right. Even as they got to my knees, I knew they weren't going to zip up over my rounded belly.

Fate had gotten me after all.

chapter 5

Things can only get better." It must be true; it was on TV. But you tell me what political party could sort out *my* problems. If I thought it would really make a difference, I'd be down at that polling booth at 7 A.M., but nobody really cares about people like us, stuck at home with only the insane for company.

We save this country a fortune, and where does it all go? Bloody subsidies for bloody London opera houses and the like. I'd vote Monster Raving Loony if I could actually be bothered, but I haven't got the energy. It's all right them offering a lift to the polling station, but I bet none of them would be prepared to change Nan's bag while I was out exercising my democratic right.

Politicians! They ought to try living in the real world.

You'll have to do a test," said Daniel, his face blurry through my tears. We were sitting in Tiggy's Italian coffee bar at a Formica-topped table covered with wet ring marks. I hadn't meant to say anything, but it was all my head was full of; there wasn't room for anything else. Besides, somehow I thought he'd know what to do. He seemed that sort.

"I *can't.*"

"Yes, you can. Look, it's probably a false alarm. I mean, you don't *look* pregnant, if it's any consolation. How far are you meant to be along?"

"About three and a half months, if I'm right." I began to draw miserable lines in the sugar with the end of my spoon. "God, I just can't be. Not me. Anyone else, but not *me.*"

"It might simply be too many Easter eggs. Or a hormonal imbalance; have you been sprouting hairs on your chin?"

"Oh, for God's sake, Daniel, it's not something to joke about!"

He drooped his head. "Sorry."

"Do you *promise* not to tell anyone about this? I couldn't bear the thought of the other girls . . ."

"As if I would." He seemed really hurt. "I don't do that sort of thing. Besides, who have I got to tell? Look, if it's not too personal a question, have your periods stopped?"

"*Daniel!* Honestly!"

"Well, it's a bit crucial, Charlotte. I mean, I'm a mere male, but even I can see there might be a connection."

"Well, yes and no. Oh, I can't start going into details, it's too gross. And especially not with you. You don't talk about things like that, it's not polite."

He shrugged. "We talk about everything biological in our house. It's with my dad being a GP. No bodily function is taboo. They used to take us to a nudist beach in Greece every year, until I started getting what my mother called *stirrings*."

"That's because you're middle class, probably. In our house everything's taboo; there are no safe subjects, so mostly we don't talk. Well, Nan does, but she doesn't count because none of it makes any sense." The knowledge of why I was here settled on my shoulders again and I slumped forward. "Oh, Daniel, what am I going to do?"

"Wait here," he said, rising to his feet. "Don't move a muscle." And he ran out of the shop.

I waited and watched through the window. Shoppers crowded past, carefree. Every other figure was loaded with personal irony: the willowy pair of teenage girls with flat stomachs, laughing at some private joke; the smart brisk career woman whose life was clearly going places; the—oh, horror!—hugely pregnant mum with a toddler on a child leash, peering into the café, her hand shading her weary brow. I stared back. Surely it must hurt when your body got to that size? What happened to your skin? Might it not split, like a dropped tomato? How did her trousers not fall down? How could she see what she was doing when she went to the toilet?

"Give the woman a break," said Daniel, sitting down again and sliding a drugstore bag across at me. I realized I was gaping with horror and looked away quickly.

"Is that what I think it is?"

"Uh-huh. Now, run to the toilets, sort yourself out, and then come with me."

"Where?"

"Do as you're told. Come on." He pulled me up and shepherded me to the back of the café.

Once in the stall I undid the cellophane and opened the box. A white plastic felt-tip thing slid out. I had a good look at it, pulled the cap off, then fished out the instruction leaflet and unpleated it. So, you just peed on the end of the stick; two minutes later it was all over but the shouting.

When I came out Daniel was waiting. "Well?"

"I haven't looked yet."

"Good."

He grabbed my hand and pulled me out onto the street.

"Where are we going?" I shouted, as he yanked me through the crowds.

"Just come on!"

We ran and ran, up Standishgate, down Market Street and Parson's Walk, into Mesnes Park Terrace, and through to the park.

"Quick!" We dashed through the iron gates and dived for the grass. I sort of fell, then rolled over and lay back, gasping. "It's not too wet, is it?" he asked, patting around with his palm.

"Yeah, it's bloody soaking but I don't care." I was still panting like mad. "What's going on?"

He squatted beside me. "Unwrap the test. Go on." He nodded encouragingly.

I sat up, drew the bag out of my jacket pocket, and held up the box. My fingernail slid under the cardboard flap. "I know what I'm looking for, I read the blurb. If the second window's empty, I'm in the clear. . . . Oh, God, Daniel, oh, God. Oh, no."

He leaned over to peer at the two blue lines. The air felt still around us. It was one of those moments when the universe pivots and you know nothing's ever going to be the same again.

Daniel looked shattered. "Oh, Charlotte, I'm sorry. I was so sure it was going to be okay. I was so sure."

Don't touch me! I thought, but he didn't. He set his jaw and gazed out to the treetops. I could tell he didn't have a clue what to say, and I wished to God I could snap my fingers and make him vanish.

I don't know how long we sat there on the damp grass. I wasn't thinking proper thoughts, just giving in to a squeezing sensation round my rib cage and a feeling like my heart was going to explode. I just kept staring at the sun going in, out, flirting with the clouds, but there was no heat. I was chilled right through.

"Your teeth are chattering," said Daniel, wrenching his focus back to me. "Maybe we should go."

I hate you, I thought. If it wasn't for you, I wouldn't have known. It's your fault, you weirdo four-eyes bastard. I was waiting for the sky to cave in, or one of those giant pointing fingers to come pushing out of the heavens. *It could be you—and it is!* How could things be going on as usual around me, the woman walking the Airedale, the kid wobbling around on a bike, when my life was over? It wasn't fucking *fair*.

But then I thought, it could still be wrong, the test. It only said 98 percent accurate. That meant two in every hundred *weren't*. So, say they sold, I don't know, five hundred a week

nationwide, somewhere in Britain ten women would be shit-
ting themselves for nothing. And one of them might be me.
After all, I *had* had a period, so that proved it. It was probably
okay after all. I'd sneak one of my mum's water tablets when I
got home, see if I could shift some of this potbelly. Because, at
the end of the day, I was me, *me*, and there was no way *I* could
be pregnant. Encouraged, I began to hunt in my pocket for the
instruction leaflet.

"I think," said Daniel cautiously, "your next step is probably
to get checked out at the doctor's. You might need to act quite
quickly, depending . . ." He trailed off.

I think I went a bit mental.

"What the fuck is it to do with *you*?" I gave him a shove, and
he nearly toppled. His glasses fell off and landed in the wet
grass, and that made me hate him even more. "It's *my* body! *My*
problem! You have no idea about *anything*. Just . . . just"—my
arms were waving pointlessly—"get out of my *head*!" As Daniel
tried to wipe his spattered lenses on his sleeve I struggled up,
clutching the white plastic stick with its parallel lines of doom.
"And *you* can fuck off too!" I told it, ramming it into the soil
like a tent peg and stamping it down. I turned and stalked off,
toward the wobbly kid.

"I don't know why you're so cross with *me*," I heard Daniel
call; then he muttered, "I'm not the one who got you pregnant."

I broke into a run.

The trains in my head came back again last night. Details change, but the dream's recurring in its basic plot: I'm trying to go somewhere (although the exact destination's always pretty vague), but the train I'm on never gets there. There's always some crisis: I'm on the wrong train, or it won't leave the station, or it turns into a wheelbarrow. Sometimes it never comes at all. I wake with a terrible sense of panic and loss.

Not hard to interpret that particular sequence of symbols; any quack psychologist could work it out. I wonder, though, if I ever got my life together, would the trains actually get there, or would the dreams simply stop?

Sometimes in the morning, before I get up, I lie for a few seconds and my heart's strung out with nostalgia for something I can't even identify.

I got to work at ten after nine that Monday, even though I'm not technically paid till half past; I wanted a clear field. It was eerily quiet. Everyone was in assembly (except for Sylv, who's let off the daily spiritual injection to man the phones). I tiptoed past the main office, turned the corner, and trotted quickly down the long corridor. That morning's hymn floated out to greet me.

"The trivial round, the common task,
Should furnish all we ought to ask,"

sang the children flatly, northernly. And yes, when I peeped through the double doors Mr. Fairbrother was standing at the front, hymnbook aloft, a trumpet and a traffic cone at his feet (he likes his visual aids, does Mr. F; "I hear and I forget, I see and I remember," he's always quoting at us). So I had about five minutes. I hurried back up to the reception area, peered round the corner—all clear—and scuttled across to Mr. F's office.

Once inside I dumped the shopping bag containing the borrowed rain gear on his chair where he couldn't miss it. I'd wondered about a note with it, but what do you say, "Sorry I puked on your shoes?" My eyes traveled around the room for a moment. Shelves of box files and books, union memos and selected children's artwork displayed on a corkboard; on the floor by the far wall a giant ammonite, an inflatable hammer, a monkey puppet, a hamster cage, a devil mask (as I said, he does like his props); in the corner a box of confiscated soccer balls, cap guns, poking devices, et cetera. On his desk was his parents' wedding photo and a selection of horrible ornaments bought for him by various kids over the years. It was the room of a kind man. Oh, how I had messed up!

Time to go. I listened at the door, then opened it slowly.

"Everything all right?" Sylv's voice made me jump about a mile in the air. She was standing across the corridor, lipsticked coffee cup in hand, waiting for me. "He's in assembly. But you know that."

I could have told her. I could have beckoned her into the office, closed the door, and taken her through the whole sad story; she'd have loved that. Sworn her to secrecy (a slim chance but a chance nevertheless). But I couldn't do it. I said, "I was just checking Lost Property," and she stared at me so hard her eyebrows nearly disappeared into her hairline. Oh, piss off, you poisonous old witch, I nearly said. Nearly.

The morning seemed to last forever. By ten I was sitting in

the quiet corner with the remedial group helping them fill in work sheets on Area. We'd all drawn around our hands and agreed that mine was the biggest, and I was trying to count away the recollections of Sunday with square centimeters.

"How old are you, miss?" asked Dale. They do that, remedials, constantly try to distract you with personal chat.

"That's rude," said Lisa promptly. "You shouldn't ask a lady that."

"I think she's about twenty-five," persisted Dale. He had a long face with a large jaw and chewed his pencils compulsively.

"No." I smiled. "I'm a bit older than that."

"Fifty?" offered Lisa. "You've a look of my gran, and she's just had her fiftieth birthday."

"When's your birthday, miss?" asked Dale, spitting splinters of mashed-up wood across the table.

"Mine's next week," said fat Philip, waking up. "I'm gettin' a Furby."

"You big poof," said Dale. "You big girl."

The groups moved around and I helped put up some backing paper for a display on Transportation. Mr. F's disappointed face and Sylv's peevish one were printed on every sheet of construction paper. Each time I pulled the trigger on the staple gun it felt like I was driving staples into my own temples. Finally I asked Pauline if I could get some aspirin.

"Then go and sit in the staff room," she said. "There's only ten minutes to break, I'll clear up here." I must have looked really poorly.

Sylv's the guardian of the aspirin unfortunately, but, hooray, she wasn't in the office, so I unlocked the cabinet and helped myself, swigging them down with a mug of cold water. From there I went straight to the staff room, where I heard through the half-open door, *"Saw them embracing in the car park of the Feathers, apparently."* So I did a smart U-turn, walked back along the corridor, and met Mr. F coming in the opposite direction.

"Thanks for the—um, bag," he said, as he drew near.

"Oh, no problem. Thanks." I couldn't look him in the eye. Keep walking, I told him silently. He did, and I pushed out through the swing doors into the playground and breathed again. My whole body felt hot and I knew my cheeks were burning. Maybe it was the menopause, come early. That'd be just about my luck.

The bell went and children began to trickle out. I walked across the playground over the patches of slush and perched with the edge of my bottom on the low wall by the gates, wishing I had a coffee. "Hey, miss?" Dale appeared at my elbow. There were tiny flecks of red paint all over his lips off the crayon he'd been eating. "Look! I did you a card. For your birthday. You can save it, like, and bring it out when it's time." He handed me a folded piece of centimeter-squared paper with two pencil figures drawn on the front. One was lying down in what appeared to be a pool of blood. "It's okay, he's a baddie," explained Dale, pointing. "The other's Gravekeeper, he saves the world." He spread his arms out like wings, then let them flop to his sides.

"Nice trick if you can do it," I said, opening the card up. *To a grat teasher,* it said. *Meny happy retuns.* You're not supposed to touch the pupils, the times being what they are, but I leaned forward and gave him a hug. On these slender shafts of sunlight, sanity seems to turn, at times. "You've made my day," I told him warmly. He stepped back slightly. "No, really. You've redeemed the moment, you've given me the impetus to lurch forward into the next inevitable crisis. You've provided a tiny spark of light in a tunnel of gloom. Dale, you are a superhero within your own galaxy."

"Steady on, miss," he said.

I waited a week and did another test, also positive, so that was that. Then I sorted all my clothes out and ended up with a capsule wardrobe of sweatshirts and baggy pullovers and tube skirts and leggings. Standing naked before the mirror now, there was no doubt. My whole body had started to change. It wasn't mine anymore. It belonged to the thing inside.

At school I avoided Daniel—avoided everyone, really. Spent a lot of time in the library, books open, looking out the window. Well, how could I join in the common-room chitchat about clothes and boys and weight and fallouts? In the smart corner it was all Tony Blair and his New Vision, but I couldn't engage with any of it. The very word *Labor* turned my insides to water. None of it seemed real; it was as if there were a big glass wall between me and the others. I'd realized in the park that nothing was ever going to be the same again, but it was taking time for the extent of it to sink in. I mean, I couldn't see past the pregnancy. There was the immediate problem of trying not to look fat, and (more hazily) steeling myself for the hoo-ha when everyone found out, not least my mother, who was definitely going to have some kind of breakdown. On the very far horizon was the prospect of giving birth, which I'd heard was quite painful, and I wasn't very good with pain. But after that? I knew there was going to be a baby at the end of it, but I couldn't get my head around it. Not *me*, not a *baby*.

Unless I decided there wasn't. But, as Daniel, damn him, had pointed out, I was going to have to get my skates on if I wanted to go down that route. I didn't even know what they did. Vacuumed you out, a girl had once told me. It didn't sound too awful in that respect, but even I could see there was probably more to it than a quick trip to the Outpatients'.

I think it was the toes that were bothering me. We'd had a video on pregnancy, in Year 10. It showed the fetus wiggling about, sucking its thumb and kicking its skinny legs with their little splayed toes; then the narrator had said, *See if you can guess how old this baby is.* The teacher had paused the tape and we'd had a go; most of us thought about five months. Then she switched the video back on and the answer had been fourteen weeks! *See how the heart, with its four chambers, is already beating,* the narrator had continued. *In fact, a heartbeat can be detected at just six weeks of development.* The miracle of creation. It was a joke.

So what a mature and sensible person would have been doing at this stage of the game was weighing things—the fucked-up life versus the other, differently fucked-up life—and seeing which she thought she could honestly cope with. What a mature person would do was tell her mother, see a doctor, get a counselor. Face up to it all, and pronto.

But I was frozen. Because it still couldn't be true; it couldn't be me who was going through this. I was going to slide the pregnancy under the lining paper of the chest of drawers in the spare room of my mind. Something would turn up, surely.

Mr. F came striding across the playground, kids buzzing around him like flies.

"Here," he said. "No sugar." I took the steaming mug from him and studied the ground while he scanned the sky above my head. "Don't worry about Sunday. These things happen. I was once very ill after a bad sausage roll." He nodded at my bare forearms; my coat was still in the staff room. "Don't catch cold, will you?"

He walked away and was immediately accosted by a very small Year 1 boy, tugging at his trouser leg and pointing over to the soccer field. Mr. F bent down to hear the tale, and it was like a scene from *Goodbye, Mr. Chips,* except that Mr. F looks more like Syd Little than Robert Donat.

I'd give them break time to get it out of their system; then I was going back inside.

I was having a conversation with Daniel in my bedroom. He wasn't actually there, I'd just conjured him up for the purposes of rational debate.

"I know you *want* to see Paul again. But all I'm asking is, Have you thought through the reasons behind it?" Daniel sat scrunched up in the beanbag chair, his knees to his chin. I was at the desk, doodling boxes and clouds on the inside cover of *Sense and Sensibility.*

"He's got a right to know," I said sulkily. I wanted to see Paul so much it was like a toothache; I couldn't keep still, couldn't get comfortable. Today was Sunday, which always makes things worse. There's something about Sundays that makes you rattle around inside yourself, even in these exciting days of flea market sales and extended shopping hours. Mum had gone to Do-It-All to get some bubble wrap, and Nan was downstairs playing dominoes with Ivy. I'd paced up and down my room so much I had a stitch in my groin; I thought I was going to go mad with indecision. Hence Daniel.

"He will know, sooner or later. You can't keep it a secret much longer. Unless you—"

"Yes, all right," I said testily. "I know the score."

"What do you honestly expect his reaction to be?"

I wasn't ready to answer this question, even from myself. We tried again.

"In an ideal world"—Daniel pushed his imaginary glasses farther up the bridge of his imaginary nose—"what would you expect his reaction to be?"

That was better. "Well, he'd be totally supportive, for a start. He'd say, 'Whatever you want to do, Charlie, I'll stand by you.' "

"And what *do* you want to do?"

"I want . . . I want not to be pregnant in the first place!" I heard my voice rise to a wail.

Daniel sighed heavily. "Come on, Charlotte, grow up now. Are you saying you want an abortion?"

"I—" Suddenly, out of the corner of my eye, I saw the door handle turn and my heart jumped in horror. The door swung open and Nan shuffled in. "Ivy's doin' some toasted tea cakes. D' you want one?"

"Oh, Nan, thank God it's only you. I thought it was Mum."

Nan smiled blankly. "Toasted tea cakes," she said.

"Oh, no, you're okay. I'll wait till later. I'm not hungry."

"Eeh, I don't know. Not hungry. I could eat a buttered frog." She chuckled at her own joke and retreated, pulling the door closed after her. I waited till I heard it click, then turned my attention to Daniel again.

"Well, are you going to . . . ?"

"It depends what *he* wants. If he came with me while they did it, if he was really nice and we got back together and he let me talk about it afterward, and he never mentioned Jeanette Piper or Chrissy . . ."

"If pigs went flying past the window."

"Oh, ha-fucking-ha." I vanished him, then sat in a huff drawing cartoon bombs and lightning bolts.

Julia and Anya materialized on the bed, unbidden.

"Isn't it the absolute worst thing you can think of, though?" Anya was saying.

"Oh, yeah. Well, cancer would be pretty bad, and losing both your parents in a car crash."

"Or being permanently disfigured, with, like, acid or something. You know, having a glass eye or whatever."

"Or being a quadriplegic."

"Yeah."

"But being pregnant's pretty horrendous. I mean, your whole life messed up. Can you imagine what your mum would say?"

They both pulled manic faces and Julia put her hands round her throat and made strangling noises. "I'd just die. Wouldn't you?"

"Oh, God, yeah. Awful. Completely fucking awful."

"What I don't understand, though"—Julia wound a strand of glossy hair round and round her finger—"what I don't get is, how she let it happen. I mean, she's supposed to be so clever. She got an A in that last History midterm, the one she was supposed to have messed up."

"Yeah, I know. And I tell you what, I didn't even really know she had a boyfriend. Actually, she can be a miserable bitch sometimes, she never tells you anything. To be honest, I still had her down as a virgin."

"They say it's the quiet ones." Julia snickered. Anya began to giggle; then Julia started too. "Oh, shit, we are awful. 'S not funny. Poor Charlotte."

"Yeah, poor old Charlotte."

Three identical culs-de-sac run off Barrow Road; Paul's house is down the second. Not much had changed since I last went, except the bus shelter now had no roof at all and the form was completely slatless, just two thick concrete stands five feet apart rising out of the tire-marked grass. I remembered when I was a little girl, three old men in caps and mufflers used always to be sitting there, smoking away, gossiping. They were sort of like custodians of the highway, Neighborhood Watch. Nan knew who they all were, used to say how do and get a nod. Then after a few years there were two, then only one old man, sitting on his own, clouded in blue smoke. One day there was no one at all, and after that the bench started to get taken apart. I think maybe Bank Top didn't used to be so crappy; something went wrong with the people.

The Alsatian had gone too. The yard was bare except for a chewed rubber ball and a length of chain.

Mr. Bentham let me in; I could tell he was surprised.

"Paul! Paul!" he shouted up the stairs. "You've gorra visitor!"

Paul's face peered over the banister and he mouthed *fuckin' 'ell* when he saw me. But when he didn't move I climbed up after him.

By the time we got inside his room I was out of breath and sweating.

"What d'you want?" he asked gracelessly.

I saw with a pang that he was still as handsome, that the Man U duvet looked sex-rumpled, that someone had bought him a white teddy with heart-shaped paws that he'd stuck on top of his computer.

"Can I sit down?"

He just shrugged, so I stayed where I was, shoulder to shoulder with David Beckham. The moment twisted slowly on its long thread. I couldn't make my mouth work, though my brain was racing.

"Nice bear," I said finally, like an idiot.

"Oh. Yeah." He snickered awkwardly, looking all around the room, everywhere except at me. "Shit, y' know, seems really weird—" He allowed himself a glance in my direction.

All those times I was here, I was thinking, *and the last few weeks, we never knew; I had cells dividing inside me: 2, 4, 8, 16, an exponential time bomb. Cells all drifting to their allotted place like synchronized swimmers. Shape-shifting: amoeba to blackberry, shrimp, alien, baby. There's a baby under this sweatshirt. Hello, Dad.*

"Hey, are you all right? You look a bit—funny."

I took heart from what might have been concern in his voice and stepped forward. "Paul, I—no, I'm not all right. I, I'm—" My hand dipped automatically to my stomach and his eyes followed it, then widened. Then his brows came down and his whole face went hard.

"Paul?"

"Oh, no. Oh, no, not that one. I do *not* want to hear this! I do not fucking want to hear this!" He turned away and put his hands on the back of his neck, blocking me out. Any minute now, I thought, he's going to put his fingers in his ears and start humming.

"Paul, you've got to know—"

"Fuck *off*!" he shouted over me. "Don't try and put this one on me. This is *your* fault. Christ! You stupid, stupid bitch!" He thumped the wall, then leaned on it, shoulders hunched, still with his back to me. He looked like a three-year-old whose mum has refused to let him go on the Tigger ride outside Tesco's.

There was silence while I fought the urge to run down the stairs, through the door, and across the continent; run forever, run the pregnancy away.

"I'm sorry, Paul, it's true."

"Aw, Jesus." He groaned and finally turned back round to face me. "You've gotta be wrong. It's not like we didn't use anything. Loads of girls have scares, it dun't mean a thing. You've just got yourself in a state."

"I did a test."

He put his hand over his mouth and swore behind it.

"It *is* yours."

He took his hand away from his chin and stared at me. "No, Charlotte. That's where you're wrong. It's yours. It's all yours. I don't want fuck-all to do with it."

At least you know where you stand. At least you know where you stand.

I don't remember walking back home, but here I was under the duvet in my bedroom. Maybe I'd been asleep, because I was very hot and my mouth was dry. Maybe it had been a dream—maybe it had *all* been a dream!—but no, my hand strayed down over my bump, and Paul's parting shot still rang in my ears. I'd put my Walkman on, but it'd made no difference; Paul was louder. That exact intonation would be etched into my brain all my life, long after his features had become vague. I'd probably die with that last sentence replaying itself.

I snuggled down farther into the bed. When I was very little and Mum and I still got along, she used to let me make a nest at bedtime out of the duvet. Then she'd peer in and pretend she couldn't see me and that she was going. I'd shoot out from underneath, all flushed and ruffled, and shriek, "Story!" and she'd pretend to be incredibly surprised. She used to read to me every night, long after I could read myself. If only I could be little again. You don't appreciate it at the time.

I must have drifted off again, because the tape was on side two and Nan was shaking me gently.

"A shut mouth keeps flies out," she was saying, when I lifted up the earphones.

"You what?"

Nan settled on the bed and leaned over to stroke my hair.

Normally I'd have had to fight the urge to squirm away; not that I don't love her, I just get really touchy about my personal space sometimes. But this time I lay there quietly, glad of the sympathy. After a while she said, "You're havin' a baby, then."

I nearly jumped out of my skin. *"Nan!"*

"Don't you worry, it'll be awreet. We'll see you through." She fished under the duvet for my hand and took it in her gnarled fingers. The flesh moved loosely over the bones, as if it was ready to come away. I shuddered and closed my eyes, tears brimming out from between the lashes.

"Oh, Nan."

"Charlotte, love." She gripped my hand tighter.

"*Please* don't tell Mum. Not yet. I can't face her."

She half smiled. "I know all sorts as I've never towd." (Of course you do, I thought.) "Don't fret, I'll not say anything till you're ready."

Beside my ear the Walkman played:

> *You walk out of trouble*
> *Into trouble*
> *Out of trouble*
> *Into trouble*
> *And this is your life*
> *This is your life*

"Oh, Nan, why is everything such a mess? Why me?"

"Eeh, lamb," she said, "you'll be all right, you'll see. God's good."

"How *can* I be?"

But she just shook her head and carried on stroking my hair. I closed my eyes, let the earphones fall back.

My mother was eighteen when she had me; Jimmy was born two years later. But she couldn't hold my father. Harold Fenton were a restless soul; his own mother couldn't make moss nor sand of him. I think he loved us, though. He wouldn't marry my mother, but he gave us his surname for a middle name, so's everyone would know who we were. Nancy Fenton Marsh. I hated it, still hate it today. Fillin' in forms and such; whose business is it anyway? Because in them days, the sin fell on the children as well as the mother. But there was a lot of it about.

She was always short of money, that's why she had to take in washin', an' it were a right palaver in them days: two washtubs, a coal boiler, scrubbing board, wringer, it took forever. She never had a home of her own, either. The summer before I was born she'd sit out every evenin' in her parents' backyard wearin' her nightie and her dad's overcoat; there was nothing else that fit. She said it was a terrible labor: when they held me up and said, "Polly, it's a girl," she told them she didn't care if it was a brass monkey, so long as it was out.

Once, when I was about six and Jimmy four, we were waitin' at a bus stop to go to Wigan an' a smartish woman came and stood alongside us. There was a bus comin' and my mother just bundled us on. I said, "Mam, this isn't our bus, where are we goin'?" "Never you mind," she said. It turned out this woman was my father's latest fancy piece. We went all the way to Worsley before my mother came to herself. He had a lot of women, she told me before she died, but she said he was her man and that was that. "At least he never drank," she used to say.

She'd be thinkin' of her father, Peter Marsh. Her mother, Florrie, had a grim time of it even though she had a husband. They'd married because she was expectin', and then, after my mother, she had three children die in their first year. The doctor told her not to risk any more or she'd damage her own health—all she could think about was that at last she could sleep in the front bedroom with Polly, away from him. He was mean, you see; she always struggled to get money out of him because he spent it all on drink. She used to send Polly to the colliery gates to try to get some of his wages off him before he went in t' pub (he never came straight home when there was brass to spend), but that would get him in a rage. I think she was relieved when he went to join the Loyal North Lancashires in 1917, except when he got there, there were so few of 'em left he had to join up with the East Surreys. He sent some beautiful silk postcards, though, GREETINGS FROM FRANCE, all embroidered with flags and flowers, and his slow big pencil writing on the back. Then he was hit by a shell, or at least he jumped into a hole to avoid one and got buried by a wave of mud. They'd just been wondering how to break it to him about Polly's baby—me—when they got the telegram. He was only forty-two.

My father tried to join up as well at seventeen, but it'd finished by the time he got there, typically. I don't suppose he were too bothered. My mother's big fear was that she'd be made a widow too, but never being married she wouldn't have qualified. She lost him young, though; two days after his thirty-first birthday he was knocked down in Manchester, outside the Corn Exchange. And I did miss him, even though he'd been in and out of our house like a cat. We both cried over him. He was my dad. And you need your dad when you're growin' up. Well, I think you do, anyway. Family's everythin' when it comes down to it.

I woke with a jolt. The tape had finished and my earphones were hissing. I unhooked myself and struggled out of the duvet.

"I can't have this baby, Nan. I've decided."

From the end of the bed Nan snored gently. I folded the covers over her and tiptoed out of the room.

chapter 6

I went on a blind date with Pauline's brother's friend from tae kwon do class. "He's got a smashin' personality," Pauline had said. Ugly as sin, then, I thought. But it was worse than that. When I walked into the Working Men's and saw him propped against the bar it was like that old music hall joke, Don't stand up—Oh, I see you already have. He came about level with my nose. That wouldn't necessarily have been a problem, only he looked like Woody Allen and talked like Andrew Dice Clay. I sat through fifty minutes of filth, then he said, "I've got good manners, me. Tits before ass," and laughed uproariously. "Prick," I hissed, picking up my bag. "Ah, get away, you love it really, you ladies." He grinned. "Have you ever actually *had* sex with anyone?" I asked nastily. That shut him up.

"His twin brother's on a kidney machine; you have to make allowances," said Pauline the next day.

I gave her a hard stare. "Why? Why should I? No one does for me."

She just turned away and started counting Tesco's computer vouchers. Bitch.

My God, you're here!"

Daniel was sitting in the window of Tiggy's, looking anxious.

"Did you think I wouldn't be?" he asked.

"Well, under the circumstances . . . I'd have stood me up, without a doubt." I slumped down beside him. My bulge nearly came up to the edge of the table. "I don't know what to say. I've been such a bitch."

"No, no. Well, yes, actually."

We laughed nervously.

"Sorry."

"Hormones under the bridge. This thing's too important to fall out over." Fingers through hair, worried frown. "So, you really have decided, then?"

"Oh, yeah." I kept my voice low. "It's not practical. I could no more look after a baby than fly to the moon. Think about it. Mum's life would be in tatters; I'd have to throw in my university place and stay—God—stay at home for *years*. I can't bear thinking about it. And I know I'd make a terrible mother, I'm just not the sort. I've been really stupid. I should just have been sorting things out. I mean, the father . . ."

My voice began to quiver and my eyes pricked.

"Say no more."

An enormously fat chef carrying a tray of dirty cups squeezed past our table, his apron straining over his stomach. "Keep your hair on, we're short-staffed," he barked at an old woman in the corner. Everyone turned to see. The woman stuck two fingers up at his back, then swept all the packets of salt and pepper into her handbag.

"Now, *he* looks pregnant. You're a positive sylph compared to him. Look, I'll get you a milk shake while you cast your eye over these." Daniel began pulling some folded sheets of paper out of the pocket of his jeans.

While he was at the counter, I looked through the pages he'd printed off the Internet. *An abortion is legal until the 24th week of pregnancy,* I read. *There is an initial consultation with a doctor, but the woman can also see a counselor if she wishes.* Hmm. Now there was an idea. I didn't want my head screwed up anymore than it was already. On the other hand, they might try to persuade me to change my mind, and now I'd made the decision there was no way I was going back on it.

"Banana," said Daniel, putting the tall glass down on the table. "They're all out of chocolate. Drink up, anyway. You need calcium or your teeth will fall out. And you don't want to be toothless on top of everything else, do you?"

I tried to smile.

In order to qualify for a same-day procedure, the woman must be under 19 weeks pregnant. If she is more than 19 weeks, she must stay overnight at the hospital or health care center.

Same-day procedure!

It is generally accepted that there is very little risk associated with abortion.

"How far along are you?" asked Daniel gently.

I thought back and counted. "I'm fairly sure. Eighteen weeks, I think. So I might be just in time. I could go to the clinic in the morning and be back by teatime, tell my mum I'd been to Manchester shopping."

Buy some extra-large pads, pretend I had flu and rest up for a day or so. Maybe it wouldn't be so bad after all.

Daniel looked uncomfortable. "Yeah, you might just about be okay. Only, they have this funny way of calculating."

"What do you mean?" My heart began to thump.

"It's something I've heard my dad mention. They don't cal-culate from the actual date of—er, conception." He dropped his gaze. "They take it from the start of your last period. So you—"

"You *what*?"

"So—well, that means you're not actually pregnant for the first two weeks or so of your pregnancy. As it were."

"You've got to be wrong about that. That's ridiculous, it doesn't even make sense. I've never heard that one before."

"Forget it. I'm probably wrong."

As soon as he said it, I knew he was probably right. "So what you're saying is, that would make me nearer twenty." I put my hands over my face and dragged them down over the skin. What a fucking mess.

Fat Chef came out from behind the counter again and began shouting at two boys for breathing on the window and drawing pictures of penises. "If yours looks like that you need to see a doctor," he bellowed. "I'll be phoning your headmaster. Which school d'you go to, when you're not playin' hookey?"

"Best go before he sits on us!" one of them shouted, and they slid out of their seats and barged past us, colliding with the table and sending the sauce bottle spinning on its axis. We watched it lurch and fall. Tomato ketchup blobbed out slowly, mesmerizingly.

Stupid I may be, but I'm not daft. I knew that nineteen-week cutoff point must be there for a good reason: a later operation was going to be a lot more traumatic than an early procedure. I'd been really ill having a wisdom tooth out once, vomiting everywhere and swollen up like a hamster. My insides still scrunched up when I thought about it.

Did they use a general anesthetic? It would be best if they just put you under so you didn't know what was going on, but what if they didn't? What if it really, really hurt and you *saw what came out* and it lived in your head forever and ever?

"Do you know what they do, exactly?" I made myself ask.

"No. The website didn't go into details. Just what's on those pages."

I couldn't tell if he was lying or not. We looked at each other for a long time, but he held his gaze steady. Panic rose suddenly in my throat like nausea, catching me off guard. *Not me! This can't be happening to me! I can't cope; there has to be another way!*

I struggled to get a grip. My mum has these breathing exercises, they use them in anger-management courses; she does them if we have a big row. She doesn't know I use them too. In through the nose, count five, out through the mouth. I had—*breathe*—to stop the scary thoughts—*breathe*—and face up to—*breathe*—the practicalities—*breathe*. There was no other way. *Breathe*. It was going to be all right if I kept my head.

"What you could do," Daniel was saying, "is tell your mum you're staying over at a friend's—a girlfriend's, obviously—"

"Which is something I never do."

"Work with me, Charlotte. You could tell her it was a special occasion, an eighteenth or something—"

"I'd have to skip school. They'd want a note."

"It's half-term, the week after next."

"What if she rang up my friend's house to check?"

"Take your cell phone."

"I haven't got one!"

"Take mine, for God's sake!" Daniel sounded exasperated. "You could tell her your friend lent it to you so you could always be reached, even if you got in very late. And give her a false number for the home telephone; then, when you get back, say—if she's tried it—that you must have made a mistake."

Once again I looked at him with respect. "God, you're a good liar."

"Sign of intelligence." He cocked his head, eyebrows raised. "So, are we set?"

I closed my eyes and took another long deep breath. "You are so . . . God, I don't know what to say."

"It's no big deal. Just providing information." He drained his cappuccino and leaned back.

"Well, yeah, then, I think I am—er, *set*. Bloody funny word for it, though." I scanned the papers again while I waited for my insides to settle down. It looked as though everything might work out okay. Outside, the two rude boys had returned and were busy writing FAT BASTAЯD on the steamed-up glass.

Then something on the papers caught my eye.

For details of our fees please click on our home page.

"Hey, Daniel, is this a private clinic?"

He nodded.

"Well, I can't afford it. How much is it going to be?"

"About five or six hundred pounds."

The milk shake straw pinged out from under my fingers. "You're joking."

"It's no big deal—"

"Pardon me, it bloody is!"

"If you'd *listen* for a minute. I was going to say, my grandfather left me a few thou, it's sitting in a savings account doing nothing."

"Oh, God! No way. I am *not* taking your money for this. No way. That's final."

He put his hand out to me across the table, but I didn't touch him. "Charlotte, what choice do you have? You can pay me back when you get your student loan, whatever, if it'll make you feel better."

"National Health Service?"

"If you want to start from scratch and check out that route, it's up to you. But to be honest, you're leaving it all a bit late."

I wanted someone just to sort it out for me, take it all out of my hands. I felt utterly weary.

"Can you book me in, then?"

"I'll telephone as soon as I get home."

Like he said, what choice did I have?

This is the way my world collapsed.

I'd gone on a mug hunt. Opened the kitchen cupboard, and there was only Nan's china cup with roses and an eggcup with Blackpool Tower on it. Ridiculous, as we have about twenty mugs in this house.

I knew where they'd all be, so I steamed upstairs and rapped on Charlotte's door. No answer. I didn't seem to have seen her properly for weeks; she kept disappearing off to her room with sandwiches and endless bloody yogurts. She was supposed to be studying for exams, but I'd thought she might be brooding over that boy, so I'd left well enough alone.

I stood and listened: nothing. I hadn't heard her go out, but she obviously wasn't in her bedroom. (Can I just say I don't normally go barging in; for one thing, I'm always frightened of what I might find—justifiably, as it's turned out. Oh, *why* did I have to be *right?*)

I opened the door slowly, sniffing the stale teenage air, and looked around. Mugs, yes, several, dirty, dotted about; her sweatshirt on the floor in a heap; Charlotte, *Charlotte*, on the bed, half sitting up against the headboard with her Walkman on and a book on her lap.

Her lap.

Through the thin T-shirt I saw, for the first time, the outline of her belly rising in an unmistakable swell. The paperback was perched on top, so it looked like she was using one of those beanbag trays for the elderly. Her head whipped up and she stared. And the look in her eyes was mine, eighteen years ago.

Out of the corner of my eye, I saw something move and my whole body jolted with shock. I was *sure* I'd locked the door, but there she was, like that vampire Nosferatu only with permed hair, pointing a sharp fingernail at my belly. Ohgodoh-godohgod. Worst-nightmare-scenario, major panic for about five seconds, and then, weirdly, something else. Something else taking over.

The guitar solo on my Walkman faded out and a voice in my head spoke over it. *Don't panic. This is the worst it gets. What can she do to you, other than shout? And you're well used to that, it's water off a duck's back, isn't it? And, listen, you're her equal now, in this situation. You're one woman talking to another. She can't accuse you of anything she hasn't done herself. Keep calm and say what comes into your mind.*

Eighteen years ago, sitting at the table in tears and Nan kneeling at my side trying to hold my hand, except I kept pulling it away. Nan saying over and over again, "Tha'll be all right, we'll sort it out." Me saying—shouting—"How *can* it be, for God's sake?" She was frightened—I think I bullied her a bit after Dad died—but very sure. Very sure.

Then I was ready, and from then on it wasn't like me speaking at all.

You *stupid*—"

Charlotte wrenched her earphones off. Her face was twisted with some emotion, but it didn't look like shame.

"Oh, Christ, don't start."

"What do you mean, Don't start? I cannot *believe* what I'm seeing"—I pointed in fury at her stomach—"that my own daughter could have been so bloody bloody stupid—and, and *loose!*"

She put the book down deliberately on the duvet and shuffled herself more upright. "What, like you, you mean? Exactly like you, Mum, or had you forgotten?"

She was too cool by half. I wanted to strangle her with my bare hands.

"Oh, no. How could I *possibly* forget? That's the point. All that sacrifice and now this slap in the face." I clenched my fists so hard my nails dug into the palms. "You should have taken notice of me, of my mistake! I thought, Jesus wept, if there was one thing I'd taught you, it was not to throw your life away—"

"Like you did."

"Exactly!"

Her eyes were flashing anger back at me, as if *I'd* done something wrong.

"So, in fact, you wish I'd never been born? Isn't that

what you've been burning to tell me for the past seventeen years?"

All that sacrifice. "Well, you said it."

"Well, then. That makes two of us, doesn't it?"

The words flew out and collided in midair. There was a moment of deafening silence.

Then Charlotte threw her book against the wall and it dropped down on top of her pot of pens, scattering them across the desk. At the same moment Nan walked in, wide-eyed with fear. She pushed past me and tottered over to the bed.

"Eeh, love," she said, putting her hand on Charlotte's shoulder.

Rage boiled up inside me at the gesture. Just who should be getting the sympathy here?

"Get *off* her!" I shouted, and they both flinched but stayed where they were. *"You,"* I barked at Nan. "It's *your* fault, all this. We wouldn't be in this mess if it wasn't for you. Get out and leave us to it."

They moved closer together and Nan lowered herself down on the edge of the bed. She put her arm round Charlotte's bulk.

"Talk sense, Karen," Nan muttered.

I thought I was going to hit her.

"Talk sense? Talk sense? That's the pot calling the bloody kettle, isn't it? There's no one comes out with as much rubbish as you, and it's me who has to put up with it on a daily basis. It's a wonder I'm not crazy."

"Are you sure you're not? Anyway, it's not Nan's fault, Mum. Whatever else, it's nothing to do with her." Charlotte's face looked small under her bangs, but very fierce.

"Oh, isn't it? *Isn't it?* Well, I'll tell you something you don't know, lady."

"Karen," said Nan faintly.

I didn't even look at her.

"For a start, it was Nan who made me keep you. Just hang on, she told me. Have the baby and then, if you're still not suited, put it up for adoption, there's plenty of women who'd jump at the chance. Of course, once I'd had you she knew I'd never be able to give you up. She said she'd look after you—"

"She *did*!"

"Only some of the time. And that's not the point. She *changed my mind*, ruined my life. I had such plans . . ."

"Oh," said Charlotte tartly, "put another record on. Come on, Mum, we all know it was *you* who fucked up. You can't blame it on anyone else. Not even Dad."

"A lot you know. You're not even eighteen. You wait till you get to my age and the best years of your life are behind you and you know there's no redeeming them; see how you feel then about *decisions that were made for you.*" It was true what they said about a red mist coming down in front of your eyes. There was a buzzing sound too, and my heart was leaping with extra surges of boiling-hot blood. I stepped forward shakily and pointed down at Nan. "She isn't even my real mother."

Nan turned her face into Charlotte's shoulder and I waited for the thunderclap. She just stared back, cool as you like.

"Did you hear what I said? I'm adopted. *Nan isn't my mother.*"

"Well," said Charlotte, "same difference. She brought you up, didn't she? What's that make her, then?" She was breathing fast and clinging to Nan, who had her eyes shut. "At least she *wanted* you, which is more than I can say for *my* mother. From where I'm standing it looks like *you* got a pretty good deal. Now, would you get out of my room, please? I'm supposed to be watching my blood pressure."

To my amazement, Mum turned on her heel and swept out. I'd thought she was going to hit me, at one point, or have a heart attack. Her cheeks had gone really pink and her eyes all stary. My own heart was pounding in my chest and my throat was dry.

After a minute, Nan and I untangled ourselves. She fished a hanky from her sleeve, wiped her eyes, and blew her nose. Then she began rooting in her cardigan pockets.

"Have a mint," she said, offering one up in a shaking hand. "She doesn't mean it. She loves you. That's why she could never give you up." She wrestled with the cellophane wrapper.

"I don't care," I said, and at that moment it was true. My insides were churning, but my head was clear. I gripped the mint in triumph. "Oh, Nan! I can't believe I said all those things to her face. I've wanted to say them for so long. It feels great. How did I manage it? It was like I was possessed."

Nan turned to me and smacked her minty lips. Her bottom dentures jumped forward suddenly, and she popped them back in with her index finger. "Pardon," she said. We both began to giggle with nerves.

Then the door flung open and Mum was there again.

"How *dare* you laugh at a time like this!" she shouted. She held up a photo frame in front of her face. It was the one she keeps on her dressing table: me on a stretch of mud at Morecambe in a white sun hat and knickers, hair blowing across my face. "Look! You were five when this was taken, and just *look* at you! Picture of innocence! And it turns out in the end you haven't the sense you were born with. All those times I've warned you!"

Nan and I sat and watched as she tossed the photo onto the desk, where it sent more pens clattering off and knocked over the clay elephant I'd made in Year 7.

"Bloody hell, Mum. You've broken its trunk off."

"You're having an abortion."

I could have said, Yeah, actually, I am, in two days' time. You can come along and cheer if you like. But at that very moment two things happened. Nan drew in her breath and put her hand over my bump, and I felt the baby move.

It wasn't the first time, I realized now; there'd been flutterings before, like when a nerve twitches, only deep inside. But I hadn't understood what they were until this moment.

"You're having an abortion," Mum said again.

If it had been a request; if she'd sat down and held me like Nan was doing; if we hadn't said those awful things to each other five minutes ago. But Fate gets decided on littler things than that every day.

"You're wrong, Mum." Flutter flutter. "I'm keeping this baby."

Nan's arms tightened around me.

"Don't talk nonsense. You're not fit." Mum leaned forward and spat the words at me. And if I hadn't decided by then, that would have swung me.

"Well, I'm a damn sight *fitter* than you. At least I won't make this baby feel guilty all its life." Flutter flutter. "At least I won't try and make it responsible for my own shortcomings. If you didn't want me, eighteen years ago, that's fine. But I'm not going to do to this baby what you did to me. Poor thing. It deserves a better chance than I had."

Can fetuses clap? I was sure I could feel a round of applause down in the left side of my pelvis. Washed in adrenaline, the thing was going berserk.

Mum's face had gone that nasty color again and her legs were trembling.

"You'll change your mind. Or I'll never speak to you again."

"There's worse things than babies," said Nan. "They're nice, babies are."

"Damn you both," said Mum.

There's worse things than babies, dear God in heaven there are.

It was all drinkin' in th' olden days, an' fights all t' time. The children used come runnin' across the fields shoutin', "Harry Carter's fightin' again," an' we'd all go an' watch. He lived at Top o' th' Brow, an' he were always after the women even though he was married. His little boys would be pushin' through t' crowds an' shoutin', "Don't fight, Daddy," but he never took any notice. He was forever askin' Herbert Harrison's wife to go with him, an' she'd always tell her husband on him; it was like a game. They just wanted an excuse. One time I was stood wi' a big crowd watchin' them stagger about the street and Dr. Liptrot came up alongside me. He didn't see me, though, he was glued to th' action. Finally Herbert Harrison knocked Harry Carter down, and then he turned an' walked off. Harry got up, rubbed his chin, an' stumbled toward us. I ducked away, but as he drew level Dr. Liptrot patted him on the shoulder and said, "Now, then, let that be a lesson. Fightin' dogs come limpin' home." Harry stopped for a second, looked at the doctor, then hit him so hard he knocked out both his top front teeth.

It wasn't just the men who drank, neither. My grandmother Florrie used to have a big oak sideboard with a long dark patch on the top. Once she caught me an' Jimmy playin' with matches outside on the flagstone and she dragged us in and pushed us right up against the drawers of this sideboard. "Do you know what made that mark?" she said. I shook my head; I'd only have been about seven, and she could be very fierce. "A neighbor set herself afire with an oil lamp," she told us. "She was dead drunk, an' she came runnin' out into the yard and staggered in here, all in flames. She laid her arm along this sideboard, an' that's why there's a mark." She put her face close to ours. "So think about it." "Did she die?" Jimmy asked. "Of course she did," said my grandmother, and she clipped us both hard around the ear.

I never saw it happen myself, but as soon as I knew the story it was in every dream I had for months. Jimmy never said anything, but I know he dreamed it too.

There was a lot of drunkenness in them days. My grandfather was always on a spree, my mother said. He used to knock his beer over and lap it up off the tabletop like a dog; he were terrible. And when he ran out of money he'd go and stand outside the pub and wait for people to treat him. He had no shame. He sent my mother, even as a little girl, to the Wagon an' Horses with a jug for him, when he was too lazy to get his own ale.

His friends laughed an' called him a "character," but Florrie had another word for it. At his funeral do, when they'd had a bit, some of 'em were singin':

> *"Me father was a hero;*
> *His brav'ry made me blush.*
> *They were givin' free beer up at Bogle*
> *An' me father got killed in the crush."*

My mother said it was disgustin', an' they were all tarred with the same brush.

Then after, two of his mates from t' colliery were tellin' tales about him, how he'd gone to t' pictures once to see a Charlie Chaplin. He'd not been gone more than an hour an' he was back in the pub, an' they said, "Wha's up, Peter, was it not a good show?" An' he said, "They turned all the lights out, so I got up an' came home." They were all doubled over laughin'.

"Aye," said another man, "an' there were a time when we went to see the Minstrels at Southport, an' a chap came on and sang 'Danny Boy' an' he was really good, so all th' audience started shouting, 'Encore! Encore!' An' Peter called out at t' top of his voice, 'Never mind bloody Encore, let the bloody man sing again!' "

Someone else said they remembered Peter Marsh coming out of the voting booth once, very pleased because he'd said to himself, "Well, I'm not voting for '*im*'—an' put a great big cross next to t' candidate's name. Was he soft in the head, or was it just the drink? No one seemed to care. It didn't matter, 'cause he was such a character.

Florrie wasn't laughing, though. She had twenty-two years of his meanness with money and his not bothering about the babies she'd lost. She never married again; I think she'd had enough of men. So she lived with her daughter, Polly, and then me when I came along, and it became *my* dad who had us all on a piece of string wi' his antics.

There were times as Jimmy hated our father, hated his comings and goings and the fact he would never marry our mother. "He loves you in his own way," Mam used say. "He gave you his name."

"That just makes it worse!" said Jimmy. She had no answer to that, 'cause it was true. I think she felt it was her fault she couldn't keep him.

So as he got older Jimmy started to go wanderin', all over the fields an' down by the canal. He'd walk an' walk, as if he were lookin' for something. An' he ran errands for people an' made a bit o' money that way. He used to see a lot of Mrs. Crooks at Hayfield House; she was a widow and had never had children of her own. "I'll pay thee Friday," she'd say to him, an' she always did.

Then one day, he should have been at school, Harry Poxon saw him at the side of the canal, leanin' over with a stick. "You'll fall in," he said. That was the last time he was seen alive. They looked for five days before they found him, under the bridge at Ambley. Mrs. Crooks sent forget-me-nots for his coffin, and all the school lined up an' sang "There's a Friend for Little Children."

He was only ten when he died.

Three o'clock in the morning, and there's somebody standing at the bedroom door.

"I can't sleep. The baby's kicking."

"Go back to bed, Charlotte," I mumble, still only half out of a dream.

But it isn't Charlotte, it's Nan.

chapter 7

All night I'd been dreaming I was drowning; now I'd wak-
ened to the image of my baby lying face up, motionless, under
water, and a terrible chill of knowing it was somehow my fault.

Then as my head cleared I thought about how its body was
actually floating inside me now, this very minute, hair flowing
round its huge head, and how everything would all gush out—

I couldn't face school. I lay in bed till eleven staring at the
ceiling.

"I'll tell them I've had flu," I said to Mum, when I finally
made it downstairs.

"Say what you damn well please," she replied.

So I walked out through the front door, down Brown Moss
Road, Gunners Lane, and out onto the Wigan road. I was going
to walk until I dropped off the edge of the world.

By the Cock Inn I turned right and started down the public

sidewalk to Ambley, past the golf course and Hayfield House behind its screen of trees. I didn't know where I was going, didn't care. Crows cawed overhead, and sparrows flirted in the dust on the rutted track. Elder flower and dog roses were still thick among the hedgerows; you could smell the fertility in the warm air.

I turned off the track, scrambled down the canal bank, and began to make my way along the towpath. A barge chugged past, castles and roses round the door, Jack Russell perched on the roof. The middle-aged woman steering smiled and nodded. Now there was an idea; I could always go and live on a boat, sail off up the Manchester Ship Canal and start a new life. A blackbird ran across my path *chuck-chuck*ing, and the baby fluttered. You stupid girl, I told myself. That's exactly why you're in this mess now, starting a New Life.

As I drew level with the Fly and Tackle, I realized I was thirsty. I fished in my pocket to see if I had any money and extracted £3.30 in loose change. I climbed up the worn stone steps onto road level, checked for traffic, and crossed over.

After the brightness outside, the interior of the pub was dark and I had to blink a few times before I could get my bearings. I'd passed the place enough times on the bus, but I'd not been in before; it was a bit of an old fogy's place, popular for Sunday lunches and real ale. Squinting, I made out movement behind the bar. A fat bald man was drying glasses and singing "Born in the USA" over the jukebox. There were sweat stains under the armpits of his shirt.

"Have you got a telephone?" I asked, hovering by the door.

He pointed to an annex by the Ladies' and carried on being Bruce.

Inside the booth I checked my watch and dialed Daniel's cell phone number. *Please have it switched on,* I prayed. There was a click.

"*Hell*-o."

"Daniel, it's me! Hey—what's that moaning sound?"

"Hey. Just a minute, I'll move somewhere a bit quieter. . . . That's better. They're doing some sort of charity karaoke at one end of the lounge. Just what you need after a hard morning's physics, some boil-ridden Year Ten apeing Noel Gallagher at top volume. Are you all right? I saw you weren't in homeroom this morning—"

"Yeah, I'm fine, just not feeling very schooly today. Look, have you got any frees this afternoon?"

"Surely you mean *study periods*? Actually, I have one genuine and one by default, because Mr. Chisnall's away at a conference so he's given us work to do in the library. I do hope you're not going to suggest skipping class."

"Too right I am. Can you get away at all?"

"What, now?"

"Yes, please. It's a bit of a crisis. Another one. Sorry."

"No problem, I'm on my way. Are you at home?"

"God, no. Do you know the Fly and Tackle?"

"At Ambley? We went there two Sundays ago for my mum's birthday. Nice line in pies, dire jukebox. Okay, I'll be with you in . . . twenty minutes. Don't do anything foolish."

He rang off. I got two halves of cider and went outside to wait.

I sat at one of the wooden tables and watched the glinting cars hunching over the little stone bridge and the water sliding under it. The banks were lush and the trees bent low with green fruits. Two swans glided past sending a V of ripples behind them that broke the reflection of a perfect sky. If only I'd had a camera. The scene was idyllic, something like the picture on the front of Nan's old toffee tin she uses for storing buttons. I would come back here, I promised myself, and take a picture of this place; maybe even do a painting, and give it to Nan. She'd like that.

At last Daniel's shiny red Kia, last term's present for passing his driving test, bobbed over the bridge and disappeared into the parking lot. Thirty seconds later he emerged through the back door into the beer garden, blinking. If only he'd do something about his hair, I thought meanly.

"There's a man in there auditioning for *Stars in Their Eyes*," he said, lifting his long legs over the bench and laying his jacket down carefully.

"I know. *Nuts in Their Head,* more like. They'd have to strap him into a corset to get him to look like Bruce Springsteen. And put a paper bag over his face. Here." I slid his glass over.

"Cheers." He took a long drink. "Now, this crisis. You've not changed your mind again?"

"God, no. I still want the baby."

"Thank Christ for that. I canceled the clinic when you phoned. Anyway, being realistic, you're probably too late."

"I know. I've done it now, haven't I?"

"Yep. So, I brought you this." He reached into his jacket pocket and pulled out a banana.

"What is it with you and fruit? I've had two apples today already. You're turning into a food fascist."

"No, it's not to eat; well, you can if you want, I suppose. This is your baby."

We both looked at it, lying on the table. It was mottled brown and there was a fingernail scar at the stalk end.

"I hope to God it's not."

"I don't mean it's banana *shaped*, I mean it's about that size. I looked it up on the Internet."

"Oh, my God, really?" I put out a hand and stroked the clammy skin, then picked it up and held it against my stomach. "Wow, weird."

"You still don't look particularly pregnant, you know," said Daniel, peering at my bump. "A bit fat, maybe. I wouldn't guess, just seeing you."

"Yes. Well, that's why I wanted to talk to you. I want to, now I've decided; there's no point in hiding anymore. I want to tell them at school. And I'm terrified, and I don't know how to go about it. I mean, I could just walk in wearing my T-shirt, that'd be a dead giveaway, you know, no sweatshirt or anything to cover it. They all think I'm crazy, still wearing winter stuff anyway, I'm nearly passing out with heat exhaustion in some lessons, and I have to keep saying I'm cold. Or I could take Julia aside and ask her to tell everyone; she'd love that, all the drama. Then I'd be waiting for the summons, Mrs. Lever poking her head around the classroom door, lips pursed, asking ever so politely if I could pop along to the Headmaster's office, while everyone looks at each other and whispers. *Or* I could go straight to the Headmaster—or some other teacher, maybe— and ask them to handle things. They could have, you know, a special assembly on it and I could be shuffling about outside the hall listening. Oh, God, either way is going to be completely awful." I put my head in my hands. "What am I going to *do*, Daniel? How—*how* am I going to cope with all the fallout?"

"You will. You're that sort," he said confidently.

"What do you mean?" I asked, through my fingers.

"Well, um"—his hands fluttered—"hmm . . . okay. Have you ever smoked?"

"No. Never even tried a cigarette."

"Why?"

I took my hands away from my face and considered. "Well, I weighed up the pros and cons. Stinky breath, needless expense, appalling health risks, grief from adults, looking like a slut, versus maybe losing two pounds and joining in with everyone. I decided it wasn't worth it. Why d'you ask?"

He grinned and slapped the tabletop. "Have you any idea how few people think that way? You are *so* unusual."

"I am?"

"You know you are. Most people want to fit in at any cost, whatever the risks; you, you don't give a damn."

I was staring at him.

"Can I be totally honest with you?" He looked straight into my eyes.

"Be my guest." I wondered what the hell was coming.

"I think you're driven by stubbornness."

A vision of my mum flashed up, and for a second I thought I was furious. Then I started to laugh. "Go on."

"Well, you're incredibly self-contained, aren't you?"

"I—oh, I wouldn't say . . . in some respects, maybe."

"Oh, come off it, you know you are. You've got friends, yeah, but you don't care whether you sit with a group in the lounge or on your own."

"That's not true! You make me sound like some kind of freak.

Honestly, Daniel, I'm just a normal teenager—apart from having a bun in the oven, obviously."

"No, that's not it. What I mean is you're not afraid to swim against the tide. You're an *individual.* That's why—" He broke off and studied the canal for a while. "Anyway, I'm not saying you're in for a picnic, but if anyone can cope with this, it's you."

He really did know how to make you feel better. "Damn you for being right."

"My pleasure. Can I get you another drink?"

"Lemonade, I suppose. Have to think of the banana's welfare. Don't want the little thing pickled."

When he came back, I said, "Don't suppose I'll have much time to be self-contained after the baby's born."

"I don't suppose you will. Have you thought of any names yet? You could start talking to it, you know, it can hear you in there."

"Honestly? God, that's so spooky." I looked down at my stomach and spoke to the bump. "Chiquita if it's a girl, Fyffes if it's a boy. What do you think of that, then?" No response. "Too disgusted to reply. Oh, Daniel, it's so nice to be able to *talk* to someone about all this. Mum can't even bear to look at me; half term was hell. Mind you, I did get a lot of studying done. . . . Do you think I should tell a teacher, then?"

"If you can find one you like. Mrs. Stokes?"

"Oh, ha-ha. No, I was thinking of Mrs. Carlisle, she was my class tutor in years Ten and Eleven. She's a bit of an old hippy so she won't be too shocked. She always gave me nice pastoral reports."

"She could even have a word with your mother," suggested

Daniel, under the impression that Mum was in a rational enough state to be spoken to.

"Well. Let's not get carried away. One step at a time, eh, Chiquita?"

"So you'll be in Tuesday?"

"I've an appointment at the hospital tomorrow, so it'll be Wednesday. God forbid I should miss exams."

"I'll have chocolate and Kleenex ready."

He really got me thinking. Was I not normal?

I remember seeing Charlotte Church on television last Sunday, hair shining with cleanliness. "I'm just an ordinary teenager," she kept saying. Yeah, right. So what's an ordinary teenager? I can't see that she has a lot in common with, for instance, Gary Whittle, who I went to primary school with and who I remember once tied a firecracker to a cat's tail. He's in a Young Offenders' Institution now. And she's certainly nothing like me and my ever-expanding bulge of shame. The only thing I can see teenagers have in common is that they've waved twelve goodbye and haven't reached twenty yet.

Imagine:

General Studies Paper I:
Section I, Arts and Society

Q I: How normal are you?

Intro: Need for both individuals and society (esp. media) to stereotype across age range, class, ethnic group, occupation, etc.;

usually collection of negative characteristics; allows person to feel superior and in possession of all significant facts on basis of flimsiest evidence.

Para 1: Teenagers pigeonholed by jealous middle-aged and elderly. Threatened not by teenagers themselves but by reminder of their own mortality and wasted chances. Unflattering characteristics projected onto young include:

Para 2: Moodiness. Unfair accusation; not confined to any specific age group. My mother is queen of moods. If sulking were an Olympic sport, she'd get a row of perfect 10s. A grown woman who can outdo any adolescent.

Para 3: Materialism. Unfair again. Rife throughout society— IKEA on a Sunday! No point *my* being materialistic anyway, as we have no money.

Para 4: Vanity. Unfair. Self-obsession an insecurity thing, not age-related. In fact, older you get, more you focus on looks, e.g., Grecian 2000, Playtex corsets, super-strength Dentu-fix, etc. Teenagers aren't the ones spending £70 a bottle on La Prairie face cream.

Para 5: Habitual drunkenness. Inaccurate! A quarter of our 6th form are Muslim, for a start. Also Dave Harman = Jehovah's Witness & Alison Gill teetotal therefore mother killed by drunk driver last yr. To judge by what staggers out of Working Men's every Sat night, worst offenders are 50-plus.

Para 6: Pimples. Even this boring old chestnut wrong. Supply teacher in science labs this term has pimples *and* wrinkles; must be at least 40, poor woman. I only get them on my back and shoulders, so doesn't count.

Conc: Can't stereotype teenagers as you can old people. No such thing as typical teenager. Therefore, if there is no such creature, I can't be judged as either normal or abnormal. QED.

I was sitting in a government office overlooking the town hall square, sulking. Across the desk sat Mrs. Joyce Fitton, my Adoption Society social worker. I'd already written her off as a waste of time.

"What have you found out?" I'd asked, as soon as I'd sat down.

"Nothing yet. That's not why you're here. This is a counseling session, so we can be sure of where you want to go." Mrs. Fitton wore glasses on a chain and had a big motherly bust. She talked slowly and kept stopping to smile. I wanted to smack her.

"This place could do with a good clean. Those venetian blinds are thick with dust," I said rudely. I was so disappointed.

"I can see you're very angry, Karen. With your birth parents?"

No, with you, you stupid old bat. I took a deep breath.

"I just can't cope with all these delays. I thought today you'd have some information for me." I thought today you'd have found my mother and solved my life for me. I imagined you handing over a big thick file containing photos of my real mum, a résumé of her life so far (including the empty hole I left in it), pictures of her lovely house (polished wood floor, French windows, field with ponies at the bottom of the garden), and a beautifully written letter on Crane's stationery saying how much she wanted to see me.

"You need to have a clear idea of what you hope to get out of any contact you might make. And be sure you can handle the possibility of rejection and disappointment."

"Oh, I'm good on those." God, I sounded bitter.

Mrs. Fitton took her glasses off and gave me a long look. "Of course we may decide, after careful discussion, that you don't in fact want to find your birth parents," she said. "Some of these situations are potentially quite damaging, you know. I would say"—she put her glasses back on and began to sort pieces of paper on the desk—"that unless you have the right—um, approach, you're leaving yourself open to a lot of harm. Not that I want to be negative."

I took the hint. "Yes, absolutely. You're just doing your job. So, do you think you can find her?"

"I think there's a very good chance, yes. And your father, if you want."

"To be honest, I haven't really thought much about him. It's my mum I feel drawn to."

She smiled again. "That's usually the case, Karen. Even with men. There's something very special about the person who carried you for nine months, then went through labor for you. Most people assume there's going to be a special bond."

"Isn't there always?"

"Usually. Now, have you discussed this issue with other members of your family?"

"Oh, yes."

"And what have their reactions been?"

"Everyone's totally behind me. I have a very close relationship with my adopted mother; we can talk about anything." So long as it's bullshit. "And my daughter and I are more like friends, sisters, that sort of thing."

"So you anticipate their welcoming your birth mother into their circle?"

"Oh, absolutely." I won't let them anywhere near her.

Mrs. Fitton wrote some notes in a small hand.

"And what do you expect to get out of finding your birth mother, Karen?"

Ah-ha, I'd been expecting this question somewhere along the line, and I was ready.

"I just want to ask her about her experiences, tell her about mine. Talk to her as one woman to another. I'm not trying to, ha-ha, replace my own mum, God forbid. I'm not looking to her to solve my problems or anything mad like that." I rolled my eyes. Crazy idea.

"Have you got problems at the moment, then?"

Damn and blast. "No, nothing to speak of, you know. Only ordinary, everyday little problems, like everybody has. The washing machine breaking down, the trash men not coming, that sort of thing."

She nodded sympathetically. "Someone keeps taking our trash bin, would you believe it? We've had to paint our number on the side."

I chuckled.

"Well, you sound as if you've given this whole business a lot of thought."

"Oh, yes." That bit was true, at any rate.

"Are you happy then if I go ahead and contact the mother and baby home on your birth certificate?"

"They've closed down." It slipped out. "I—I tried there first, phoning, but it's a business school now."

She didn't even blink. "Yes, they relocated. We've dealt with them before. They should have all your records. Then we can make another appointment and go over the papers, and see where we go from there. Maybe think about your dad, too."

"How long will that take?"

"Couple of weeks, not long." She smiled once more. "You seem like a level-headed young woman, Karen. I'm sure you'll cope with whatever we turn up."

Level-headed? Didn't these people take psychology exams? Gullible old trout. Still, I wasn't going to own up to being a bag of neuroses. I watched her fill in a Post-it note and stick it onto her computer, next to a small orange toy with goggle eyes. Imagine getting to that age and still believing the best of people. Bloody odd.

We shook hands. As I was going out I said, "I'm sorry I was so rude about your blinds."

Mrs. Fitton smiled. "We get a lot worse than that here, believe you me," she said.

I'd have liked Nan to go with me to the hospital, only she couldn't. I could just imagine the consultation with the midwife. "So, Charlotte, how many weeks pregnant are you?"

Nan: "Do *you* believe they've sent a man to the moon? Load o' rubbish."

I'd have liked to take Daniel, but it was too much of an imposition. The potential for embarrassment was colossal ("No, this isn't actually the father, he's only come along to hold my urine sample"), and besides, he had an exam that day.

I suppose I could have taken Mum, if she wasn't still a quivering mass of rage. We nearly came to blows last week when she gate-crashed my doctor's appointment.

"Folic acid? Never mind bloody vitamin pills, tell her what a stupid girl she's been. Tell her, Doctor. Did you know she was supposed to be going to university?"

Fortunately, Mum's fairly scared of health professionals so when he told her to shut up, she did. In fact she hasn't spoken to me since.

The midwife I saw at the hospital was really nice. Very young, not much older than me, I think, and that helped. The first thing I asked her was, "How can you have a period and still be pregnant?"

She sketched me a little womb on a notepad and a little egg implanting itself.

"As the egg burrows in it sometimes breaks a few blood vessels. That'll be what you had. Not much blood, just spotting; is that right?"

I nodded glumly. The things grown women keep quiet!

"I bet you didn't know whether you were coming or going." She smiled. I think she must have guessed, looking at my birth date and the absence of a partner, but she didn't say anything at first. It came out when she was strapping the black Velcro sleeve round my arm to take my blood pressure.

"My mum's on the way," I lied. "She must have been held up."

"And your partner?"

The sleeve tightened and the blood pulsed in my fingers.

"Is a grade-A bastard. He's history."

There was a hiss as the air seeped out and the sleeve went slack.

"I see. We do get a few of those." She unstrapped me briskly. "Do we know anything about this bastard's health? His blood group, any serious illnesses in the family, that kind of thing? I only ask because of this form we have to fill in."

"Nope."

"OK, then, not to worry."

Like I said, she was really nice.

After she'd filled in pages and pages on my diet and progress, we listened to the baby's heartbeat, *pyow-pyow-pyow-pyow* through a special microphone. Then it was time to go and drink a pint of water and wait for the scan.

The scan. Night after night I'd dreamed about that scan, and always there was something wrong. The baby had no head, or it looked like an octopus, or it was too small.

Outside in the waiting room were a whole lot of bloated women. Some of them were reading magazines, and some were trying to amuse hyperactive toddlers; nearly all of them were with someone. I sat down near a lone black lady with a soccer-ball-up-the-sweater profile and tried to catch her eye. She smiled when she noticed me, that secret club smile pregnant women pass around between themselves.

"Have you been waiting long?" I said.

"About half an hour."

"How far along are you?"

"Thirty-seven weeks. The baby's turned the wrong way around, they're going to see if they can persuade him to do a somersault. Otherwise I might have to have—"

She broke off as a tall man in a suit came and sat down next to her. He put a hot drink down on the table, kissed her cheek, then reached over and patted her stomach. I edged away, feeling miserable. It was important not to think about the nightmares.

I rooted in my bag for the funky little paperback I'd been given by the doctor: *Emma's Diary*, a week-by-week guide to pregnancy. I wanted to see what it said about birth defects. As I pulled the book out, a scrap of paper fluttered down onto the tiles. I got down on my hands and knees to pick it up and recognized Nan's swirly writing.

> *Don't think you're of little importance,*
> *You're somebody, somebody fine.*
> *However you tumble, and get up and stumble,*
> *You're part of a vision Divine.*

A vision Divine. My eyes blurred with tears and I scrambled back onto my seat. Oh, Nan.

Forty minutes later, just as my bladder had passed from painful to critical, a little gray-haired nurse called me into a dim room, hoisted me onto a table, and pulled my shirt up and my leggings down to my pubic bone. I stared down at the slightly flattened bump as she squirted cold gel on my skin and then stood back for the doctor to get in there with his probe thing.

"Look at the screen," whispered the nurse, beaming.

And there, in flickering white profile, was a head and an arm.

"It's sucking its thumb," she said.

My God. So there was a baby in there after all. It was all true. The fetus squirmed about as the doctor pressed hard into my flesh for what seemed like ages.

"Don't hurt it!" I called out in alarm.

"It's fine," he murmured, and carried on methodically, taking down measurements every time the machine went *beep*. "Sorry, when was the date of your last period?"

"I told the midwife, I don't know." Who keeps track of these things?

He moved the probe around, and two waving legs came into view. "And you haven't had a dating scan . . . well. . . ."

The image froze.

"What's the matter?" I felt panic rise. Next to my hip the machine made a sinister whirring noise.

The nurse leaned over. "It's okay, he's just taking a nice picture for your notes. You can take a copy home if you want."

"Is there something wrong? Is my baby all right?"

The doctor flicked a switch and the screen froze again; then the overhead lights came on. "You're fine, and your baby's fine. I'd say you were about"—he glanced over at my notes—"about twenty-six weeks. So I'm going to put your due date down as the sixteenth of October."

"Oh, my God, that's my nan's birthday!"

The nurse grinned and helped me up off the table, but the doctor was busy writing on my file.

"Can I ask a question?"

"Sure," he said, without turning round.

"Can you tell whether it's a boy or a girl? I'd really like to know. For the names and stuff."

He glanced over his shoulder at me.

"It's not hospital policy to disclose the sex," he said briefly, and turned back again. I wondered how he could be so un-moved by the miracle he'd just revealed.

"You'll have to knit lots of lovely white things," twittered the nurse, squeezing my arm. I'd have liked her as a mother, I de-cided. "Now, I'll bet you're desperate to pee. I'll show you where the toilet is."

And then I was on the bus going home, the grainy flimsy photo clutched in my hands. There was another universe-upside-down moment, when for the duration of that ride I and my baby were at the center of creation, and the feeling that we two were all evolution had been working toward for millions of years overwhelmed me. Nobody on the 416 seemed to notice my fantastic revelation, but that's the way the world works, isn't it? We miss amazing things every day, right under our noses. Maybe it's for the best. If we went around being amazed all the time, we'd never get anything done.

I bounced into the house and went in search of Nan, but there was only Mrs. Crowther from Crossroads reading last night's *Bolton Evening News*. "She's having a nap in her room," she told me. "At long last. She's been up and down like I don't know what. Something's botherin' her."

I shrugged and went to find something to eat. In the kitchen I smoothed out the little picture again and drank in the detail. Just its top half, the face in profile, a big forehead. I wondered who it looked like and a pang of memory, Paul's shining face and floppy hair, skewered me where I stood. Would he not like, would he not want to see . . . ? But that was not Paul I remembered, not the real Paul, who was scum. This baby didn't need a fantasy father.

I wanted to phone Daniel, but a glance at my watch told me he'd still be taking his exam, so I made a giant cheese sandwich and went upstairs to do some more thinking.

When I opened the door and saw what was on the bed, I couldn't believe my eyes.

One of the things that's bothering me most about this baby business is that it means I'm on my way to being old. Thirty-four: it's no age, is it? You see TV presenters older than me (occasionally). I want to throw out my pullovers and leggings and start again, wear spaghetti straps and combat pants and little butterfly clips in my hair. Would I really look like old mutton dressed as a lamb? How *can* I be a grandma? Yet once this baby's born I'll feel as if I've started down the slippery slope that ends with Werther's Originals, *The People's Friend,* and death. I didn't think I was even middle-aged really, but look, here I am, Grannie Karen. So even less chance of finding a man. I mean, it's not exactly an alluring chat-up gambit: Why don't you come back and see my grandchild? I bet Charlotte never thought of that, did she. How did I ever manage to produce such a selfish daughter?

Laid neatly across the bed were three blouses, a pair of jeans, and a long floaty skirt. I went over and had a closer look. MUM-2B said all the labels. It was maternity wear! My first set of decent clothes for six months. I tore off the saggy size-14 leggings I'd bought off Wigan market and pulled on the jeans. They were really clever, sort of stretchy at the top and then skinny in the legs like real jeans. It was great to have something that felt comfortable again. I struggled out of my T-shirt and put on the nicest blouse, a floral job, and all right, I looked a bit mumsy, but what could you expect in the circumstances? The point was everything fit in the right places and didn't feel like it was going to fall down or cut me in half. Next I tried the skirt, also great, with the same blouse, then another, then the third; then I took off the skirt and put the jeans back on, and it was then that the front door opened and I heard Mum's voice in the hall.

"Mum!" I shouted down.

"Just a minute," she called back. I heard her talking to Mrs. Crowther, then the door closing again. Finally her footsteps on the stairs and she was in my room.

"Well?" She sounded sharp, and I faltered.

"All these clothes . . ."

"Yes?"

"Did you buy them?"

"How else do you think they got there?"

"Oh, Mum, thanks so much—"

She cut me short. "I ordered them from the catalog. If you don't like them, don't pull the labels out and I'll return them. You can pay me back in installments; we'll have to work it out."

Even the news that they weren't a gift didn't dampen my gratitude.

"It's so nice of you. . . ."

"Well, let's be honest, you were beginning to look a complete sight in that other stuff." She turned to go and I stepped forward and grabbed her arm.

"Oh, Mum, I've got to show you something—" I picked up the photo from the pillow and held it out shyly.

She took one glance and then her eyes flicked away. She wrenched her arm free and walked out, slamming the door.

Sometimes it's hard to see what a woman sees in a feller. I loved my dad 'cause he was my dad; we didn't see him so often, but when we did he was great wi' us. He made Jimmy a boat out of wood with a mousetrap inside it, so's when you pressed a button at the side it flew apart. We used play with it for hours out on the flagstone out back. For me he made a little chair— I have it now—wi' spindles an' turned legs. When I got too big for it, it worked for my dolls. An' although he could be sharp-tongued, he only twice laid a finger on me an' that was for sayin' "Good shuttons" to the milkman—I didn't know it was rude—and for mouthin' *What a face our cat's got* at my mother; she saw me in the mirror. He would never have touched our Jimmy: he thought the sun shone out of him; we all did. He had his father's charm wi' none of the arrogance.

But when I grew up, an' especially when I got married, I began to see what a terrible time he'd given my mother. Grandma Florrie hated him; hated the way he'd turn up at the house an' expect to stop the night, but she never said no because Polly'd be beside herself wantin' him to stay and so would we. Sometimes his mother, Grandma Fenton, would come around, an' the two old women would sit on the horsehair sofa and moan about his behavior.

We felt sorry for Grandma Fenton. Fancy havin' produced a son who hated women. She'd been in service when she got caught and she'd never say who the father was, although it was pretty obvious it was the chap who employed her; he wouldn't have anything to do wi' it, I suppose. So when Harold was young she had a poor time of it, no benefits in them days, of course. She used have a stall against the Victoria where she sold nettle beer, brandy snaps, and treacle toffee. An' she were a nice woman; it was a shame. She'd have done anything for Polly. She never got much love from her son.

I know I've been lucky. Bill was a wonderful husband and father. And the more I see of the world, the more I think there aren't so many of 'em about.

I'd been putting it off—frankly I'd rather have driven six-inch nails into my kneecaps—but it had to be done. Steve had to be told about Charlotte's situation.

I wouldn't say we were on bad terms; he's too lazy to harbor a grudge. For him the past is the past; he's not fussed about the way our marriage turned out. He always seems quite pleased to see me (which is about once a year) and quite pleased when I leave.

He lives in Harrop, at the bottom of the hill; you could walk it, but it'd be a heck of a climb back up. I took the Metro and parked it up the entry at the end of the terrace.

"Hey."

He'd seen the car and was standing at the door in his stocking feet. He'd grown a mustache since I'd last seen him, and it made him look older. Still as lean as a whippet, though, still that sharp-featured face and cheeky grin.

I walked up the overgrown path and went through the dark hall, picking my way past cardboard boxes, to the back sitting room.

"Have a seat. Kettle's just boiled."

There were more boxes and some bundles of newspaper on the floor, lots of used crockery dotted about, a pair of jeans folded over a wire rack by the unlit gas fire. When we'd first split up I'd been appalled at the way he lived, but now I just left him to it. I suppose a bit of peeling wallpaper border never hurt anyone, as long as it wasn't in my house, obviously.

"So what's this all about? You sounded a bit rattled on the phone. Is it something to do with Charlotte?" He handed me a mug with a picture of Cindy Crawford on it and sat down opposite.

"Yeah. God, there's no easy way to say it. She's got herself into trouble."

"Wha', at school? I thought she was a gold-star pupil."

"No, you fool, *into trouble*. She's pregnant."

"Oh, bleedin' 'ell." Steve put his cup down on the carpet and shot me a twisted grin. "Not our Charlie. I thought she had more sense."

"Apparently not."

Steve shook his head. "I can't believe it. Not our Charlie.

She's such a smart girl. Smarter than us, I thought. What did she think she was doin'?"

I shrugged and lay back against the sofa wearily. "It's not like I haven't warned her a thousand times. But you know what she's like, so deep. So difficult to talk to. I wasn't even absolutely sure she had a boyfriend for ages, she's so secretive. And she's far along, it's too late for an abortion. She hid it from everyone." It wasn't my fault, I wanted to add, but then Steve would never have thought like that anyway. I was justifying to myself, not him.

"An' this lad, what's he got to say about it all?" Unconsciously, he drew himself up and squared his jaw.

There was a pause.

"I've not really pursued that line," I said awkwardly.

"What do you mean? Haven't you been around to his house, had a talk with his parents? Because it seems to me he's got some explaining to do."

I couldn't tell him I'd been too wrapped up in blaming Charlotte and my own inadequacies to dream of doing anything other than get rid of the pregnancy. When this plan failed I was so drunk with fury I couldn't think straight. I couldn't even bring myself to say good morning to Charlotte, let alone have a rational discussion about the role of the baby's father. In any case, I secretly didn't blame him, I blamed her, because whatever they say, there'll never be equality of the sexes till men can get pregnant; she was bright enough to know she'd be the one to get caught, so she should have taken care of it. Men'll just try for what they can get where sex is concerned; they don't think it through. That's for us women to do. So as far as I was concerned, it was her fault.

But Steve had scented a villain and his blue eyes were bright.
"What's this little bugger's name and where's he live?"

"Paul. Paul Bentham. He lives round the corner, off Barrow Road, apparently. He used to go to school with Charlotte when she was in primary school. Cocky so-and-so. He dumped her about three months ago, and that's why I thought she was so moody, still pining for him. I never dreamed—"

"Well, I'm going to pay this Paul Bentham a visit and tell him exactly what the state of play is. He can't just walk away; I didn't, did I? You've got to face up to your responsibilities, even at that age. Little shit." He thumped the arm of the chair. "Upsetting our Charlie like that and then running off. Poor girl. Is she all right?"

What about me? I wanted to shout. *I'm* not all right! I want to jump on the next bus to Manchester airport and flee the country, except the whole house would collapse without me. Christ, I can't even pop down the shops without checking Nan's bag or Charlotte's sanity; I feel like that Greek guy who had to hold the world up on his shoulders.

But I hadn't come around to moan. There's no point with Steve, he blocks it out, which is partly why we used to have such god-awful rows. He never understood that women like to complain for the sake of it, to get things off their chest, and don't *want* to be given practical solutions and courses of action. They just want sympathetic attention, and lots of it.

So I said, "She's fine. I'm not worried about her at the moment, she's"—a bitter laugh escaped—"really into the pregnancy now and pretty upbeat. Though I think it'll all go awry when the baby's born."

"Well, it does, doesn't it?"

"Exactly."

There was a silence while we both remembered the unholy fuckup we'd made of the postpartum months.

"Well, she's got you to look after her," said Steve, and a big spear of guilt ran through me. "So what d'you want me to do? I'm no good at talking to her. . . . She scares me a bit, if you want to know." He laughed sheepishly. "She's so bloody clever, and she's taller than me an' all." He ran his hand through his hair. "I don't know her well enough."

I could have made a nasty remark here, but I was too aware that the feelings Steve was trying to articulate were basically my own. In any case, I needed more aggravation like I needed a hole in the head.

"I could probably find some extra cash," he continued. He gestured vaguely at the cardboard boxes. "I'm looking after some stuff for a guy at work, and there'll be a few quid in it at the end for me. I don't mind passing it Charlotte's way."

"I can't pretend it wouldn't be welcome. Money doesn't buy you happiness—"

"But at least you can be miserable in comfort," he finished, and we grinned briefly together. "Right-oh. It's not a problem."

"I didn't come around here to scrounge, though."

"I know you didn't."

"I thought you needed to be included. She might—she might still want to come around and talk it over with you."

A look of panic crossed Steve's face. "Oh, bloody hell. Look, I'll tell you what I'll do. I'll go around to see this boy and I'll see if I can sort something out. I mean, I can't make things any worse, can I?"

I gazed at my cup and considered. Cindy Crawford simpered out at me from under a film of tannin.

"Probably not. Just make sure you don't lose your temper," I said.

I did it: the big school revelation. At four o'clock Scan Tuesday I phoned Mrs. Carlisle and told her the whole sorry story. She said to give her half an hour to think about it; then she called back and said what they'd do was let me take my exams up in Mrs. Duke's office, out of the way, and I could come and go during lesson time so nobody would see me. So that's what I did, sloping in and out of the building like a bulky shadow. For the college boards I had to have a teacher sit in with me, but for the final exams I was just left alone to get on with it; me, a bottle of Evian, a packet of mints, and my little curly photo. I've never felt so focused.

At the end of the last exam, Mrs. Carlisle came and had a long chat with me. She'd brought me a syrupy mug of real coffee, unaware that even the smell of instant made me heave. Still, it was something to do with my hands while she went on about deferred university places and child-care options for next year. She'd done a lot of research. "You mustn't let go of your dreams." She said it twice. I didn't even know what my dreams were anymore.

On the last day of term she gathered the lower sixth girls together and told them the situation. I'd had every intention of going in and saying good-bye; Daniel thought I should. But when it came to it I couldn't face the glare of publicity and spent the morning down the canal bank at Ambley again, throwing leaves in the water and watching them float off to freedom.

That was on Wednesday; on Thursday I had a phone call from Julia asking me to meet her in town for lunch, and I thought I owed it to her so I went.

The thing about Julia is that she's brimming with social aplomb. She must get it from her mother, a girlish woman with a bright lipsticked smile who can talk to anyone. I remember last Open Day there was a woman with no hair, I think she must have had cancer, and Julia's mum just breezed up to her and started chatting away. I was working at the refreshment stall and I'd been dreading this woman coming over in case I said something like, *Do you need a wig?* instead of *Do you need a tray?* So, I have to admit, if the shoe had been on the other foot and it was Julia who'd been pregnant, I'd have been struck dumb with embarrassment.

No such problems for Julia. She came rushing over to my table and gave me an enormous hug around my neck and then said, "Look at *you*! You look *amazing*! Your hair's really glossy and your skin's absolutely *glowing*! Fantastic!"

She sat down and ordered, then produced a plastic bag containing a fluffy toy from Anya, a card signed by the sixth-form girls, and a book on pregnancy month by month from Mrs. Carlisle. I was completely overwhelmed.

"Anya wanted to come too, but we thought it might overwhelm you seeing us both together. But she says she'll call you next week. We'd have been in touch before but Mrs. Carlisle told us when you were first out you thought you had mononucleosis and didn't want to get out of bed. But, wow, you're doing great. Everyone's really excited, and they all send their best wishes." She sat Anya's little fluffy-rabbit thing up on its hind paws. "Sweet! So, how you doing?"

I'd been feeling not too bad until the presents, but the unexpected kindness slew me. My face went red and my voice strangled with the effort of not crying.

"It's really nice—," was all I managed.

"Say no more." Julia was brisk. The drinks arrived and a plate of cakes. "God, don't you just *love* these chocolate muffins? I could literally eat them till all my buttons popped off. Fantastic. Oh, you missed some major gossip over the last few weeks. Did you know Denny's been suspended for selling funny cigarettes to Year Nines? One of them nearly set fire to the toilets, apparently, trying to light one of his homemade ciggies. God knows what was in them, because it wasn't tobacco. Martin Ainsworth reckons it was dried seaweed. Some of the kiddies lost their voices, that's how the teachers knew something was going on, they'd all come back in after break croaking like frogs. Anyway, at least it wasn't proper dope because he'd have been out on his ear, you know how twitchy the Headmaster is over drugs."

It was relaxing to have her rattle on like this. It made me pretend I could be normal again, with the usual teenage concerns and excitements. She made me laugh in spite of myself, and the baby inside me jumped and squirmed.

". . . So then Jimbo told Simon that he'd seen Abby and Dom eating each other's faces in Fatty Arbuckle's, and Simon went absolutely ballistic and told Abby she was a slut in front of everyone in the lunch line, so Dom jumped on him and there was this huge fight, tables everywhere, and Mr. Barry had to drag them apart and make them go to separate rooms to cool off and their parents were called in. It was really hectic." Julia stopped to draw breath. "So you can see you've missed loads. I don't know how anyone's gotten any work done. I certainly didn't. My report card was a disaster. Like I really care." She took a big bite of cake and winked at me.

"Mine was brilliant," I said gloomily. Mum had been in a terrible temper when it came through the mail. It was one of those no-win situations, like every year when the General Certificate of Secondary Education results improve and the press goes, "Oh, standards must be slipping." But if ever the results were down on last year's, it would be, "Oh, we see standards are slipping," and the *Daily Telegraph* would commission a special shock report on how stupid today's teenagers truly are. So if my exam marks had been bad, Mum would have been beside herself because I was throwing away my chances. The fact that they were better than I could ever have expected made the pregnancy even more of a disaster because I was clearly destined for great things. Or would have been.

"Julia," I said. "What happened when Mrs. Carlisle told you about me?"

She paused for a fraction of a second only. "Well, we were all really surprised, and a few people looked at me because they must've thought I knew about it—"

"You can understand why I couldn't say anything?"

"Yeah, yeah, of course. A big thing like that, you need to get your own head around it before it becomes public property. Then the twins asked if they could send you a card, and Mrs.

Carlisle said she thought that'd be very nice. That was it, to be honest. Oh, a few people have asked me whether you'll be around next year. Will you?"

"I dunno. I don't know what it's like having a baby around. If it's not too much hassle I could put it in day care or something and come back in January. Maybe sooner. I don't want to have to repeat the year, not with all those bozos from Year Eleven coming up. The teachers could send me work and I could get Special Consideration for the exams. Oh, I don't know. It goes around and around in my mind. We'll have to see."

Julia was nodding; then she said, "And of course, somebody asked me who the father was . . . I told them I didn't know, but I don't know if they believed me. Obviously you don't have to say anything if you don't want to."

I could tell she'd been burning to get this question out. Well, she'd been pretty good with me so far. It would be a relief to say something at last.

"I don't think it's anyone you know. A lad I used to go to school with years ago: Paul. But we're not together anymore. He didn't want anything to do with me once he'd found out. I had it *so* wrong. You'd think, if you'd . . . if you'd slept with someone—that you'd know them pretty well. That's what I'd thought anyway, silly me. I hope—I hope he gets run over by a truck, very slowly, so his ribs crack one by one and you can hear his screams all the way to Blackpool. I hope he moves to the other side of the world and I never see him again. Oh—"

A pain shot through my groin.

Julia was on her feet at once.

"Charlotte! Are you all right? Do you want me to get someone? Shall I phone for a doctor?"

I shifted on the chair. "It's okay, stop flapping. I think it was a fluke. Ooh!" This twinge bent me over and made me gasp.

"Stay where you are, I'll get an ambulance."

"Come back!" I shouted, as Julia shoved her chair out of the way and prepared to do a mercy dash. "I'm not going into labor. At least, I don't think I am. The pain's in the wrong place. It's down here. Ow."

Heads were beginning to turn, and the panic that always overtakes me if I inadvertently become the center of attention began to well up. There was another twinge. I had to get out, and quickly.

"I need to go home," I said. "Can you walk me to the bus stop?"

"To the bus stop? You must be kidding. I'm driving you home. But don't you dare give birth on my mother's new seat covers. We'd never hear the last of it."

Julia drove me back from town with exaggerated care, glancing over at me continually. Was the seat belt too tight? Were the pains coming every three minutes? Did I want her to turn the car around and go to the hospital? I kept saying no, and gradually the pains went away. She began telling me about her holiday plans and her new bedroom, and then we were pulling into Brown Moss Road, both of us heaving a sigh of relief.

She stopped the car. "You gave me a fright, missus. Are you okay now?"

I nodded.

"You're not just saying that?"

"No. Honestly. Thanks."

"Do you want me to walk you to the door?"

"No, really. I feel fine now, it must just have been—"

We both caught sight of him at the same time. Julia turned to me, puzzled.

"Who's that man bleeding onto your doorstep?"

"Oh, God," I said. "Ohgodohgod. This is why I never bring anyone home."

chapter 8

I wed a bid wrog," my dad said through his hanky. "I'b sorry, Charlie." Mum had him sitting on the sofa, leaning forward and pinching his nose; she has to deal with nosebleeds all the time at school.

"Don't keep swallowing," snapped Mum, "it'll make you sick. Spit into this if you have to." She thrust a Pyrex bowl under his chin.

"I can't believe you went around there. Why didn't you say anything to me first? What was he like? Was he really angry?"

Part of me was horrified that Dad had crashed my private life like this, after years of sitting on the sidelines. But part of me was grateful that someone should finally have thought to give Paul a good beating; it was about time. If that's what had happened. It didn't look too promising.

"Aggry? He shit hisself when he realized who I was. I told hib the score. Dobody walks away frob something like that. Be a ban, I said. Face up to your responsibilities."

"Is that when he hit you?" said my mum. I knew what she was thinking because I was thinking it too. He looked pathetic, with his red hanky and his head bowed, a button hanging off his shirt. Beaten up by a seventeen-year-old, nice going, Dad.

Through the muffles of clotting blood we finally got the tale, though how much he'd brushed it up I wouldn't like to say.

He'd gone around late afternoon when he knew Paul would probably be in (and I guess hoping his old man wouldn't). A "little lad" opened the door and then shouted for Paul, who came down the stairs unsuspecting. Dad started his speech, which quickly turned into a shouting match, during which Paul maintained first that the baby wasn't his and then that, since it was my decision to keep it against his wishes, he couldn't be called to account. (I broke in to argue at this point, but my mother shut me up.) After a few minutes of hurling insults at each other, Paul had turned to go back upstairs and my dad had completely lost it, lunged forward, and grabbed Paul around his legs. Paul fell face-first onto the step—"He'll have a swollen black eye toborrow"—and in the struggle to get away kicked out, making contact with Dad's nose; "It was nothing, a lucky blow." At this point Mr. Bentham appeared on the landing, bleary with sleep and taking out his earplugs, "though he soon looked sharp when he saw me." He ran down and hoisted Paul upright, checked him over briefly, and propped him against the banisters. Meanwhile Dad had been shouting about his son's behavior, and despite Paul's denials, the finer details of the situation had begun to dawn on Mr. Bentham. He'd apparently turned to take a swipe, seen Dad's berserk blue eyes and bloody nostrils, and let his arm drop to his side. (I suspect this bit is true. Mr. Bentham goes in for a quiet life.) Then he'd told Dad to get out of his house and, if he wanted to take it further, to get a blood test done. "I will, don't worry. We'll have Social Services on you. An' you should see that that boy of yours gets a good hidin'," my dad had told him, and stormed out.

"So, full of sound and fury and signifying nothing," I muttered. My mother leaned over and cuffed me round the ear.

"Less of that, madam. A thank-you would be nice, after what your dad's been through. Even if it was a waste of time."

Dad shot us a despairing glance and I immediately felt sorry. A proper daughter would have got up off her backside and given him a hug, but of course that was impossible, so I just gave him a thin smile instead. "Thanks, anyway. Hope your nose doesn't hurt too much."

He took the hanky away experimentally. "I was trying to help."

"I know you were. He's a big nothing."

"Well, I must admit, I don't know what you ever saw in him, love. I thought he were an arrogant little shitmouth."

The baby elbowed me sharply and I thought, You poor bugger, that's your father we're talking about. What an inheritance.

"Do you mind if I go upstairs and lie down?"

Mum and Dad shook their heads, and I dragged myself up to my room. Next door Nan was snoring and mumbling. I flopped onto the bed. The baby kept kicking.

"It's probably something called 'round ligament pain,' " said Dr. Gale. "Nothing to worry about. Your muscles are having to hold up a tremendous weight; it's not surprising they're putting up a bit of a protest."

We were in the backyard of Daniel's enormous house enjoying the sunshine. They'd installed me in a lounge chair in the shade of a beech tree; later on, under that same beech tree, Daniel would try to kiss me and I would refuse, thus spoiling a perfect day.

"That's what the midwife reckoned. All the joints are under such pressure I'm bound to get some aches and pains. It was really scary, though. My friend thought I was about to give birth."

"You'll be fine," Dr. Gale smiled. "You look perfectly healthy to me, anyway."

He was nice, Daniel's father. Tall, like his son, but more assured, quite distinguished. Lovely newscaster accent. I bet all his menopausal women patients harbored fantasies about him. He made me feel relaxed despite the fact that I'd never met him before, and I was seven months pregnant, and I didn't know what he'd been told about me. I suppose he sees all sorts in his practice. The sun shone warm on us both, and bees crooned amid the lavender at our feet.

Inside I could hear Mrs. Gale and Daniel preparing the evening meal. I'd have called it tea, but here it was dinner, and it happened at seven, not five. I remembered Mum trying that one out on us a few years ago; Nan was nearly eating the tablecloth in frustration and I kept sneaking custard creams, so by the time the food was on the table I didn't want it. "Eeh, I can't be doin' with this every night," Nan had said. Big row.

I wondered what Mum would make of the Gales' Edwardian villa. Actually she'd be struck dumb with envy and inadequacy as she ticked off their Minton floor, the polished staircase, the quality art prints on the walls. By the time we reached the dream kitchen her jaw would be on the floor, as mine was. Kitchens aren't my thing, I tend just to breeze through on the scrounge, but even I could see this one was like a show home. It was huge, for a start, with a quarry-tile floor and immaculate counters and—yes, Mum would have died—an Aga cast-iron oven *and* a conventional high-tech built-in oven. Then there were all those little tasteful touches that I've seen on the front of Mum's magazines: bunches of dried herbs hanging from the ceiling, gleaming copper pans, a hodgepodge of Victorian tiles along the back wall.

"Mum does cake decorating for weddings and parties," said Daniel dismissively. "She works for that marriage counselor organization too."

He'd taken me out through French windows into the lovely garden and introduced me to his father, brought us drinks, and left us alone to have a chat.

"So, have I set your mind at rest?" asked Dr. Gale. "You don't want to be brooding and worrying just now, especially over something that's perfectly normal. Try to keep yourself calm. Calm mums-to-be make calm babies, so the research has it."

"Really?"

"Oh, yes. You think about it. There are all sorts of chemicals passing between you, including all the ones your body releases when you're under stress. In the later stages of pregnancy it could have an effect on the fetus's eventual personality. And at this point—well, you've got a viable baby in there now."

"What do you mean?"

"I mean that if you went into labor tomorrow there'd be a good chance the baby would survive, provided it got immediate and proper care. It'd be a skinny little thing, but it would have all its parts, more or less."

I laughed and stroked my bump. "It's certainly pretty active."

"Good." Dr. Gale took a sip of his drink and looked out over the lawn.

I wish I could move in here with you for the next three months, I thought.

Dinner was grilled trout and salad, and guess what? Mrs. Gale had grown all the parsley and dill herself. I thought of Mum's herb garden two summers ago, a row of pots along the back windowsill. Most of the herbs grew fantastically tall and then fell over; some of them didn't grow at all. Nan kept putting her used tea bags in the pot nearest the drainer, which didn't help.

"Daniel tells me you're hoping to study English at university," said Mrs. Gale pleasantly. I say *pleasantly,* but really she was gritting her teeth to stay nice. I could sympathize. There was her precious son bringing home some pregnant slut who clearly didn't know which knife to use and, having wrecked her own life, was hatching God knows what plan to wreck his.

"I'd like to go to Oxford," I said, through a mouthful of fish.

"We wanted Tasha to apply, but she had her head set on

Birmingham, for some reason." Grimace. "Still. Daniel'll probably apply to Lincoln. David went there." Mrs. Gale nodded at
her husband.

"Smashing. Is that a nice university, then? Isn't it very hilly?"

Dr. Gale coughed politely. "I think you've misunderstood. I
went to Lincoln *College,* Oxford."

How we all laughed. I gave up the battle with the fish and
put my cutlery down. I'd begun to feel sick if I ate too much at
one go.

"Gillian went to St. Hilda's. We met at a May ball."

"How romantic," I said, meaning it. These were people
who'd got everything right, done their lives in the right order.

"Yes, she was with a chap I detested. Ended up punching
him in the mouth." He smiled at his wife and raised his glass.
"Marvelous days."

"And you were with Elise Osborne, owner of the most irritating laugh in Oxford," replied Mrs. Gale smartly. "Finished
with that plate, Charlotte?"

I helped clear away, and we ended with fruit, which is also
something that never makes an appearance in our house, owing
to its generally sitting in a bowl till it goes moldy and is thrown
out. Poor Mum. She'd love to do this: Italian bread, wine, five
cheeses, grapes. She used to try different foods on us, but she's
given up now. Nan's preferred dish is belly pork, two disgusting
bow-shaped pieces of meat covered in a thick layer of fat that
Nan eats with her fingers; she'd have it for breakfast, lunch, and
dinner if Mum'd let her. Alternatives are a nice bit of tripe,
steak pudding, whist pies, or potted shrimps. Oh, and tinned
salmon. Should Mum ever be foolish enough to serve up some-

thing mad like rice or pasta, it ends up in the garbage bin, untouched. How Nan got through the war I'll never know.

I'm a grazer and don't like sitting down to meals. I eat yogurts by piercing the lid with my thumbnail and drinking them down in the light of the fridge door. Makes no mess, you see. You'd think Mum would be grateful for this low-maintenance approach, but no. If I want a cookie I have to go through all the trouble of extracting a plate from under a tower of cups or bowls—quite often I'll have scarfed the cookie by the time I've gotten the plate down—and then there's the washing up and putting away again for what would have been a twenty-second eating experience. As if a few crumbs mattered. If she had a life, then they wouldn't.

So we all sat around and ate fruit nicely. And apart from a few sly looks from elegant Mrs. Gale, the meal was great.

"Coffee?" she asked at the end.

"Not for Charlotte, she's gone off it."

"It's true." I didn't tell her what I'd told Daniel, that I thought it tasted of piss. "I'll have another grape juice, though, if that's okay."

Daniel moved around to pull my chair out for me. "And I'll have some more of that wine. We'll take it outside."

It was still nearly as light as day but cooler out on the patio. I breathed in the evening and felt rejuvenated. Banana baby rolled and wriggled inside me, making strange shapes I could feel under my palms. The greens of the lawn seemed to glow under the evening sky, and my eyes fixed, unfocused, on a cloud of midges swaying over the pond near the hedge. It must be so much less stressful being this far up the social scale, to have the space and the cash and the knowledge about the world. I thought of Mum and wished I didn't have to go back home.

"It's a lovely garden. God, that heady scent. . . . Makes me think of Keats: *I cannot see what flowers are at my feet.* Although presumably that wasn't because he was straining to see over an enormous bloated belly." Baby heaved, a blackbird began singing near us, and for a moment I felt as though I were on a film set. "You're so lucky, you know."

Daniel helped lower me onto the steps and sat down beside me. "Yeah, I suppose so."

"No supposing about it." I wondered whether to count his blessings for him—nuclear family, pots of money, social poise—but decided it might be in bad taste. In the end I said, "Your house is incredibly calm."

"Is it?" I looked at him but he was gazing at the horizon.

"Oh, yeah, amazingly. Well, compared with my place, it is. So is Beirut, probably." The bird finished singing and flew away, a cutout black shape across the streaky sky. "Don't you like it here?"

"Not much." He rested his chin in his hand. "Actually, I was quite happy in Guildford."

"Why did you move?"

He sighed. "Dad got an offer he couldn't refuse from an old university chum. He wanted to start up a practice with my dad as a partner. Dad said it was fate, went off to see, and liked the place. So we all upped stakes and followed. If it had been one year earlier or later we probably wouldn't have gone, they wouldn't have wanted to disrupt my education, but I'd just finished exams. Conveniently." There was a bitter note to his voice. "I'd chosen my options for Year Twelve and I was looking forward to a great year with my mates—I had some, down there—Miles and Toby. We used to have some great laughs. They weren't like those geeks I sit with in the common room; God, they're so boring they even bore themselves."

I moved away slightly and stared at him.

"I had no idea you were so fed up."

"We e-mail each other, but Miles has got a girlfriend now, so I don't expect I'll be hearing much from him for a while. Anyway, it's not the same."

"Maybe you'll move back there," I said, "if your dad's job doesn't work out."

"I don't think so." He picked up a piece of gravel and flicked it out over the grass. "You see, my mum was having an affair, so we won't ever go back."

I drew in my breath. "God."

"He was one of her clients. She broke every rule in the book. She'd have been chucked out pronto, but luckily for her everyone involved decided to keep their mouths shut. He went back to his wife. We had a family conference about what to do, not that anyone was very interested in what I wanted. Then this job offer came up. Dad reckoned it was the only way to keep the family together. But he's still really angry, and so's she, for different reasons. Insane! In some ways it might have been better if they'd split up. I don't know. It pisses me off the way we pretend, like this evening."

It was shocking to see him like this. I hadn't thought of him having his own problems, he was just someone who supported me through mine. I edged nearer again and put my arm round his shoulders.

"It's the wine talking. No, it's not the wine talking, it's me."

"Oh, Daniel."

"You're the only thing that keeps me sane, I think," he said, and in a swift movement turned his head and kissed me on the mouth.

I didn't stop to consider, it wasn't a conscious decision, but I pushed him away and put the back of my hand to my lips. The sour tang of wine and guilt. He jerked backward and stared, then dropped his head down so I couldn't see his face.

"Sorry, sorry, sorry. Stupid—"

I couldn't make out the rest.

"No, *I'm* sorry, Daniel. I really am. Sorry."

Behind us the French windows slid open; then we heard the click of his mother's heels on the patio. A chill breeze passed over my shoulders, and at the end of the garden the leaves of the beech tree stirred suddenly.

"Have you two finished with your glasses?"

"Oh, yes," said Daniel. "We've definitely finished."

They phoned me at work, on the last day of the semester. The kids were all high as kites, clearing display boards and turning out drawers. Year 6 were running around the building trying to find drawing pins to prize off the walls because Mr. F had promised a Mars Bar to the child who brought him the most.

Sylv took the message, so she was beside herself with importance by the time I hit the office at morning break.

"Social Services called. They want you to make an appointment to see a Joyce Fitton as soon as you can. Here's the number. Is it about your adoption?"

"Yes," I said. I didn't have the energy to lie.

"Oh, Mr. Fairbrother, Karen's found her birth mother."

Mr. F, who had just popped his head around the door to ask for the stapler, looked at me in surprise.

"No," I corrected, "Sylv's a little ahead of herself. I've got an appointment with Social Services, that's all. They might have some information; then again, they might not. A lot of it's talking: you know, assessing."

"Assessing what?" asked Sylv.

"Can I break in here and ask you to find a file on the computer?" said Mr. F. "Only it's quite urgent. See you later, Karen."

I backed out gratefully and went to phone from the staff room.

I hadn't spoken to Joyce on the phone; it was another woman who took down my name in the appointment book, so I didn't know what she'd found out. Surely, this time she'd have the address of my mother. The desk was a sea of papers, and this time there was a plastic carrot stuck on the computer. It didn't look very professional to me. Someone had had a go at the blinds, though.

Joyce put her glasses on and opened a cardboard folder with my name on the front.

"I'm not able to disclose the address of your birth mother today, Karen," she began.

I felt like shouting, Fucking hell! What do we pay our fucking taxes for? Fucking social workers! What do you do all day, sit around and drink coffee? 'Cause you don't do any fucking work, that's obvious.

"What's the delay?" I managed.

"Are you disappointed?" Joyce inclined her head sympathetically.

"I seem to have been waiting forever."

"It's hard, isn't it. Well, what I can give you now is a contact for your mother, someone who does know where she is and, if you like, can act as an intermediary."

"Why? Doesn't she want to be found?"

"It's a little complicated." Joyce put the file down and leaned forward, elbows on the desk, hands clasped. "After she left the mother-and-baby home she went to stay with this lady, who was like a kind of foster mother. She offered the girls who didn't have any support in the area a halfway house, until they'd got themselves set up with a job and lodgings or decided to go back home. When your mother left she kept in touch over the years; I don't believe she had anything more to do with her own family back in Wigan. She settled in London and—er, changed her name."

"You mean she married?"

"You need to speak to our contact, Mrs. Beattie, Mary Beattie. She's expecting you to call and arrange something."

"Right, well, you'd better give me her address."

Joyce handed over a sheet of paper.

"What you can do, as I said, is use her simply as an intermediary; you don't have to meet your mother at all if you don't want to. You could just exchange letters through Mary without giving your own address."

"Why would I want to do that?"

"I'm only telling you your options, Karen." Joyce folded her hands over the closed file. "And obviously I'm here if you feel you want to talk it through afterward."

All this bloody mystery; what a fuss over nothing. They make a job for themselves, social workers. Still, at least I could sort things out myself now, and we'd get on a damn sight faster.

"Thanks," I said, standing up and putting the paper in my handbag. "I'll have to run, I've got a date."

"Good luck," said Joyce.

I walked out under a gray sky and hurried off to the municipal gallery to meet Mr. F.

It was a collection called Dogs in Art.

"I like paintings to look like something recognizable, not a chaos of splotches. I don't know if that makes me old-fashioned." Mr. F, Leo Since-We're-Not-at-Work, was standing in front of a large picture featuring a woman in a white nightie holding a cocker spaniel. "I don't particularly care, either. Have you seen this little fellow? We used to have a spaniel when I was a boy."

"What was it called?"

"Kipling. My father named him."

"We had a black cat called Chalkie. My dad named him too. The funny thing was, he went missing the week my dad went into the hospital for the last time. Neither of them came back. Chalkie wouldn't have known what to do with himself without my dad for company anyway; he used to sit on the workbench while Dad tinkered in the shed. Dad used to say he was teaching him how to hold a nail in his paws."

"He sounds like a nice man."

"Oh, he was. He really was."

We walked on in silence, past a dachshund on a riverbank and a gun dog lying next to a pile of pheasants.

"And how did the interview with Social Services go? If you want to talk about it."

"Oh, yeah, there's no problem. Well, at least I think there's no problem. They're being a bit cloak-and-dagger about making actual contact, but I've got the address of a woman who knows her, so it's up to me now."

"So you'll be off down to London?"

"Ah, well. . . ."

We walked on past a St. Bernard standing silhouetted on a mountain ridge and a medieval whippet sitting at the feet of a knight.

"It's weird, but I feel . . . almost scared now the end's in sight. No, maybe not *scared,* but kind of reluctant to take that final step. I keep thinking about my childhood; memories I thought I'd forgotten have started popping into my head, some of them in dreams. Nan on a picnic with a caterpillar stuck to her tights. The time she helped me win the Easter bonnet competition at school. I wonder if—if I'm kind of rejecting all that by looking for my real mother. Because they weren't all unhappy times."

We stopped in front of a Great Dane standing over a tiny baby. "In fact, the more I think about it, I actually had quite a nice childhood. Before Dad became ill, the most frightening event I experienced was Doctor Who fighting the Sea-devils. The only betrayal I can remember was finding out the label on my teddy bear's blanket said Pure New Wool and not Mr. Fuzzy's. It only went sour between me and Mum after Dad died, and some of that was probably my fault. See, within her limitations she's been a good mother. We just weren't matched, that's all."

"Are you feeling disloyal?"

"Yes."

"Come and have a cup of tea and a muffin."

Leo led me out of the gallery—"Unashamedly populist but very enjoyable nevertheless," he told the woman at the desk—and across the road to the Octagon.

"This is something I remember." I stirred the sugar around in the bowl with a teaspoon. "Did you believe in sugar stealers when you were little?"

"I'm not sure what you mean."

I started to smooth out the granules with the back of the spoon. "Those floaty seeds—dandelion clocks and such—we all thought at primary school that they were insects, or something and lived on sugar. I was always finding them in our pantry. I really thought it was true for ages."

Leo laughed. "No, I can't say I've heard that one. Tell me another."

I chopped patterns in the smoothed-out grains while I thought.

"Okay, what about those green glass chips you get on graves."

"What about them?"

"Well, if you take even one of them home with you, the ghost of the person whose grave it is will come and haunt you in your bedroom until you put it back."

"Did you ever try it?"

"No way. Too scary. But a boy in our class did and he swore

he was woken in the night by an evil old woman. He lived with his grandma, though, so that was probably it."

Leo was chuckling and wiping his eyes. "Stop, stop. You'll have me choking on my muffin."

"And there was a big craze for giving yourself love bites on the arm. Of course we were only eight; we didn't know what they were. Some lads had completely purple forearms. I'm amazed nobody contacted Children's Services. Then a girl called Sharon Dawes said her mother had caught her doing it and told her it would give her cancer, so we all stopped overnight. Except for Christopher Flint, but he was crazy. He got sent to a special school in Little Lever."

We were both giggling now.

"Sounds like Gavin Crossley," said Leo. "I can't see him being with us much longer, the rate he's going."

"Oh, he was much worse than Gavin. He pushed a wardrobe on top of his brother once, and fired an air gun at Mrs. Porter from the newsagent's when she refused to give him a paper route."

"Village characters."

"Happy times."

"So do you think you'll go to London or not?"

"God knows. I'll flip a coin. No, I won't; I'll count the currants in my muffin. Evens says I go, odds I stay." I took a knife and began to saw. "I can always change my mind later."

I never had no new clothes when I was a girl except for the lace-up shoes I wore on a Sunday; it was all hand-me-downs.

So at field days—Walkin' Days, they're called now—I used have to go at the back o' the line, even though the only time I ever missed church was when I broke my arm. I'll tell you who always walked under the banner, it was Annie Catterall in her fancy white frock, an' she never went to Sunday school nor nothin'. It was only 'cause her parents could afford to take her out. One time my friend Lily Alker took a ribbon off a banner; I don't know how she managed it 'cause her father was an invalid. She'd perhaps lent a frock to someone. Anyhow, they were gettin' to th' end of the procession and this ribbon broke. Annie pocketed it, took it home, an' made hair braids out of it. When she got found out she was stripped and sent to bed, besides gettin' a good hidin'. So perhaps I was best off marchin' at the back.

The worst whippin' I ever got was when I took all my mother's buttons to play in t' street. We used make a circle in the dirt an' try an' flip these buttons in, an' if you got a button inside you could have your pick of all the others. I got in a row many a time for it, but you don't think when you're young. They used play piggy too, an' cock-on-big-or-little. Piggy was the best, though I don't think they play it now. You used put your piggy, which was a fat peg of wood with a whittled end, on a brick on the floor so its snout was hangin' over th' end. Then you got a stick and you walloped it so it flew in th' air. Some big lads could make it go right along the street. They used guess how many strides away it was. Sometimes the Co-Op held races down the Chantry, but I never won anything. I could never run, me. I got a doll once, but that was only 'cause everyone did; I still finished last.

But they were poor days. When times were good Grandma

Florrie made gingerbread an' barm cakes, steak puddings and calf's-foot jelly with a crust on top. A tripe man used come around the streets too, shoutin'. But in the years after the war, when I was still only little, my mother had to go to the church for charity loaves; you could have two a week. An' there were always people singin' in the streets, beggin', and miners squattin' at street corners 'cause they had no work.

My mother was marvelous, now I think about it, because me and Jimmy never felt it, all that poverty, not really. I wish I could have known her longer.

A nya had called to say she was going in to school for her exam results and did I want to meet her there.

"The twins are going for a picnic in the park after, if it's not raining. They're dying to see you. So am I. Come on, shift yourself."

I thought I was too miserable to lift my head off the pillow, but I went in the end. Missing Daniel was like a pain; worse than splitting up with Paul, which had been a series of stabs to the chest. This feeling was a deep, dull ache all over, as if I were about to come down with the flu.

I wondered if I was going to bump into him at the office. Theoretically students come between 10 and 12 to pick up their grades, but in practice there's a seething crowd of hysterical teenagers at the front door by 9:50 and a mad rush when the head of sixth comes down to open it. I slid in with the general melee at 10:03, so I didn't have to wait around being gawked at. Generally, the students who come later are the ones who know they've done either really well or really badly. A lot of posturing goes on: class jokers pretending to be amazed they didn't do even worse, huddles of girls patting and hugging tearful friends in an agony of embarrassment at their own success. The teachers stand around and offer congratulations where appropriate and avoid eye contact where it's not. The air is electric. I hated it last year, hated it again now.

For those few minutes my pregnancy was completely forgotten. Anya and I stood in isolated pools of agony, tearing open the slips, gazing, absorbing, then shrieking at each other, at anyone who'd listen.

"I got an A!"

"Oh, my God, so did I!"

Anya put her arm round me, no mean feat, and we tottered out onto the drive like two drunks. Mrs. Carlisle hurried after us.

"Well done, both of you. Looking forward to next year." She smiled at me. "This is for you, my home phone number. You can call me at any time and we can get together to talk about how things stand." She passed me a sealed envelope. "Don't let it fall into the wrong hands. I don't want obscene calls all summer!"

"She is *so* nice," said Anya, as we walked slowly out of the gates toward the park. We passed the twins on their way in, mad with nerves, but there was still no sign of Daniel. It occurred to me he might be away or have arranged for them to be mailed. But I couldn't stop scanning the faces as one car after another drove past us over the ramp and crawled round the quad.

"Do you want to talk about the baby?" asked Anya unexpectedly. "Now, I mean, before the twins come out. Because we weren't sure whether you'd like to or not, and we didn't want to get it wrong."

Poor Anya. It must have cost her an effort to say that.

I shook my head. "Thanks. No, I don't, not this afternoon. I think I'd like to just be me, not Mrs. Pregnant. Do you mind?"

"No, not at all." There was relief in her voice. I wished then, so keenly, that I could have shed the pregnancy for a few hours, unstrapped the bulge and hung it up in the wardrobe. I wanted a break, time off for good behavior, one last good laugh with the girls, and then I'd be ready to go back to it in the evening. It was so *part of me.* I looked awful now and felt breathless most of the time, couldn't bend down, constantly needed to pee. . . . You're a big parasite, I'd told the baby in the bath. Let it hear, I didn't care.

When the twins caught up ("two Cs") we strolled to the park and sat around the sunken garden, eating. And although there was this great black hole in the conversation, everyone including me trying to avoid the topic that was screaming in our faces, it was good because there were so many other things to talk about. Teenage things, trivia, plans, gossip. I couldn't exactly join in, but I could listen and laugh and tease.

An ice-cream van rolled up, and Anya and I went to get cones for us all. The sun was pretty hot now, and there was a shimmer over the grass. As I cast my eyes over the red-and-white flower beds sloping up to the entrance I spotted Daniel walking quickly toward us. I didn't know what to do, and anyway I had an ice-cream cone in each hand, so I was a bit restricted. I smiled, then looked away in case that was too much.

One of the cones began to melt and drip over my fingers, so I twisted my hand round and tried to lick it off. Daniel broke into a run.

"No!" he shouted.

"What's up with him?" I turned to Anya, but she only shrugged.

Without losing speed he charged at me and, like a jousting knight, knocked the ice cream from my grasp. It splatted onto the ground, cone upended, and began to merge with the gravel.

He overshot, blasted through a flower bed and staggered to a halt several yards away, panting. Anya pulled a loony face at me.

"What the hell do you think you're doing?" I asked. This was some bizarre revenge for rejecting him.

He came up to us, wild-haired and grinning.

"That was a close one. Didn't your midwife tell you about listeria?"

"Yeah. Deadly bug. It's in blue cheese and pâté and I don't like either. So?"

"And in soft ice cream from vans, if you're unlucky. Can't be too careful. Can I treat you to an ice-cream bar?"

"Jesus." I turned to Anya with a despairing look. What would you do with him?

"I'll leave you to it," she said, sniggering, and joined the goggle-eyed twins back on the bench.

What could I do? "I'll have a popsicle," I said grimly.

We must have made an odd couple from a distance, me like a barrel on legs and him a tall streak of nothing. When he gave me my popsicle he flourished his hand and bowed. I could have kicked him.

"Listen, Prince Charming, do you want me to stick this up your nose?" I hissed.

We went over and joined the others, but there were a lot of meaningful looks going on behind our backs and stifled giggles. I'll give them the benefit of the doubt and say they were still a bit hysterical from the exam results.

"Well," said Anya, after about thirty seconds, "we must be off if we're going to hit the shops. Are you coming into town with us?"

"Not a lot of point me trailing round with you at the moment. I have to be getting back soon, anyway."

I knew they couldn't wait to be on their own. They'd probably phone Julia from town and give her a blow-by-blow account of the madman in Queen's Park.

We said good-bye with lots of hugging and promises to call and good lucks; then they left. Daniel was lying along a bench chewing his popsicle stick.

"Waiting for the food additives to kick in," he said.

"I think they already have. Did you take your Ritalin today?"

"The only problem I've got is Grade Deficit Disorder," he said, sitting up and shading his eyes.

"Really? What did you get?"

"B and a C. My parents will be scandalized. Still, serves them right for moving me at a critical period of my development."

I went and sat at the other end of the bench. "B C isn't too bad. They're only exams. You can retake, can't you?"

"Yeah, yeah. It's okay; I've got the spiel worked out in my head for when I get home. You got an A, didn't you?"

"More trouble at home. My mother'll make me wear it around my neck like the albatross. How did you know?"

"Lucky guess. Well done. My dad'll be delighted; he thinks you're wonderful."

"It was nice of him to drive me back last week."

"No problem. He enjoyed talking to you. He says you're intelligent. I got a talking to, though, for being too drunk to drive you myself."

"Were you? Drunk?"

"Oh, yes." He inspected his popsicle stick and read out the joke. "What zooms along the riverbed at one hundred mph?"

"I dunno."

"A motor pike and a side carp. Nice one." He pocketed the stick and got up. "I'll give you a lift back now, if you want."

"I won't say no."

And so, just like that, we fell back into step as if nothing had happened. Maybe both of us had too much to lose.

"Do you mind if I don't ask you in? I'm exhausted. I really need to lie down."

"I've got to get home myself. Face the music." Daniel grimaced. "Bloody parents, they're a liability. See you!"

He honked his horn and I trailed up the front path, feeling suddenly depressed. Reaction, I suppose. I struggled with the door, tossed the results slip on the table, and collapsed on the sofa. Nan came out of the kitchen, beaming.

"Eeh, it's our Charlotte. You're looking bonny, love. Get your feet up, and Debbie'll make you a cup of tea. She's brought a little present for you."

I blew her a kiss.

"I do love you, Nan," I said.

When I got in, Milady was lying on the sofa admiring a tiny sleeper, Nan was massaging Charlotte's feet, and Debbie the cleaner was holding a needle and thread over her tummy.

"I can't tell whether it's swinging in a circle or not," Debbie was saying. "And I can't remember which way around it is, anyway. Can you, Nan? Is it a circle for a boy and a straight line for a girl?"

"Perhaps it's a hermaphrodite," quipped Charlotte. I know for a fact neither of them know what that is, but they both laughed.

I picked up the scrap of paper on the table and winced. It was the report fiasco all over again. Shame she didn't get an A in doing as you're damn well told.

"You do know you're throwing your life away," I snapped as I went past. She never even turned her head.

"Ooh, I just saw the baby move!" exclaimed Debbie. "Bless it."

"Can I have a feel?" said Nan.

Three days later I walked out.

chapter 9

The day started as per usual, with Nan wandering in and announcing it was morning. Up with the lark, that's my mother. Back in her bedroom I changed her bag; then she stumped downstairs and had a wash. Meanwhile I threw on leggings and a shirt. Nan returned to her room to get dressed and I trailed down to the kitchen to make breakfast. It's a kind of ballet sequence we've refined over the years, and the only one who ever throws a wrench in the works is Charlotte, rising unexpectedly early or locking herself in the bathroom for a pre-school hair crisis.

This morning I'd finished my toast and Nan still hadn't made an appearance, so I went back upstairs to see what the matter was. She was sitting on the bed in her underslip glowering at the chair.

"What's up now?" I asked. "Your Weetabix is going cold."

"I'm not wearing that." She pointed to the dress slung over the chair back.

"Why ever not?"

"It's not red."

"Oh, for God's sake. It's a lovely frock. You wore it last week." She glared at me.

"I tell you what, why don't you put that little maroon cardigan over the top? That's reddish."

No answer.

"Well, you can't go to church in your underslip. Maud and Ivy'll be here soon; you don't want to hold them up." I opened the wardrobe door and rifled through her clothes. "Wait a minute, what about this?" I pulled out a gray dress with scarlet flowers on the skirt. "This is a nice one."

"It's not red enough."

With enormous control I put the gray dress back and walked out onto the landing to check the laundry basket. Maybe her red wool two-piece could be redeemed with a squirt of Febreze and a good shake. I rooted about and found it, but there was a soup stain down the front. I flung it back in and stood there thinking. I had four choices. I could throw myself over the banisters now, this very minute; then they'd all be sorry. I could burst into noisy tears, which no one would take any notice of. I could go into Nan's room and slap her across the face— oh, I know it's a terrible thought, I'm supposed to be her caregiver and it's not her fault et cetera, et cetera, but believe me, there are times when I come so close I have to walk away and count ten. Or—and this was the plan resolving itself before my eyes as being the most reasonable course of action under the circumstances—I could run away.

I went back into Nan's room and pulled out all the spare bags and tape she needs for changing and put them on the dressing table. Then I got out the little scissors from her jewelry box and cut the right-size openings in the top of every bag.

"I'm old enough to do as I like," she snapped suddenly.

"No, you're not old *enough,* you're *too* old, that's the point."

I got the overnight case from the top of her wardrobe and took it into my room. (*We're off! We're off!*) My head started to sing a stupid song of Nan's to the rhythm of my breathing. I packed a smart suit and a pair of pumps, two pairs of leggings, and assorted tops, underwear, travel wash, makeup and a curling iron. (*We're off in a motor car!*) Walking past Nan's bedroom I could see she'd lain down on the bed and closed her eyes. I carried straight on downstairs to the bathroom, where I topped up my sponge bag; then in the hall to check my handbag and address book. (*Sixty policemen are after us, and we don't know where we are!*) Finally, I scribbled a note to Charlotte saying I'd gone to stay with a friend for a few days but I'd give her a ring that evening and if she needed help to contact her dad or Social Services. It was completely irresponsible of me. I imagined the expressions of horror when Charlotte finally roused herself to let Maud and Ivy in and they discovered the truth together. Well, they'd just have to sort it out.

I slammed the Metro door so hard the hinges all but fell off, then stuck a Madonna tape on full blast. All the way to Manchester I justified myself to the music: "Rescue Me," "Secret," "Bad Girl." I couldn't believe what I'd done.

Then, as I drew into the half-empty parking lot, the tape came to an end and a man on the radio said Princess Diana was dead.

I sat in the car for a few minutes, listening; a car crash, France, early hours of the morning, a high-speed chase. "The phone lines are open now for your calls," the newscaster said. "Please do dial and let us know how you're feeling about this terribly sad, this shocking tragedy. . . . Hello, Gemma from Radcliffe." Gemma, quavering: "I just can't believe it, she was so young—" I switched the radio off and got quietly out of the car.

I walked up to the station, past the screaming headlines on the newspaper stand, past a huge chalk heart someone had scrawled on the wall near the café, R.I.P. DI. Unreal. I bought my ticket on autopilot and went to stand on the platform, where a little group was talking together animatedly. Tight-faced fifty-something woman, nasty claw-shaped brooch on her coat; very thin man freezing in shirtsleeves; young lass in salwar kameez and anorak, towing meek child: normally they'd all be busy maintaining personal space. But this morning was different.

"In a tunnel," Claw Woman was saying. "Awful." "Those boys," murmured the young mum, shaking her head while her tiny daughter stood with her face upturned, watching pigeons fly between the metal rafters above our heads. The thin man balled his fists. "Bloody journalists. They should be locked up. They've no bloody scruples."

"It said in our paper she was just very badly injured," Claw Woman piped up. "I thought she was still alive till I put the telly on. I can't believe it."

Thin man saw me staring at his *Observer* and handed it to

me without a word. I held it up, saw the pictures, and read the words, so it was true.

Then the train to Euston slid in.

As the coach lurched out of the station, I sat alone in my corner by the window and thought about Diana and about me. I remembered all the royal wedding celebrations, all that hope and happiness in the midst of my own messed-up life, her lovely smiling face and that rumpled fairy-tale dress. Everyone had seemed united; you'd felt like the whole nation was with you as you sat in front of the telly watching that balcony kiss. I'd kept the souvenir issue of the *Radio Times* and even copied the haircut briefly. I thought she was charmed; then it turned out she'd been duped just like the rest of us, confessing and crying on prime-time TV. I'd squirmed for her. And now after so much unhappiness she was dead, shocking proof that money and elegance and class and beauty—none of them mean anything in the face of Fate.

Sadness and guilt tightened on my chest. If Diana couldn't get it right, what chance had the rest of us? Then my own failings and inadequacies seemed to rise up like a cold mist around me, so that I suddenly found myself in tears and had to stare out the window at the blurred countryside. I didn't even know her, I thought, so why am I crying?

It was turning into a surreal kind of day. No Mum, Dad in the kitchen unloading frozen meals and tins of Nan food, and all the TV stations awash with the Diana story, whichever channel you flicked to.

"I know it's a shame, but I don't know why there's all these women in tears," I muttered. "You'd think she'd been personal best friend to a hundred thousand people. I think they're putting it on for the cameras."

"I got you six of these mini pizzas 'cause they were on special offer," said Dad. He was really pissed off, you could tell. "What a flamin' fuss. I have to be at work tomorrow, you know. I've had so much time off the boss has given me a warning. But Ivy Seddon says they're organizing a roster at the Over Seventies', and I've been on the phone to Social Services and there's a nurse coming around every morning for an hour. That Cross-roads woman's here tomorrow and then there's that cleaner you have. It'll be like Paddy's market. You certainly won't be on your own, love. I'll come around every evening after I've had my tea. Anyway, your mum might not be away so long, she could be back in a day or two."

"I'm not bothered, Dad." I wasn't, either. In some ways it was a relief to have her out of the house. "She's done it before, remember. That time she found a lump in her breast and took herself off to Fleetwood for a long weekend."

"Aye. And it was nothing in the end. Do you think she really has gone to stay with a friend?"

"I wouldn't have thought so. She doesn't have any."

"It's not a man, then?"

"Nah."

"I just wondered."

"She's been horrible about the baby, you know. She wanted me to get rid of it."

Dad became very busy stacking the freezer compartment.

"Well, she was only thinking of you. She thought it would be for the best. You know, your education and that."

"I don't think I'll ever forgive her."

Nan wandered in.

"Where's our Karen?"

Dad and I exchanged glances.

"She's had to pop out for a while. Would you like a cup o' tea?" Dad unplugged the kettle and held it under the cold tap.

She sighed. "I need my bag changing."

"Over to you," said Dad.

As soon as I got off the train I found a cell phone place, threw my credit card at the assistant, and emerged with a Nokia, a charger, and twenty quid's worth of vouchers. "You've one bar left on your battery," the smart lad in the shop had said. "You're telling me," I joked, but he'd lost interest. Then I went outside onto a grass roadside, away from all the bustle, and read the instruction booklet. At last I felt ready to dial.

Unluckily it was Steve who answered, so the first few seconds were him calling me every name under the sun. When I could get a word in edgeways, I told him my number and got him to write it down and read it back; it's not that he's thick, far from it, but he's careless. I asked after Charlotte and Nan and got another mouthful of abuse, then I heard Charlotte's voice in the background asking to speak to me. I knew if I let her I'd fall apart; I'd turn straight back to the station and climb on the next available train home. So I said quickly, "Tell her I'll be home in a day or two. Battery's dead. Got to go." Then I pressed END and switched off for half an hour. If I was going to do this right, I needed to clear my head.

I retraced my steps into the station, bought a street map at the newsstand, and went down the escalator to the Underground. I stood in front of the map for ages, trying to work it out, while people barged into me and sighed with impatience over the top of my head. I reached forward and tried to trace the route with my finger, like a slow reader. Northern line, change at King's Cross to the Piccadilly. That was okay. But which *zone* was I in and how much would that make the ticket? There was a massive line at the ticket office so I spent ages studying one of the machines to a background of irritated tuttings from the woman behind me. At last I pressed the right button and a card dropped into my palm. Now, which escalator? I stood like a rock in the middle of a swirling river. An oriental man with a briefcase stood on my foot. "Sorry," I said. He disappeared into the crowds without looking back.

I made my decision, glided down past the advertisements for theaters and museums, and found myself in a windy tunnel that smelled of burning rubber. Did I want platform 1 or 2? How should I bloody know? A quick check of my pocket diary and down the tiled walkway, then finally out onto a platform with a lot of bored-looking people. Almost instantly there was a terrific noise and a train shot out and slowed to a halt in front of us. The doors hissed open. I stood back politely, and was nearly knocked over in the rush to get on.

The last time I was in London was a school trip to coincide with the Silver Jubilee. We'd worn school uniforms and our commemorative badges because, our form mistress had said,

That's what the Queen would want, not jeans and sneakers. We'd gone to stand outside Buckingham Palace, and someone had said the Queen was definitely in because of the way the flag was flying, so she might have looked out of the window and seen us.

The train came into King's Cross, where there was a teenage girl begging with a baby on her hip. I thought of Charlotte and pulled out my purse. The girl's top lip was covered in sores, but her eyes were pretty. Where was *her* mum, I wondered.

"What's his name?" I asked, smiling at the round-eyed snotty baby.

"Ellie," she said and pocketed the note neatly.

I thought about her all the way to Amos Grove.

At last I came up the steps into the sunlight, feeling bruised. I pulled out my street map and started walking. I was looking for Hemmington Grove and Mrs. Mary Beattie.

Actually, it's no big deal, changing Nan (after all, I'll be doing diapers soon). It used to freak me out at first, but now it just makes me sad. Nan lies meekly on the bed with a towel under her, her dress pulled up and her underpants and tights around her thighs. There are poor little white hairs between her legs, and the skin is loose round her belly. You peel off the old micropore tape and the used bag and put them in something like a diaper bag. Then you wipe round the weird, amazingly clean hole in Nan's flesh with a sterile tissue. You take the backing strip off the new bag and stick it down with the opening against Nan's stomach; Mum likes to make extra sure with some tape on top. Sometimes, if the skin's red, we use Nivea, but you have to be careful not to get it under the tape or nothing sticks and it's a disaster. Nan remains glassy-eyed throughout, then switches back to life the minute you pull her dress back down. So there you are. Nothing to it.

I was heading toward the trash bin after the lunchtime change when the doorbell rang. Dad was right, it was like Paddy's market. I thought it was another of Ivy's volunteers, but it turned out to be Daniel clutching a bassinet.

"One of my father's patients asked if he could find a home for it. It needs a new mattress, but it's got a stand and some frilly things to go around the sides."

"Fantastic." I took it off him and laid it on the sofa while he went to get the rest from the car. Maud and Nan crowded around to see.

"Eeh, isn't it lovely?" said Nan.

"Better than a drawer," said Maud, peering inside. "That's where my mother put me when I was born."

"Well, they did in them days," said Nan. "In't it lovely, though."

"Where's it going to go?" asked Maud.

Nan shrugged.

"It can come in my room," I said. "It'll have to. Be easier, anyway, if I'm getting up at night." I glanced out of the window and saw Daniel struggling with a stack of books and a froth of linen. "Hang on."

I waddled down the path and opened the gate for him.

"Come here, you daft good-for-nothing. Let me have some of the books, at least."

"They're from Mrs. Carlisle. She thought you could be doing

some reading before term starts. Don't take too many now, just these from the top."

"Oh, God, I must phone her. I've been meaning—" I broke off with a cry, and the paperbacks fell on the pavement.

"What's the matter?" Daniel threw his stuff back on the seat and put his arm round me.

"Get me in. Get me in, Dan."

We staggered inside and I sat down breathlessly.

"What is it, Charlotte? Have you got a pain?"

Nan and Maud were hovering anxiously.

"Shall I make her a cup of tea?" asked Maud.

"Yes, that would be excellent. Thank you." Daniel came and sat next to me and fluttered his hands. "What is it, Charlotte?"

I groaned. "It was Paul. Across the road; you didn't see him. He was walking past with a Spar bag. He saw me—" Oh, Christ, the humiliation. He'd seen me and stared, then deliberately looked the other way till he was around the corner. He'd have run if he could. Bastard.

"Paul."

"Yes."

"Dirty bugger," said Nan, miming a spit. "He'll come to his cake and milk."

"I'm not terrifically good at that sort of thing, but I'll go after him and hit him if it would make you feel better," said Daniel. "All you have to do is tell me where he lives."

Even in the midst of my personal hell, I couldn't help but smile at the image. *Excuse me,* Daniel would probably say first, *do you mind if I punch you in the mouth?* Then Paul would knock seven bells out of him.

"No, it's okay. My dad's tried that one. Silly bastard."

Daniel let out a sigh of relief, and Maud came in with the tea.

"Look, are you definitely all right? Do I need to get you to a doctor?"

"No, really, I'm fine. Just mortified, that's all." I took a sip of tea. "Thanks, Mrs. Eckersley. I could lie down, though."

"Good idea. Get your feet up." Daniel rose to his feet. "I must be going, anyway."

"Please stay," I said. "Come up to my room so we can talk."

Maud gave me a funny look and I nearly said to her, For God's sake, I can't get any *more* pregnant, can I?

"I'm sorry the room's so small," I said, as Daniel folded himself into the beanbag chair.

"What are you smiling at?"

"Nothing. It seems strange you being here, that's all." I was reclining on the bed with Nan's V-shaped pillow behind my head, trying to find the right way to lie. "The trouble with being this size is you can never get comfortable."

"I suspect you're going to get even bigger before you've finished."

"It's all right for you, Slim-Jim." I lay back.

"Shall I put some music on?"

"Yeah, will you? The tapes are on that shelf by your head. Pick what you like, so long as it's relaxing. Actually, that one on the top is good; Julia made it for me. Supposed to be my labor tape. Sound track to my agony."

"Everything's very . . . right at hand in this room." Daniel switched on the cassette player by leaning to one side and stretching across the shelf. The music started and we listened for a few minutes without speaking.

> *What sense does love make?*
> *Your brain's turned inside out,*
> *A chemical illusion*
> *That makes you want to shout.*

It was me who began. "The thing about Paul is, I hate him but in a way I still love him. No, not *him,* but the person I thought he was. He seemed great at first because he was so happy-go-lucky and I'm so serious; I actually thought he was *good* for me. Crazy. Even now I can't totally shake off the promise of those initial few weeks. My brain still hasn't caught up with recent events. I *know* he's a shit but he's the baby's father too."

"Not if he doesn't want to be. You can't force him to have anything to do with the child if he doesn't want to. You might be able to extract a few quid out of him after the birth, but that's about all."

"I know. But biologically—"

"Biology's nothing. Inserting your knob at an opportune moment."

We both blushed. The song finished and another one began.

> *You are the star—sun—moon that guides me,*
> *My lightship in the storm.*
> *You keep me safe from harm,*
> *Safe and warm*
> *Through the storm.*

"The other problem is he's practically on the doorstep, as demonstrated today. We'll always be bumping into each other. It'll be awful."

Daniel chewed his fingernail. "All the more reason to get your university acceptance sorted out. You can always defer. Put that prick behind you and get on with your life."

"I know, I know. You are right." I heaved myself up a bit and grinned feebly at him. "Actually, now I think about it, he was a prick at primary school. He was one of those boys who used to set up trouble and then walk away. It was never him who got yelled at. But he was funny and good at soccer, so he had a lot of friends. He knew all those rude songs."

" 'My Uncle Billy had a three-foot willy,' that sort of thing?"

I smirked. "It was four-foot around here. You were obviously suffering from shrinkage down south."

"Huh," said Daniel.

"Then there was the classic 'Ooh, aah, I lost my bra; I left my knickers in my boyfriend's car,' and 'Jesus Christ superstar, wears plastic knickers and a Playtex bra,' 'All the girls in Spain wash their knickers in the rain.' It was all underwear."

"The knickers-knackers-knockers school of comedy."

"If you say so. He had this joke, too: He'd go up to you and say, 'Are you a PLP?' If you said no, he'd say, 'Are you not a Proper Living Person, then?' If you said yes he'd go, 'You're a Public Leaning Post, then,' and barge into you."

"Sounds like a genius."

"And once we had this student teacher in, a really nice bloke, actually. He was always changing in and out of his tracksuit like Superman or something, and one time when he left his shoes in the classroom Paul wrote WAN KER on the bottoms with

Wite-Out. Or at least, that's what he meant to write. But he got the shoes mixed up, so when this teacher sat on the floor with us at story time with his legs out in front of him and his feet together, it actually said KERWAN on his soles. Everyone still thought it was very funny, though."

"I suspect there's a lot of inbreeding in this village," said Daniel.

Number 80 was a neat Edwardian twin with white-painted sills, a black front door, and two giant terra-cotta pots on either side of the step. I could see swagged curtains at the bay window and a fern in a Wedgwood planter. I must have stood for ten minutes just staring; I suppose I was hoping someone would come out, but no one did. Eventually I picked up my case and carried on down the road, swinging my head from right to left as I searched for B & B signs. I turned right at the bottom of the road into a street where the houses were smaller and terraced and found a bed-and-breakfast place at once.

The hall smelled of elderly dog and the wallpaper was grubby but I wasn't too bothered. It was only a base. The wheezing old lady who led me up to my room asked lots of questions but then didn't give me any time to answer, which suited me. I shut the door on her and took off my shoes; it was time to phone Mrs. Beattie. Where was my cell phone?

I psyched myself up to press the ON button, but this time the battery really was dead. Now that was fate. I threw the phone down on the bed in relief. Then I had second thoughts and put it on to charge while I unpacked and had a wash in the poky little sink. Looking at myself in the mirror, I wondered what my mother would make of me after all this time. I wanted her to be impressed, to think I'd grown up to be a stylish, together sort of woman. I wasn't in bad shape, on the whole. My skin was quite good for my age—a few lines round the mouth, that was all—and my hair was in between cuts, which is when it looks its best. I'd wear my suit and pumps and paint my nails if I had time. I lay back down on the bed and caught my breath with the enormity of it all.

My mother.

After an hour I tried the phone again. The screen lit up; it was time.

A posh woman answered.

"Am I speaking to Mrs. Mary Beattie?"

"Yes, you are. May I help you?" She sounded cool and professional, like a consultant's receptionist: I'm sorry I can't give you your test results over the phone.

"Er, my name's Karen Cooper. Mrs. Fitton from Bolton Social Services might have called about me. I think—she said you might be able to—can you help me find my birth mother? Her name was Jessie Pilkington. She stayed with you once, a long time ago."

"Yes, yes . . . Joyce Fitton did call." She paused, and I could hear my own breathing in the receiver. "Yes, well, what we thought you could do was come down and see me sometime and I'd talk you through—"

"I'm here."

"Are you actually in London?"

"Yeah. I'm staying with a friend. I'd like, if it's not too much trouble—I'd like to come and see you."

"Let me check my calendar," she said.

I wandered over to the window and gazed down at the back-yard. It wasn't so different from a small house in Wigan. It was more the *feel* of the place; it had to be London, somehow. It just didn't feel northern.

"Right." She was back on. "Can you manage tomorrow morning? Say, ten? Or is that too early? Where are you coming from?"

"Ten's fine. I'll be there."

"I'll look forward to seeing you," she said, and my heart dropped like a stone with terror.

That night was prenatal class. I plunked myself at the back and tried to look older than I was; also, as if I'd just left my loving husband at home instead of an angry dad and a crazy grannie.

The midwife held up a plastic pelvis and forced a doll's head through it. I sat there, thirty-four weeks pregnant and still thinking, *This isn't me, this is not going to happen to me. I'm not ready. I can't do it.*

"Burned your bridges now, girl, haven't you?" I heard my mother's voice say.

I sat on the chaise longue, waiting for Mrs. Beattie to make tea, feeling exhausted. All night long I'd been running after trains. One was going to America, and I said to Captain Kangaroo (because he was with me), "How can it go across the sea?" and he said, "Oh, anything's possible." I got up far too early, felt cold, got back in bed again, and painted my fingernails. I turned on the radio but it was all still Diana's death. I had a little weep—half of it was nerves—and then went down to breakfast, which I couldn't eat. My landlady was clearly a big Elvis fan, and all through the meal I kept my eyes fixed on the Love Me Tender wall clock whose hour hand was the neck of a guitar. Time moved so slowly I thought the thing was broken. Then I got dressed and was all ready to go by nine twenty, so I had to walk up and down the road several times. Even though Mrs. Beattie wasn't my mother, I'd put on the suit.

"Here we are," she said, passing me a china cup and saucer. I looked in vain for a safe place to put it down. If I spilled tea over this nice chintz! I perched the cup on my lap and took in the room.

"This is such a lovely house," I said. It was, too. Everything I'd seen, I wanted.

"It's rather big for me, now I'm on my own. The stairs are becoming difficult too."

I wondered how old she was. Seventy? Very elegant, though. Nothing like Nan. "You could get one of those stair lifts."

"It might come to that."

We sipped our tea. What was she thinking? Inscrutable, that's what she was.

"Well, about my birth mother," I announced.

She pressed her lips together, bent down, and set her cup on the slate hearth. "Yes. There are some documents on the desk, if you'd like to fetch them. Bring the side table, and we can put it between us. I need to take you through this."

My heart thumped as she separated the sheets of paper one by one.

"Do I take it you know nothing about your mother at all?"

"Only that she was very young and she wasn't married. Oh, I knew she gave birth in London. Probably couldn't wait to escape!" I squeaked with nervous laughter. My voice was too loud in that quiet room.

"Right," said Mrs. Beattie carefully. She pushed a piece of photocopy paper toward me. "I want you to read this."

It was a newspaper report dated April 1971. A man and a woman living in Croydon had been charged with manslaughter after a child had died in their care. The six-year-old's body showed signs of serious malnourishment and was covered in bruises and sores. She—it was a little girl—was described as looking like a child two years younger because of her small frame. Neighbors had become suspicious after seeing the girl foraging in garbage pails and reported what they had seen to Social Services, but somehow the messages hadn't got through. School noticed nothing because she was never there. She hadn't even been on the At Risk register when she died.

The little girl's name was Emma, and Jessie Pilkington had been her mother.

I read it and read it and read it, and it still didn't make sense. Mrs. Beattie reached out and took my hand. I was shaking.

"Would she have been my sister?" I whispered.

"Half-sister."

"Oh, God. My little sister." I started to cry. Mrs. Beattie sat back and let me, patting my hand. The clock ticked and traffic swooshed past the window; I wasn't aware of anything else. We stayed like that for a long time.

At last she said, "I have a photograph, but you may not want to see it."

I wiped my eyes. "Of Emma?"

"Of all of them. Taken from a newspaper."

"I think it might break my heart."

She put her arms round me and I felt like I was a child again, Nan holding me the first time we knew Dad was ill. There was a ticking clock then as well, and the radio in the kitchen was playing "Bridge Over Troubled Water."

I'm on your side.

"Did Mrs. Fitton know all this?"

"Yes." Mrs. Beattie wiped her eyes. "But because I'm a trained counselor and used to work for Social Services, she thought I'd be the most suitable person to talk to you about it. And, of course, I knew your mother."

"How could she do something so *awful*? I mean, your *own child*?" Charlotte: baby Charlotte crying in her crib; toddler Charlotte throwing porridge on the floor, wetting the bed; beautiful Charlotte.

"She became involved with a violent man, as a lot of women do; you'd be surprised by how many, all walks of life. She was a very . . . needy person, not at all able to stand up for herself, despite the big talk. So she stayed with this man even after he began to abuse her daughter—it wasn't his child; she'd gotten pregnant by another man, which didn't help matters. She always maintained she never actually hurt Emma herself. I don't know if that was true or not. There certainly wasn't enough evidence to convict her of direct cruelty; her defense claimed the only reason she hadn't acted to save her daughter was that she was frightened he might start beating her as well. It may have been true. She got four years; he got fifteen, but he died of cancer before he was released."

"Good."

"When Jessie came out of prison, she changed her name and moved. There was terribly bad feeling toward her from the public, as there always is in these cases, though I don't think the press was as intrusive then as it is now. She had hate mail, death threats, so she tried to walk away from what she'd done and reinvent herself. By and large she succeeded."

I put my hands to my temples. "I still can't take it in."

"It must be a great shock for you. Can I get you anything, a glass of brandy?"

"No. I'll take a couple of Tylenol; I've some in my handbag." But I knew Tylenol would never take away the cold clamping sensation in my heart or stop me from reliving those horrific phrases from the report.

Mrs. Beattie went off to get a glass of water, and I found myself opening the file again, scanning for those pictures. *Don't do it!* part of me was screaming, but I had to know. And there she was, a fine-featured little girl in a checkered dress and a cardigan, smiling away and looking as if she didn't have a care in the world. I closed the file quickly. My heart felt as if it were going to burst with grief and fury.

"So my m—Jessie Pilkington's still alive?" I asked, when Mrs. Beattie came back.

"Yes, she is. I have a contact address for her, even though I haven't spoken to her for many years now. She sends a card at Christmas, that's all."

How could a child-killer send Christmas cards? "Don't you hate her?"

"It's difficult . . . I hate what she did, certainly, but there are other factors. She's been punished, of course, she served her time. You have to remember too that she was a victim herself in many ways. Her own father—"

I put my hands over my ears. "Stop. Oh, please stop."

Mrs. Beattie took the file and slid it under her chair. I wished I could have done that with the new knowledge in my head.

"I feel like a different person," I said. "Nothing will ever be the same again." She nodded. "I need to go away now and think about this. Can I have Jessie Pilkington's address?"

"I have no right to withhold it from you."

"But you don't believe I should have it?"

Mrs. Beattie pulled her cuffs straight and smoothed her skirt. "I'm not sure you could do anything very constructive."

"All the same."

She went back into the file and pulled out an envelope. "It's in there. Think carefully about how you want to handle this situation tonight, and come and see me tomorrow. We'll talk it over together." She clasped my hand again. "You've been very brave. Whatever your life has been like, it's made you a strong person."

"I don't feel strong."

"Well, you are."

Then she hugged me again and I left.

I don't know why I did it. I should have gone straight home, but I knew I'd never settle till I'd seen Jessie Pilkington, or whatever her name was, and talked to her face-to-face. I trailed back to the B & B, collected my stuff, and set off for the Underground.

Back on the Underground, everything seemed squalid and threatening. People looked at one another out of the corner of their eyes; hardly anyone spoke. Even the beautiful young couple strap-hanging seemed to be mocking the rest of us when they laughed together. The diversity was frightening too; every race, language, class, and subclass seemed to be on our train, and it made my head spin. I unfolded the envelope and checked the address for the umpteenth time. Lewisham. What was that like, then? You hear the names of these London boroughs they don't mean a thing. Certain ones have memory tags attached—Brixton (riots), Lambeth (Walk)—but mostly it's all pretty vague. Well, how many Londoners know the difference between Worsley and Whalley Range?

Maybe she'd make it all right. She might say something that would explain and make it not so bad. It couldn't be any worse. In any case, it was what I needed to do.

It didn't take me long to figure out that Lewisham isn't an upper-class area full of millionaires. There were a lot of boarded-up windows, for one thing, and metal grills on some of the shops. Big difference from Hemmington Grove. I got the feeling terra-cotta pots wouldn't survive very long here. A filthy man with a droopy eye came up to me, as I stood turning my street map around, and shouted something in my face. I put my head down and started walking.

It took me nearly twenty minutes to find her street, Bewely Road, and it was grubby and depressing. I followed the numbers until I came to a sixties block of flats, two stories high, with colored panels, orange and blue, stuck to the bricks under the windows. There are some flats like that in Wigan, just as you get near the town center. They smack to me of desperate mothers caged up with screaming toddlers and teenagers pissing in the stairwells. Maybe I was being a snob; your house doesn't make you who you are, I should know that. But I didn't feel sure of anything much anymore.

She lived on the ground floor. I rang the bell—by now I was so nauseated and swimmy I had to lean against the jamb—and waited. The plain front door swung open and there she was.

It was the toes I noticed first; she was wearing sandals and her toenails were painted red, but dirty underneath. Leggings, a baggy T-shirt, much like I knock about in when I'm at home, and a face that was mine but old and twisted with sourness.

"I know who you are," she snapped, in an accent that was still northern. "Mary phoned me. She warned me you might turn up."

"Can I come in?" My mouth was very dry, and the words sounded odd as I said them. "I've come a long way." Behind her I could hear a television going but I couldn't see past her into the hall.

"I don't care how far you've come. You've to go away. I never asked to see you. What do you want to come rooting around and stirring up trouble for? Haven't you got a life of your own?"

"That's what I wanted to talk to you about, tell you what I've done with myself over the years. I thought you'd like to know. There're things I need to ask you."

She pushed her graying hair behind her ears and lowered her

voice. "Look, I just want you to leave. If I didn't want you when you were a sweet little baby, I'm hardly likely to want you now you're a bitter-faced thirty-year-old, am I? For God's sake. I owe you nothing."

"I'm thirty-four, actually."

She made to shut the door.

"Wait!" I wedged my shoulder painfully into the gap and forced it open again. A smell of old cooking oil floated out. "Tell me about my dad, at least. He might want to see me even if you don't."

"You'll have a tough time. He's dead." She laughed meanly.

"Well, who was he? I've a right to know."

"Oh, *rights*, is it? We've all got rights, love. Well, I'll tell you, since you're burning to hear the truth. He was an evil bastard. He just wanted rid of you. He'd have done it hisself if I'd let him; he did it to another lass. D'you get me?" I must have looked blank. *"With a"*—her face screwed up and she made a kind of clawing movement with her hand— *"coat hanger."*

I clapped my palm to my mouth and took a step back, and she slammed the door. I noticed my suit had a black mark all the way down the front.

Daniel had come around again, and we were watching cartoons before eating our frozen pizzas. It was so relaxing without Mum there.

"You won't believe this, but I need to pee *again*," I said, heaving myself up off the sofa. There was a sudden rush of water between my legs. "Oh, my God." We both stared at the dark stain spreading over my skirt. "I think I've wet myself."

"That's not wee," said Daniel.

I was standing on the platform at Euston when my cell phone rang. I nearly had kittens when it went off.

"Hello?" I was expecting another ear-bashing from Steve.

"Hello," said a polite young man. "I don't believe we've ever met. I'm just calling to tell you your daughter's in labor."

chapter 10

"Shall I phone the hospital or your father first?" Daniel asked, as I struggled with the bath towel he'd brought me to mop up the mess.

"God, *I* don't know," I snapped. I was really frightened.

"Okay. I'm going to call for an ambulance. Lie down and try to relax."

I stretched out on the sofa and willed the baby to keep moving. "My prenatal notes are on the sideboard. You might need to give them some details."

"Fine."

Daniel disappeared into the hall. I started to pray.

When he came back he looked cheerful. "They'll be here in ten minutes. Now, what do you need to take?"

"There's a packed bag upstairs. I'll come with you." I started to haul myself up.

"No. Stay horizontal. I'll figure it out."

"There are some extra things written on a Post-it note stuck to the handle," I shouted after him. "Don't forget my Walkman. And try not to wake Nan. I can't cope with her as well."

I lay there for about ten seconds, then got up. "Oh, little banana, hang on," I whispered. I shuffled to the phone, still holding the towel between my legs, and dialed Dad's number. Thank Christ; he was back.

"Yep?" he said, his mouth full.

"Dad? Can you come over right now? I've got to go to the hospital."

"Charlotte? Are y' all right, love? What's up?"

"We think the baby's coming."

There was a choking noise followed by coughing. "I thought it weren't due till October."

I started to cry.

"I'll be around straightaway," he said. "Damn and blast your mother." He hung up.

"Get back on that sofa," hissed Daniel over the banister.

When the ambulance came, I wanted Daniel to come with me.

"No, Charlotte, that doesn't make sense. I'll stay till your dad arrives, then I'll follow in the car. That way I can come and go from the hospital; otherwise my car'll be stranded here and I'll have no transport."

I started to sob, even though we were standing in the road with all the curtains twitching. *"Don't* make me go on my own. *Please* come. I'm so *scared."* I grabbed his hand and squeezed the fingers desperately.

"Has your father got a key?"

"Yeah." I sniffed.

"Fuck it, then. Come on, let's get this show on the road." And he lifted his long legs and climbed into the back of the ambulance.

"I'm going to strap this around your tummy so we can hear your baby's heartbeat," said the Irish midwife. "You'll need to lie fairly still. Do you think you're having contractions?"

They'd met me with a wheelchair, which was pretty freaky—did they think the baby might drop out if I walked up to the ward?—and pushed me along the shiny corridors at speed, Daniel trotting alongside. Now he was lurking at the foot of the bed. I wouldn't let him out of my sight. Mum was on her way; he'd telephoned her from the hospital foyer, but she thought it would be about another five hours.

I didn't know if I was having contractions or not. "There's a funny feeling low down every so often but it doesn't hurt."

The nurse nodded and pointed to a slip of paper hanging out of the monitor like a long white tongue. "This will tell us if you're in the early stages of labor," she said. There was a black wavy line drawn along the center.

"It looks like a lie detector," said Daniel.

Pyow-pyow-pyow-pyow went the baby. The midwife left the room.

"Your mother thought I was Paul." Daniel grinned.

"Oh, God, what did you say?"

" 'I certainly am not.' Then she decided I must be a doctor."

"It's the posh accent. My mum's a sucker for BBC English."

"Look, I could wheel the telephone in here, there's one outside, if you want to speak to her. She sounded fairly frantic. She said she'd never have gone if she'd realized, but that first babies usually came late." He fished in his jeans pocket. "I've got about a pound in silver."

"Put it away," I said grimly. He didn't ask again.

Ten minutes later a doctor arrived to do an internal exam.

"I'll pop outside," said Daniel, and slunk away. Poor bugger, neither fish, flesh, nor good red herring.

"My name is Dr. Battyani," said the smiley gentleman in the white coat. "I will try not to hurt you. Now, will you put your heels down, your ankles together, and let your knees fall apart." He poked about for a minute or so while I stared up at the air vents in the ceiling, and it did hurt, quite a lot. "You are only two centimeters dilated," he announced, pulling the sheet back over my shame. "But I can see from the monitor that you are having mild contractions. Although your baby is early we will not try to stop your labor because of the risk of infection. What we might do is administer a steroid injection to help your baby's lungs cope better."

My heart cringed with fear. "Will my baby be all right?"

"You are in the best place," he said, and left.

The contractions started properly about half an hour later.

"It hurts, but it's not too bad," I said to Daniel, who was reading out the *Times* crossword to me. "I have to say, so far labor's been quite boring."

"I wouldn't complain if I were you," he muttered, chewing his pen thoughtfully. "Whenever I've seen women on TV giving birth, it always looks grim. Loads of gripping onto brass bedsteads and rolling about screaming. Maybe you've got a high pain threshold. Now, what about *seed pod,* five letters?"

But an hour later, when the midwife was examining me again, I was sick as a dog. Daniel melted away again as I retched into a kidney basin and moaned. "It's really hurting now. Can I have something for the pain?"

"Well, you're getting there. Six centimeters." She pointed to the chart by the bed, which showed circles of increasing diameter. The biggest one was like a fucking dinner plate. I was never going to make it to ten, that was just plain ridiculous; what the bloody hell did they think I was made of, latex?

"OhhhhhhhhhhhhhhhhhhhHHHHHHHHHHHHhhhhhhhh-hhhhhhhhhh." I panted miserably, overtaken by a wave of agony. My God, it was wonderful when it stopped, but it was like being in the eye of the hurricane. You knew it was only a temporary respite.

"We can give you some gas and air. But you need to try and work with the pain." She was all happy and brisk, I hated her.

"What do you mean?" Why did they talk such garbage? I really couldn't deal with it.

"Keep on top of your breathing. Deep, controlled breath *as soon* as you feel a contraction coming on, then *slowly* out with the pain. Hum if it helps."

"But what about the drugs? I want drugs."

"Well, pethidine isn't a good idea with you being a wee bit premature; it can make the baby a little woozy, and we need him nice and alert. I'll sort you out with the gas and air."

"I want an epidural. It says so on my birth plan—

ohhhhhhhhhhhhhHHHHHHHHHHHHHHHHHHH-Hhhhhhhhhhhhhhhhhhhhhhh. Jesus. Oh, I can't do this. I can't."

She gave my hand a squeeze. "Of course you can. You're doing great."

Fucking five-star liar.

"The epidural!"

"Ah, the anesthetist's with another patient at the moment. We'll bring him in as soon as he's free." She nipped out.

My wail brought Daniel scuttling back in. "Charlotte, what is it?"

"What's the good of writing a *fucking* birth plan if nobody takes any *fucking* notice of it?" I shouted at the top of my voice. Let the evil bitch hear. Far off someone else was yelling too.

"Medieval women used to chew willow bark, I gather. Contains natural aspirin. Sorry. I'll shut up." He dabbed at my neck and forehead with a cold washcloth. His expression, wide nervous eyes and fixed mouth, made me think of a cod trying to smile. I could nearly have laughed.

Mrs. Happy trundled the tank of nitrous oxide in and invited me to bite on the mouthpiece. "Like the breathing, start inhaling the second you feel the pain beginning."

I took a huge great lungful and nearly fainted. Another contraction hit me.

"Is it any good?" asked Daniel, trying to read the writing on the side of the container.

"Complete bullshit," I said, when I'd stopped groaning.

It was like being in prison, sitting on that train. All I had with me was my own thoughts, one dreadful memory after another layering themselves one on top of the last, and, uppermost, fear. There was no relief. Wherever I turned my gaze there was an awful image imprinted on my mind's eye, like the mad stain on your vision after you've looked too long at a lightbulb. The pictures, some of them from the past, some from the future, blotted out the placid faces and the countryside around me. As we neared Manchester, night was falling and all I could see when I stared out of the window was my own scared white face.

I want to get up," I raved.

"We need to keep the monitor pads around your stomach. Concentrate on your breathing now. Not much longer." The midwife wrote some notes and checked her watch.

"Well, I need to take this off, then." I'd managed to get myself all tangled up in the T-shirt I'd brought. Why was it so fucking hot in here?

"Er." Daniel was hovering at the edge of my vision. "Look, Charlotte, would this be a good time to go? My dad's here and he's going to drive me back to get the car. But I'll stay if you want me to. You know I won't leave if you need me." He reached out for my hand just as another contraction swept over me.

"Charlotte? Charlotte?"

"It's fine," I managed to gasp. "Yeah, go." I needed to con-

centrate on the rhythm of the pain. I could see now why animals crept off on their own to have their litters in bushes. I
couldn't cope with his concern, his anxious questions, that
bloody washcloth.

"Sure?"

I closed my eyes; perhaps he'd think I'd fainted.

"I'd go if I were you," whispered the midwife. "You can
come back tomorrow, bring her a nice big bunch of flowers." I
saw her wink at him.

"He's not the father, you knowoooooooWWWWWWWW
WWWWWWWoooooooooooo," I howled. Her smile never
slipped.

"See you, then," he muttered, and waved limply. It felt better when he'd gone.

The 10:05 to Bolton is running"—the TV screen over my head
flickered for a second—"thirty-five minutes late. We apologize
for any inconvenience."

"But I need to get to my daughter!" I shouted up at it, my
voice echoing slightly under the iron rafters. No one on the
platform took much notice; after all, there are a lot of crazy
people around these days.

Now, Charlotte, I need you to listen to me." The voice was
coming as if from under water. "Charlotte, I can see the top of
the baby's head when you push. Lots of lovely dark hair. What

I need you to do is to push as hard as you can with each con-traction. Okay? Tuck your chin down and push through your bottom."

I was beyond speaking now, but I tried to do as I was told. There aren't the words to describe the sensations; I was only a heaving mass of muscle and pain, all control gone.

"Keep on top of it now. Down through your bottom."

I pushed with all my might, but I was getting exhausted. "I can't do it," I managed to gasp.

"Yes, you can. Come on now. You want to get this baby out, don't you?"

Stupid fucking question.

I pushed till I thought my eyes would pop but we didn't seem to be making much progress. I thought of all the women in history who'd had babies. Why did you never hear what it was really like? Had it been this bad for all of them? Some women had loads. Mrs. Shankland at the post office had *seven;* had she been through this every time?

"Charlotte." This was a man's voice. "It's Dr. Battyani again. How are you doing?" Sensibly he didn't wait for a reply. "I've had a little look at you, and I think we need to make a small cut." He didn't say where, but I knew. We'd heard about it at prenatal class, and I thought then, Whatever happens, I do *not* want one of those, no way. "It's okay"—he consulted his clipboard—"we will numb the area with an anesthetic first."

Oh, so you've *got* fucking anesthetics *now,* have you? I thought. "Nyerhhhhhh," I managed. He took this as a yes; well, maybe it was. I was so desperate to get the baby out by now they could have threatened to use a blowtorch and I'd have agreed.

The next part is confused because I was waiting for the cut, and an Irish voice said, "There's somebody here to see you," and "Come in around this side and hold her hand."

Then a huge wave came over me and I began to push again. "That's it, Charlotte, you're doing so well, the head's nearly out." There was somebody crying near my face, and when I opened my eyes it was my mum, my mum, and she held my hand tight; then the head was out, and with a great slither and a gush the whole baby plopped onto the bed in a slimy mess. I was sobbing and panting and my mum, tears running down her cheeks, looked like she'd been dragged through a hedge backward.

I collapsed against her while they took the baby and checked it over. "Time of birth, 11:42," I heard a woman's voice say. The baby squalled when they put it on the cold scales.

"Bless it." Mum choked. "I've no hanky." She wiped her eyes on her coat sleeve, leaving a smudge of mascara on the beige cuff.

The midwife brought the baby over and laid it on my chest, where it squirmed and hiccuped.

"You've got a little boy, five pounds ten." She beamed.

"Oh, a boy. I thought it would be a girl." I stared down at it—him—in bewilderment, with his matted black hair and his screwed-up puffy eyes. I'd made that. He was mine.

Everything was quiet for a moment; somehow I'd expected a fanfare of trumpets or exploding fireworks, but there was nothing except the sounds of the midwife clearing away. Dr. Battyani leaned over me and lifted the purple baby up in his large brown hands.

"We need to check him again," he said, and took him over to a table on the other side of the room.

Mum hugged me and kissed my hair while a new midwife appeared and began fiddling about down below. "I'm just after your placenta," she said cheerfully. "Then we're all done and dusted."

Together Mum and the first midwife tidied me up and put my nightgown on from out of my bag, combed my hair, and sponged me down.

"Can I have my baby now?" I asked, still feeling like I was floating.

"He needs to pop downstairs to have a spot of oxygen," said Dr. Battyani. "Just to help his breathing."

Mum and I looked at each other in horror.

"Is he going to die?"

Dr. Battyani tutted and shook his head. "He is a strong healthy baby for thirty-four weeks. But he will be more comfortable during the night if we give his lungs a little assistance. Have you got a name for him so we can write it on his tag?"

"No." I thought briefly of Fyffes. "Oh, God, Mum, I've no name for him!"

"Do not panic. We can put your name on." The doctor came over to my bed and spoke to Mum. "She needs to get a good night's rest. You can stay with her for a little while."

My limbs began to tremble with fatigue. I closed my eyes and snuggled against her, something I hadn't done since I was tiny. "Oh, Mum, I'm so glad you're here."

She leaned over me, stroking my arm.

"My father and I just wanted to say well done," said Daniel, emerging from the shadows.

"Are you a hallucination?" I asked reasonably. He laughed. Mr. Gale stood behind him. I could see Mum eyeing them up and down. "I thought you were going home?"

"Dad said I could hang around till midnight. And you got there in the nick of time."

"Didn't we all," muttered Mum.

How often do parents say we're sorry? Well, most of us don't listen, for a start, so we never even realize we've done anything wrong. In the struggle to take on the mantle of parenthood—and it is like a mantle, a big padded-shoulder superhero costume—you fall into this trap of arrogance. It starts early on when you're outside a supermarket and your toddler is screaming for something totally unsuitable he's spotted on the shelves and taken a fancy to, such as a box of Godiva chocolates. You have to be firm, obviously. You have to look as though you know what you're doing, because there's always this fear that if you don't some passing shopper will spot your deficiencies and report you as a fraud, someone who's only playing at being a parent. Then your children will be taken into foster care and your life will be in ruins.

Also, you have to convince your child that you're in charge, because this is what kids are supposed to like, firm boundaries and what have you. But listen, I don't believe they ever do think you're in charge. They know all along that what you're doing is simply steamrollering your opinions through because you're bigger and can smack harder and shout louder, and that's not really the same thing as being in charge. But you're so caught up in the role, you convince yourself that, whatever the situation, you're right, and if your children disagree they must therefore be wrong; the posh chocolates come to symbolize your superior understanding of the way the world works. And this is true up to the point where you die, so that there are even now seventy-year-olds being berated by parents in their nineties for being wasteful with money, deficient in visiting duties, slatternly around the house, and so on.

Philip Larkin wrote that famous poem about your mum and dad fucking you up; notice he didn't go on to say, *And afterward, when you're all mature adults, they can appreciate all their mistakes and apologize wholeheartedly over drinks on the patio.*

I was going to break the mold. I was going to tell Charlotte I was sorry and watch the sky crack and the earth split apart.

"I think they've forgotten about us," Charlotte murmured, resting her head on my arm. "They were pretty busy earlier on. I'm not bothered. It's nice, this, just us two. Do I look awful?"

"You've just given birth; it doesn't matter what you look like. Was that your new boyfriend, the lad with all the hair?"

"No. He's a friend . . . from school."

"Some friend, to come with you and hold your hand like that. He deserves a medal." I shifted around on the bed and gazed at her damp hair and her red eyes. She seemed so young, as if she'd woken up from a bad dream and sneaked into my room for a cuddle like she used to after Steve left. "Oh, Charlotte. . . ."

She let out a huge yawn. "What, Mum?"

"I'm so sorry."

Her blue eyes flicked onto me and her brow furrowed. "What for? You were here, weren't you, in the end? I was all right. You know, they think that gas and air has only a temporary effect, but I think it stays in your system. I could rise off this bed and drift around the ceiling." She stared up at the dirty tiles as if they were the most beautiful things she'd ever seen.

"No, I didn't mean going away. I shouldn't have done that either—"

"Where did you go?"

"Lyme Regis," I blurted out. *The French Lieutenant's Woman* had been on Granada TV last week.

"Mmm. Dig up any skeletons?"

"What do you mean?"

"Any old fossils. Ammonites, that sort of stuff. I know I'm talking rubbish, ignore me." She closed her eyes again.

"Oh, I see. No, it was very quiet, really. I had to do some thinking. But I should never have walked out like that, without any warning. It wasn't fair. Sometimes I feel like I've been following some sort of manual, a *Handbook for Being a Bad Mother;* actually, there've been times when I feel I could have *written* it."

"God, Mum, there are plenty worse than you."

I pictured for a moment a door slamming in my face and, farther back, a little shabby figure cowering in a corner, nobody there to protect her. Tears spilled over my cheeks again.

"I've been rotten to you over this pregnancy." I sniffed. "I only wanted you to have a happy life."

"I know, Mum. But let's not argue all the time from now on,

eh? I hate it when we argue, the air turns all . . . spiky. Nan hates it too." She stretched and tried to roll onto her side. "You know, I used to be jealous of Nan when I was younger, 'cause of all the time you spent looking after her. You once said to me, 'Love isn't a cake, you can't divide it up into slices.' And I said, 'No, but time is. A clock even looks like a cake.' Do you remember?"

"No." God, I had it all wrong! "I'm sorry for that as well, if you felt neglected."

"It was my problem, selfish adolescent; you were just trying to do your best. I can see that now. I can see a lot of things. I really love her, you know." She sighed, and there was a long pause. I thought she'd dropped off to sleep and I was wondering about slipping over and dimming the lights on the other side of the room. Suddenly she said, "Tell me what it was like when you had me. I've never asked."

I settled back against the metal bars.

"Well, some of it's still very clear. It was the best and worst day of my life, I think. I remember, I was in labor for nearly twenty-seven hours and they had to use forceps, which is why you've got that tiny dent over your left cheekbone. The midwife was absolutely horrible. When I told her how much agony I was in, she said, 'You should have thought of that before you got yourself into this mess.' Honestly. You'd report them today. Steve wasn't with me because he said he couldn't face seeing me in pain: lame excuse. And Nan was beside herself with worry; she was terrified of losing me, or you, because she hadn't been a widow very long, so by the time you were born she was like a wet rag. She held you first—I think she may even have cut the cord, I'll have to ask her—and then she put you in my arms. All the nurses commented on your blue eyes, and you fixed me with this fierce gaze, as if to say, You're *mine;* don't even think about giving me away. It made my insides melt, because it was the first time in all the pregnancy that I'd realized you were an actual person."

I glanced down, proud of my speech, but Charlotte was fast asleep with her thumb in her mouth.

I woke with a shock when the breakfast cart rattled past the door. My first thought was, *The baby's died in the night and they daren't tell me.* I pressed the buzzer, and a young nurse came in, carrying some charts.

"How's my baby?"

"Oh, he had a very good night. You're both going up to the ward today. You can have a shower first, make you feel more human; I expect you'll be feeling a bit bruised and battered, but that soon passes. I just need to do your vital signs while I'm here."

She took my temperature and blood pressure, and all the time I was trying to get my head round the fact that I had a baby. I was a mother. Surely it was all a mistake. I couldn't really have a baby, not *really.*

Up on the ward there were lots of real mothers, all with their babies next to them in clear plastic cribs. The space by my bed was empty. I lay there, the biggest fraud in the world, while the woman opposite picked her child up, put her hand inside her nightdress, and fished out a breast. Then she clamped the baby to her nipple and started to flick through a magazine with her free hand. It was pretty impressive. To my right, a girl about the same age as me was changing a diaper, like she knew what she was doing. I tried to peer over her shoulder but it looked a bloody complicated arrangement, and the baby kept wriggling. When she'd parceled up its tiny bottom, she put its sleeper back on, bending the minute limbs carefully, poking inside the sleeve openings with her finger to extract the curled fists. Finally she picked it up, her hand behind its floppy head, and called the nurse, who brought a bottle, which the baby drank with its eyes closed. I knew for certain I'd never be able to do any of this. I'd drop him, sure as eggs is eggs, or break his arm trying to dress him. I'd better tell them now I wasn't fit to be a mum.

Just then they wheeled him in.

"Here we are," said the nurse, parking him expertly and flipping on the brake. "Here's your mummy." There was no response from the swaddled heap. "He's still asleep." She leaned over the side of the crib and touched his head. "What a lot of lovely hair."

"Is that normal, to sleep so long?" I could feel myself panicking again.

"Oh, yes. Labor's a very tiring experience, and not just for the mum. He'll wake up when he's ready. My goodness, you'll be praying for him to go to sleep before he's much older!"

I leaned over and watched his crumpled face. There was absolutely no movement. I looked for signs of breathing but there were too many blankets round him, so I gingerly swung my legs out of bed *ow-ow-ow-ow* and started to unwrap his body. At last his chest was uncovered and I could see it rising and falling. Thank God. I got back into bed and lay there watching that small movement, up and down, because if I didn't it might stop.

He didn't wake properly until after dinner, and by then I was convinced he was going to starve to death. "Help me feed him," I said to the nurse pathetically.

I'd just got my boobs out when Mum walked in.

"Oh, Christ, you've not brought anyone with you? Imagine if Dad saw me like this, or Daniel!"

Mum rolled her eyes and drew the curtains around. "How are you getting on?"

"I can't seem to make him open his mouth wide enough." I looked down at the feeble scrap rooting about blindly. "See, he hasn't a clue. I thought it was instinct."

The midwife maneuvered him around and pushed another pillow under my arm. "Stroke his cheek, that makes him open his mouth." She took hold of my breast and sort of stuffed it between the baby's lips. It was a shock having another woman touch me like that.

I shivered. "I don't like this. It feels funny." The baby tugged at my nipple and broke away. He started to cry at a pitch that went right through you.

"I don't think you're going to be able to do this, Charlotte; it's very difficult, you know. You might be better off bottle-feeding," said Mum.

I pulled my head up, annoyed. "Give me a chance. We've not been at it two minutes. Anyway, what did you do with me?"

Mum looked smug. "Oh, you were entirely breast-fed for four months."

I frowned. "Well, he will be too. Come on, matey. Put some effort into it." I pulled his face against me and again felt that questing mouth on my skin.

"Here," said the midwife. She pulled my shoulder forward and turned his head. He shifted in my arms, latched himself on, and relaxed. "That's right." She stood back to admire the composition. "Now, can you see him swallowing? That's what you need to watch for. It's a slightly tricky technique at first; you need to persevere, that's all. Give me a shout if you need me again." Mum gave her a wink and I knew I'd been had. I didn't care.

I sat up like a queen, like a mummy, while he suckled on. "Well," I said, after we'd sat in reverent silence for a while, "pigs can do it, and cows and sheep."

"Dogs and cats."

"Mice and rats."

And we both started to laugh.

I t was the first time in all the pregnancy I'd thought of you as an actual person, and although you had your dad's blue eyes, the expression behind them was mine. Stubborn. Perhaps that's why we've argued so much, being so alike. I knew you'd be trouble, though, even then, but there was nothing at all I could do about it because I'd just fallen down a big well of love.

Baby Jesus had the Three Wise Men; I had Dad, Daniel, and Nan. Dad came first, shuffling in as if he had a poker up his bum.

"What's up with you?" I asked, amused.

"I hate hospitals, me. *Brrrrrr.* Even the smell of 'em makes the hairs on my neck prickle." He sat down in the easy chair by the bed but kept his back straight, alert for any sign of attack. "How are we, then? Oh, I see him. He's a grand little chap, in't he? Very nice. Well done."

"How have you been getting on? What did you do about Nan's bag?"

He grinned. "Oh, I phoned that woman from Crossroads and pleaded with her to send someone, I said it were an emergency, like. I told her to send a nice young nurse, preferably a blonde."

"And did she?"

"Aye. His name was Simon."

I snickered. "Serves you right."

"P'raps it does. Hey, before I forget, I brought you a book. I know you can't get enough on 'em." He pulled out a shopping bag from under the chair and extracted a Penguin Classic. "There you are. I looked at the cover an' I thought, That'll be right up Charlotte's alley. I got it off a guy at work, he has whole van full of 'em."

I picked it up off the bedspread. *Tess of the D'Urbervilles,* I read. "Oh, Dad, you are priceless!" I gave him a hug.

"What's up? You haven't read it, have you? I dunno what it's about, but it looks like the sort of thing you like."

I muffled my laughter on his shoulder.

He didn't stay long, but before he went he gave me something else.

"Come here an' I'll tell you something you'll bless me for over the next few weeks. It'll be t' best piece of advice anyone gives you. Come closer, I'll have to whisper it."

I moved closer, intrigued.

"When that baby of yours cries, you'll want to run to it right away. And that's fine, most o' the time. But there'll be some days as you can't cope and he's screaming away and you think you might throw him out the window. Well, at times like that you change his diaper, try him with a bottle, get him burped, and then you leave him. You close the door, go downstairs, and have a cup of tea. Nobody phones the police; God doesn't strike you dead with a thunderbolt; you give yourself five minutes, and then you go back. And if you're really lucky, little bugger'll have gone to sleep."

"Thanks, Dad."

"No problem."

Next came Daniel, bearing a huge bunch of flowers. There was also a book on baby care by Miriam Stoppard.

"I don't know if you have this already, but my father says it's a definitive work." He tossed it on the bed and lounged in the chair. "I can't believe how normal you look after all that trauma."

"Get away, I look like a dog. And I feel as I'd been run over. Just as well he's so good." I nodded at the crib.

Daniel rose and peered across. "Skinny little chap, isn't he? Dad says he wouldn't have had a chance to lay down all his fat stores but that he's a good weight for his age." He poked the baby experimentally but it didn't stir. "Does he do any tricks?"

"None at all. Very disappointing. Oh, yeah, he does black poo."

"Lovely." He sat back down again. "Decided what to call him yet?"

"Nope. I was going to have a chat with Mum about it. She might know some family names I could use." I looked across at the cot again and got another electric shock of disbelief. "It feels so weird having him here."

"Yeah, I know what you mean." Daniel took his glasses off and began to clean them on his shirt. "I'm sorry I was so crappy toward the end."

I turned to him in surprise. "You weren't. You were great. I'd never have got through the first few hours on my own."

"Yeah, but when you started having those terrible pains . . . I didn't know what to do, and it was awful watching you like that and not being able to do anything. Plus, I think in retrospect I should have worn a placard round my neck saying NO, I'M NOT THE FATHER. There were one or two embarrassing moments with nursing staff. One of them asked me whether . . ." He gave an awkward laugh. "I'll tell you some other time. Hey, did you ever actually use Julia's birthing tape?"

"Oh, that. No, I forgot all about it. Actually, being strapped to the monitor was bad enough, I couldn't have coped with headphones as well."

"You can listen to it now; it might help you relax."

"Good idea," I said. But even as he was digging in my suit-case I realized that I couldn't put my phones on *and* listen for the baby. It was going to be a very long time before I wore my Walkman again.

Nan came in the evening. She looked smart, as if she were going to church, in a red two-piece and pearls. You could tell she was worked up, though.

"Where's little thing," she quavered. Mum guided her around to the crib, and she gazed at the baby in total adoration. "Eeh, little lamb. It's like our Jimmy, safe and sound. In't he beautiful? Eeh. How can they hurt 'em, honest? Oh, Charlotte love, he's beautiful." She gave me a perfumy kiss and Mum installed her in the best chair. Her whole attention was focused on the crib. "They're all as matters, really, babies. Han't he got a lot of hair? He does favor our Jimmy."

"Who's Jimmy? He can't favor anyone, can he?" I mouthed at Mum.

"No," she whispered, "but don't say anything."

I watched Mum watch Nan and I thought she seemed different with her, somehow. Nothing I could put my finger on, but sort of calmer. I might have been imagining it, of course; I was brimming with hormones.

"Can I hold him?" asked Nan, her face shining.

I glanced at Mum. "Will she be all right?"

"She'll be fine. I'll keep my arm round him. Let her, Charlotte, it'll mean such a lot."

Mum scooped him up and laid him gently across Nan's lap

so that his head was cradled in the crook of her elbow. He was coming round and his blue eyes were peeping. Nan sat stiffly as if she hardly dared breathe.

"Have you got any further with names yet?" asked Mum.

"No. I keep thinking, *Who does he look like?* but then getting depressed . . . I don't *think* he looks like Paul, do you?"

"I only ever saw him twice, if you remember, and that was nearly a year ago. But it doesn't matter, even if he does. Who you are is the way you were brought up, it's nothing to do with your genes. I'm sure of that." She had a strange expression on her face.

"If you say so. But you'd better tell the scientists so they don't waste any more time on research. Anyway, I hope to God he isn't like Paul, I hope he's a nicer person than that."

"We'll bring him up right," said Mum. "He'll know the difference between right and wrong."

"And if he doesn't we'll smack his bottom."

"No, we won't," said Mum quickly. "We'll find other ways. You shouldn't hit children, not for any reason."

It took a second for this revelation to sink in. "Bloody hell, Mum," I said, outraged, "I wish you'd thought like that when *I* was small. You never had any problem slapping *my* legs. My God, there was that time in Stead and Simpson's—"

"I know, I know. I'm sorry." Her mouth had gone all funny, as if she was going to cry, so I left it. Maybe these hormones were infectious.

Nan began to sing to the baby in a wobbly voice.

"How can I be poor
When there's gold in your darling curls?

How can I be poor
When your dear little teeth are like so many pearls?
Your lips to me are rubies,
Your eyes are diamonds rare,
So while I have you, my baby,
I'm as rich as a millionaire."

"Oh, Nan, that's lovely. He hasn't got golden curls, though."

"He hasn't got teeth, either, but I don't suppose he's going to put in a complaint," Mum said.

"What should we call him, Nan?"

"Eeh, tha'll soon be spittin' in t' fire," she told the baby. "Tha will. Yes, tha will." He stared up with round unfocused eyes as she waggled her head at him.

Mum opened her handbag and pulled out her diary. "I made a note of some family names for you." She flicked through the gilt-edged pages to find the scrap of ribbon. "Here we are. There's Bill, of course; William if you like. It'd make Nan's day if you called him that." She smiled over at Nan but got no response; Nan was too wrapped up in a baby bubble to notice. "Harold, you could shorten that to Harry; that was Nan's father's name. Jimmy, or James, of course; that was Nan's little brother."

"I didn't know she had a brother."

"He died very young. I think he was knocked down by a tram. Or that might have been her dad, I'm not sure. She's had a tragic life, really, because her mum died when Nan was only in her thirties, and she lost her father when she was a teenager."

"Like you."

"Yes, like me. He'd have loved that baby, you know." I saw

her eyes flick over Nan's pink-and-white head and over the tiny black-haired scalp inches below. The baby's skin was still mottled dark purple; Nan's was pale and blue-veined and liverspotted. Mum heaved a great sigh that turned into a yawn. "Sorry, love, I'm done in."

"*You* are?"

"I know, I know, I remember what it's like." She peered in the diary again. "Oh, and then there's Peter; that was her grandad, so your great-great-grandad."

I shifted my bra strap and winced. "They're a bit like icebergs, families: all that hidden history."

"I don't think icebergs are anything like as hazardous, though," said Mum, closing the book.

ℳy very first memory is rocking our Jimmy in his cradle by the fire and gazing into that terrible red glow deep down in the coals, while Grandma Marsh sang to lull 'im to sleep.

> *"Th' art welcome, little Bonny Brid,*
> *But shouldn't ha' come just when tha did."*

She always called him Bonny Brid; well, he was, a little angel. I was never jealous; I just couldn't wait for 'im to grow up so's we could play together. By eight he was the best in our street at spittin'; he'd fortify himself with pop beforehand, then give the others peanuts, casual like, so when it came to it they were dried out; he won all sorts that way. An' if I were feeling down he'd sing "Tickle me, Timothy, Tickle me do" till I cheered up; he were always full o' fun. That time he got under t' table playin' Pirates and pulled t' leg so th' end dropped down, I told me mother it was me even though her best cup were broken. I ought to have tekken more care of him. If I'd been with him that day down by the canal—

Out of the corner of my eye I became aware of movement. "Nan?"

Nan was slowly slumping forward, the baby sliding down her lap. My heart thumped with fright but Mum made a grab for him and caught him as he began to roll. I saw a thread of saliva hang from the corner of Nan's mouth and stain her red top.

"Quick, Charlotte," said Mum, dropping the baby back in his crib and rushing to Nan's side. "Press that buzzer of yours and get a nurse." I hesitated for a second, stunned at the sight of Nan deflating like a balloon. "Do it!" she shouted. "I think Nan's having a stroke."

They say it's a tunnel with a light at th' end, but I found myself on the canal bank at Ambley, wi' Jimmy.

"All right?" he says, big grin on his face.

"You're looking well," I say, "considering." He just laughs and puts his arm through mine.

He tugs me over in the direction of the bridge—it's a beautiful day, all reflections in the water, very peaceful—and as we get near I can see all sorts of folk sitting on the opposite bank having a picnic. They've a blanket and some bottles of ale, a basket full of barm cakes and pies and things. There's a lot of babies lying on t' ground, waving their legs in the air or sitting up and patting the grass round them, chuckling to themselves the way babies do—and the odd thing is, not one of 'em's crying. One's crawled over an' gotten a barm cake and it's chewin' away; must have a tooth coming. There's a little girl laid out on her front in a summer frock and cardigan, blowing bubbles at them out of a basin of soapy water; she's got a bit of wire bent in a loop. Jimmy's arm tightens on mine and I squeeze back, all warm. I'm dying, I think, and it's lovely.

"Look," says Jimmy, pointing under the trees, and it's Grandma Marsh and Grandma Fenton; Grandma Marsh is holding up a length of red wool while Grandma Fenton winds it into a ball. They're rambling on so much neither of them notice me. Jimmy digs me in the ribs and makes a face, so I give him a hug.

"You haven't changed," I tell him. He shrugs. I want to ask him about our mum and dad but something tells me to wait.

A tenor horn starts up and I know it's Bill before I spot him. He's at the water's edge, standin' very still and straight. He doesn't wave, never takes the horn from his lips, but he's playing for me, "Stranger in Paradise"; the notes dance across the water like light, like a language. There's such love in the air, you could get drunk on it. There's no rush. He'll wait for me.

We're nearly at the bridge.

"Come on," says Jimmy, "just a few yards now." He pulls me along by the hand and his eyes are shining. I want to run, because suddenly I've all this energy, maybe I could just jump the canal, but as I put my fingers on the top of the stone wall darkness comes up around the side of my vision and everything falls away. And while I watch, there is a pinpoint of light, tiny, getting bigger. It's coming toward me very fast, very fast.

chapter 11

$\mathcal{M}$rs. Hesketh! Nancy! Can you hear us?"

You've to go away. It's hurting my eyes. I'm dead.

I sat in that hospital corridor for hours. Might as well have moved in, the amount of time I was spending there. One floor up in another wing I'd sat with Charlotte while she gave birth; now I was waiting to see whether my mother was dying. Sorrow and joy a few hundred yards from each other. Turn left, up the stairs, and through the double doors.

Over my head the strip light hummed. My eyes were sore from lack of sleep. Even when I'd managed to snatch a few hours it had all been trains again, exhausting, only this time I'd known where I was headed; I was trying to get back home. I would have, too, if that bloody platform hadn't turned into Chorley market.

I kept having to blink to stop the reflections in the night-sky window from flickering. Every time a hospital cart went past, it felt like the rubber wheels were trundling right over my heart, the rattling and clanking dislodging bits of my brain. I wondered whether little Emma had been to the hospital, sat in the ER, while nurses tended to her broken bones and exchanged glances over bruises. Why hadn't anyone done anything? Why hadn't *Jessie*? Every time I tried to think about that, a gulf of incomprehension opened up in my mind and I saw her face again, hard, sour, in the crack of the door. It was fear in her eyes at the end, not anger; she'd been afraid of me. She'd always be running away from the past; there'd be no rest. Nor should there be.

I wondered if he'd suffered at the end, that man. I hoped he had. I hoped he'd had terrible pain for a long time and then gone to hell. I could understand now these stories of ordinary people hiring hit men. In the face of such evil, what else is there to do but wipe it off the face of the earth?

You try not to think about life's darkest things, but sometimes they just flood into your head and you can't stop them. In a place like this, in this no-man's-land of time, you've no chance. Because being in a hospital reminds you how every second sees someone off or ushers someone in, souls squeezing in from the dark or flitting out into it. There are supposed to be ten ghosts behind every living person, aren't there? And what about the ones waiting to be conceived, baby ghosts of the future? If they knew what pain was waiting for them, how many would choose not to be born? Awful images were flying into my mind, one after another. War reports on the news, Diana in a hospice with a little bald boy, National Society for the Prevention of Cruelty to Children posters, even that mocked-up TV ad for immunizations where the tiny baby rolls about on the edge of a cliff. Curtains closing on Dad's coffin. A strange sea in front of Buckingham Palace.

The hospital clock ticked on, taking lives with it, and the dead lined up to be remembered. I'd been waiting forever. I ached to hold Emma and make it all right; she was there, surely, just by me; I could feel her. And behind Emma all those other children who cry at night from fear or pain or loneliness crowded around and reached out little hands to me until I thought I was going to scream—

"Could I have a word?" The doctor was a young Indian woman, very pretty, slightly beaky nose. I looked up at her stupidly and struggled to my feet. My handbag dropped down my arm onto the floor, but I was too tired to bother. We stood facing each other and I searched her expression, trying to guess. There was a lash on her cheek and a stray hair coming down over her forehead. I wondered if she ever wore one of those red spots on her brow. All this in a fraction of a second. Make eye contact, I pleaded, because if you don't, I'll know it's bad news.

Nan was in a room off the main ward on her own when we went. I wondered if that was a bad sign. She certainly had enough wires and tubes coming out of her.

"They won't know what damage has been done to her brain until she comes around," Mum had told me. "But she might be able to hear us—they say it's the last sense to go—so watch what you say. She's no teeth in, so she looks a bit grim."

I'd forgotten she was so small. There didn't seem to be anything of her under the covers, and her hands resting on top were like little turkey claws.

"Mum?" I whimpered, but she shushed me and patted me forward.

"Let's get his lordship installed first." She hoisted the baby's car seat onto a chair—he was blotto from the journey—and drew one up for me. Then she sat down herself and started unpacking all the goodies people had sent. "I thought I'd tell her about them even if she couldn't see them; something might filter through, and she'd be so pleased everyone was thinking about her. Now. Mum?"

She leaned over the bed and raised her voice.

"Mum, Charlotte and the baby are here; they've come to see you. And I've brought some presents and cards. They're all asking at church after you; your name was read out for special prayers. The vicar sends his love."

She fished in a shopping bag.

"I've all sorts in here for you, shall I put them on the bed? No, probably not, they might interfere with one of these tubes. Anyway, Ivy's given you some lemon-scented tissues; they'll be useful." She plunked them on the bedside table. "I've brought a stack of *Woman's Weekly* from Maud, and a perfume stick. Mrs. Waters from the library's sent you a big bag of mints, here, and Reenie's given me a pot of honeysuckle hand cream for you. I could put a bit on for you now if you like."

There was absolutely no response, it was awful, but Mum just chattered on.

"There's all sorts of cards, too, I'll read them out in a minute. Oh, there's a bottle of Lucozade from Debbie, and Nina from Greenhalgh's brought around a tin of Uncle Joe's Mintballs—"

I sniggered with nerves.

"What?"

"Sorry. It's the name. It always makes me laugh."

"What, Uncle Joe's Mintballs?"

"Yeah." I was fighting giggles; it was that or tears.

Mum smirked; I think she was on the verge too. "Well, you know what they say about Uncle Joe's Mintballs, don't you?"

"No."

Mum lowered her voice. *"Uncle Joe's Mintballs keep you all aglow, Give 'em to your granny and watch the bugger go."*

We stared at each other for a second and then burst into hysterics. I laughed until my ribs hurt, we laughed so much Mum went red and I got hiccups; then she knocked the tin off her lap and it rolled all the way to the door, which was hilarious, and the baby woke up and Mum tried to pick him up but she couldn't undo the straps, which was also incredibly funny.

And then Nan opened her eyes and said, "Blast id."

I screwed my eyes up tight. If I didn't open them, maybe I could go back. I could almost feel that warm stone under my palm. When I'd looked down at Jimmy he'd got dandelion seeds stuck in his bangs, and I wanted to brush them out with my fingers and feel his bonny hair again. But a wall of black had come up between us and I knew he was gone, Bill was gone, all of 'em. I'd missed the boat. I couldn't stand it.

Wake up, Nan, and give my little boy a name. We're waiting on you to christen him. We can't go on calling him Banana baby forever, he'll get teased at school." I chafed her small cold fingers under their tape while Mum went to call for a nurse. My mouth was dry as I watched her eyelids flicker and wince. "Nan? Nan!" She sighed deeply but made no other movement. If she dies now they might think it's my fault, I thought. "Come on," I hissed. The baby suddenly sneezed twice, and I felt Nan's body twitch. I put my face close to hers on the pillow and saw the lashes flutter and a huge tear roll out and pause, then spread into the wrinkles of her cheek. Her lips pursed and I could see she was trying to say something. The lines round her mouth deepened.

"What, Nan, what?"

The breath came out of her in little pants but no words. I dropped her hand and ran for Mum.

Let me get back, I wanted to say. Give me something, quick, while I still remember how to get there. If I can just go to sleep and if they'd just turn this blasted light out. I tried and tried, but I couldn't make my mouth work.

W hat's she saying?" Mum asked me, as the nurse held Nan's wrist, counting.

"I couldn't tell. Her teeth . . ."

The nurse adjusted some machines and wiggled tubes, then unhooked the chart at the end of the bed and made some notes. Nan snorted a little and moaned. The nurse put down the chart and bent lower, putting her ear to Nan's lips, frowning. We waited. She straightened up.

"Apparently she's won a vacation. For two. I'll just fetch the doctor."

T hat wasn't what I wanted to say at all.

I t was baby's naming day and Nan's birthday. The nurses stood around the bed clapping while I took a photo with one of those disposable cameras: Nan in a new bed jacket holding a cake on her lap. The walker was just visible in the corner, but to cut it out of the picture I'd have had to chop Nan's arm off. I told her this.

"Might as well chop it off, all the use it is," was her comment. "Do you know why they clap when someone old says their age? It's because you're not dead yet, that's all."

"I see it hasn't affected her speech, then," muttered Dad to me.

"No. She's been lucky, really. If you call not being able to walk properly or feed herself without stuff going everywhere *lucky*. She's getting very frustrated, though, stuck in bed. She used to be so active. How many eighty-year-olds do you know who can still touch their toes?"

"Aye, well, she's short. She doesn't have so far to bend down."

"Stop it. I think she's really depressed."

Dad looked chastened. To be fair, he's not good at tragedy. He only came because Mum put the pressure on, how it might be Nan's last birthday and she'd always thought so much of him.

"So how's she going to go on when they kick her out of here? I mean, Karen's got her hands full with you and the baby, never mind hauling miniature pensioners about. What's she going to do?"

"It was the best place for her t' 'ave a stroke," said Ivy loudly, grasping Dad's arm. She nodded at Nan. "I was sayin', it was the best place for you. You've some beautiful flowers."

"Blood and bandages." Nan pulled a face at a vase of red and white carnations. "They're bad luck. I've told the nurses but they don't do anything."

"Let's have one of you, William, and me on the bed with her," said Mum. "Steve"—she handed him the camera—"if you'll do the honors." Mum and I settled on the metal-framed bed either side of Nan, with Will like a fat white grub on her lap. "Ready."

"Right-oh. Say Cheese."

"Eeh, it's a poor do," said Nan, closing her eyes.

If the times had been different I'd have felt completely disorientated by Nan's uncharacteristic gloominess, but you've got to be realistic. It was chaos in our house, and you can only take on so much at a time. I was going all out to be a better mother in the most trying of circumstances, I mean, the house looked like several bombs had hit it. Nan was out of the way for the time being, true, but I was trailing off to visit nearly every day and Charlotte had me going up and down those stairs like a demented yo-yo.

"Mum, Mum, my jeans still won't do up!"

"That's because you had a baby six weeks ago. Your figure'll come back, give it time. Dry your eyes and we'll have a cup of tea."

"Mum, Mum, his stump's fallen off!"

"Well, they do. Wipe around his tummy carefully and watch you don't catch it when you're changing his diaper."

"Mum, Mum, there's all bits in his poo!"

"That's normal. Come on now, Charlotte, stop worrying about *every little thing*."

"Mum, Mum! *Mum!* I've forgotten how to give him a bath!"

"Oh, for Christ's sake, Charlotte, just have a go! His head's not going to drop off!" Five minutes' bloody peace with the *Bolton Evening News,* that's all I wanted.

I can't believe how Charlotte's changed; she used to be so damned independent, and now she's on my back all the time. Secretly, though, it's quite nice. I like being able to tell her what to do and have her listen for once. She hangs on every word, asks me constantly about when she was a baby. We talk like we haven't done for years. When the baby blues hit she went down like a rag doll, completely useless. He'd got jaundice, and I *told* her it was very common and not serious, but she kept yammering about him turning into a banana; I thought she was going mental. Then she came out of it and two days after we were joking about the size of her boobs. "Look at this, Mum," she said, holding up one of her old bras against her massive chest. "It's like a fairy bra." We were doubled over, laughing. She's doing ever so well, really. There'll always be rows, the habit's too ingrained, but I really do feel as if I've been given a second chance with her.

People think I'm coping, but I'm not.

All these secrets women keep. Actually, I can understand why; after you've given birth you feel as if your body's been turned inside out and left hanging on the line for a week. If word got out what it was really like, nobody would get pregnant ever again. I'm certainly not up for it a second time, no way, Will'll have to resign himself to being an only child. I'm such a mess down there it's horrific. I can feel these knobbly stitches; they're supposed to dissolve on their own but I'm not convinced they will. I touch myself in the bath, and it's not my body anymore.

My breasts aren't mine. They've changed into tender, meaty bags of milk, and they go knobbly too if Will sleeps through a feed. Then I have to go and milk myself into the bathroom sink like a big cow. It sprays out in tiny jets, it's too weird.

The baby's weird, too. He's got pathetic scrunched-up little legs and a huge tummy now, and eyes that scan your face as if they're going right inside your head; I hope to God they're not. His willy's funny, a tiny soft teapot spout of a thing. When you're cleaning the poo off it you think it's impossible that one day it'll be this huge hard veiny stalk with wiry hairs all around. Mum says he's a good baby to what I was, he only wakes once or twice in the night and goes back down after a feed, but it's killing me getting up to him at all hours. How do people manage without sleep? Sometimes I lie awake in the dark, waiting for him to cry, and I wonder if he can read my thoughts and whether that starts him off.

Once, and I haven't told anyone this, he was crying and crying in his crib and it was half-past three in the morning. He had gas but I didn't know; I thought he was doing it to spite me. I picked him up and he carried on screaming into my ear, and my whole body started to tremble because of the urge to shake him hard. A good shake will show him, make him stop, I thought. Then I came out of it and remembered what Dad had said, but as I went to put Will back down he let out a huge burp and stopped crying immediately. I went down and had a cup of tea anyway.

He is a sweet baby. I call him Will, Mum calls him William, to Nan he's Bill or sometimes Bonny Brid. Dad refers to him as *t' little belter*. I can change his diaper now, no problem. I sing him songs by Oasis; he's gaining weight, and he might have smiled for the first time today. Mum said it was a smile, anyway.

But I'm still a fraud. I put him to the breast and look down at his fragile skull and I think: I don't love you yet. I wouldn't want any harm to come to you, I'd fight off a tiger with my bare hands if you were in danger. And yet there's a gap inside me where I'm sure I should be feeling something more. You shouldn't just be *fond* of your baby, should you?

What have I done?

The house is full of cards, and people troop up the path almost daily with bits and pieces for the baby. Mr. F sent a book of lullabies from around the world; Debbie's sister brought a bag of clothes, 3 to 6 months, she'd finished with. All Mum's friends from the Over Seventies' have given something, knitted cardigans and teddies and what-have-you. Mrs. Katechi from the Spar gave us a scrapbook entitled *Baby's First Year*. Pauline came with a bag of gifts from the staff and kids; even a couple of parents had chipped in. A lot of it's secondhand but that doesn't matter. William's not going to complain, is he?

Charlotte wanted to know why everyone was being so nice.

"I don't know half these people. Why have they brought me presents?"

I was writing thank-you notes at the table, but I stopped and put my pen down. "Do you know, it's funny, I remember thinking exactly the same, but I can understand it now. It's because a new baby's a blank sheet. It's not made any mistakes like an adult has. People want to get in on that innocence and celebrate it while it's there. It's very attractive, that unspoiled life, sort of magical. It gives us all hope. The baby's got a chance of getting it right where we've failed."

Charlotte snickered. "Steady on, Mum. Isn't it just that babies are cute?"

William, who was lying naked on his changing mat with his chubby legs kicking, snorted and sneezed.

"Maybe. That's only my take on it. Hey, you'd best put his diaper on before he wees. It goes a long way with boys, I've discovered."

"I know, it's like a fountain." Charlotte knelt—she's getting so capable with him—and started to strap him up. "Yeah, I can understand people being nice with *him;* who wouldn't be? But I thought some of them might be a bit off with me—you know, not being married and that. The older ones, anyway."

"Oh, love, there probably isn't a woman alive who doesn't think, *There but for the grace of God.* The older ones especially, I shouldn't be surprised, because when they were young it was a lot easier to get caught."

Charlotte snapped the last snap on William's suit. "Oh, God, imagine, Mum, imagine Ivy Seddon . . . and Maud Eckersley . . . on their backs, in the grass!"

"Stop that now, madam, you've a nasty mind. I've got to give them both a lift to the hospital this afternoon. I think all those hormones must have affected your head. Hell's bells, what an image, though."

"But they must have been young once. They must have courted and that."

I put the last card in its envelope. "Oh, I don't think so. Sex wasn't invented until the 1960s, you know. Before that everybody behaved themselves."

"Did they? Did they really?"

"What do you think?"

When Mum asked me what I wanted for my birthday, I said, "Sleep." It was true. All I wanted was to get my head down for a few hours. You could stick your parties and your presents. I thought she'd roll her eyes and suggest a gold locket, but she only said, "You'd best be expressing some milk, then."

So on the morning of my eighteenth birthday the fairies came and spirited Will away, and I slept on in a tangle of sheets. I slept till noon, woke up, and went back to sleep again. This second time, though, I started to have a very strange dream. I was on the London Underground, and a dwarf with a black beard was crushed up next to me. He kept looking at me and licking his lips, so I tried to move away but the crowd was packed too tight. Then he reached up and started squeezing my breasts hard. Harder and harder he squeezed, until it really hurt; then I woke up.

I was lying in a pool of my own milk. It had soaked right through my bra, my T-shirt, and the bottom sheet. My breasts were so hard I could have lain on top of them and been a foot off the mattress. "Bloody hell," I said, in some pain, and stumbled out of bed. I staggered to the landing, blinking in the light, desperate to find my baby and have him relieve some of the pressure before I exploded.

"God, Mum!" I shouted, as I reached the bottom of the stairs. "Where's Will? I've got to give him a feed; my boobs are like two rocks. And I've got milk all down me."

I opened the door to the living room and in my thick-headedness took in a small crowd: Daniel, Julia, Anya, Mum,

Ivy and Maud, Mum's boss (?), Debbie, Dad, a banner, balloons, cocktail sausages. "Happy birthday," I heard Daniel say
weakly.

I turned and fled upstairs, locking the bedroom door behind
me. Ten seconds later Daniel knocked.

"Come on, Charlotte, I'm sorry, we're sorry; let me in."

"Go away!" I shouted. "I want Mum!"

She came, with fat-chops Will slumped against her shoulder.
"Here you are." She handed him over and he started rooting
immediately. "Get yourself settled first." He latched himself on
and began to gulp. "He's missed his mummy, haven't you? He's
been fine, though, good as gold all morning," she added hastily.
"Now, are you all right? I'm *ever* so sorry—"

"What do *you* think? Standing there like I'm in a wet T-shirt
contest in front of everyone, no makeup on, my hair like a
bird's nest, how would you like it? God, Mum, how *could* you?"

"It was meant to be a surprise."

"Yes, well, it was that, all right. Stop smiling! It's not funny,
it's *not*. Christ almighty. *Why* didn't you come up and warn me?
It was awful. I don't think I'll ever set foot outside this bedroom
again. I'll get agoraphobia, and it'll be totally your fault."

Mum patted my knee. "Come on, nobody minds. I did keep
coming up to check on you, every fifteen minutes. I was going
to let you come around and then say Daniel was here, so you
could get your lipstick on. But last time I looked in on you,
you seemed to be sound asleep and it didn't seem fair to wake
you; then Maud wanted to know how long to put the appe-
tizers in for and I got waylaid. We only caught a glimpse, for
heaven's sake. Nobody minds, honestly."

"I do."

"I was trying to do something nice for you, Charlotte; give me a break." Mum looked weary suddenly. "I get tired too, you know. In fact, with having to take care of William here all morning *and* sort out a buffet, I'm absolutely spent. But I wanted it to be nice for you because it's your eighteenth; it's special. I think I'll take your present back to Argos. You don't deserve it."

"What is it?"

"You'll have to come downstairs and find out."

Will put his palm on my bare chest and spread his fingers ecstatically. I put my hand out to meet his and he caught and gripped my thumb. His hair was still thick and dark, and none of it had dropped out as Maud had predicted.

"You funny monkey," I said to him, "you don't care what state I'm in, do you? You haven't a clue. Oh, hell. All right, I give in."

"Don't put yourself out or anything! Honestly! Everybody in that room just wants to wish you a happy birthday; stop being so horrible." She took wriggling Will off me while I hunted around for clean clothes.

"It's not my fault I'm bad-tempered, you know, it's the hormones."

"Nonsense. You can't go on using that excuse forever. Now, I've brought you up your toothbrush and I've even filled Nan's jug and basin next door for you so you don't have to trail through the living room to the bathroom; you can make yourself decent up here."

"Am I a miserable cow?"

"At times."

"Why can't we have an upstairs bathroom like normal people?"

"When we win the lottery. Now get a move on."

Actually it was Daniel who gave me the best birthday present, although Mum's was pretty amazing.

She wheeled it in on the hostess trolley. "We thought you had enough things for the baby. This is just for you."

"For your studies," said Dad shyly.

"It's a good package." Daniel handed me the scissors, and I started to undo the tape. "Though you might want to upgrade at some point."

So I knew it was a computer before I'd got all the paper off. "Oh, God, how did you . . . ?"

"Your dad put some money toward it, and Nan. We don't want you to forget your plans for the future."

I circled the huge boxes in awe. "But you already got me the car seat. I don't deserve this."

"Yes, you do," said Dad and Daniel in unison.

"No, you don't," said Mum.

"Where's it going to go?" I thought of my room, the tiny desk, the two square yards of floor space.

"We can maybe move the display cabinet out of that corner. We'll have a chat about it later." Mum went into the kitchen and came back with a trash bag. "Help me get that styrofoam into here before it goes all over."

"When's this cake going to get eaten, then?" asked Dad.

Julia and Anya (box of goodies from the Body Shop) stayed till Dad left for his next shift, then Debbie (photo album) had to catch the bus. Maud and Ivy (gift certificate to the bookstore and arnica cream) tottered off to an evening service at church, which left Mr. Fairbrother (*The Little Book of Calm*) and Daniel (nothing as yet). Mum started to ferry crockery through to the kitchen, and Daniel jumped out of his chair as if he'd been stung by a wasp.

"I'll do that, Mrs. Cooper, you sit down."

Mum flushed with pleasure. "Well, that would be very nice. Just leave everything out on the drainer, and I'll put it away to-morrow."

"I'll pour us all some wine," said Mr. Fairbrother.

I sat in the kitchen to keep Daniel company and rocked Will, who went to sleep.

"I wonder if everybody's life turns so weird after having a baby, or if it's just mine. I feel as if all the things I was certain of before have been blown away."

"Such as?" Daniel groped in the water for the dishcloth.

"Mum. She's almost human these days; that break must have done her some good. Nan not being around; that's *really* strange, I mean she's *always* been there. Part of me misses her like mad and part of me's dreading her coming home. I mean, a three-month-old baby *and* Nan under the same roof. Chaos. Mum'll go all cranky again, it's a shame, and there's every chance Nan'll get cranky back, now she's on this new medication." Will mewed unexpectedly, then settled again. "Then there's Dad being around so often; that's pretty unnerving. He doesn't change, though, he's still charming and useless. And this bloke Mr. Fairbrother—"

"He wants us to call him Leo, he said earlier."

"Leo, then. What's he doing buzzing about the place? He's too old for Mum, surely. Not her type at all."

"I thought he seemed okay. I don't think your dad liked him, though."

"No, well, they're like chalk and cheese. And then Julia and Anya coming; I was really touched. Did you arrange that?"

Daniel tried to push his glasses up and got foam on his nose. "Might have done." He blew the bubbles off, and they floated down like snow to settle on the tiles. "I was going to take you out to Pizza Hut and ask them to come along, then your mum phoned and told me about this—"

"She phoned your house?"

"She was chatting to my dad for ages before he put me on."

"Oh, God. I am sorry."

Daniel shrugged. "I wouldn't worry, he's a natural flirt; it doesn't mean anything. My mother calls it his bedside manner." He emptied the bowl and filled it up again, ready for the pans. "She'd like this Belfast sink. Thirties, isn't it? She'd probably kill for these original black-and-white tiles too."

"She wouldn't like having to traipse through the kitchen to have a bath, though."

"I was wondering about that. I suppose the bathroom was added on after the house was built."

"I know Nan and Grandad moved in here before the war, but I don't know if they used a tin bath and the outside privy or whether it had been updated by then. I'll have to ask her. Mum remembers there being a range in the front room, where the gas fire is now, but that went in the seventies."

"It's full of character, your house. Full of history."

"Get away. You can say that because you don't have to live here. I'd swap you any day."

Call-me-Leo appeared in the doorway, holding two glasses. "Are you having your wine in here?"

"Stick it on top of the fridge for now." I got up carefully; Will was totally out. I carried him through into the living room and laid him in his bouncy chair. With his head thrown back and his turned-up nose he looked like a piglet in a onesie.

"Bless him," said Mum. I could see the bottle of wine was well down.

"Can you look after him for a bit longer? Birthday treat?"

She nodded. I went back to the kitchen and picked up my glass. "Leave that now, Daniel. Come on."

He smiled. "I was hoping you'd say that."

Up in my room he turned all serious.

"I've been waiting to give you this," he said, putting his hand in his jacket pocket. "I didn't want to do it in front of everyone." He pulled out a small black cube, about the size of—well, a ring box. Oh, hell, I thought. "Take it," he said, placing it in the palm of my hand. Any minute now he was going to sink to his knees and ruin everything. I swallowed and opened the lid.

"Oh, Daniel!"

"They're your birthstones. You *have* got pierced ears, haven't you? I forgot to check."

I was laughing with relief. "Oh, they're lovely. Brilliant. I'll put them in now." I stood in front of the wardrobe and fitted the tiny pins through my lobes. The blue gems glittered as they swung in the light. "I like my ears. One part of me that hasn't changed shape recently."

Behind me Daniel glowed with pride. "You look fantastic," he said.

I turned around and since we were standing so close together it wasn't much of a stretch to reach over and kiss him. He put his arms round me and we fused together, lips, hips, and toes. If this were a film, I thought, music would be swelling and the camera would be circling us in a long close-up. He kissed really well, surprisingly well. Maybe he'd left more than friends behind in Guildford; I'd never thought to ask.

"Come and lie on the bed," I said quietly.

"If you're absolutely sure." He looked into my eyes. "Are you?"

"Yes."

We lay for a long time necking and writhing against each other. He ran his fingers down my back, seemed to know instinctively not to touch my breasts. His kisses on my skin were light and shivery, but he scrupulously avoided contact below my waist, even though I was grinding my hips against his crotch like a complete floozy. Suddenly I wanted him to touch me, really touch me. I didn't care about the flab or what the stitches looked like, I just needed his fingers. I guided his hand down, past the waistband of my skirt, under the hem of my underwear, an electric path. I thought I was going to die with lust.

All the time he was gazing into my eyes and moving his hand really gently, so gently. I knew I was soaking wet; I knew too that the sensation was better than anything I'd ever felt with Paul. No thrusting or stabbing, no jagged nails, just his feathery fingertips slicking over and over the exact spot it felt most good. The pleasure got more and more intense, became a different feeling altogether; he had to keep going, he mustn't stop, I closed my eyes and came, came, came on his hand, in waves of the most exquisite, fantastic, glorious—

"Are you all right?"

I opened my eyes. "Oh, my God. That was unbelievable. I never knew what it was like. Oh, God." I collapsed back onto the pillow. "You're brilliant. You knew exactly what to do."

"I've been reading up on it," he said modestly.

I buried my face in his chest. "You and your bloody Internet."

"Ashley Carter, actually, historical novelist. One of my mother's trashy paperbacks. She keeps them in the bottom of the wardrobe; she thinks I don't know. It might all be crinolines and fans on the front, but it's hot stuff between the covers, I can tell you. They've been quite an education to me over the years." His face was pink and he'd taken his glasses off, which made him look different and vulnerable. I had a sort of leap of love for him then and reached over to hug him again. I felt the hardness at his crotch against my belly.

"Is there—is there anything I can do for you?" I asked.

"I should think *so*." He sighed, lying back as I unzipped his trousers.

I haven't dreamed about the London visit at all, and I was expecting nightmares. Maybe it's because I think about it all the time so there's no need for my subconscious to drag it out at night. Emma haunts me like a little ghost, her big eyes, her wispy hair. I see her everywhere, as a child in the kids at school, as the adult she never had a chance to be. There's a weather girl on GMTV who reminds me of her for some reason, something about the arch of her brows. My heart does a stupid jump when she comes on.

What can I do, Emma? I ask her, but she just looks sad and frightened. She's become my imaginary friend; any day now I'll find myself setting a place for her at the table. And sometimes in the night my heart bulges against the mattress with emotion, and I feel as if the love in me could flow out like a huge sea and bathe all those children no one wants, their little limbs, if only I could get to them. What can I do?

As for *her*, she's a bad sensation that crawls over my memory from time to time, often unexpectedly. The gaps between flashbacks are getting longer, though. Maybe, sometime in the future, a whole day will go past and I won't picture her at all. Did Nan ever actually *know* Jessie Pilkington? It seems impossible: such goodness meeting such evil. In any case, I found my real mother. Surprise, surprise, she turned out to be Nan after all.

I was thinking through all this again while I sat in the consultant's waiting room, ready for him to deliver her long-term assessment. I was all set up for an argument: *Don't you dismiss my mother as a bed-blocker! She's paid her National Insurance contributions all her life, she's only asking for what she's entitled to. If it takes her a long time to recuperate, then so be it; you'll just have to make arrangements. Don't we care about old people in this country anymore?* No consultant was going to walk all over me.

And yet, when I met him, Mr. Hammond turned out to be perfectly reasonable.

"Take a seat. Now, Mrs. Coper."

I laughed out loud. "Oh, I wish! It's *Cooper,* actually."

"Oh, dear, that wasn't a very good start, was it?" He amended his notes. "I see you've been looking after your mother, Mrs. Hesketh, for—thirteen years, is it?"

"Yes, I suppose it will be. . . . Although to be honest, she looked after me for a while. I suffered from mild postpartum depression; then it came back when I got divorced, so when I moved into Mum's I was a bit of a mess. She was marvelous with my daughter, got her in clean clothes every day, packed her lunch for school when I couldn't manage; it's not a time I like to think about. I'm not very proud of myself."

Sudden mental image of me sitting at the table with tears running down my face and Charlotte's paintbrush in my hand. Nan's hand patting my shoulder and saying, "Nay, they don't put children into care just because their mother's done a bit of painting." From upstairs we can both hear Charlotte thumping about, furious with me because during the night when I had more energy than I knew what to do with, I'd filled in every damn page of that magic painting book I bought her; she's not got to do even one tiny bit. "I couldn't stop myself," I keep saying, "it was like a compulsion." And Nan keeps patting, and Charlotte keeps thumping. Oh, I did weirder stuff than that; don't know why that incident popped into my head.

When I came back to myself, Mr. Hammond's eyebrows were raised above the steel frame of his glasses and I realized my mouth was open, God knows what he thought of me. I pulled myself together and carried on.

"So it's only in the last—oh, I don't know—five or six years she's been bad. It's difficult to pin down exactly when the balance tipped from caring to being cared for. For ages she was just forgetful; we figured it was just old age. I can't really leave her on her own now in case she sets the grill pan on fire or floods the sink, but then again some days you wouldn't credit it; she's as right as rain and you wouldn't guess there was anything wrong with her. I gather that's pretty normal, is it, with dementia?"

Mr. Hammond gave a slight nod. "It can be."

"Weird, isn't it? You never know which side of her you're going to get, is she putting it on or not; sometimes, you know, I could—" I clenched my fists in front of my face, then laughed to show it was just a joke. Wonder if he was fooled? I suppose he's seen enough caregivers to know the score. He kept nodding anyway, didn't call the police. "But I've been able to manage because she's been so independent physically. She could get in and out of a bath, no trouble; climb the stairs; dress herself; marvelous, really."

Mr. Hammond clasped his hands and looked sympathetic. "I'm afraid things are on a different footing now," he said.

"I guessed so."

"You have to understand that for the foreseeable future Mrs. Hesketh is going to be significantly disabled. At the moment nurses are helping to feed, dress, and toilet her. She's going to need a lot of care."

There was a silence while I took this in.

"What about physiotherapy?"

"That may have some long-term benefits, but it isn't going to work miracles."

"Will she be able to climb the stairs?"

Mr. Hammond shook his head. "She won't be able to *walk* without assistance. She was quite severely affected by the stroke. So what we have to decide, together, is how to provide the level of care that your mother needs to achieve the best possible quality of life."

So this was my penance for rejecting her and trying to find something better. I was going to have to fireman's lift her every time she needed a wee, for the rest of her life: spoon-feed William with one hand and her with the other. My heart sank to my boots.

"She wants to come home. She'll have to come home eventually, but can you not keep her another month or two? My daughter had a baby in September and the house is upside down, as you can imagine, and we're going to need more help from Social Services. . . . Can you see to that for me or do I have to contact them myself?"

"I'm still not sure you understand the full picture," he said gently. "I don't see how you can cope on your own. Your mum will need a *lot* of care."

I thought of her bedroom, of carrying her downstairs to the toilet in the night, or of trying to fit a bed in the living room (then where would the table go, where would we eat?). Maybe if we shifted the sideboard—but where? Could we make Nan's room into a study-cum-dining room for Charlotte to work in? It would be funny eating upstairs, and taking food all the way from the kitchen and then the dishes back again. . . .

"Do you work?" asked Mr. Hammond.

"Part time. Why?"

But he didn't have to say anything. My life was telescoping before my eyes.

"I think you should consider a nursing home," he said.

"Oh, I'm sorry, that's out of the question. We'll find a way of managing," I replied. I knew that however grim the situation was, there was no way I could hurt Nan any more than she was already. It was an impossible idea, Nan not being around.

As I got up to leave an idea I'd been trying to suppress for a long time rose to the surface. Mr. Hammond seemed a kind man. "Can I ask you something?"

"Go ahead."

"Do you think my getting divorced all those years back might have triggered the dementia? She was really cut up about it; family's everything to her."

"No."

"Oh. Thank you." I got as far as the door. "And—er, is there any chance that her stroke might have happened because I had a few days away on holiday the week before?"

"No."

"Oh. I thought I'd ask."

"Good-bye, Mrs. *Coper*," I heard him say, as I closed the door. I didn't know what to make of that.

I walked through the hospital building, past the maternity unit with its soft colors and posters of happy breast-feeders, past the children's ward with its giant Tigger mural, to the gift shop, where I bought a family-size bar of chocolate. I wolfed it down unhappily; then I went to see Nan. She was trying to turn over a page of *Woman's Weekly*, licking her thumb and index finger and fiddling with the corner. "Damn useless," she was muttering. But her face lit up when she saw me, and that was something. "Eeh, it's our Karen. You look bonny. Have you brought that baby today? He's so lovely, little thing."

"No, Mum, I'll bring him tomorrow."

She looked vacant for a second, then she was back again.

"Ooh, it is lovely to see you, I can't be doing with hospitals, everyone talks rubbish. And you look bonny; have you a new frock on?"

"No, Mum, it's C and A. I got it when we went to Chester that time. Do you remember? It poured down, so all we did was go in shops."

"Aye. No, not really. Have you brought that little baby, then?"

After that I went back to Steve's and accidentally slept with him.

"You're full of surprises, you." Steve shifted so he was leaning up on his elbow. "I'd have changed the sheets if I'd known."

"Oh, God." I closed my eyes in irritation. "Why do you have to be so disgusting? You're never any different."

"It's part of my charm."

When I left the hospital I had been too upset to go home, so I went shopping. After an hour wandering round Debenhams, I still didn't feel like going back, so I stopped off at his house. I was hoping for a cup of tea and half an hour to get my head around things before I talked to Charlotte. What I got was Steve fresh out the bath, clean-shaven again, and slightly tipsy still from the night before. "I'd best sober up, I'm back at work in two hours. I hate these evening shifts. I could do with workin' part time."

"You could do with packing up altogether." I laughed. "I've never known anyone as lazy."

He scratched his head amiably. "Aye, well, life's too short. So, what can I do you for? Everything all right with our little belter?"

I told him about the consultant. "You see, Nan's so trusting, she's like a baby herself. I couldn't put her in a home, it would be cruel."

Steve pulled at the belt of his dressing gown. "Aye, it's a tough one. Can Social Services not sort something out for you?"

"I don't know. They'll have to, won't they? Oh, the thought of having to go through all those different departments again and fill in all those assessments." I didn't want to have to go near their offices again either, in case I bumped into Joyce Fitton and had to face the look of pity in her eyes. "It's been one thing after another this year. I must have broken a mirror or run over a black cat."

"I've been thinking," said Steve (and he moved chairs to sit next to me), "this in't the drink talking, you know, this has been on my mind for a while."

"What has?"

"All it is, I've enjoyed helping out a bit more: you know, being around, involved. It's nice to see more of Charlotte now she's not so hoity-toity all the time; it's done her good to roll her sleeves up and change a few diapers. I'm not much of a one for babies—"

"You can say that again."

"No, fair enough, but the boy'll need someone to play soccer with him as he grows up, and I'd quite like to be—well, around."

"You are. You've been quite helpful at times. What are you trying to say, Steve?" I was aware of his arm pressing against mine and the smell of his aftershave.

"Are you seeing that feller?"

"Who, Leo Fairbrother?"

"Yeah, th' headmaster." He rubbed his lip where the mustache had been. "Is he your boyfriend?"

"No." This was true; absolutely nothing had happened between us, and it didn't look as though anything was ever going to. I had no idea what Leo was up to, but it didn't seem as though a great seduction was on the horizon. I'd more or less given up. "What about you? What about that woman from Turton, that one who ran the London Marathon?"

"Oh, her? She was nothing."

"Nothing as in nothing or nothing as in bad-tempered?"

"Both, really. She wanted me to go jogging, can you imagine? I said, The only way you'll get me to jog is to put a pub at the finishing line. She weren't amused."

"That's you, all right." I nudged him good-humoredly, he nudged me back, and it turned into a clumsy embrace. His face loomed into mine, his lips hit my cheek, then my mouth, and my face went into shock. "Bloody hell, Steve, what are we doing?"

He stopped. "Why? Do you not like it?" He had a point; it was very nice. I'd not slept with anyone for over a year; some of the men at the Over Seventies' were beginning to look pretty tasty. "No strings, come on. It'll do us both good."

"I can't sleep with you. Don't be ridiculous."

"You know your trouble?" said Steve, kissing my neck where he knew I liked it. "You look for problems. Sometimes you just have to go with the moment. Stop analyzing everything." His hand dipped under my collar and eased down my bra strap, making my nipples tingle with anticipation. His dressing gown fell open. "You don't know what you do to me."

"I've a fair idea," I mumbled, as he unbuttoned my top.

chapter 12

Does this mean I'm back in, then?" Steve pulled his jeans on and fastened them round his skinny waist.

"Back in where? Have you seen my tights?"

"They're here, stuck on this lamp shade." He threw them over. "Back in the bosom of my family."

I wriggled my hand down inside each leg to turn the tights right side out. "Get off. It's not like you live in Australia, is it? You *are* part of the family, whether I like it or not; you're Charlotte's dad, and she needs you around at the moment."

"I were thinking, though." He sat down on the edge of the bed. "We could have another go, couldn't we? I don't mean move back or anything mad like that, but we could meet up for a drink sometimes and—and . . ."

I located my shoes, slipped them on, and stood looking

down at him. "No, Steve, no way. It would be too complicated."

"Complicated? I'm about the least complicated guy you
could have. There's nothing complicated about me, now is
there? Go on, admit it."

I sighed. "That's not what I meant. The answer's no."

"Awww. I've got you a smashin' Christmas present an' all."

"Bribery won't get you anywhere. We haven't bought each
other Christmas presents for thirteen years. I'm not going to
start now." I picked up his mucky hairbrush and tried to
smooth my hair without actually touching the bristles. "Let's
quit while we're ahead, eh? You can come around when you
want, but no more of this nonsense."

He put his face under mine and grinned. "It was good,
though, wasn't it?"

The first place we went to was at the bottom of the village:
Bishop House. The air had been freezing, the sky looked like
tracing paper, and the paved drive was slippery under the pram
wheels. The light was failing too, even though it was only mid-
afternoon. As far as I was concerned, Bishop House had just
been a big Victorian pile behind some horse chestnut trees on
the bus route to Bolton, but now there was every chance it
could be Nan's new home.

"You see," Mum had said over breakfast, "I'm not sure I
can give her the care she needs. She's not doing well, and she's
never going to get completely better. That's what the doctors

say. She needs qualified nurses around her twenty-four hours a day."

I stared out of the window, trying to take in the news. The Ribble bus went past, and I remembered the trips with Nan to Wigan on the top deck, and the Pick 'n' Mix from Woolworth's we always used to choose together. I really enjoyed going shopping with Nan as a child because there was never a row *and* I got my own way and a bag to put it in. She loved my company and I loved hers, simple. Then, as I got older, things changed; I changed. For all those hours she'd spent cutting pictures out of catalogs for me and helping me make pastry animals, suddenly I never had the time for her anymore. God, I'd let her down.

"I could help out. Couldn't we put in one of those stair lifts Thora Hird's always muttering about? They do walk-in baths too, I've seen them advertised during *Countdown*. If the two of us work together—"

Mum shook her head. "You've more than enough on your plate. It's all you can do at the moment to wash your armpits in a morning and put your sweater on right-side out. Well, isn't it? You don't understand the level of attention she'll need, *I* didn't at first. You're thinking of the old Nan, Nan as she was. She's a different person now." She was speaking in a slow, sort of rehearsed way that made me think she'd been over the arguments again and again.

"I feel as if she'd died; it's horrible, Mum."

"You mustn't think like that, Charlotte." Mum stirred her coffee rapidly, but she didn't elaborate.

We sat in gloomy silence while Will watched us seriously from the hearth rug. I tried to get some cornflakes down, but they stuck in my throat. I'd really thought, once Nan was out of danger, it was simply a matter of time and she'd be out of the hospital, back home, and making a nuisance of herself. I mean, here we were on the verge of the twenty-first century. They could send cameras to Jupiter and Saturn, so why couldn't medical science sort out her wayward limbs? It was unbelievable that Nan wasn't coming home.

"We'll find somewhere nice with some young male nurses she can flirt with. Everyone'll love her. She'll be happy as Larry once she settles in."

I was still wondering about this as the huge front door of Bishop House opened and the smell of pee hit us. I noticed Mum had got baby spit-up all down the back of her sleeve, but I knew she was so keyed up it was probably better not to mention it. We pushed Will up the wheelchair ramp and parked him in the hall while the young girl who had let us in went to fetch the matron.

"God, it's hot in here," said Mum, unwinding her scarf. "You'd better unwrap William before he cooks."

As I was fiddling with the baby's blankets, a tiny old man came out of the TV lounge and moved shakily toward us. He fixed on my mother and snapped, "I need to go to the toilet!"

Mum raised her eyebrows at me. "I'll see if I can find a nurse."

"You don't understand, I need to go *now*." His eyes were watery and desperate; he made me want to throw up.

"Hang on, Mum." I popped Will back down and ran along the hall, around the corner (only four old ladies playing cards in a side room), doubled back, and checked up the stairs to the landing, but there were no staff in sight. "Nurse!" I shouted.

"Nu-urse!" a white-haired biddy in a blue dressing gown sang back at me cheerfully. She waved at me over the banisters till I got to the bottom. "You'd think they'd have a bell or something . . ." I called as I stalked crossly back to the pram, but Mum and the old man had vanished. I hoisted Will out again and went to sit on the stairs to wait. Finally she reappeared, frowning.

"Honestly! That poor man."

"You didn't—?"

"Well, of course I did, once we'd found where the toilet actually was. He was terribly upset. Did you manage to find a nurse?"

"Nope. So, did you have to *wipe his bum*?" I couldn't believe what she'd just done. I was full of appalled respect.

"*No,* only his willy." Mum checked her watch. "What can that woman be doing? Don't look so funny, it's only what I have to do at school sometimes, only on a bigger scale. The little kids are forever having toilet incidents. If it had been Nan, you'd have wanted someone to help her, wouldn't you?"

That shut me up. We waited for another five minutes under the feeble Christmas decorations stuck to the light fittings; then the young girl came back.

"Mrs. Street says she's very sorry but she's been delayed." She lowered her voice. "A resident passed away this morning, and she's with the daughter now. But I can show you around till she's free."

We walked along behind the girl, whose hair needed washing. It was a sad route. Every door opened like a blighted Advent calendar: a lady on her own, slumped in an easy chair, watching *Bodger and Badger* on children's TV; three old women all asleep where they sat, canes laid on the floor; a bald hunched man looking out of a bay window at the gathering dark. The furniture was cheap and nasty, house-clearance stuff in white melamine or black ash, and the carpet was that rough, corded type; some of it was stained. In one room we passed a lady was lying in her bed shouting, "Help! Help!"

"Do you not need to go in to her?" asked Mum.

The girl smiled. "No, she's all right, our Mrs. Wallis. She always does that, then when you go in and ask her what's up she says, 'Was I shouting?' She's fine, really." She shut the door on Mrs. Wallis's cries. "It's a lovely place for them; they get their meals delivered and their own rooms, and there's always company. We do bingo and concerts too. The children are coming from St. Peter's next week to sing carols in the dining room. It's a nice home, this one."

I searched for irony in her face, but there was none. I grasped Will to me and he rooted against my shoulder and whimpered.

By the time we got outside we were nearly hysterical with the horror of it all. I could see the relief on my mum's face in the security floodlights. Her breath came out in a frosty cloud.

"We can't send her there!"

"Oh, thank God, Mum. It was *awful*. The thought of her in with that lot . . ."

"I know. And yet, do you know, I think the staff were trying their best. It's just so sad . . ." She shook her head. "That commode, though!" She started to giggle.

"Well, *I* didn't know what it was, I thought it was just a seat. I was tired; you try carting Fatso here around for forty minutes. I thought my legs were going to give way."

"It wouldn't have been so bad if it had been empty. . . . Your face!"

"All right." I was laughing too; it was the nerves. "But we're not sending Nan there, are we?"

"No."

"Good. Merry Christmas."

"Merry Christmas, Charlotte. Incidentally, did you know you've got spit-up on your shoulder?"

From inside the depths of the pram, Will's eyes glittered.

"You little soiler," I told him.

I'd made up my mind, to be honest, or at least I thought I had: Come hell or high water, there was no way my mother was going in a home. But it was Leo who said, "Have you investigated Mayfield?" Apparently his father had had a couple of weeks' respite care there, and they'd both been impressed. "More like your four-star hotel," he told me in the Octagon bar after we'd been to see *An Inspector Calls.* "Very upbeat, not at all depressing, even though some of the residents are pretty laid-up. I know it's farther away than you'd want, ideally, but you've always got the car, and it's only fifteen minutes or so. Worth a look, anyway, I'd have thought. I'll come with you if you like."

So I took his advice but went with Charlotte. It was a family thing, after all.

Mayfield was modern orange brick and overlooked a superstore, but inside it was clean and airy. The only detectable smells were furniture polish and dog. BLOSSOM WHERE YE ARE PLANTED proclaimed a tapestry over the vestibule door.

309 The Bad Mother's Handbook

"Mum, have you seen this?" Charlotte pointed to a six-foot-high cage full of birds all going berserk because a tortoiseshell cat was lounging across the top and dangling a paw over the side.

"They're the best of friends, really," said the matron, a smart woman in navy who met us in the hall. "They just enjoy scolding her, but she's too well-fed and lazy to do any harm, even if she could get at them. Aren't you, madam?" The cat flicked an ear at her but otherwise made no movement. "Oh, and there's Bertie as well." Bertie was a yellow Labrador, who came up to the pram and laid his head on William's blanket. "Everyone loves Bertie." Matron patted his flank. "I have such a job trying to stop our guests from overfeeding him."

Charlotte stroked the dog, and he wagged his tail so hard his back end nearly went over. *Nan would like him,* she mouthed at me.

I don't know what it was, whether the paint they used was brighter or the windows were bigger, or perhaps it was because we were seeing the place in the morning rather than at dusk, but it was different from Bishop House. There were still some very poorly old people there, but there seemed to be more activity. Even the television watchers were arguing among themselves. How Old Is Too Old to Give Birth?

"We like Mr. Kilroy in here, don't we?" said Matron. "What is it today, 'I Had a Baby at 60'? Good God. What do you think about that, Enid?"

"I reckon she's crazy," said a lady in a pink cardigan. "I put the flags out when I had my last one, and I was only twenty-six. Takes me all my time to look after myself, never mind a baby."

They all went mad over William, though. Enid wanted him on her bony knee.

"See the doggy? Can you see that nice doggy? That's my Bella, that is."

Bertie trotted up to each outstretched hand in turn before exiting.

"Off on his rounds again," said Matron. "He's everyone's pal. So, what else can I show you?"

I put out my hand to shake Matron's. "I think we've seen enough, haven't we, Charlotte? Thanks for the tour, we're very grateful. And you do have a place available?"

"At the moment." She touched my arm gently. "These decisions are never easy, but sometimes it really is for the best. Have a think and get back to me."

Bertie raced past us, pursued by a woman on a walker.

"Honey! Honey! Come back here!" she was shouting. "Damn dog's got my paper," she complained, as she passed Matron.

"Never mind, Irene, gets you your daily exercise, doesn't it?"

She let us out, and we stood on the porch for a while looking out over Morrison's.

"What do you think?" Charlotte asked me.

"I think . . . it wouldn't be so bad," I said. We walked slowly down the path onto the main road to where the Metro was parked. "I only hope Nan agrees."

You wait for years to overtake your parents, and then when you do it's no kind of victory. When I was little and being told off, I'd think, *Just you wait, when I'm grown up I'll show you.* Sometimes Dad used to pull rank on me—Why? Because I say so—

and I hated it. But nothing prepares you for the day when you realize your parents are weaker than you. It's like having the ground fall away from under your feet.

I sat by Mum's bed, holding her hand for a long time before I spoke. I was talking to her, though.

Mum, I said in my mind, *I want to tell you something, a secret you should know.* She breathed evenly in her sleep. *It's something I've only just found out.* The funny thing was, in profile she did look a bit like me. We had some of the same lines and wrinkles, anyway. *Listen, Mum, you know when I got pregnant? I think*—the idea formed itself properly into actual words—*it might have been Freudian.* The way she was lying made her skin smooth out, and she seemed years younger lying there next to my face. *Do you understand what that means? What I'm trying to say is, deep down, part of me was too scared to take exams and go off to university, start a new life away from everything I'd ever known. I didn't know it then, it wasn't conscious, but I can see quite clearly now. I think getting pregnant was a way of avoiding all that risk. So I would never have got rid of Charlotte, for all I moaned at the time. And I don't blame you. I don't blame anyone. It's the way life works out.*

When she woke up I was going to tell her about Mayfield.

There were little yellow chicks all over the house suddenly.

"What're these for?" I asked Mum, who was producing them at fantastic speed. "I didn't even know you could knit."

"Nan taught me years ago; you don't forget. You can knock one of these off in an hour. Ivy showed me. Then they fit over a Cadbury's creme egg, can you see?" She put her fingers inside the chick's body and filled it out. "If you're not doing anything, you could sew some eyes on those two over there. There's black wool in the basket."

"I've got to change Will, he stinks. Anyway, why are you making them?"

"The Child Protection Agency. I talked it over with Leo. We're going to have a big drive at school next term to help battered children and see how much we can raise with lots of different events. I thought we could have an Easter fair and sell these, say, a pound apiece? Or could we get away with charging more, what do you think?"

"I think you're nuts," I said, hoisting Will onto his plastic mat and undoing his snaps. "We're in the middle of Christmas, never mind Easter. I don't know how you've got the time." I undid the diaper. "Oh, God, look at that. It's gone up his back."

"Well, I thought if I did two or three a week from now till March, and buy a couple of eggs every time we go shopping. . . ."

Will chortled with delight as I wiped him down. "It's not funny and it's not clever," I told him. He grabbed his genitals and grinned. "Perv," I said and strapped him back up.

"Then I was wondering about a duck race on the canal at Ambley, and a sponsored walk, and maybe cake sales every Friday by the back doors, because if we have them outside then the cleaning staff won't complain about crumbs. . . ." Mum's needles clicked busily.

"You're turning into Nan, you are," I joked.

"Don't even think it," she said.

I presume it's her way of coping. Apparently it was really

hard to get through to Nan about not coming back here, and whenever Mum thought she'd finally broken the awful truth, Nan would gaze up at her and say something like, "I can't wait to get home to that baby." In the end she gave up.

Oh, another funny thing I found: talk about turning into Nan, Mum left some papers in the bathroom, of all places; a pack about returning to education. I wonder what's going on there, and if Leo Fairbrother put her up to it. He seems to be behind a lot of stuff these days. I didn't say anything, though. I don't think I was meant to see it. I left the pack where it was, and it was gone next time I looked.

On Christmas Eve Daniel came around to have a talk.

"What's going on here?" he said, surveying the chaos in my bedroom. "Is this really the best time for a major clear-out?"

"Mum's idea. She wanted me to move into Nan's room, but I don't want to, so we're setting it up as a study-cum-nursery type thing. If you think it's bad in here, you should see next door. Come and have a look. It's so weird."

Mum had pushed Nan's wardrobe against the chest of drawers to clear a wall, and the bed was piled high with old-lady underclothes and spare bedding. The carpet was darker in an oblong where the wardrobe had been and there were some spectacular cobwebs across the newly revealed wallpaper. God knows what kind of tarantula hybrid had been sharing Nan's room for the last few years.

"The desk's going along there, and the bookcase. And Will's moving in the New Year. I thought he could have his crib under the window." I squeezed around the bed and looked out over the frosted Working Men's. It would have been nearly beautiful, but for the fact that two lads were going from one vehicle to another, inscribing rude messages on the sparkling windshields. I opened the window catch and shouted down, "There's two Gs in BUGGER, you know. What's Santa Claus bringing you, lobotomies?" They whipped their heads up, saw me, and gave me the finger. I gave it back and shut the window again. "Nice to see community spirit's alive and well. Christ, it's bloody freezing out." I pulled the curtains shut quickly and hugged myself warm. "Don't know what's going to happen to the bed, though. It seems really disrespectful to start messing about with Nan's stuff when she doesn't even know she's not coming back. Like she was dead, only she's not."

"Maybe your mum could put it in storage."

"Maybe." I perched on one side of the mattress and Daniel perched on the other. "It's what we're doing to Nan, after all."

He reached across and squeezed my hand. "Chin up," he said, in a pathetic attempt at a northern accent, and grinned.

"Watch it, you."

"By 'eck."

"Fuck *off.*"

He pursed his lips and fluttered his eyelashes. "Ooh, Mr. 'Igginbottom, is that a ferret down your trousers or are you just pleased to see me?"

I picked up some big ecru underwear and threw them at him. "Stop it, will you? I want to be miserable for a minute. You don't understand, Nan's always been here."

"So you said."

He held out his arms and I crawled across the bedspread to him. He pulled me against his chest and I found I was shivering.

"Well, she has. And I never really took her on. I thought she was a nuisance half the time. It's too late." I sagged my shoulders and exhaled slowly. "I've been a rubbish granddaughter. Why don't we ever say the things we should to the people we care about?"

"Like you said, she's not dead yet. Sort it out, if that's the way you feel. Look, I'm not trying to be unsympathetic, but simply by producing Will you've probably done as much for her as any doctor. Go and see her. Talk to her." He gave me a squeeze, then took my face between his hands. "And listen, there's one thing you should know that's more important than anything else right now."

I searched his eyes. "What?"

"That there's a damn great spider on your shoulder."

I yelped and shot off the bed, pulling at my sweater and staggering into the wall.

"Hold it!" shouted Daniel, and launched forward, clapping his hand over the dark shape that squatted between the tufts of the candlewick bedspread. "Gotcha!" He held it up as if for inspection. "Oh, no, it's got away!" he yelled, as the black blob leaped out of his hands and at my feet. I screamed at the top of my voice and threw myself against the wardrobe. The hairy mass flopped onto the floor. And lay still.

"You total bastard," I said, and picked it up.

Mum appeared in the doorway, the old cross expression back on her face, like it had never been away. She wears it well.

"Will you two make a bit less noise? I've just this minute got the baby down." She wiped her brow with the back of her hand like a poor woman in a Victorian melodrama.

"Sorry."

"Sorry, Mrs. Cooper." Daniel cocked his head on one side and raised his eyebrows earnestly; it made him look about twelve.

Mum huffed.

"It's all my fault I'm afraid, Mrs. Cooper, I was being very immature." Daniel's neck craned into an even more humble posture.

"Yeah, he was, Mum; actually, it was his fault. He threw this—God, it's not funny!—fake mustache at me." I held it up for her to see. "What's it doing in here? I don't remember having any pirate costumes as a kid."

"Let me see." She held out her hand and I placed the thing in her palm. "Oh." She smiled, turning the mustache over in her fingers so it was tape-side up. "You'd never believe it. This was Nan's."

Daniel's eyebrows shot up. I snorted. "Get away."

"No, honestly. She used to do a lot of plays for the Mothers' Union, comedy ones, in dialect. She was always the man, for some reason."

"But she's such a midget!"

"I think that was part of the joke. She'd be paired up with some hefty woman as the wife; hen-pecked husband, that sort of thing. Seaside postcard couple. They used to perform over at the Working Men's, in the days when it wasn't quite so seedy."

"God, really? Did you ever see her?" It was fascinating, this Nan I never knew.

"Oh, no; it was only when I was very little. Apparently she was very good, though. Had the audience in tears a time or two, with laughter. Ask Maud, she'll remember." She passed the mustache back to Daniel as if offering him a canape. "Here you go, lad, try it for size."

Daniel took it politely and pressed it against his lip. "What do you think?" he tried to say, turning to me, but the mustache fell off and dropped down between his legs in a spider-type action. I half expected it to scuttle off across the rug.

"Gerrr*oss*! You look like the love child of Gene Shalit and Cher. Don't *ever* grow one of your own, promise?" I bent double and fished it off the floor. "If you do, you're dumped, okay?" I put the mustache to my lip; it smelled musty. "Imagine Nan dressed as a man, though."

"Wherever did it come from?" asked Mum, stepping forward to shift some of the ancient pillowcases and sheets. Some of them still had cellophane wrappers on. "Did it drop out of these? Oh, wait a minute, what's this?"

She lifted some linen, and nestled in between the layers was a pink raffia knitting bag with wooden handles. It had been squashed under the sheets so long it had left its shape imprinted in them, top and bottom, like a fossil. A ginger mustache was sticking out of the top, and as Mum picked the bag up a thick wooden peg fell out and rolled against my thigh.

"And this is?"

Mum frowned. "A piggy, probably."

"A what?"

"Some game they used to play in the olden days."

The ghosts of Nan's past crowded around to see.

"I wonder what they did with it," said Daniel, attempting to spin it on the bedspread.

"Hit it with a bat and ran after it, I think." Mum rummaged

in the bag and brought out a little plaster figure with a flat white triangle where its nose should have been. She held it out for us to see.

"They called these Kewpie dolls, with their potbellies and molded hair. This'll be old, you know."

"Worth anything?"

"Wouldn't have thought so. Seen better days, haven't you, love? Never mind, so have we all." Mum put the doll on the bed and emptied the bag carefully between me and Daniel, then she knelt down so she was on a level with it all. Papers and cards, odds and ends, had spilled out. A pair of pink baby bootees caught my eye.

"Oh, sweet! Were these mine?"

"No. They were mine. And the lamb rattle." Mum looked sad as she touched them.

"These must be from World War One," said Daniel, flicking carefully through a bundle of postcards with embroidered fronts. "Amazing. This is real social history."

Mum handed me a letter to Santa she'd written when she was six or seven.

"Purple felt-tip? Bit sloppy, that. And what's that zombie thing in the corner?"

"Zombie?" Mum imitated outrage. "That's a drawing of Barbie. My whole happiness hung on that doll, you know; I thought it would complete my life. Even though it was in the days before she had all these posable limbs and waist-length hair, what have you. It's all gone completely nuts now, of course; they do Barbie penthouse apartments, camper vans, beauty salons, discos. . . . Takes all the fun out of it. I used to cut up shoe boxes and line them with wallpaper; stop sniggering, Charlotte. And you couldn't get Ken outside the States, nobody would import him, so I made do with an Action Man I got from a garage sale. His gripping hands came in useful many a time." Mum smoothed out the letter wistfully. "Tell you what, though, I wish I'd kept that doll, it would have been really collectable. Nothing like those interchangeable pink-and-blond bimbos you had when you were tiny. This one had black hair cut in bangs and an op-art dress, à la Mary Quant. Quite scary, actually, but it could have been an heirloom."

"Cool," I said, then laughed. "God, Mum, how sad are we?"

"Do you realize these cards have seen actual bloodshed?" Daniel broke in. "This thumbprint here; it might even be blood. Wow. You should take them into school. Mrs. Carlisle would love it." He turned one over and started to read.

"No." Mum took it gently out of his hand. "Sorry. I want to look through them first. They might be personal. Nan's grandad was killed out there, you know."

The light in the room shifted, and the air in the chimney sighed. Daniel gazed at his knees in embarrassment, so to make him feel better I undid the safety pin on the crepe bandage I'd found and began to wind it round his wrist. He didn't seem to object so I carried on up his arm, tying a neat knot at the shoulder. After a minute he shook himself out of his mood and started a retaliatory action with a bobbin of thin pink ribbon. His fingers wove the satin in and out between my fingers, his long bony fingers mixed up with my thin girly ones, and I thought, I love you, you stupid fool.

And then Emma was leaning into me, I could almost hear her breathing at my shoulder. So I reached under the papers and there was a New Testament with a black cover, very plain, but with a gap in the gold-edged pages like a half-closed eye. I opened it up a fraction and caught a glimpse of a pink slip of paper, *Certified copy of an entry . . . General Register Office . . . caution.* My adoption certificate. They didn't see anything, the pair on the bed: too busy mucking about with ribbons. Well, let them. It didn't matter anyway. I closed the book and pushed it back in the bag. Next to me, Emma sighed again.

Mum came over all moony suddenly and said she wanted to be on her own for a while, so I took Daniel back to my room. There was even less space than usual, but he managed to wedge himself into the corner nearest the door; I didn't tell him that at the bottom of the trash bag by his elbow was all the memorabilia from six months with Paul. I'd squirted hair mousse over the handful of cards, notes, photos, and tickets before dumping them; now the room smelled like a cheap salon: The First Cut, perhaps. Daniel's nose wrinkled but he didn't say anything. I picked up a dog-eared magazine article entitled "Perfect 10: Nails to Die For." "God, look at this! Imagine having *time* to paint your fingernails!" I dropped it in the plastic sack. "A lot of this seems totally out of date now. From another era."

"I can see what you mean. Oh, this is no good; if I don't move soon I'll seize up." Daniel uncurled himself awkwardly and picked his way over the mess on the floor to install himself on the bed. He lay down and put his hands behind his head, very at home. "So. Now the dust has settled, what are you going to do with your life?"

I shrugged. "There's only so much dust *can* settle with a baby. Mum still wants me to go off to university, but it seems impossible at the moment. Mrs. Carlisle thinks I should have a year out to retake the exams I missed; she has this idea that she can send me assignments through the mail and I would just come in for a few lessons a week. Apparently the Headmaster's okay with that."

"And you?"

"I really want those A's. I worked hard enough for them. But it's going to be a bloody funny year." He caught my rueful gaze and held out his hand. I stepped over and sat next to him.

"Come here." He pulled me down, wrapped me in his long arms, and kissed my hair. "Listen. I won't go, I've decided. I'm not leaving you, Charlotte."

"Don't be daft," I mumbled into his chest. "You had your heart set on Oxford."

He snorted. "Some chance. With an offer of three A's it's not very likely. Dad can pull all the strings he wants, it's not going to get me in unless my papers get mixed up with some other poor bastard's. Anyway, that's not important anymore. You and Will are what matter."

I moved away and touched his face. "It *is*, Daniel. If you don't get into Oxford, somewhere else'll take you; you're too bloody smart. I bet Durham or Manchester accept you. You've got to go and get that degree. *I'd* go if it was the other way around."

"Would you?" He looked surprised.

"Oh, I don't know." Faintly from downstairs we heard Will begin to cry. I tensed to go to him, but then he stopped; Mum must have nipped down and picked him up. I let my muscles relax again, but my mind was racing. "It's all too difficult. My brain's not what it used to be."

"How about I defer my place and take a year off? I might be able to swing some sort of job at the engineering works; could your dad put in a good word for me?"

I laughed. "My dad? That really would ruin your chances. No, don't. We'd still have to part at the end of the year, unless I got in to the same school, and there's no guarantee of that." Daniel looked mournful. "Come on, it's only what happens to thousands of couples every year. And in the end they either make it or they don't."

"We will."

"Yes."

"I don't want to leave you."

This was getting out of hand.

"Daniel!" I shook him by the shoulders, pushed him against the mattress, and climbed astride him. His eyes were wide and miserable. I blew in his face but he only turned away. "All right, you!" I growled, putting my mouth close to his ear. "Stop being such a silly bugger. It's not till next September, anyway! You might meet some fancy piece and run off with her long before then. Snap out of it! Lighten up! Because if you don't I'm going to have to take your trousers down and interfere with you."

There was a pause.

"Did I tell you how depressed I've been?" he said.

Afterward we lay quietly, and I combed his hair with my fingers.

"You really should get this chopped, you know."

"Do you think? I've always thought of it as my finest feature."

"No way." I ruffled his mop. "You look like Young Einstein."

He gripped my wrist and kissed it. "I know you think I was being over the top before, but this is the first time in my life—well, certainly the first time since I left Guildford—that I feel like I belong with someone. Does that sound crazy?"

"No, 'cause I think I feel like that too. It's . . . trying to find out where you fit in. I've never felt very good at that. Mind you, this household hasn't been exactly conducive to forming settled relationships. It's been such a battleground, and with three of us it was always two against one, different combinations. You won't have had that, with there being four of you."

"No, but I know what you mean about the rows." We shifted into spoons, and he put his arm across me and talked into the back of my neck. "About a year before we left Surrey there were shouting matches every night, and actually there were just the three of us then because my sister had left home. Then, after the rows, came the freezing silences and the 'Tell your mother that I won't be in for dinner' and 'Tell your father that he'll have to cook his own, then' routine, with me in the middle. I never want to go through that again. If they ever start up I shall leave. I'm old enough now."

"Move in here. See how the other half live." I reached back and dug him in the ribs.

He sighed. "All us damaged adolescents, all over the country, trying to create our own families. I hope to God we succeed."

The feeling hit quite suddenly; perhaps postpartum depression's catching. I'd spent a long time going through Nan's bag, although I didn't look at the certificate again. There were four suspender ends, and seven Robinson's Golly vouchers paper-clipped together, and an empty cotton spool with nails hammered in for French knitting (Nan had drawn a smiley face in pen on the side); there was an award for long service at the paper mill with my dad's name on it; there was a Temperance Society newsletter dated 1899, God knows whose that was; there was my first baby tooth folded in greaseproof paper in a cookie tin; and a scraggy bit of needlework I'd done in junior school, all lumpy knots underneath.

I thought of Nan: as a young woman, a girl, and as she was now. The present didn't wipe out the past; she had been those other—young—people.

Then Will began to cry again so I gathered it all together and took the bag downstairs with me. And as I hoisted him up and held his squirmy bulk to my chest, it seemed to me that time split clearly down the middle, and I realized what I'd so nearly done.

Once, when I was about seven, I'd found a sparrow's nest in a vacant garage on the edge of the housing estate. There were three blue eggs, perfect as a painting, against some white fluff and gray-brown feathers. The mother bird was going frantic, chip-chipping at me from the rafters above, so at first I just looked, but finally the urge to cradle the smooth warm shells against my palm became too much and I picked them up. They felt precious and thrilling. I carried them carefully back home and took them straight to Dad. I assumed he'd be as excited as I was.

His face went angry, then sad, when he saw what I had. Deep lines came from his nose to the corners of his mouth; it was much, much worse than if he'd shouted at me. He marched me back in silence to the nest and made me roll them gently back in. Then we stood for a while, waiting to see if the mother bird would come. "You see," he'd whispered, "she might be able to smell you on 'em; then she'd be too frittened to come near."

"Does that mean the babies'll die?" It had only just dawned on me that that's what the eggs were; I mean, you buy eggs in the supermarket like a packet of cookies, don't you? Then when you eat them it's yellow and white goo inside, not tiny birds. I felt terrible. Dad nodded almost imperceptibly and I burst into tears. We waited a good thirty minutes but no mummy bird appeared.

"Don't give up hope," he said comfortingly, as he took my hand to lead me home, but I wasn't crazy. I knew eggs had to be kept warm. I knew what I'd done.

"Thing is," he explained, as we got past the church, "if you take even one egg you're not killing one bird, you're killing millions."

"How come?" I'd been wiping my nose on my cardigan sleeve all the way, but he didn't yell at me for it.

"Because that bird would have had babies, and those babies

babies of their own, and so on and so on, down the generations. Ad in-fin-i-tum."

It wasn't like him to heap coals of fire on my head, so I knew
he thought it was serious. All the rest of that summer I trailed
back and forth to the garage in the hope that I could deliver
some good news and wipe the slate clean, but each visit the
eggs were still there, proof of my guilt. At the beginning of autumn the whole nest disappeared, I don't know whether it was
lads or gales or a fox maybe; do they eat rotten eggs? I stopped
going, anyway.

To make it up, Dad bought me a pair of binoculars for my
birthday the next year and took me up the Pike to see if we
could spot the albino jackdaw (we did!), only the effort of climb-
ing winded him and it took us a long, long time to stagger back
down again. I think maybe that was the beginning of him getting ill. I can still remember Nan's face as he finally tottered in
through the front door. So all things considered, I never really
got into bird-watching.

But baby Will lying so trusting in my arms, delicate flaring
nostrils, little screwed-up yawn; I so nearly destroyed you. I was
so nearly *such* a bad mother. I can't believe what I almost did
with your life and your mother's. Every time I look at you, I'll
feel the weight of what might have happened: all that future
wiped out. Your first tooth, your first step, your first word, your
first day at school. And so I should. I'll make it up to you, Will;
I'll be such a good grandma, I really will, really.

Strange thing: I heard Mum crying in the night when I got up to do Will's feed. She was sobbing and it sounded like she was talking to herself too. Anyway, I didn't go in. I was exhausted, and I wouldn't have known what else to say. She'll just have to work the Nan thing through.

I've kept thinking of something the vicar said at Bill's funeral: *The door is always open. It is never closed.* I wish I'd asked him what he meant but he's dead now, Mr. Speakman.

What did he mean?

It turned out to be a weird Christmas, all right, even though it started off fairly normal. It was the first Christmas with Emma, for a start. Throughout the morning she hung at my elbow, round-eyed. You're never going away, are you? I asked her silently, and she shook her head.

Nan came home for Christmas dinner, thank God, or I'd have spent the day under a cloud of guilt. I cut the food up for her while the plate was still in the kitchen; Matron had tipped me off about that. Then I chopped Charlotte's up too, so she could eat with a fussy Will on her knee. We got through that all right, although pulling the party snappers proved to be a bit of a challenge and the noise made Will bawl. He worked himself into such a foul temper Charlotte finally took him upstairs, where he went to sleep at once. Then Steve arrived with his Brilliant Present.

"I'm not stoppin', my sister's expectin' me. I wanted to drop these off, though."

There were some CD-ROMs for Charlotte, a bottle of dubious perfume for Nan, a ridiculously large teddy for William, and a spiral-bound notebook for me.

"What's this?" I asked, turning it over and finding only a W. H. Smith's price label on the back. True, it had a nice picture of Lake Windermere on the front, but I didn't see that was anything to get excited about.

"Take a look inside. There's twenty of 'em. Took me ages."

I flipped a few pages over.

1 voucher for 1 hours babysitting
signed
Steve

"Good, in't it? A chap at work saw it on Oprah Winfrey, an' he said it had gone over well." He stood back and waited for the applause.

"Thanks. Really, that's a great present. I appreciate it."

Steve beamed. "I thought so. Only don't make it a Saturday afternoon 'cause of the soccer. An' I'm out Tuesday and Thursday evenings. Fridays can be tricky, too. But apart from that . . . I'm all yours! Hey, by the way, how much did you pay for that tree? 'Cause I know a chap at work selling 'em for a pound a foot. He gets 'em off highway reservations, digs 'em up at night, so it's not like it's stealing or anything. I'll get you one out next year."

When he'd gone, Charlotte wanted to know what the deal was.

"It's just a way of getting back in with me; I know what he's up to. But don't look a gift horse in the mouth, eh? I don't suppose he knows what he's getting himself into." We looked at each other and snickered. "I'd like to be a fly on the wall when he has to change one of William's demon diapers."

"Or when Will pukes all down Dad's back."

"Quite."

"This scent smells of toilet cleaner," said Nan. "Put it under the sink with the Vim."

Daniel arrived shortly afterward like some kind of rogue Santa, bringing with him an entirely new future.

I could tell he was on pins from the word go.

"I got all these for Will," he said breathlessly, unpacking a stack of garish toys from the Early Learning Center. "Dad says a baby's brain goes on developing for months after birth, so he needs plenty to stimulate him." He pressed a plastic cow in the stomach and it mooed. "That'll get those neurons sparking."

"Have you been running?" I asked.

He only gave a nervous giggle and handed me a huge poinsettia. "For your table," he explained. "Although I have to say it looks extremely nice already."

We all turned to the scene of devastation that was the remains of the turkey dinner. A trail of gravy bisected the white cloth, and Nan had wiped her hands on her paper hat and crumpled it up in the gravy boat. Dead jokes lay curled next to a set of jacks, a metal puzzle, and a fish key ring.

"Yeah, right," said Charlotte. "We did have a centerpiece, but I set it alight and melted the robin."

"Jolly good. Now, take these; I haven't finished yet," said Daniel, producing more parcels with the flourish of a conjurer. I began to wonder if he was drunk.

There was talc for Nan and a snakeskin belt for Charlotte to match some boots she had. She was delighted.

"Are you taking your coat off or what?" I laughed.

"Yeah, sit down, for God's sake, Fidget Britches," said Charlotte. "And while you're here you can settle a debate." She pointed at the silver tinsel tree with folding arms we bring out every year. "Is that or is that not a middle-class Christmas tree?"

"Be quiet," I said, without much hope. "I've got to go and strip the turkey."

"Hang on a minute. What do you say, Dan?"

He shuffled himself backward into the settee and shrugged. "I'm not entirely sure what you mean."

"Well," said Miss Clever, "Mum thinks we should start having a real tree because it's classier, even though it's a lot more hassle."

"I *like* them," I said. "I like the smell, it's atmospheric. We'd have had one this year, but what with one thing and another I never got around to it."

"Only," Charlotte went on, "I told her that in real middle-class homes they care about the environment too much to cut down trees on a whim, so it's actually cooler to have an artificial one."

"I think they're both rather fun," he said, "if you have to have a pagan anachronism in your front room."

"Well, what sort of tree do your parents have, Daniel?" I asked, rising to tackle the mess on the table.

"Norway spruce. But my father has a synthetic one at his office. I don't know if that counts."

"*See?*" said Charlotte, but actually I thought *I'd* won that one.

W hat was all that about trees?" asked Daniel, when Mum was in the kitchen sawing the last bits off the turkey.

"You're a bonny lad," said Nan, attempting to lean over and pat his knee. "I'm nearly ninety, you know."

"Splendid."

"They think as 'cause you're old you're not so gradely reet." Nan sat back with a satisfied look on her face.

"Do they? Do they really?" He turned to me.

"Oh, yeah. Well, I was winding her up. Mum's such a daft bat at times. Listen."

> *"While shepherds washed their socks by night*
> *All watching ITV,*
> *The angel of the Lord came down*
> *And switched to BBC,"*

sang Mum over the noise of the radio, then, *"Bugger bugger bugger!"* Evidently the turkey was putting up a fight this year.

"Have a toffee," said Nan brightly. But I knew she couldn't open her handbag so I got down on the rug, fished some out for her, and began unwrapping the cellophane.

"It's Mum's fixation about being middle class. It's stupid. I keep telling her we're probably all middle class these days."

"I wouldn't have thought it mattered."

"Ah, well, that's because you're *real* middle class. It's the half-and-halves, caught in between, who obsess about it. Nan knew where she was, working in the mill and proud of it; I'll probably go off and get my degree—eventually—and earn my twenty-thousand-plus a year, so I'll be all right." Daniel's eyebrows moved up and down rapidly. "Yeah, well, if everything goes to plan, that is. Sorry, didn't mean to sound so smug. But Mum's in the land of the class-dispossessed: part-time school assistant living in former public housing. She's aspiring to something, but I don't know what."

Daniel squirmed and opened his mouth to say something, then changed his mind.

"The irony is, she's just become middle class and she doesn't even know it." I placed the naked candy on Nan's lap and clambered back on the sofa. "Shall I tell you why?"

"I'm utterly intrigued."

"It's the fact that, instead of spending her energy moaning about things, she's now getting up and actually doing something to make them better. As long as I can remember, she's droned on about how life ought to be different and I always thought, *Well, why not see if you can change it, then?* And I never had a satisfactory answer, unless you count 'We don't do that kind of thing,' 'That's the way it is,' 'We put our heads down and slog on.' But your middle-class person says, I'm going to write to my MP, make a schedule, lobby the congressmen, hold a meeting. Middle-class people *act*, they don't suffer."

"Too much of a generalization," said Daniel, hugging himself like a man who's been accidentally shut in a freezer. "I know plenty of whining middle class. Half my father's patients probably fall into that category."

"Huh. It's my theory and I'm sticking to it."

"Mrs. Waters is fed up 'cause she's having a hip op," Nan piped up.

"No. She said she's fed up with her son playing *hip-hop*." I snickered, then felt mean when she looked confused. "He plays his music loud," I explained.

"Well, they do, young 'uns. You do."

"I don't—"

There was an extra-loud clatter and a yelp from the kitchen. I got up to investigate.

"Do you think your mother's going to be long in there? Because there's something I want you all to hear," he blurted out. "Together. I think."

Radar Ears was back in the room like a shot.

I was expecting an old-fashioned film: Mrs. Cooper, may I have the honor of asking Charlotte to be my bride? It would be a shock, but quite a nice one. I mean, a doctor's son. I came through wiping my bleeding thumb on my apron, all ready to play the understanding mother.

He stood up as soon as Mum walked in.

"Eeh, are you going?" mumbled Nan, through a mouthful of candy. "You'll want a coat on, it's bitter out."

He shook his head, embarrassed, and moved so that his back was to the fire. Me and Mum sat in front of him like an interview panel while he straightened his fingers, spread them out, and put his palms together. Then his hands dropped to his sides and I thought, *Oh, God, what's coming now?* Because I really hadn't a clue. He raised his head and began.

"I should have said this earlier, when I first came, but I didn't know how—I have something I need to tell you both. At least, I think I should tell you—I mean, there's no question whether I should tell you, it's whether I should tell you both together, or just you, Mrs. Cooper, or maybe you, Charlotte, and get you to speak to your mother."

"Maureen Tickle had a broken ankle for six weeks before they x-rayed it," said Nan. "She'd been walking on it an' all. Exercise, the doctor told her, honest to God." Her lips snapped shut and she stared at Daniel's knees.

"Go on," Mum prompted him. She was gripping her thumb so tightly the tip had gone white.

"Right, well. The thing is, I may have been out of order, acting behind your back, in fact I probably was, and you're going to be very angry. My father will be furious with me when he finds out; he'll say I did it all wrong."

"*What,* for heaven's sake?" I tried to catch his eye but he was looking over the tops of our heads.

"They've a new woman at the post office, great big teeth like a rabbit."

"Shut up, Nan, just a sec."

"It was meant to be a surprise. I've been doing some research on the Internet. I thought you had a right to know—"

Daniel pulled out an envelope from his jeans pocket and made as if to offer it to Mum, then pulled it back and held it to his chest. "But I can see now I should have gone to you first because it was to do with your family, no business of mine—"

"*Please*, Daniel, tell us." I rose from the sofa, and he let me take the envelope out of his hands. I started to unfold the contents, a printout from some website or other, an envelope paper-clipped to the back, and for a moment I thought, *Christ, he's found Mum's birth mother; bloody hell, what a can of worms that'd be.* I sat back down quickly, not sure what to do. But then my eyes focused properly. *www.nationalsavings.co.uk,* the footer read. A photo of a smiling woman with her arms in the air, over the legend *Congratulations!*

Mum leaned against my arm, scanning the page. "Is it ERNIE?" she asked, and swallowed. She undid the paper clip.

"Don't get too excited, chaps." Daniel grimaced with emotion. "It's not the national lottery jackpot. But it's better than a poke in the eye with a blunt stick. Tax free, as well." He was rocking on his feet; I think he'd have liked to run for the door and take off down the street.

"I'm sorry to disappoint you, Daniel, but I don't think we have any premium bonds. You must have typed in the wrong letters or something." Mum's voice was quavering because, like me, she'd spotted the line where it said *£10,000!* "This is somebody else's prize."

"Lucky bastards," I said, with a feeble laugh.

"No, no. That's what I was trying to tell you. It was absolutely the wrong thing to do, to go behind your back. When

I spotted the bonds I should have handed them straight to you—"

"What bonds?" Mum's hand was really shaking as she undid the flap of the envelope.

"The ones out of that old bag. In Charlotte's grandma's room. They were in with all those silk postcards." Daniel's face was flaming, his hair spectacularly on end where he'd pushed his fingers through it over and over again. "Oh, hell, I can't believe I behaved so crassly; I should have just handed them over at once. I had this idea it would make a nice surprise."

"Is there a James Bond on this afternoon?" asked Nan. "He's a swanky chap." Everyone ignored her and she closed her eyes.

Mum spread the yellowed bonds out on the sofa between us. ISSUED BY THE LORDS COMMISSIONERS OF HM TREASURY, the one nearest me said. *£1.*

"So Nan's won ten thousand pounds?" I laughed. It was a hysterical thought. "My God, she'll be able to buy cartloads of belly pork!"

Nan opened her eyes and started to giggle too, though I don't think she had a clue as to what was going on.

"No, hang on a minute," said Mum, waving the page and breathing hard.

"What now?"

Mum frowned. "Well, there's no name on the bonds themselves . . . but it says Miss *Karen* Hesketh on the card that's with them. Does that mean . . . ?"

"Oh, my God! I bet Nan and Grandad bought you these when you were a baby! How many are there?"

Nan was smiling broadly.

"Twenty pounds' worth. That would have been a fortune in those days." Mum got up slowly and knelt in front of Nan, holding up the scraps of paper under her nose in a fan. They looked a bit like banknotes. "Did you? Did you buy these for me when I was born?" Nan went on smiling but said nothing. "It's very important, Mother. Do you understand me? Did you buy these—for *me*?"

"They're date-stamped April 1963, if that's any help," murmured Daniel politely.

Mum put the bonds into the dip of Nan's skirt and took Nan's hands in hers. "Oh. . . ."

Nan patted her daughter's head absently, sighed, then closed her eyes again. "It were a good big turkey," she muttered. Her lips parted and she was asleep immediately, head lolling onto the antimacassar. How do they do that, old people, just drop straight off? Mum rocked back onto her haunches and Daniel helped her to her feet.

"Okay, Mrs. Cooper?"

She looked him in the eye. "Are you absolutely sure this money's ours? Because I don't think I could stand it now if you were wrong."

He stared right back. "Mrs. Cooper, I wouldn't have said a word till I was one hundred percent positive."

"No, you wouldn't, would you?"

"No."

So Mum cracked open a foul bottle of wine one of the kids at school had given her at the end of term, and Daniel had one glass and then went because he said we had a lot to talk about. After I closed the door on him I went back into the room, and

Mum and I looked at each other and burst out laughing. "Oh, my God," Mum kept saying. "Oh, my God!"

I knew Charlotte had in her mind a huge shopping spree; she'd have blown the whole lot on clothes *easily,* might have taken a few months but she'd have done it. But it was my money. I told her that straight off. Her face fell.

"Well, can we at least have the bathroom done? You said you would."

I shook my head.

"Well, *what,* then?" She was looking for a fight, it was quite funny to hear. Well, all that tension had to go somewhere. "You're not going to stick it all in the bank for a 'rainy day,' surely? Come on, Mum, life's too short."

Emma nodded at me.

"I will share this money with you. In fact, I'll split it down the middle, fifty-fifty." Her eyes lit up: £5,000 to spend in Top Shop! "But listen, we need this money to do something very important."

"What?"

"It's going to get us both through college."

You could see the cogs going around.

"Both? Are you . . . ? D'you know, I *thought* there was something going on with you and college. Bloody hell." She was shaking her head. "Will they take people so . . . people like you?"

"Get away." I made as if to give her a kick. "I'll be a mature student. Yes, all right, stop pulling faces, it's not that funny. There are thousands like me, apparently, I've been looking into it. I just never thought it was really an option, what with the cost. But as soon as Daniel told us. . . . Oh, Charlotte! I still can't believe. . . . There are debts to be dealt with, quite a few of those, credit cards, catalogs—"

"My computer."

"Your computer. But the rest is going to pay for a teacher training course for me, at Manchester Metropolitan, and your English degree, wherever you decide to do it. Because you have to go on and do it now, Charlotte."

I felt so full of energy, like I really was ready to step into this new millennium everyone kept going on about.

"I never had any intention of not applying," she said, a bit haughty. "But I can always get a loan."

"I could throw this glass of wine over you. Don't be so crazy! Why get in hock when there's a big lump of cash sitting there for the purpose? *And* it'll help fund a place for Will at the best nursery we can find. If you're all right with that."

" 'Course it is; God, don't ask me. You'll be burdened with the little star while I'm away; it's for you to decide." She combed her fingers through her hair and sighed. "Bloody hell, Mum, it sounds crazy, but ten thousand's hardly going to be enough, is it?"

I took a swig of wine. "It won't cover everything, no, but it'll give us a damn good start."

"You going to tell Dad? He gave us some out of that bogus compensation claim that time."

"He didn't, actually. Although it wasn't his fault; he was supposed to get thousands, but the claims company took most of it in fees. Serves him right, painting on bruises with eyeshadow. So, no, I think we'll keep quiet for now. Not that he'd begrudge it going on your education, he really wouldn't. He's proud of you." *Even if he does find you scary.*

She kicked off her mules, stretched out on the sofa, and put her feet in my lap like she used to do when she was very young. It was such an ordinary, intimate gesture, but she'd never have done that six months ago, when we hated each other. I looked down at her neat young toes and for a second remembered her as a baby, a startling memory of fat feet pressing into my naked thighs as I held her up, giggling, by her baby armpits. All that clean, innocent skin, this little piggy.

I came out of the dream and tuned back in.

"What I don't understand, though," she was saying, "is why the Premium Bond people didn't contact us. Is it like the lottery, and it's up to you to check your numbers?"

I took her toes between my palms and she squeaked and wriggled; what a shock that we could be like this again. I was overwhelmed with the desire to bend right over and give her an enormous hug, thank her for having once been such a beautiful baby, but she'd have thought I was crazy. Instead I just said, "Yes, I was thinking about that. They're supposed to write. We should have had at least one letter, the October or November before last. I wonder what happened to it."

From the armchair, Nan smacked her lips and muttered. Charlotte turned her head round to look, then made a despairing face at me.

"Oh, God. She could have done anything with it, Mum. Toasted it, pushed it under a carpet, stuck it behind a pic—" She gave a funny sort of giggle. "Well, who knows? They could have sent us a whole load of *Congratulations!* and she'd have destroyed them one after the other. Like having a vicious dog lurking behind the letter box. Who knows *what* vital communications we've lost over the last couple of years. But then, you'd think they'd have used the telephone—"

"Which she won't ever answer."

Charlotte clapped her hand to her brow. "And if we were tied up and missed the call—"

"They don't keep trying forever. There are thousands in unclaimed prizes, apparently, Daniel said."

"Thousands of people with grannies who eat the mail?"

"Maybe." I thought of what the New Year was to bring, the bed waiting for Nan at Mayfield. Remembering was like having a family Bible settle on your chest. "Anyway, that's one problem we won't have to deal with anymore."

Leo came in the evening, after Nan had gone back. I told him about the money; I wasn't going to at first, but then it just came out. He was delighted for us, as I knew he would be. He *is* a nice man.

There are a lot of things money can't touch, of course.

It was so weird leaving Nan in that home. We got her set up in her room—a pleasant one with a bay window and a tree outside that hid most of the parking lot—put her slippers by the bed, her underclothes in the drawers, her knickknacks out on the shelves. She didn't have much with her. Big photo of Will on one side of the bed, Mum's wedding on the other, but the prime spot went to a blown-up print of her and Grandad sitting on a bench—they look about twenty—having a cuddle. She's got white stockings on and black shoes with a bar across, and her hair is straight and shoulder-length. She's looking into the camera, only half smiling, as if she has something on her mind. He's looking at her, his arms tight around her shoulders, shy grin. His legs are out in front of him, and you can see four little studs at the front of each sole. They are so *young*.

"You'll be able to watch the birds, Nan."

"Aye."

When we walked away she was sitting on the bed like a lost child. Matron was chatting away to her, but she wasn't taking much notice.

"I don't think I can stand it," said Mum, clinging to the doorjamb.

"Come on. Quick, before you chicken out. If she's really unhappy after a few weeks, you can think again, but you've got to give it a try. The doctor said it was the best place." I took Mum's sleeve and pulled her away, down the corridor. Bertie trotted past us, tail beating. I watched with my fingers crossed, and he disappeared into Nan's room.

"I need a drink," said Mum.

"Do we not need to get back for Debbie?"

"I told her half past three, and it's not half past two yet. She's got my cell phone number if William acts up."

So we found a wine bar and sat there for nearly an hour, two women sharing a bottle of Chardonnay.

Charlotte had been pestering me about filling in the family tree at the front of William's Baby Record book. I'd drawn a blank after three generations, so I told her to ask Nan. "Take those old photos in the shoe box while you're at it. I've been meaning to get them labeled for ages. And leave William here with me or you'll never get anything done."

When she came back, she was bubbling with excitement.

"God, it was crazy, Mum! They had a full-scale emergency on when I got there because this old biddy reckoned she'd seen her friend eat a bit off a starter log. They had an ambulance out, the doctor, everyone running round looking for the First Aid book, do you induce vomiting or not. Then in the end it turned out to be a chunk off a Thornton's nougat box. Matron had to have a sit-down after. Never a dull moment at Mayfield, she says."

"And how was Nan?"

Charlotte started unpacking the shopping bag of photos. "Amazing. It was like switching a light on, Mum; she just came to life. We talked for hours, and it was so interesting."

She pulled some photos out of an envelope and laid them on the table. I stuck William under his baby gym and came to see.

"That one's their wedding day."

"I guessed that."

"Yeah, but check out that hat! You can hardly see her face. Is that the locket she still wears?"

"Probably. Gosh, doesn't my dad look dapper with his button-hole. . . . He was no age when he died, it was such a shame." I picked up the picture and held it to the light. The dad I'd known had always been tired and short of breath; here was a young, happy, vigorous man starting out in life.

"And did you know he'd been engaged to someone else when she met him?"

I put the photo back down, surprised. "No. She never said anything."

"Yes, really. She stole him away! Can you imagine Nan doing something like that? I guess she was a bit of a minx when she was a girl." Charlotte shook her head in mock disapproval.

"She must have really been in love." I thought of my own wedding album, stuck underneath the wardrobe in shame. "And she was right too, they were devoted to each other for over forty years."

"My God, that's fantastic." Charlotte picked out another, Nan in a gaberdine-type coat and a group of young girls in pinafores. They were standing, along with a big, stern man wearing a watch and chain, in front of a vintage bus. "Nan said that was a sightseeing bus. They called it Whistling Rufus, and they went on trips to Blackpool and Southport in it. She couldn't remember who those people were, though."

"Looks like a school party. Unless—no, she's about eighteen there so she'd have left school. It must be millworkers. She always said she had some good times at Jarrod's, but they don't seem so happy there, do they? Maybe good times are relative. . . ."

But Charlotte wasn't listening. "Have you seen this one, Mum?" In her hand was a very faded, creased, and yellow photograph of four people: a little girl, standing, with ringlets, hands folded in front of her; a grim old lady, sitting, in black silk and wearing clogs with their curved-up soles; a boy, younger than the girl, standing awkwardly in a dark outfit with a large white collar, something like a sailor suit; and a pretty, anxious woman in her twenties, perched on a straight-backed chair, an oval locket against her white blouse. "Do you know who they are?"

We huddled together and gazed at the four solemn faces. Only the boy was smiling, as if he couldn't keep his energy and youth from spilling out.

"Well, that's Nan," I said, pointing to the girl. "And that'll be her grandma next to her."

"Florrie Marsh, that's right. I've written it on the back. She looks a right old battleax, doesn't she? The other woman's Nan's mother, Polly. She's sad there because Nan's father kept leaving them, apparently, then coming back again. He was living with some woman in Chorley when that picture was taken."

I thought Polly looked tired to death. "Poor thing. Awful not to know where you stand, and humiliating, especially in those days. Nan would never tell me much about it, too ashamed, but I knew there was something funny about the setup. Well, well." I put my finger gently to the boy. "I can guess who he is; what a little angel." His dark suit was spoiled by a white crease in the paper running the length of his body. "Terrible to die so young."

"Nan's brother, Jimmy. Aww, see, one of his socks is coming down."

"Did she say anything about him?"

"He drowned in the canal."

"Really? Poor lamb."

"She cried when she told me, I think they were pretty close.

But she was all right after," she added hastily. "I started telling her about Will puking into Ivy's shopping bag, and she cheered right up."

We shuffled the pictures together, and Charlotte slid them back in their envelopes.

"I tell you what, Mum," she said, as she put the lid back on the shoe box, "I'm going to take that portable tape deck and record some of Nan's stories, because they're really interesting: How We Used to Live and all that. I could keep the cassettes for Will when he's older, his family history."

(My family history, I thought.)

"It's like"—Charlotte put the box at the bottom of the stairs and came back in—"you know when the TV's on but you're recording a different channel to the one you're watching? It's like that with Nan. What you see on the surface isn't what's going on inside. We think she's crazy half the time, but it's just that she lives in a different dimension from the rest of us." She rescued Will from where he had wedged himself against the hearth and held his face up to hers. He laughed and tried to swipe at her hair. "Well, her time frame's different, anyway. Nan's past *is* her present. I mean, there's not much this decade has to offer her, is there? You know, if someone in their twenties was widowed and then disabled, everyone would talk about how tragic it was, but because Nan's old she's expected to get over it. She's an amazing woman, actually. I guess there's more going on with Nan than anyone ever realized."

I was listening to Radio 4, and they were interviewing Kate Adie about what it was like to report on the conflict in Bosnia.

She said what made it difficult sometimes was that the people there had no concept of an incident being the result of a single moment's action; when something happened it was because of an accumulation of events, sometimes stretching back for decades. She was sent to cover a massacre that had taken place in a small town near the main fighting.

"What happened here yesterday?" she asked an eyewitness.

"In 1943 . . . ," the man began.

Everyone's history is the product of someone else's; what we think of as our own experience is only what's been bestowed on us by others. You can't walk away from that.

And why should you?

Snapshots from the Future

Will stands up on his own for the first time, falls over, and bangs his head on the marble hearth. For ten seconds I think he might be dead, and in that gulf of horror I realize how much I love him, after all. It must have snuck up on me when I wasn't looking.

Mum comes home from school with the news that Leo Fairbrother's getting married, shock announcement. Some well-to-do fifty-something he's met in Italy, Maria Callas lookalike, though she actually comes from Oldham. How will Mum take this terrible blow? To be honest she seems fine about it; maybe they really were just good friends. In the event, Mrs. F provides Mum with twice the social life (teaches her bridge, invites her to wine-tastings) and passes on her old Aquascutum and Jacques Vert, all contributions gratefully received. Now they go to the Octagon as a threesome (though I think it stops there).

I come in quietly through the back door. It's Reading Week at university, so no one's expecting me. I can hear voices before I get inside.

Mum is sitting on the toilet with the door open, blowing up a balloon, while Will rushes around the kitchen shrieking. "Mummee!" he yells, when he sees me.

"Good God, is there no privacy in this place?" she moans, her voice echoing off the tiles.

I put my bags on top of the fridge and lie down on the floor so my son can climb all over me, giggling. It's good to be home, but only because I don't live here. Maybe I'm a bad mother for not being around all the time, but, hey, I'm doing the best I can. What more can any of us do?

It's a Friday teatime in November, and I'm phoning home as usual.

"Shall I put Nan on?" asks Mum. "She's been to a funeral today, so I brought her back for tea."

"Go on, then."

There's a scuffling and someone says, "Bloody hellfire," then the sound of heavy breathing.

"Hello? Hello?" ("There's nobody there," she tells Mum. "Yes, there is," snaps Mum, "have some patience, for God's sake.")

"Hello, Nan."

"It's dark here. Is it dark where you are?"

"Yes. I'm only in York."

"They've a big bonfire at the Working Men's. Are you having a bonfire?"

"We've got some fireworks for later."

"Are they?"

"Nan?"

"It was a beautiful sermon."

"Nan."

"What?"

"I LOVE YOU!"

"I love you too." ("Here, Karen, I've got myself stuck with this wire all around me.")

Acknowledgments

For their encouragement and guidance:
David Rees, Kath Pilsbury, Ursula Doyle, Leslie Wilson,
Katherine Frank, and Simon Long.

For helping to get the ball rolling:
Judith Magill, Adrian Johnson, Lynn Patrick,
and Peter Straus.

For invaluable practical support:
the Headmaster and staff of Abbey Gate College.

For inspirational background material
and a whole lot of Oldham Tinkers LPs:
Mum and Dad.

the

BAD MOTHER'S HANDBOOK

Kate Long

A Reader's Guide

A Conversation with Kate Long

Printed with permission from Kinokuniya, Japan

Kate Long wrote her first novel in her spare time, at night after her children were asleep or on the weekends. It became an instant number-one bestseller in her native England, was serialized on a national radio station, and sold in over twenty-three countries, including Japan. Here she does an interview for the Japanese bookstore, Kinokuniyu.

Q: Briefly, where were you born and brought up? Where did you go to school? Which university did you go to and what did you study?

A: I was born in Pinner, England, adopted at six weeks and brought up in Wigan. I spent seven miserable years not fitting in at the local primary, then won a scholarship to Bolton School, an independent girls' school, which is where Monica Ali went. I loved it there. I left to do a degree in English Literature at Bristol University, and won several prizes there for academic study. I was invited to stay on and do a Masters in Literature or Ph.D. but I'd had enough of academia by then and wanted a break.

Q: What made you decide to be a teacher? How long did you teach, and what age groups and subjects did you teach? Would you say a career as an English teacher is a good foundation for a novelist? When did you decide to give up teaching, and was it a hard decision to make?

A: I'd been helping out in classrooms for as long as I could remember—mainly my mum's, but also when I was at Bolton School in their prep department. I liked it, it was fun. At university I visited a local primary every Wednesday afternoon and took groups for extra reading or math work. In my final year it occurred to me I could do this and get paid for it. So I applied to Rolle College at Exmouth, and got a degree in junior teaching. My first job was in a primary school in Guildford where I stayed for two years, and then I went to the cinema and saw *Dead Poets' Society* and decided I wanted to move into secondary teaching and use my degree again. So I got a position in a small independent high school outside Chester and taught English. I stayed there for thirteen years and really loved it. It was a wrench (and a risk!) to leave teaching but I just couldn't do two jobs and look after the family as well. I now do an afternoon a week in my son's primary school—can't leave the education system alone.

Teaching's a great career base for a novelist because you're training in communication all the time, and also you have the summer holidays in which to get down to some serious writing.

Q: Did you write stories as a child? When did you take up writing seriously and what prompted you to do so?

A: I've been officially "good at English" since I was young. I was inspired by *Kes*—it's a film about a poor boy who brings up a kestrel (a hawklike bird) and how his relationship with the bird transforms his life—and I wrote a poem about a kestrel and was short-listed for a competition with it—I'd have been about thirteen. It was like a switch going on, seeing that film. And because I was a complete loner till I was eleven, always had my nose in a book.

I might have started writing because I went on a teaching course in about 1990, 1992, and did some fiction writing there and got enthusiastic feedback from the group. Or I might have started because I used to suffer from insomnia. Then again, it might have been the moment I picked up a glossy magazine and saw a story in it by someone I went to university with. (How dare she?) It was probably a combination of all three.

Q: Can you describe the process of writing *The Bad Mother's Handbook*?

A: I'd read several books that were about "juggling mums" but, disappointingly, they all depicted women from wealthy, upper-middle-class backgrounds. So I had a bit of a mission; I wanted to write about the lower-middle-class mum, and also what it's like to be a carer for a disabled person. I suppose I wanted to say, "Our lives are important too, us ordinary, unglamorous folk."

It took me a summer holiday to write about 80 percent of it, and then another year to finish and polish. Not only was I teaching in that year, but I had a young child and an infant to look after, so I used to have to write in the evenings after the boys were in bed—as long as I didn't have a pile of papers to grade or I wasn't out at a parents' evening. But only having a small slot like this in which to write was actually a help because it stopped my procrastinating.

Q: Tell me about your typical writing day, when/how often/ how much do you typically write?

A: It takes me about eight or nine months to prepare a manuscript to the point where it's fit to submit to my agent. I do about 3,000 words a week, about 600 words Monday–Friday mornings, and the odd sentence or two on the weekends. If I don't write regularly I have trouble getting back into a rhythm.

Q: How do you begin a novel? Do you do research?

A: I have to write a synopsis first. But I wouldn't embark on something as long and complex as a novel without having it pretty well planned out first. I do change direction sometimes as the novel develops, yes, but never dramatically. Like most writers, I find my characters arrive fully formed, but I still have to sit down before I start writing and fix their details; I use a set of questions, like a resumé, to help me do this. That way I don't make so many factual errors, such as accidentally changing someone's age by putting in the wrong date for them starting school. I have done bits and pieces of research; my optician has told me everything I needed to know about age-related macular degeneration, for instance, and I spent a lot of time watching reality TV for the background to the third novel. I find if you ask, people are usually prepared to tell you about their jobs or experiences, and of course the internet is wonderful. I've been in touch with a lady I found online, and she's been able to tell me some details about what it was like to grow up in Wigan, England, in the 1920s. And a lot of the anecdotes in *TBMH* came from tape recordings of my grandparents.

Q: Was your second novel already written when you got the publishing deal? Can you give me a brief idea of what the book is about? What are its main themes?

A: Here's the official description of my second book, which Ballantine will publish in 2007:

Katherine's father, Poll's adored only son, was killed in a car crash when Katherine was a baby. According to Poll, the crash was the fault of Katherine's mother, who disappeared shortly afterwards, never to be seen again. Poll is pushing seventy, half-blind, and utterly poisonous. Her ambition is for things to stay exactly the same forever, and for Katherine never to leave their small town of Bank Top; indeed for her to leave the house only when strictly necessary.

Katherine has other ideas, especially when on her birthday she receives a mysterious parcel of glamorous, grown-up clothes—so unlike the ones Poll makes her wear. And then the handsome and self-assured Callum turns up, claiming to be a cousin she never knew she had. Katherine can feel that change is coming; the omens are all around her. In the meantime, she cleans up after Poll, revises for her exams, watches daytime television, and surfs the net at the library trying to find out how to be bulimic. What she doesn't quite realize yet is that life won't always wait for you to catch up.

Q: Do you have any favorite authors who have particularly inspired you?

A: Alan Garner is a writer who I deeply admire, and Jeanette Winterson. But the one who switched me on and made me want to write is Kate Atkinson, possibly because her style is so fresh, possibly because I happened to read her at the "right time." I know she too wrote while bringing up small children. And of course I had a background in the classics—Austen, the Brontës, Dickens, Hardy, et cetera. I'd say immersing yourself in quality writing—poetry and prose—is the best thing any aspiring writer can do, because you can't help but absorb good practice. Read widely, read for enjoyment.

Q: Now that you have established a new career as a novelist, how real does it all feel to you? Did you expect, five years ago, to be where you are today? Where would you like to be, in your writing career, in five years' time?

A: The exciting thing is, I don't know where I'll be in five years' time. It could all have bombed, in which case I can say I had a good bash at it and it was fun while it lasted. It might carry on at the same pitch, which would be fantastic. I never expected to get published in the first place because the odds are so stacked against it. Does it seem real? Well, light is slowly dawning and I'm not getting bouts of panic like I used to. I hate to sound like a '70s car sticker, but I think we all of us have to take each day as it comes.

Reading Group Questions and Topics for Discussion

1. How are the sections in Nan's perspective different from what you'd expect? How did they affect your understanding of Nan throughout the book?

2. Karen says she feels she's been living the wrong life. Have you ever felt the same way?

3. Do you think that discovering the truth about her birth mother helped Karen make her life "right"? How?

4. Do you think Charlotte is an admirable character?

5. Compare the men in the novel: Paul, Danny, Mr. F., and Steve. Do these characters remind you of people you know? Are they realistic?

6. Did you expect Karen's relationship with Mr. F. to turn out differently? Why do you think the author chose to end this way?

7. Which character do you identify with the most: Karen or Charlotte? Why?

8. Was Karen too hard on Charlotte? How do you think you would have reacted in Karen's situation?

9. What, if anything, do all three women—Nan, Karen, and Charlotte—have in common?

10. Do you think this book has a surprise ending? If you had to write an alternate ending, what would you write?

11. What does the novel have to say about the choices we make in life, or that are made for us?

12. According to the novel, has life gotten easier for Western women over the twentieth century, or harder? Do you agree with the novel's presentation?

13. Do you think *The Bad Mother's Handbook* is an appropriate title?

Read on for a preview
of Kate Long's

SKY MESSAGES

Available from Ballantine Books
in July 2007

"One day I'll die," Poll's always going, "and then you'll be sorry, my girl."

No I won't. I'll put the bloody flags out. I'll tie a red satin bow round Winston's neck, dance stark naked up and down Mesnes Park, and put an ad in the "Celebrations" column of the *Wigan Observer*.

> *She always had a lot to say*
> *She had a tongue sharp as a knife*
> *But now my grandma's passed away*
> *I'm off to start a whole new life.*
> In remembrance of Pollyanna Millar,
> evil-minded shrew and dog-botherer.

That night, after Poll had groped her way along the landing from the bathroom, I wrote in my diary:

New Year's Resolutions

1. Stop eating (lose 10 kg by Valentine's Day)

2. Get everyone at school to call me Kat, not Katherine, as it sounds cooler

3. Try to make friends with Donna French
   X X X lush lush

4. Decide what to do about My Future

Then I lay down on the bed, under Dad's old posters of Blondie, and tried to block out the bad thoughts that always gather about this time by doing A-level essay plans in my head. Finally I turned out the light and blew Dad a kiss, like I always do. It might be mad, but it helps.

I share my room with two dead people. As well as Dad, in his jar on the windowsill, there's Great-grandma Florence, who was Poll's mother, in the bottom of the wardrobe inside a black and gold tin. I never think about her, to be honest, except when I'm hunting for shoes.

The rest of Poll's family are buried in the Bank Top cemetery, a sloping field down which the gravestones are moving imperceptibly, along with the wall that's supposed to keep them in. If you climb up on the war memorial in the middle you get a good view, a clear view anyway, of the dirty brick town of Harrop below, with its derelict paper mill and defunct loco works. Surely this can't be where the occupants of the cemetery are headed? I can't see the attraction myself.

My big dream is to be normal. I need to ditch the socks and frocks and be more like other girls, but it's not easy with a grandma like mine.

"Makeup? What do you want to wear makeup for? You'll ruin your skin. You'll end up looking like a clown or a prostitute, one or t' other. Smear some Vaseline on your face, that's all you need at your age. I were a married woman before I owned a lipstick."

We have this bollocks continually.

It's dawning on me, now I'm reaching my eighteenth birthday, that actually a lot of things Poll says are rubbish, e.g. that mending your socks while you're still wearing them brings on terrible bad luck. "It's sewing sorrow to your heart," she always moans. "You'll rue." She also reckons that washing your hair while you're having a period sends you mad, and that sleeping with a potato prevents cramps.

When I was younger I believed her, so therefore all the other kids assumed I was mad too and wouldn't have anything to do with me. I couldn't catch a ball either, and I wore a hand-knitted school cardigan instead of a bought one from Littlewoods. I pretended I didn't care.

"Not everyone has a mother and a father," I would recite when they cornered me on the rec. "Me and my grandma are a family too."

"Piss off, Fatso," they'd say. "You don't even call her Grandma. How weird is that?"

"She doesn't like it."

"She doesn't like you. You're mental. Your mum killed your dad and then ran off. Weirdy-weirdo." Then they'd run away screaming and screwing their index fingers into their temples. Weirdy-weirdo would skulk by the bins for a bit and then go and stand by the teacher till the bell went.

The trouble with Bank Top is that everyone knows everyone else's history.

Poll doesn't want people to feel sorry for her—which is lucky, because in general they don't. She's as blind as she wants to be: Some days, you'd hardly know she has a problem; others, she's all but bed-ridden. "It's like having a black spot pasted on the front of your eyeball," she says. "If I look at your head, now, all I can see is an empty space." She's got peripheral vision, though, so you'd be unwise to try anything sneaky.

The Rehab Officer likes to stay upbeat. "Here, we prefer the term *partially sighted*," she says when Poll goes to be assessed for extras e.g. hand-rails, magnifiers, large-button phones. Not that she bothers with most of these aids; after all, it's what I'm there for. I'm just a two-legged guide dog.

When she first began to lose her sight she was given this handy booklet, *Coping with Age-Related Macular Degeneration*. It's full of top tips for someone with a reasonable take on life:

- *Use strong lighting throughout the house, particularly on stairs.*

Poll says, "If you think I'm getting an electrician in you've another think coming. Pass us that flashlight." Our sockets are loaded to buggery and we have nine table lamps in the living room alone.

- *Tell others clearly what you need.*

No problems with this one. It's all I get, all day and every day. I shop, cook, clean, wash, iron after a fashion, lay her clothes out for her every night and put her eye drops in. She doesn't need the eye drops; she just likes the idea. She needs the ICaps dietary supplement pills, but she won't take them, of course.

- *Use your cane as a signal that you need help.*

Or as a weapon. She may only have limited vision but she can always locate an ankle bone from a good height.

- *Don't dwell on your difficulties. Treat your visual impairment as a challenge to be overcome.*

To be fair, she isn't much into self-pity. Anger, petty-mindedness, pig-headedness; now those she does a treat.

- *Get to know your neighbors; build up a community around you.*

Don't know if Dickie the Dogman counts as a community; he certainly hangs round our place enough. Poll thinks he's marvelous because he's always posting tat he's got off the market through our dog-flap; loaves with big holes all through them, unperforated toilet roll, bacon that's about 90 percent fat. And they have these long gossip sessions in the kitchen while Wolfie lolls about on the flags and tries to chew his own paws off.

"You know that woman up Nettle Fold who did Maggie's daughter's wedding dress?"

"Oh, aye?"

"She's a medium."

"A medium what?"

"No, she talks to spirits."

"Oh, right. What, part-time?"

"I suppose so. Maggie said she's snowed under with alterations for people."

"So can she tell the future?"

"Maggie says she can."

"It's a pity she didn't let on about the groom knocking off the chief bridesmaid, then, in't it?"

I never used to mind Dickie Dogman, in fact I thought he was quite funny when I first knew him. He came on the scene when I was about five, after he knocked on the door and offered us some sand he'd found. "Mek a nice sandpit for t' littlun," he'd said. "Oh, go on, then," Poll had said, unexpectedly. The pit was a disaster; it stained my arms orange and was a total cat-magnet. But somehow Dickie stayed on the scene. He knew a lot of jokes, and he could do tricks with matches.

Sometimes I'd go with him over the fields while he walked Wolfie, or the other dogs he had then. In the spring he'd help me catch tadpoles which would go in a jar on the kitchen top for about two weeks, then Poll would knock them over, or pour melted fat on them, or swill them with bleach. In the autumn Dogman enjoyed identifying fungus, then smashing it up. "That's fly agaric, that is. We'll have that bastard for a start." I have a really clear memory of him sitting on a stile once and a red admiral butterfly landing on his coat sleeve. "Look at that," he said, watching it dip its wings and unfurl its tongue briefly. "The miracle of nature. Oh, it's fucked off." But his favorite crop was dirty magazines, which grew all along the hedgerows near the lay-by. For a long time I thought he was just litter picking.

As I hit puberty, I began to see Dogman for what he was; a dirty old man. I kept catching him staring at my breasts and licking his lips. From the time I was fourteen, I never had a cold without him offering to rub Vicks on my chest. Then, one day last year, something really horrible happened.

I came out of the library to find him sitting on the form outside, talking to someone on his mobile. He had his back to me and he didn't know I was there. Wolfie wagged his tail at me but still Dogman didn't notice. He was engrossed in conversation.

"Well, you know me," he was saying, "I like 'em big. Yeah, completely topless, nips and all." His shoulders shook with laughter. "She didn't know I were there, it were first thing in t' morning. Yeah, massive. Round the back, through t' kitchen window. Hey, hang on, it's not my fault if she parades round wi' no bra on. I was just standing innocently by the back door, me."

As he was sniggering down the phone, I remembered Saturday and how I'd run down at half-eight to let Winston out for a wee in the garden. I'd not finished getting dressed, but you don't hang about with Winston because his Westie bladder's old and unreliable. Not ten minutes later, Dogman had appeared at the back door with the glad tidings that Lidl were selling off dirt-cheap TVs, and did we want him to get us one. I thought he seemed agitated at the time, but I put it down to the amazingly low-price deal.

So ever since then, I've tried to avoid him, he gives me the krills. But it's not easy; he virtually lives here. He's Poll's number-one best friend.

Dogman's not the only pervert round here, either. I've seen a penis, and I was only about eight. This elderly gent stopped me in the street near Flaxton's Chemist and asked me to help him get his puppy out of a drainpipe. "I know where 'e is. I can hear 'im whimpering. What's your name, love? Katherine? Well you've lickle 'ands, Katherine, you'll be able to reach in an' cotch 'im reahnd 'is collar."

"I'll be late for school," I'd said. Because I *thought* it sounded suspicious.

But he'd taken my arm and hustled me down the ginnel to the yard behind the shop, a scruffy walled area full of rubbish bags and cardboard boxes, and indeed there was a drainpipe sticking out of a mound of earth in the corner.

I stood there straining my ears for the sound of distressed dog and he told me to get down and put my face right up to the pipe. "Call his name. Go on." So there I am, down on my hands and knees, shouting, Beaver, Beaver, all the time peering into the dark anticipating the scrabble of tiny claws. When nothing happened I turned my head to ask what he thought we should do next and blow me, he had his tackle out. It looked exactly like he was yanking a plucked chicken head-first out of his flies. "Ave a shufti at this, Katherine," he leered. I was out of that yard like a pinball off a spring. I still can't go into a butcher's round Christmas time.

I ran straight back home in tears, and Poll was the nicest

she's ever been to me. She made hot chocolate and got the biscuit barrel down and we cleared the whole stack of Dogman's Kit-Kat misshapes between us. I didn't even have to go back to school that day, which was a major coup.

"I keep telling you it's a dangerous world out there," said Poll through a mouthful of wafer. "Let's get that packet of Jammy Dodgers open an' all."

One time we had someone keep ringing up then putting the phone down. You'd go, Who is it? Who is it? And there'd be silence; it was dead eerie. Then a few weeks later the nasty language started; I never heard it myself but Poll told me bits and pieces, stuff to do with underwear mainly. She's not one to bother normally, hard as nails our Poll, but it did shake her up. She used to tense when the phone rang. A few times she said, Don't answer it, so I didn't. But one time she picked up and went white, must have been more than knickers. She put the receiver to my mouth but with her fingers over the earpiece, and told me what to say: I had to shout, "Leave us alone and get a life!" I enjoyed that. Most excitement I'd had in ages. And the best thing was, the calls stopped.

So Bank Top becomes the world in miniature, except it's even worse Outside with serial killers and exploding skylines and famine and anthrax-in-a-bottle.

"Yes, it's a sad world," Maggie, Poll's bingo friend, was saying last week over dinner. "All our age are dropping like flies. I went to three funerals last month. And May Powell died last week, it was in t' paper."

"May Powell? May Powell as we were at school with?" Poll looked up from her soup.

"That's the one. Th' undertaker's daughter. She was right snooty at school, do you remember? Not that I'd wish her dead. Does anyone want that last crumpet?"

Poll shoved the plate across the cloth toward her. "She used to say her father put her in one of his coffins if she'd been nowty, and closed the lid on top of her."

Dogman snorted his tea, as if this was the funniest thing he'd ever heard.

"Eeh, and they'd go complaining to Social Services these days for summat like that." Poll shook her head despairingly. "You're not allowed to punish your child at all without some-body poking their nose in. Then they wonder why the kids are running wild. In them days, a parent had some authority. And really, it didn't do the children any lasting harm, did it?"

"No," said Maggie. "Of course it didn't."

"So how did May die?"

"Committed suicide."

"My life's been full of tragedy too," Dogman piped up. "Hang about." He pulled out a hanky and blew his nose hard to clear out all the tea, deliberately making a trumpet noise.

"Has it, love?"

"Oh, aye." He wiped his eyes. "I lost my father really young, in an accident."

Maggie looked at Poll in surprise. "What happened, Dickie?"

"It was terrible. You know he used to work at the brewery?"

"I didn't, no."

"Well, he did. He were in charge of one of t' vats. Anyroad, the big paddle they use for stirring got stuck, so he climbed up to see if he could free it. And he fell in."

Poll put her hand to her mouth. "Oh, Dickie. I never knew that."

Dogman nodded glumly. "My mother was distraught. She said to t' foreman, 'Were it at least a quick death?' And the fore-man said, 'Well it would have been, but he got out three times to go to t' toilet.' "

"Ooh, Dickie," chuckled Poll. "You're a caution."

I tell you, we have some hilarious times in this house.

Life seems to be particularly dangerous for our family around the time of our coming of age. We get the key of the door and the hammer of doom at the same time.

The week after his twenty-first birthday, Poll's father lost his arm up to the elbow in a nasty bleach-works accident. We have the photographic evidence; a mild-looking man with sunken eyes and one flat sleeve stuffed into his pocket. The hand he still has is resting on a little table and there's a roll of paper poking out of his fist. "His Certificate in Textile Technology," Poll pronounces as if it were a Nobel Prize.

Then of course there was Roger, my dad, eighteen and smashed to pieces in the car that was his very special birthday present, a scarlet Mini Metro Vanden Plas. We all know whose fault that was. (Well, actually we don't, because although it was mostly my mad evil mother having a fit and grabbing the wheel just as a juggernaut was coming in the opposite direction, there's also the school of thought that if he hadn't been bought the car in the first place—which was Vince's bright idea—then the accident could never have happened.) So cars are deadly too and that's why I can never, ever have driving lessons because I will either kill myself or some other bugger, in fact best to stay off the roads altogether if possible (Poll once saw a schoolboy run over by a Selnec bus).

Poll's Aunty Cissie lost her fiancé in the war a fortnight before she came of age; she and her sister were actually cutting up old sheets to make streamers when they got the telegram. She's in her eighties now and she never had another sweetheart, so that was her life over with.

Poll herself go through her twenty-second year unscathed but only, she reckons, because she had a premonition that she'd drown, a recurring dream from childhood that she was stranded on a bare rock with a towering wave about to engulf her. She went to a clairvoyant in Blackpool who confirmed it, so she's made sure she's always stayed well away from water, and thus has cheated Fate.

And therefore because I'm almost eighteen now, and I've had no helpful dreams about avoiding accidents, I ought to be particularly nervous. I could leave Bank Top if I wanted to, I have somewhere to go. But is it a trick? Maybe Destiny has got something unpleasant lined up for me. Sometimes I lie awake at nights gripped with a fear I can't put a name to.

I don't know which is worse: fear or boredom.

Funnily enough Poll thinks she's going to die this year as well. "Threescore and ten I am. Living on Borrowed Time."

Yes, well, I think. Play your cards right. It could be arranged.

KATE LONG lives in Shropshire, England.
This is her first novel.